HESTER TAKES CHARGE

HESTER TAKES CHARGE

HESTER'S HUNT FOR HOME • BOOK 3

LINDA BYLER

Good Books

New York, New York

Good Books books may be purchased in bulk at special discounts for sales promotion, corporate gifts, fund-raising, or educational purposes. Special editions can also be created to specifications. For details, contact the Special Sales Department, Good Books, 307 West 36th Street, 11th Floor, New York, NY 10018 or info@skyhorsepublishing.com.

The characters and events in this book are the creation of the author, and any resemblance to actual persons or events is coincidental.

Good Books is an imprint of Skyhorse Publishing, Inc.®, a Delaware corporation.

Visit our website at www.goodbooks.com.

10 9 8 7 6 5 4 3 2 1

Library of Congress Cataloging-in-Publication Data is available on file.

Print ISBN: 978-1-68099-192-5
Ebook ISBN: 978-1-68099-194-9

Cover design by Koechel Peterson & Associates, Inc., Minneapolis, Minnesota

Printed in the United States of America

TABLE OF CONTENTS

The Story   1

Glossary   382

Other Books by Linda Byler   389

About the Author   391

CHAPTER 1

In the meadow, the varieties of green were a shock to Hester's senses after the dull brown of the past autumn, followed by the gray-white world of winter. The city of Lancaster had been assaulted by the elements, or, in Bappie's words, by God's displeasure with all the goings-on.

But now winter was over. The long, dark evenings had faded away; the sound of melting snow and ice was a song. The steady, musical tinkling of raindrops splashing from the eaves formed small streams of water that ran into the streets. There they pooled with the gray slush and were joined by the mud from horses' hooves and steel-rimmed buggy wheels.

Hester's store of herbs and tinctures had fallen to an alarming scattering of almost-empty sacks and a few half-filled bottles of various remedies. The winter had brought much sickness. Hester continued her services with herbal remedies, steadily gaining more knowledge about administering them. The word around town was about a child who recovered from lung fever after the doctor had given up. Some had abscesses heal. For others, sore eyes and flaming, pus-coated throats were relieved by the mysterious tinctures the "Indian lady" carried in her huge, black carpetbag. She dressed in the traditional black shawl and full bonnet of the Amish.

Oh, there were those who held their hands to their mouths sideways, palms inward, rolling their eyes in a pious manner and hissing to one another that this Indian maid was involved in black witchcraft. Look at the color of her outerwear. All black. That bonnet hiding those large black eyes—it gave them the shivers, so it did. They fetched the doctor whom they trusted, not some big-eyed, dark wraith that walked the brick sidewalks of the city without fear.

She held her head high now, they said. Her strides covered the distance efficiently, the long-legged, easy gait of an Indian, but give her a few decades, and she'd be a hunched-over old crone. Then people would see which spirit she possessed.

But to those who knew and loved her, Hester was the beautiful Indian widow who had been married to Isaac King's William, until the fearful, flooding night when his horse threw him against the stone wall of the bridge, injuring his head, and he was taken to the bosom of the Lord.

Now she resided with an unmarried woman, an old maid, Barbara King, called Bappie. Her temperament was as colorful as the wiry strands of auburn hair that eluded her starched white covering. The ever-expanding town of Lancaster, in Pennsylvania, was their home. Theirs was a solid house, and it adjoined a brick-encased one, which housed Walter and Emma Trout and their two adopted sons.

Bappie did not have a solid reputation within the Amish church. Its *Ordnung*, with its stringent rules and regulations in the late 1700s, barely allowed these two single women to live within the town's boundaries. For one thing, Lancaster was a place of the world, where taverns dotted the streets and worldly churches sprang up like mushrooms. There were Baptists and Methodists and Lutherans and those Dunkards who almost drowned the people they baptized, when everyone knew three splashes from the holy cup was sufficient.

No, Bappie was pushing the rules, what with the successful hawking of her vegetables at the farmers' market on the square, even if she grew all of them on her own plot of land.

As for Hester and her practicing of herbal medicines, the ministers left that alone. They were glad when a healing occurred, but they shrugged their shoulders for the most part, saying if it was from God, it would grow and prosper. And if not, the practice of using the herbs would dwindle away since no good came of it.

Hester sat cross-legged, the pleated skirt of her red dress and gray apron holding a large amount of freshly snipped herbs. Here, where the meadow sloped down to a swamp, the moisture stayed plentiful all year long. The abundant growth of plants was far beyond anything she had ever hoped to find.

There was figwort, comfrey, yellow daisies, dandelions, March turnips, dove's foot, elecampane, eyebright, featherfew, and a profusion of artichokes, hemp, and hyssop. The list went on and on, but discovering so many wild artichokes brought an eager shine to Hester's dark eyes.

Many people in the town carried their water from a communal well. But during the winter, rather than brave the cold and driving snow and ice, they drank very little good, cold water, resulting in bladder and kidney troubles. The juice of the artichoke helped immensely with this problem.

Hester had brought three large baskets, lined them with cloth sacks, and labeled each with the herb it would contain. She plied a pair of sharp scissors, snipping away dead leaves and cutting roots from stems, stacking them on a neat pile beside the cuttings. So engrossed was she in her work, with the breath of a song on her lips, that she did not notice a lone figure walking at a brisk pace, until he caught sight of her red dress and white muslin cap.

He stopped, hesitating. The mellow spring breeze ruffled the thick blond hair on his head, moving it gently. He reached up to brush a few stray strands from his vision, then lowered his hand.

His breath came faster, lighter. His one hand clenched into a fist, and then his other one, as emotion shook him. Inner turmoil took hold—a mixture of knowing and wanting, followed immediately by the sure sense that he must be willing to sacrifice his deepest longing. He told himself that he must allow time and patience—God's way—to be his guide. Hard as it was, he believed that God's understanding was far beyond his own. The young man walked on.

Hester hummed, her large, dark eyes liquid with contentment. The unbelievable softness of the day, the vibrating colors around her, enfolded her, healing the cold and the bitter anguish of children dying during the unforgiving winter months. She had felt so helpless in the presence of too many tallow candles, giving only flickering light in the dark and hopeless hovels of the poor.

She looked up just in time to see the tall figure and to watch his retreat, her hands restless in her lap. Slowly she bent her head and lowered her heavy lids as the scissors fell from her nerveless fingers. Would she always wonder? Her heart fluttered, feeling captive within the confines of her body. She had built a protective shell around herself so she could somehow live with her sense of failure as William King's wife. Yet now she felt a rising of hope that she had tried so hard to do away with.

How many months had gone by since that brisk fall day? Whenever she remembered it, the day was filled with color—brilliant yellow, vivid reds, and deep orange. His hair was thick, like spun gold. His shoulders like great oaks. She blushed deeply, thinking of the fine bronzed hair on his forearms, exposed where the gray, homespun sleeves had been rolled up.

"I am Noah."

Involuntarily, she had stepped backward. Always protecting herself. She knew in that instant that she needed to put the hard shell securely in place. The shell grew out of her own shortcomings.

He was her brother. He *was*. Over and over, she recounted their meeting of a few months earlier, every spoken word, every emotion, every light that came from his blue eyes.

Noah belonged to her childhood in Berks County. They had lived together with Hans and Kate, Isaac, Lissie, and dear tiny Rebecca who died in infancy, buried in that stone-cold place. Solomon had been born, and then Daniel. Eventually, ten children in all joined the happy home. Hans and Kate had found her, a wee Indian baby, by the spring, left there by the shame of an Indian girl, her mother. Noah had been born barely a year later.

Now, after all these years, he had come home from the war and found her, his sister. Yet after that day, the sister part was almost laughable. She was not a sister in any sense of the word, but so much more.

And then, like a thundercloud, there came an unwelcome darkening of the glad light within her. In an instant, she had shrunken within herself, leaving her words cold and clipped.

Hester bent over the herbs in her lap, holding the palms of her hands tight to each side of her face to cool the heat in her brown cheeks. She squeezed her eyes tightly as the shame of remembering that day shivered up her spine.

She had not been prepared for the pure rush of longing, the strong desire to lay her head on his solid shoulder, to feel his powerful arms enclose her, allowing her to come home to the safety they held. She had wanted to stay within a place that carried a memory of Kate, who had created her deep sense of well-being. Her mother's love had brought her kindness and generosity, rooted in deep and abiding trust.

She had caught herself, in time, thank God, when the sight of Noah tempted her to believe she had returned to the safety of her childhood world. How close she had come to allowing herself the freedom of revealing any love, even a sister's foolish devotion! How unintelligent was she, she asked herself. Hadn't she married a fine young man? Suddenly the bile of resentment she felt toward William rushed back, rebelliousness against his devout ways. For William had been raised in the strictness of the Amish *Ordnung*, which he took very seriously, keeping every demand to the letter and requiring the same from his wife.

But she had failed him. Not with her outward appearance, and certainly not in the view of his family (apart from his impossibly demanding mother), but with her inward seething. Her strong urge to hurl her mug of tea at his self-righteousness was probably a mortal sin. Only when he was on his deathbed did she come to believe this.

No one could persuade her otherwise, not Bappie nor Emma nor Walter. And so she had thrown herself into her work with passion—gathering and preparing herbs, grinding roots, boiling leaves with whiskey, bottling concoctions, living the knowledge handed to her by the ancient Indian grandmother in Berks County.

When Noah met her that day last fall, she had told him in words covered with cold, hard ice, that she lived with Barbara King, that she was a very busy woman, and that she had no time to sit with him and talk of the past.

In that moment his eyes had turned from warm gladness to a navy blue, then faded to a weary gray of disbelief, and his eyelids drooped low, as if losing sight of her would soften the coldness of her words. When he walked away, his shoulders were hunched in defeat, but only after his kindness had returned long enough to wish her a good day.

Was he able to summon, like Kate, concern for someone else's well-being, even after such a cold dismissal? Instead of firing back, he had collected himself, wished her the best, and without another word, walked away.

It had taken Bappie no more than 30 seconds to make her indignant appearance, raining cold, hard questions, thick and fast. "Who was that?" "What do you mean, 'your brother'?"

This was followed by a snort of disbelief, a swipe of fiery red hair beneath her covering, and a solid planting of her roughly clad feet with her arms crossed tightly in front, covering strings flapping loosely at her back, in disregard of the required bow under her chin.

When Hester repeated, "My brother," Bappie sent another derogatory look her way, along with an expulsion of sound, which left no doubt about the meaning of either the expression or the noise.

"He'd pass for my brother a lot more than yours."

"He's not . . ." Hester floundered, then turned away.

"You mean he was brought up in the same house by the same parents. He wasn't found by the spring with you."

Hester's head dropped forward. She had so wanted to forget Noah's appearance and the hope he had stirred within her. But Bappie's words rang true and strong, reminding her of what she couldn't deny or understand.

Bappie tossed her head, stuck the tines of the manure-encrusted pitchfork into the dry earth, loosened her hands, and dusted them off with a firm whack before rubbing them along the sides of her apron.

"I'd say you were pretty rude to the poor chap."

Miserably, Hester acknowledged this.

"You need to make it up to him. If he comes visiting, I'm going to invite him in, and . . ."

Hester broke in mid-sentence, her eyes flashing. "No, you're not, Bappie! This is my life, my situation, and absolutely not your business. I mean it. You stay out of it."

Bappie's eyes narrowed. "Well, if he's only your brother, you sure are fired up. All right, if that's how you want it. What's his name?"

"Noah."

"Hm. Just like Noah and the ark. He'd make a spectacular Noah. Just like you imagine that stalwart man of God."

Hester felt the color rising in her face and thanked God for the honey-brown color of her skin. At least Bappie couldn't see her reddening, for all her self-effacing shrewdness.

And now almost six months had passed without a word, an appearance, or any sign of Noah again. Over and over, she had told herself, it was not a good sign for a man to leave his faith or disobey his parents, let alone go to war. Had he ever committed himself to the church at all? Perhaps he had been excommunicated. If so, she had good reason to have spoken coldly. She wanted to shun him, keep him out of her life, out of sight. And yet, on this fine spring day, she relived that last meeting with

Noah when she saw a man walking alone, too far away to be recognized with certainty.

She picked up the scissors, then let them drop away. She gathered up a handful of fragrant herbs and rifled through them idly. She smoothed back a few dark hairs, picked up the scissors again, and slowly cut away the stems of a wild strawberry plant.

She thought of all the decaying teeth she had witnessed, the grayish, unhealthy color of so many of the children's gums. The juice of the strawberry root was so good for this foul ailment, but most of the children resisted the bitter taste. Worse still, in Hester's mind, was that the mothers supported the children's yells of disapproval.

She would try mixing in a bit of honey or maple syrup. Motivated now, and inspired once more, she settled her memories. Her sighs turned to quick breaths of anticipation as she resumed cutting with renewed energy.

Back home, in the soft, evening glow of the warm, spring sunshine, Bappie had worked herself into a fever of housecleaning. She had flung open the two front windows that faced the muddy street. The white muslin curtains that usually hung over them flapped softly on the washline in the small backyard.

When Hester dropped the three baskets on the back stoop, she heard windows sliding up and down and the wooden stool being knocked around. She figured if she wanted something to eat she'd have to cook it herself.

"I'm home!" she called.

No answer. Only the scraping of the stool across the oak floors.

Hester shrugged, opened the pantry door, and dug out some dried apples and a bit of hard cheese. She knew there was a ham knuckle down cellar. Her mouth watered, thinking of *schnitz un knepp*, Bappie's favorite and an old Pennsylvania Dutch dish Kate had made so well.

Hester could still see the deep pleats spread over Kate's ample hips, the wide comforting swell of them as she moved efficiently for such a large woman, seeming to float from stove to hearth to dry sink and back again.

Kate's *schnitz un knepp* was one of Hester's most comforting memories. Kate would boil the dried apples to perfection until they were soft and brown, then mash them thoroughly with a potato masher and crumble the ham into the apples, its salt flavoring the sweetness of the fruit and creating the special taste of this dish. The fluffy dumplings on top tasted of both the ham and the apples.

Wishfully, Hester put the ham knuckle in the pot with the dried apples. Wouldn't it be wonderful to see Kate just one more time?

Her thoughts were interrupted by Bappie, holding her arm above her head, leaning on the doorway, her eyes drooping with tiredness. "I didn't know you were home."

"I called out."

"I was cleaning windows."

"Mmm."

"What's for supper?"

"*Schnitz un knepp.*"

"Mm. Good. I'll polish the floor real quick."

"Don't hurry. This takes a while."

Hester sliced a thick slice of dark brown bread, spread a good portion of butter across it, and bit out a huge chunk, closed her eyes, and chewed with appreciation. She was so hungry.

She heard Bappie's maneuvering in the front room, smelled the lye soap, and smiled as she poured boiling water over tea leaves, inhaling the goodness of the spearmint. It was good to come home to Bappie, her friend and coworker, like a mother, sister, and brother, all wrapped up in one.

She had nothing to complain about. Her life here in the city was more than sufficient to keep her comfortable and content. Walter and Emma, kind and accommodating, offered assistance any time, although Hester knew all too well that as the portly couple aged, she and Bappie would need to help them more and more frequently.

The fading light created an aura of gold covering the white plastered walls, the heavy oak ceiling beams, and the well-worn floorboards in a deep, rich color. The stovetop gleamed cozily, the steam from the cooking ham and apples rising fragrantly.

A red and white cloth covered the table, where a brown, earthenware pitcher of purple violets stood in the center. Bappie's sampler, an embroidered piece of fabric with a tree, her family's names, and the words "Home Sweet Home" beneath it, hung on the wall above the bright table.

A rush of sweetness enveloped Hester. For only a moment, she allowed herself the thought of his golden hair and his thick, solid form seated at the kitchen table, infused with warm light.

"His." She could not think "Noah." It was far too intimate, and Bappie might detect a faint blush on her cheeks.

But different memories crowded in then, Hester helpless in their wake. So many meals, so much effort. Lighter bread, crispier chicken, vegetables left boiling too long, or not long enough. Tea that was not strong enough, or harvested too soon. Always after this derision, her husband bowed his dark head, closed his eyes in severe concentration, and moved his mouth with sincerity as he silently thanked God for his food.

Hester often didn't pray at all. She figured God saw the blackness of her rebellion, so he wouldn't want her praise, would he? She was powerless to stop her anger and hurt. She seethed behind her calm, unperturbed face, wanting to throw her heavy ironstone plate at her husband's pious demeanor.

"Her William," he had been, as she was "his Hester." He owned her, possessed her, was proud of her to the world, or appeared to be. It was only when they were alone that he displayed so much criticism. It fell like a shower of bricks, painful, unprotected, crushing. At other times she could manage to wave it away like a swarm of bothersome gnats.

But here it was again. How could she hope to have happiness with any man after having been married to William? Better, much better, to leave marriage and love to those who were truly sweet and good.

With a grunt and a scrape, Bappie scuttled past, a bit bent over as she carried the wooden bucket and scrub cloth, her face contorted and red, her hair only a shade darker, as she went to the back stoop and sloshed the water across the backyard.

Flopping ungracefully into a kitchen chair, she shoved her backside down, sprawled her legs in front of her, threw her arms across the chair back, and lifted her face to the beams across the ceiling. "Whooo!"

"You drive yourself too hard, Bappie."

"It's not as if I had any help."

Hester, mixing the flour, milk, and shortening for the *knepp*, gave her a sidelong look. She decided to say nothing, knowing that when Bappie got into this mood, she became as prickly as a porcupine if you crossed her path.

"Tomorrow I'll be home. We can houseclean the kitchen together."

"But our bedrooms aren't done. You know how long it takes to empty and refill the ticks. It's hard work, getting all that straw to stay in the cover. And it takes them a long time to dry after they've been washed. I was thinking of getting up at five to start the fire under the kettle and to get the bedding on the line as soon as possible. Do we have enough kindling? If we don't, I'll have to split some tonight yet.

"It's hot in here. Why don't you put a window cloth in the window and get some air in here?"

And so they ate their meal while Bappie planned and worried, eating an alarming amount of the dried apples, ham, and dumplings. She soon became quite relaxed, her mood mellowing as she finished up with the sweet spearmint tea. They needed to get out to the farm to check the peas, onions, and radishes, she said. But if they did that, when would the housecleaning get done?

It was important to have the first peas, she stated emphatically, because when the market opened, the wealthy women of the town were always willing to pay an exceedingly high amount for a half-bushel of spring peas. Of course, if they planted the peas too early, there was a danger of frost, which would be no gain at all, if those pea stalks froze. All the profit would be lost, and all they'd eventually have to sell would be some sun-bleached peas that were grown in too-warm temperatures.

Bappie was rambling on.

"We should actually move out there. Emma could find a renter for this house. She would likely be able to charge more then we pay. If we'd live there . . ."

Hester broke in. "Bappie, that house is a hut at best. You know it's not big enough, and it would cost far too much to make it decent. No."

"You're just scared out there in the wild."

"No. No, I'm not."

"Why don't you want to move?"

"I just don't."

"It's your doctoring and herbs and stuff."

"No."

"Yes, it is. I saw all those baskets of weeds out back."

"They're not weeds."

"I know." Bappie smiled good-naturedly, then placed a hand on Hester's forearm.

"You're a gifted herbalist, I know. And I respect that more and more as time goes on. You help me tomorrow, I'll help you Thursday, then Friday we'll go to the farm. All right?"

CHAPTER 2

THEY SCOURED AND SCRUBBED THE FOLLOWING DAY, THE SWEET spring breezes touching the rooms with magic. They filled the washlines with curtains and bedding. They put fresh straw in the heavy covers, called ticks, then laid them on top of the sturdy ropes that held the wooden beds together and supported the straw ticks. They washed the windows until they gleamed, and wiped down and scrubbed the floors.

They sang and talked as they worked companionably. Sometimes quiet spread across the room, comfortable and relaxed, an atmosphere that comes only after years of togetherness.

Hester pushed up the window from her bedroom and called to Emma, who was pegging a tablecloth on her washline. "Hey, neighbor lady!"

Emma's shiny, round face looked around, confused, till Hester called again. Looking up this time, the rotund little woman's face broke into a wreath of wrinkles, her eyes almost closing as her cheeks pushed up on them when she smiled. Her white ruffled house cap bounced sideways as she shook her finger at Hester.

"You gave me a scare, young lady!"

Hester laughed, glad to see Emma again. "It's a lovely day, isn't it, Emma?"

"Ya! Ya!"

Although Walter and Emma went to the Lutheran church, she was from Germany and spoke the Pennsylvania Dutch dialect fluently. She spoke English well, but a smattering of Dutch messed up many good and proper English words. Sometimes Hester gave up being serious and attentive and burst out laughing at all the wrong pronunciations.

"Hester, you and Bappie come on over. It's time for *mittag*. Me and Walter have a wonderful goot piece of pork sausage. Come."

Walter, Emma's impeccably mannered husband, bowed and scraped his way down the hallway into the kitchen, his face pink and shining with the pleasure of having Bappie and Hester at his table.

Hester noticed the pull of his wide suspenders, which put an alarming amount of pressure on his trousers. She winced to notice the snug fit around his protruding middle, the button straining at the waistband. His shirt was buttoned properly and was flawlessly white. A ring of gray hair encircled his otherwise bald and shining dome.

"Certainly, certainly, come this way. How grand! How grand!" Pulling back the chairs with a flourish, his pudgy fingers placed lightly at their elbows, he seated first Bappie, then Hester, in his perfect English manner.

He offered them each a white cloth napkin, but Emma waved him away.

"Ach, now, Walter. *Veck mit selly.* We're just plain old Dutch people from Deutschland. We chust eat; we don't need them cloths."

With that, she tucked into her perfectly browned piece of sausage, rolled it into a slice of bread, and topped it with pungent horseradish. On her plate was a stack of fried potatoes, well salted and peppered.

Walter lifted a piece of the fragrant sausage, holding it at different angles to the light that filtered through the small windowpanes, his eyebrows lifted in appreciation.

"Fine sausage, this. The best in Lancaster. I told Harvey, now, 'I don't want any of your lesser quality with too much grease.' I am suspicious that he is trying to elevate his profits somewhat, by adding undesirable portions of the hog to his sausages. I told him of my fears, and I do believe his face took on a red color, although my words were spoken with care toward his feelings."

"Ach, Walter, you're too easy on that butcher. Everyone knows he puts too much of the pig in his sausage. It's good, so chust eat it, and don't be so bothered."

Hester cut a small piece, chewed, and swallowed, but was glad to finish the too-much-discussed piece of meat and eat the fried potatoes. Either way, it didn't seem to harm Bappie's appetite; she seemed to be enjoying her lunch immensely.

"Would you ladies care for some of our sauerkraut? We have the best. It accompanies the sausage in such an excellent manner." Walter rose to bring the blue crockery bowl filled with steaming sauerkraut to each one, carefully ladling huge spoonfuls onto their plates, his eyes shining, his face beaming with anticipation.

It was at that moment that Bappie chose to bring up the subject of moving out to the farm, asking if they could find renters for the house that Emma had vacated when she become Walter's wife only a few years before, since both had been left behind by the passing of their spouses.

"Ach, *du yay.*" Poor Emma was completely taken off-guard, the abrupt announcement almost more than she could comprehend. Walter stopped chewing, wiped his mouth carefully with the snowy white napkin, cleared his throat, and reached for his water glass.

"I don't mean to be impertinent, but why would you do something like that?" His eyebrows shot up in consternation and stayed there, wrinkling his forehead like pleats in an apron.

Bappie explained her case. The garden needed closer watching in the spring, much more than they had given it in the past few years.

Yes, the house out there needed attention, but they would try and do what they could themselves. Perhaps some men in the Amish community would be good enough to volunteer their labor.

"Ach, you Amish. Always for free. You ask too much of each other. They'll want some sort of payment, you watch." Clearly, Emma was unhappy with the thing Bappie was planning.

Hester stayed quiet, surprised that Bappie approached the old couple with her plans quite so soon, although she knew it was her way—think once, then get it done, plowing through life with full determination.

Walter sat back, his chin wobbling as he valiantly fought the overflowing emotion in his eyes. "But, it will

never be the same, you know. No more friendly banter across the backyard fence, no more impromptu visits
like this. My heart would indeed be heavily burdened
were you to carry out these plans."

Emma sighed and lifted forlorn eyes to Hester. "You
don't want to go."

Hester shrugged her shoulders and looked to Bappie
for help.

Bappie took the situation in hand, stating matter-of-
factly that, yes, they did want to go, only because of the
garden, and yes, they would miss them as neighbors, but
it was time. They would have no problem filling their
house, as the town of Lancaster was booming, with
buildings going up so fast. There were always people
needing a home.

There was nothing for Walter and Emma to do but
to let them go, difficult as it was. Bappie and Hester
ate the good, flaky crust of the dried huckleberry pie,
drank their tea, and bade them a good afternoon, promising to stay another month till they found someone to
help them with the renovations of the tiny, dilapidated
farmhouse.

At the door, Walter cleared his throat, drawing himself up to his full height. "My dear ladies, let it be known
that I consider you two as salt of the earth, two of God's
best women ever placed on the face of this earth. I value
your friendship with utmost esteem."

Emma harrumphed beside him, short and squat and
thoroughly disgruntled. "Ya, well, Walter, hush. I'm not
sure I'd say that. I think you're making a mistake. You'll
regret it, living out there."

With that said, she stepped in front of Walter and shut the door firmly.

Hester walked quietly behind Bappie. Neither one spoke as they made their way to the back door.

"Was Silver fed?"

Hester nodded.

"We'll have clean beds and curtains when we move."

"You should have given me a bit of warning. I thought you meant in a year or so."

"And let that pea crop go to waste again? No. I meant now."

Hester said nothing.

They worked silently the remainder of the afternoon, although Hester's heart was no longer in her work. Why clean like this if she didn't need to? Why let someone else enjoy the fruits of their labor? She felt a twinge of the same rebellion she had felt when William berated her, but figured she'd better stay quiet, with Bappie so determined and all.

The truth was, she did not want to live in that little house. It was dark and cold and mildewed. There weren't enough windows. She didn't like the eerie quiet, nor all the hooting and hissing and warbling sounds of the night creatures. She felt alone there and unprotected.

She thought of staying by herself in this good, solidly built house beside Walter and Emma. The safety of the surrounding people, the town police, the passersby, the work she did with the herbs. Could she stand up to Bappie? Did she want to?

She could not generate enough income to pay the rent on her own, that was sure. The people she served with the herbs and medicines so often had very little money, or none. She could not count on her own income to make her way, so she supposed she really had very little choice of her own.

Bappie was good to her, sharing the profits from the vegetables in the summer. They worked well as a team, and as long as they could manage together financially, she had better appreciate Bappie's good way with business. And so she slept in her clean bedroom on the sun-kissed, freshly laundered ticking, grateful for the home she had with a companion she trusted. She only hoped they could make that disgusting little hovel into a house fit for living.

She was awake at first light because of an energetic robin chirping directly outside her half-opened window. She lay a while, breathing deeply of the fresh, crackling straw beneath her, listening to the sounds of the town awakening. Horses' hooves made a dull, sucking sound as they stepped through the ever present spring mud, the rains turning the streets slick with it.

Horses pulled graders across the worst of it and hauled the muck away, but there was still always a layer of mud, sometimes thicker than other times. Men called to each other or to their horses, the early risers who were on their way to their various duties, the menial tasks that kept the town growing.

So many buildings were going up, with endless hammering and sawing and loads of fresh, yellow lumber being hauled in by the great Belgians and Percherons. Many of the Amish preferred mules, hearty, long-eared creatures that worked tirelessly on very little feed, with many of the qualities of a donkey.

Hester heard the gong of a bell, the breakfast call at the hotel for the laborers who worked in construction. Perhaps she could find a job there as a server, carrying great trays loaded with food to the hungry men. She soon discarded that thought though, as she imagined the strange men, the low wages, and the backbreaking work. Better to stay with Bappie, even if she would have to drive Silver into town or ride with the person who came to fetch her when the need arose.

She sat up, drawing a hand through her disheveled hair as a wave of unworthiness attacked her. Despair that was cloying squeezed the life out of the beautiful spring morning.

Lowering her head, she whispered, "Dear Lord, my Savior, be here with me now. You know I need you to revive my spirits. I don't like changes, and now I have no choice. Help me to submit to thy will always."

She whispered the "Amen," then rose, determined to shake off the lethargy. She needed to throw herself into her work, forget her own foolishness, and be thankful.

She dressed, flicked a comb through her heavy, jet-black hair, set the large muslin cap on her head, and went downstairs.

The house was cold, and Bappie was nowhere about. Lifting the lid on the cookstove, she threw in a few small pieces of kindling, watching to make sure the bit of red coals would ignite the dry wood. A thin column of smoke was accompanied by a light crackling, so she replaced the lid and put both hands, palms down, on the welcoming warmth of the cookstove top. She shivered, then added a bit more wood to build up the fire.

Going to the pantry, she brought out the tin of cooked cornmeal mush, found a knife, and sliced a dozen good thick slices. She set them to fry in the melting white lard she had placed in the black, cast-iron frying pan.

Now she'd see if there were eggs beneath the brown hens. Grimly, she drew on a pair of heavy gloves, knowing all too well how every hen wanted to stay sitting on top of her prize eggs in the spring, hoping to hatch chicks. The hens would peck and flog and scratch with their feet, resisting any attempt to gather their brown eggs. Bappie was better at this than she was, but the mush was frying, and there was nothing better than fresh eggs to eat with it. Hester went through the back door with the egg basket, biting her lip and hoping for the best.

Another wonderful day had dawned. The maple tree in the backyard was bursting with delicate, purple buds. Clumps of green grass already grew thickly alongside the fence separating their yard from Walter and Emma's.

A wagon clattered by, the driver perched on a crate and rocking from side to side with each step from the horses, his hat on the back of his head, a piece of hay stuck between his lower teeth, singing at the top of his lungs. He caught sight of her, grinned and waved furiously, his large, farmer's hand flapping madly until he disappeared behind the fence.

Hester waved in return, then shook her head, a small smile playing around her full lips. That was the one thing she would miss the most, moving to the farm.

The inside of the small chicken coop was dry and dusty, with that special, warm chicken smell she loved.

She eyed the eight chickens on their wooden boxes. Every last one sat with their feathers puffed protectively, sitting like queens on thrones, their round, lidless brown eyes watching her balefully.

"Chook, chook, chook." Hester murmured soft words, trying to make peace with these sitting biddy hens, soothing them so they would allow her to reach softly beneath them and steal their eggs. Bappie simply grabbed them by the neck and flung them into a corner, where the poor hens shook themselves, looking dazed and confused for some time, before they gave up and pecked at the cracked corn.

"Chook, chook, chook." Tentatively, she reached out.

Wham! The hen's aim was true and as sharp as a knife. The beak's impact drew blood just above her wrist, where the glove gave way to the soft skin on her arm. After that, it was all chaos as the irate hen left her nest and flew directly into Hester's face, her dusty wings beating and thrashing.

Blinded, Hester screamed as she stumbled toward the door of the chicken coop, swinging the basket back and forth for protection. She stepped through the door, her arm held over her face, then ran into a person, shoving him backward as she reeled to the side. "Oh, oh. My goodness, I'm sorry."

Lowering her arm, her large, dark eyes wide with fright and embarrassment, she looked up directly into eyes that she knew well. Now they were half-closed as laughter welled up, then broke out in a deep, rumbling sound that carried her straight back to Noah and Isaac and the place of her childhood.

"Noah!" Caught so completely off-guard, she let her eyes shine with the gladness, recognizing his laughter, and savoring the warmth that welled up in her heart because of it. But only for an instant.

"What are you doing in our backyard?" The words were only fringed with coldness, but it was there.

The smile never left Noah's face, nor did his eyes leave hers. The unguarded moment was like a cold drink of water to a man dying of thirst, coming at a time when he realizes there is no more strength, no hope of keeping himself alive.

"I'm sorry. I never meant to intrude or disturb your morning." The smile lines stayed around his serious blue eyes, as if the moment of recognition lingered, shoring up his courage.

Ruefully, Hester bent her head, her hands going to the front of her dress, dusting the clinging bits of straw and a few stray chicken feathers.

Noah watched the slim, tapered fingers, the small brown hands that never left his dreams. He could still feel the soft blows of those lovely fists—pure joy—when she lost her temper and came after him with all the fury of a wronged Indian brave. How long had he loved her? Always. Since the age when he understood that she was not his sister in the way that Lissie and Barbara were. Then came years of holding up his head, facing life with the knowledge that a wall stood between them, impenetrable because of his father.

Hans lived in the same house, an upright and pious member of the Old Order Amish church, who taught his children well, led them in the path of righteousness, and loved Kate, his good wife.

Noah and Isaac knew that obedience and hard work were always rewarded by the approval of their father, their taskmaster. They knew nothing else. Hans assigned their duties, taught them to feed the livestock, milk the cows, plant and cultivate and harvest. They were taught to fell trees, dig stumps, haul manure, and butcher the steers and pigs. For a time, they attended a one-room school where the stern schoolmaster, Theodore Crane, led Noah and Isaac into the wonderful universe of books, sums, and knowledge of the wide, unexplored, and unknown world around them.

But always, it was there.

The first time Noah understood his father's feelings toward Hester, he pushed it away, allowing disbelief and denial to make tolerable what he suspected. He told himself that he was the suspicious one, the one who needed to straighten himself out, to stop watching for his father's admiration of anything about Hester that seemed inappropriate.

Hester became the light in Noah's life. His memory of her was like a written journal, the pages turned with the soft sighing of his love. Hester in an old blue dress, the hem torn out, trailing ridiculously in the dirt and the dusty corn fodder, or in the mud bordering the still and brackish waters of the creek on a dry summer's day. Her tightly braided hair like black silk, the dry winds teasing stray tendrils around her brown face. The way she would squint her lustrous brown eyes, puff out her

perfect lower lip, and expel a short quick breath to blow
the hair out of her line of vision.

Like a young fawn, she was. As quick and graceful,
easily outrunning anyone, boy or girl, in a footrace. How
his heart would swell to watch her pull ahead every time,
her long legs beneath the skirts that hampered them,
churning determinedly, her arms pumping out her competitive spirit.

There was Hester sitting by the hearth, tired and
sleepy, her heavy eyelids drooping, and still she rocked
the cradle with one foot as she sang to yet another wee
baby Kate had brought into the world. She had loved
them all, her large eyes dark and liquid with awe after
another birth, each new, tiny bundle containing the
delight of Hester's young life.

She held the babies, bathed them, changed their
thick flannel diapers, and carried them to Kate, large
and quiet, resting on the high bed, which cracked and
groaned under her considerable weight. After Kate had
begun to feed the baby, Hester would softly, sometimes
hesitantly, lay her dark head on Kate's ample shoulder.

Always, Kate's free arm would leave the baby, slide
quietly around Hester's waist, and draw her a bit closer.
Hester would lift adoring eyes to her mother. Her mother,
not in the true sense of the word, but with love binding
them as securely and tenderly as any bond could.

Noah had often felt like an outsider, watching this
with the keen eye of the sensitive observer he was. In his
young heart, he longed to do what Kate had just done—
draw Hester close and let her lay her head on his shoulder. Being too young to fully understand this longing, he

dismissed it as jealousy, a childish stirring to be equally as close to his mother himself.

He asked Isaac about his feelings. Isaac waved Noah away as if his longing was only a burst of dust from the cornfield, annoying, unimportant, and soon to end. Slender, brown-haired Isaac, who was a shadow behind Noah, copied his brother's ways, never noticing any difference between his feelings for Hester and for little Lissie.

So Noah figured he must be wrong, allowing these feelings to stir in his body or his heart—he wasn't sure where they came from. He just knew they were there, like a jewel he always guarded securely, but with a painful edge that tormented his innocent well-being.

Hester's restless hands fluttered at her waist, her fingers connecting and clenching tightly there. "Why are you here?" she asked none too kindly.

Hesitantly, Noah looked around, first to the small barn where Silver, the driving horse, tossed his head impatiently, nickering for his morning allotment of oats then to the back stoop, with the oak door leading into the house.

"There is a-a lady, a *frau* who talked to me yesterday. She is in need of a man to help her at a farm she owns. I understood her to say she lived on Mulberry Street, but . . ."

"It isn't here. This is not the right place. We, she, I don't believe your services will be . . ."

CHAPTER 3

THE BACK DOOR WAS FLUNG OPEN, FOLLOWED BY BAPPIE, her red hair wet and flattened into submission by a steel comb, her muslin cap pinned securely. The brilliant purple dress she wore, with a black apron tied around her narrow waist, did nothing for her femininity. But her smile was wide and welcoming, her dark eyes eager to acknowledge this powerful, young man, only as a means for her to forge ahead with her plans.

"You found me! Good."

"Yes, good morning, Barbara? How are you?"

Bappie became flustered then, blinking furiously, color washing over her face, a pink tide that gave away her fierce denial of any attraction for men, any man. In her mind they were all alike, and she didn't need them. She waved a hand in front of her face, as if his manners were a mosquito whining about her head.

"Doesn't matter how I am. How soon can you start?"

Noah remained quiet, then looked at her.

"Well, I'm working for Dan Stoltzfus right now. He's building a barn west of town. I don't know his plans from one week to the next."

"You mean Bacon Dan?" Bappie asked.

Hester, remembering the frying mush, slipped away across the yard to the back door.

Noah exercised all the willpower he possessed to keep his attention on Bappie's question without turning his head to watch Hester enter the house, his whole being willing her to stay with him.

He nodded. "Flitcha Danny."

"He doesn't say two words a day, hardly, does he?"

Noah shook his head. "He's a man of few words, that's for sure."

Bappie's lips compressed into a firm line, and her eyes narrowed as her thin hands curled into a fist and came to rest on her narrow hips. Noah could see her mind was churning. "So we need to get out there. You tell Dan we need you for the next two weeks at least. He can get someone else to help him. I'll pay you double what he does. I can about guess you're not getting very high wages. Why are you here? Just home from the war or what? Are you Amish? Are you staying around? Not married. No beard. Where are you staying? Out at Dan's?"

Noah laughed. "Whoa, whoa. I'm a man. One question at a time. You know we men have to think a while before we answer."

"How come you know Hester?" Bappie asked, charging ahead to get all her questions out there so her curiosity could be folded away and disposed of before planning his work schedule.

"She's my sister, from my childhood in Berks County."

"She's not your sister."

"No, well, yes. My mother, Kate, found her by the spring."

Bappie waved impatiently. "I know all that. So you're Noah."

"Yes."

"I heard so much 'Noah this, Noah that.' What was the other brother's name?"

"Isaac."

"Yeah. That's it. He was younger, I guess, right? Sort of an afterthought, as far as Hester's concerned. It was all Noah."

Bappie untied her apron in the back, then retied it, as if that would prepare her a bit better to finish the conversation and move on to a solid commitment from him.

"Do you know how to repair a shake roof? We need an addition to the house and a porch. I need gates repaired and doors, and a new floor put in."

"In two weeks?"

"Well, I'm going to make a frolic for the neighbor men. They can erect the walls for the addition and put the roof on in a day. You can do the rest."

Noah thought he might be able to but said nothing, only shaking his head slightly from side to side.

"I think you can. Me and Hester will help. Hey, she's in there frying cornmeal mush. Why not come in for breakfast? I'll probably have to get the eggs. Go on in."

Noah hesitated.

Bappie entered the chicken coop, extracting chickens from their boxes with an expert flick of the wrist, grabbing their necks, and flinging them across the floor. She gathered eight large brown eggs while he stood and watched, terrified of entering the kitchen alone. Hester would not want him at her table, of that he could be certain.

"Thanks for the invitation, Barbara, but. . ."

"Oh, don't start. You're hungry. You haven't eaten. Two eggs for me, two for Hester, and four for you. Come on."

With an upward arc of her arm and an inclination of her head, she led the way across the yard.

Noah was a coward. His stomach roiled; his breath came in quick, short spurts. "No, I'll . . ."

"Oh, come on. I'm making *panna kuchen*."

Noah followed her hesitantly, then made the inward decision to listen to Bappie and go in. It was, after all, a business meeting, and surely Hester would be civil, or at the least, distantly polite.

He was right. The kitchen was pleasant, sun-filled, clean, and cheerful. The violets in the pitcher on the red and white tablecloth reminded him of the large stone house in Berks County. Unbidden, he felt his throat tighten, his eyes stinging. Too much had happened since then. He didn't know if he could ever risk remembering those days.

Hester did not look up when they entered. She was placing knives and forks on the table beside two white ironstone plates.

"Add another plate, Hester. He's staying for breakfast."

Hester said nothing. A slight nod was her only acknowledgment. Irritation flickered across her perfect eyebrows, then disappeared.

Bappie drew a bowl from the kitchen shelf, measured flour, and melted lard, all the while talking faster than her hands moved.

"It's because of the early crops in the garden that we're moving out there, Hester and I. Put your hat on that hook by the back door. You can wash up in the bowl there. There's water in the bucket. Soap's there somewhere."

Noah turned, removed his hat, and placed it where he was instructed. He poured some lukewarm water into the bowl, rolled up the sleeves of his blue shirt, and soaped his hands.

Hester glanced in his direction. His eyes caught hers in the small oval mirror above the dry sink, but she stepped aside as swiftly as a frightened moth. He lowered his head and resumed his washing.

"Here, Noah. You sit here. Right here by the door. Hester, you fry the eggs, and I'll finish the pancakes. Noah, do you mind pouring the buttermilk?"

Hester set the pitcher on the table quickly before she slid away to the stove, turning her back to him immediately. Bappie watched, pursing her lips.

"For people who knew each other as brother and sister, you two sure don't have an awful lot to say to each other, do you?" she blurted out with all the tact of a sledgehammer.

Noah said nothing. Hester remained at the stove, rigid with annoyance.

"Oh, well, whatever dumb fight you had, you may as well forget about it now."

Hester began to breathe again when Noah said easily, "Oh, no fight. It's just strange, having known one another all those years, and now, we're grown up. We've experienced living and found out the world is a lot more complicated than we could have imagined."

"Yeah, yeah, well, get over it. Get on with your living. Life isn't easy. Nobody's going to carry you around on a satin pillow, careful of your comfort, or lack thereof, mind you. The way I see it, you have to stay ahead of the wolves—meaning hard times, unkind people, death, disease, whatever God slaps in your direction."

As if to add emphasis to her basic wisdom, Bappie flipped the pancakes high, letting them settle back into the pan with a dull sound.

"Get the maple syrup, Hester. Is there any butter?"

Wordlessly, Hester obeyed, lifting the iron latch on the narrow cellar door and disappearing through the opening like a ghost.

They bowed their heads in silent prayer and folded their hands in their laps, the way they had done since they were two years old.

Hester had no idea how she would eat anything, although she planned on doing it even if she choked. He was not going to have the satisfaction of seeing her completely ill at ease and painfully aware of him seated at this too-small table.

Noah was tall and wide and powerful, completely filling his chair. His hair was blond, clean, and well cared for. His face was as she remembered it, except now it was a man's face, tanned by his days in the sun and chiseled by the strength of his work. His blue eyes were calm and nearly closed as he smiled, the light in them the same as the light Kate had possessed.

Kate was interested in whatever the world around her had to offer. And she felt kindness toward all living creatures, not only her husband and children, but aunts and cousins, the elderly and the wayfarers, and most of all, the animals, even the wild ones that ate the strawberries and the beans.

Oh, she would say, the bunnies needed those beanstalks. It was probably a mama bunny with a whole nest of little ones at home. Or the birdies needed a few strawberries to take home to their young.

Hester cut her fried egg with the edge of her fork, swallowed, then softly laid the utensil beside her plate as she reached for her glass of water. She sipped, keeping her eyes lowered.

"Hester, pass the bread, please." Bappie stopped talking to Noah long enough to ask this, her eyes wide with a question in them.

Noah sensed Hester's misery immediately. Laying down his fork, he looked directly at her. "Hester, if I'm making you uncomfortable by being here, just say so. I'll leave and not put you through this. I know it seems odd, the way I show up so suddenly."

Hester looked at Noah, searching his face for sarcasm or loftiness, the tones William used when speaking to her.

When she found only blue earnestness and kindness, it was her undoing. Quick tears welled in her dark eyes. Taking a deep breath, she calmed the beating of her heart.

"No, no. You're welcome here at our table."

Noah acknowledged her well-spoken words with a dip of his blond head.

"Thank you, Hester. I heard you are widowed. I knew your husband only slightly. He was older than I. That must have been very hard."

Hester nodded.

Bappie snorted, lifted an alarmingly high pile of pancake pieces into her mouth, chewed, swallowed, then sat back, lifting her fork for emphasis. "Well, Noah, don't think she mourned too long. Hester was married, yes, but not in the way most folks are. William King is a nephew of your stepmother, Annie King, before she became a Zug, when she married your father, Hans. So what does that tell you? There's a mean streak in that family, you mark my words. Just like a breed of horses that bites and kicks, you ain't ever gonna get it out of them, and that's right."

Noah's eyes widened, as what he had heard changed and softened his features. Hester looked up at that moment, but her eyes fell away quickly, unable to fathom the tenderness she witnessed in Noah's blue eyes.

Bappie completely failed to see all this. She was squeezing her eyes shut tightly and flapping her tongue in the most eccentric manner after scalding it viciously with her cup of boiling tea. "Shoo, this is hot!"

The spell was broken, but Noah was rewarded by a soft laugh from Hester, her perfect eyebrows lifting in the way that he still remembered. If only he could some-how win her trust.

What was William like? Had she suffered? Why had she left Berks County? He told himself he needed to take one moment at a time, one day, one week. But he could never leave her now. He had to find out more about her life after she had disappeared, leaving Hans in a state of wildness, a fury he could fully understand.

"Well," said Bappie, after cooling the afflicted tongue in her water glass, "William wanted a whole bunch of children, that's what it was. They never had any. It was hard on his pride and rode on that Frances's back like a growth."

"Bappie, it's all right. It's in the past. Noah, William was very devout and held fast to the tiniest requirements of the *Ordnung*. So I was not always obedient. The Lord couldn't bless us because of my rebellion. The marriage would have been good otherwise." Hester's voice was soft and low, the words thickened by the constriction in her throat.

Bappie reared back and placed her cup of tea on the table with a bang, so that some of the scalding liquid splashed over the side, wetting her fingers, which she rubbed across her apron.

"See how she is? That's like saying the snake wouldn't have bitten me if I would have stayed out of its way. She blames herself, and that is simply not truth."

Noah knew there was not much he could say to this, so he drank some of his tea, biding his time. He knew Hester well enough to know her mind was not easily changed. He also knew Bappie would be the help he needed and wanted, if he could ever hope to tell Hester of the love he carried in his heart all these years.

But she had spoken to him and called him by his name.

"Well, Hester, I can't say. I wasn't there with you. Unfortunately, after you left I joined the French cavalry to fight with the Indians against the British. I was young, wild, rebellious far beyond anything you can imagine. Nothing in my life mattered much at all. Isaac stayed home on the farm. Annie's hands got so bad, Lissie had the whole work load, and Dat, well, he become demented, of sorts. He was never the same after you left. They say he is better, but shakes with the palsy. Isaac pretty much runs the whole farm now, with the younger boys' help."

An expression of raw longing passed over Hester's face. "I miss the farm in Berks County," she whispered.

Noah swallowed, feeling mist rising in his eyes. He had never loved her more completely than at this moment. How long would he need to wait?

The days after Noah was a guest for breakfast passed in a haze of remembering for Hester. Dreamy-eyed, she walked absently from room to room as the rain fell steadily on the house on Mulberry Street. It was a good rain, a cold rain that soaked into the earth and brought plenty of moisture to the energetic growth of the new spring plants. It fell relentlessly from scudding gray clouds and turned the small, meandering creeks into swollen, brown torrents of dangerous, swirling currents. The streets of Lancaster became avenues of mud, the dirt clinging to wide, steel-banded wheels and the hooves of the horses.

Bappie hitched up Silver in the pouring rain and drove the distance to the farm as determinedly as she did everything else. She wore her shawl and bonnet, sniffed righteously when Hester refused to accompany her, and returned with a severe headache, sodden clothes, and a bad temper. If this rain kept up another few days, the garden would be drowned, she informed Hester gruffly as she shed her clothes on the back stoop and ran barefoot through the kitchen and up the steps, her wet petticoat clinging to her narrow form. Like a stick, Hester thought, holding her hands to her mouth to stifle the giggle that rose in her throat.

"Start a fire!" Bappie bellowed down from the top of the stairs, followed by a tremendous sneeze, a quick intake of breath, and then another sneeze. "Ah, shoot! Must have run on to some goldenrod."

"Not in the spring," Hester called back.

"Start a fire."

"There is one."

"Well, poke it up. Get it going. I'm cold. I'm so cold my teeth are chattering."

Ah-hah! Hester was delighted. For the first time since Bappie had come into her life, she was coming down with a cold. At least Hester sincerely hoped she was. Bappie merely tolerated the herbal remedies that Hester was so deeply convinced of, no matter what she said.

Oh, Bappie pretended to support her, but now if she came down with a fever or a severe cough, Hester would have the opportunity she had so often wished for. She smiled impishly, rubbing her hands over the increasing flames as the rain splashed against the window panes and slid to the sash, ran down the clapboard siding and into the street, where it joined the brown puddles and piles of dirt turning into mud.

Bappie come down the stairs, blowing her nose into a large square handkerchief, warm brown socks on her feet and a clean shortgown pinned down the front, but no apron. Going to the hickory rocker, she yanked it as close to the stove as possible, lifted a small nine patch quilt from the basket, and covered her shoulders securely, clutching the two ends with her hands.

She shivered. Her feet flew off the floor as another sneeze racked her body. "Whew! It's freezing in here."

"Want some tea?"

"What kind? Not that stuff you make for sick people. Horsehair, or whatever it is."

Hester's laugh rang out loud and true, an honest laugh of happiness and humor, appreciating Bappie's unsuccessful attempt to hide her discomfort.

"You're getting sick, Bappie."

"Puh! You wish I would."

"How did you guess?"

"Well, you can forget it, Hester. I'm not going to swallow those foul-smelling tinctures and teas and rub that greasy stuff all over myself. I just got wet, that's all."

In the gloomy light of late afternoon, as she sat wrapped in the quilt, sunk into the depth of the rocking chair and glaring balefully out of the folds of the cover, Bappie looked like a trapped raccoon.

Once, Noah and Isaac had set a snare beside the Irish Creek in Berks County and caught a large, furious raccoon. When they found it, it was well on its way to chewing through the rope that held its two front feet and was glaring at them with brown eyes that closely resembled Bappie's. Hester had cried and made them let it go. She wasn't sure if Isaac ever forgave her.

Now Hester smiled. "I'll make you comfrey tea."

"I hate that stuff."

"How about fennel?"

"Worse."

"Spearmint?"

"Only with sugar."

So Hester brought Bappie a cup of tea and a slice of toasted bread. She crumbled some ham into a pot, added beans and water, and set the mixture on the back of the stove to simmer. As she swept the kitchen and dusted the cupboard, she was surprised to see that Bappie's head had fallen forward on the quilt. She was fast asleep, snoring lightly.

Hmm. That was strange. Bappie had never taken a nap as far as Hester could remember, not even on Sundays. She must be exhausted after that long, wet ride.

The kettle hummed quietly, the fire beneath it popping and crackling. The gloom in the kitchen deepened, so that Hester got up to light a few candles. She shivered. It felt just like the night William was thrown from his horse—that awful, rain-filled night, with the wind howling around the eaves, lifting loose wooden shakes with a mournful, whirring sound, sending shivers of foreboding up her spine.

She had prayed for William's safety. She wanted him to return out of harm's way, having carried out another selfless deed that aided in the growth and well-being of the fledgling Amish community. Her William, strong, dark, and highly esteemed by the ministers, an exacting and noble young man, if ever they saw one.

Why, then, had she rebelled so bitterly against him in her heart?

Oh, she didn't do it outwardly. She was absolutely the picture of humble submission, her hair sleek and controlled, her muslin prayer cap large, covering her ears and tied closely beneath her chain, her mouth kept in a demure, straight line. When she spoke, her voice was well modulated; she never spoke an unkind word to anyone.

For the most part, the Amish were kind and accepting of the Indian girl who was William's wife. There were some, of course, who shook their heads, compressing their lips and speaking quietly of William and Hester's inability to conceive. Well, of course they would have problems. *Der Herren saya* was withheld, likely, because Hester was an Indian. It wasn't the way God intended *vonn anbegin*. They were sure Isaac and Frances hadn't blessed the marriage. But then, that William was smooth. It was easy to tell he had a way with his mother. With her "wearing the pants" the way she did, what was Isaac to say? Not that he ever had very much to say to anyone, poor man.

Hester had desperately wanted William to live, to wake up from that agonizing sleep that hovered so close to death. She did not understand why, when his heart beat so strongly in his chest, he could not wake up.

The guilt of her rebellion held her by his bedside, keeping a tormented vigil, her whole being crying out to God in groanings that could not be uttered, as the *Heilig*

Schrift taught her. She felt the rain and the wind, the howling, the dangerous waters in her soul, a chastening so firm and exact from a God who was angry, taking William as a sign of his displeasure.

Wretched and regretting the day she was born, Hester lived in anguish those ten days that her William lay unable to wake from the battering of his head.

Had Kate lived and been there to hold her, to tell her those thoughts were not good, to bind her to the comfort of her great, soft dress by the sweet arms of her love, Hester would not have had to endure those days of self-inflicted torture. But Kate was dead. There was only Frances, William's mother, appearing like a tall, dark ghost, bearing displeasure and blame in the form of her own sorrow. Frances's keening reached to the rough-hewn beams of the bedroom and swirled around Hester's ears like the high, raucous cry of the crows that battered her senses.

Some semblance of peace had been restored by the quiet voice of her father-in-law, the hesitant Isaac, who spoke quiet words of assurance, urging her not to lay blame on herself. He, too, had lived many years with the pious Frances, having had no choice but obedience to her harsh will. He felt his subservience might bring *der saya*, recognizing his sacrifice for loving a woman who was so often held aloft by the sails of her own grandeur.

"*So gates. So iss es,*" he had spoken softly, shaking his head as he urged Hester to accept the situation. His words to Hester had partially healed the raw wound of William's disapproval, but never entirely.

CHAPTER 4

In her heart, Hester resolved never to love again. She was not a good judge of what was true and kind in a man. And so, because of her past, she clung to Bappie, the strong and independent spinster.

She would never return to Berks County, the home of her heart. Her father, Hans, had made life unbearable after she finally realized the affection he felt for her was not what he wanted her to believe, but a kind of love that was unacceptable. She found it hard to fully forgive him, since she felt she had to leave the only home she had known.

Hester stood, stretched, and yawned. No use getting all dark and gloomy like the kitchen was. Lighting two more candles, she set one on the high shelf, filled a bowl with good, hot bean soup, and sat down at the table.

She lifted a spoonful, pursing her lips to blow on the steaming soup. In that moment, Bappie fell sideways in the rocking chair, mumbled, righted herself, and then looked at Hester, her dark eyes glistening with an unnatural light, her face almost as dark as Hester's. Lifting a hand, she clapped it weakly to her forehead and said that her head felt like one big potato.

Quickly, Hester rose. She felt the heat before her hand touched Bappie's head. "Bappie, you have a fever. A high one."

"It's from the stove. It's too hot sitting here with this quilt. I'll be all right. Just get me a drink of cold water."

Hester did. Bappie gulped it down thirstily, then promptly leaned forward and deposited it all over the clean oak floor. She groaned and held her head, apologizing gruffly before sagging against the back of the rocking chair, her eyes closing again.

"I'll clean the floor," she whispered, her pride carefully in place.

"I'll get it." Hot, soapy water and a clean rag were all Hester needed. It was a job she frequently did, having been to numerous bedsides of the sick.

She tried to persuade Bappie to go upstairs to bed, arguing that the rocking chair was no place for a person with a fever. But Bappie would have none of it. Stubbornly, she sat upright, refusing to take anything Hester suggested.

Bappie's coughing began around midnight, a tight, scratching sound that wouldn't stop, ejecting Hester from her bed as if someone had dumped it sideways. Holding the hem of her thick nightgown in one hand, the handle of the pewter candleholder in another, she made her way down the stairs to Bappie's side.

Again, she felt the heat before she touched her forehead. Instinctively, she knew Bappie was very sick. She had to get her out of this rocking chair and into a bed, but there was no possibility of maneuvering her up those narrow stairs.

Coughing furiously, Bappie waved her away. "Go back to bed." She simply dismissed Hester with a wandering wave of her thin hand.

Her mouth pinched in a determined line, Hester went to Bappie's cedar-lined wooden chest and began to remove the heavy sheep's-wool comforters. Stomping down the stairs, with the candle flame flickering, she wrestled Bappie's pillow, her large heavy nightgown, and more warm socks to the first floor.

She stretched out the blankets on the floor, put the pillow on the end away from the stove, then approached Bappie with one purpose. She would help her out of the quilt, her dress, and the rocking chair, and get her onto the floor where she could lie down. Then she would spoon some medicine down that stubborn throat.

Taking a firm grip on the quilt, she dragged it away from Bappie's shivering form, as she grabbed at it weakly. "I'm cold, Hester. Stop it. Stop taking my quilt."

"Get up." Hester's words were as solid and unmoving as a stone wall.

Bappie shook her head, then reached down for the quilt.

"Get up." Hester began removing the straight pins that held her dress closed as Bappie fought her hands.

"Stop it, Bappie, you're sick. This is not your choice this time."

When all the pins had been removed, Hester raked the dress off her thin shoulders and immediately lowered the good, heavy nightgown over her head. She stuck the now unresisting arms into the sleeves, like dressing a child, and buttoned it securely under her chin. She smiled to herself as she thought Bappie might have elevated her chin only a fraction, like an obedient youngster.

Well, that was just fine. Bappie had never experienced this side of Hester. She helped her to the bed she made on the floor, lowering her carefully, then covered her with the warm sheep's-wool comforter, adjusted the pillow, and slid a cool hand expertly across her brow. Hot! Bappie was so feverish. Somehow she must get this fever down.

Going down cellar, Hester opened the wooden plug on the small vinegar barrel, held a cup underneath till it was partially filled, and went back upstairs, closing the door softly behind her. She tore a clean portion of white muslin from the length in the lower cupboard drawer, soaked it with the cold vinegar, and approached Bappie. Lowering herself to her knees, she leaned forward, speaking quietly, "Listen, I'm going to apply vinegar compresses to your forehead and the tops of your feet. Just lie still, all right?"

"Phew! You're not putting anything anywhere. Go away."

In answer, Hester clamped a cool, vinegar rag on her forehead. Bappie promptly ripped it away with her thin fingers. Hester put it back, holding her head in a vise-like grip.

And so it went all night until the light of morning appeared, gray and ghostly, creating squares of color where night had erased them, Hester resisting Bappie's pride and ignorance of the dangers of a fever as high as hers.

Hester dozed in the rocking chair next to the fire, which was now only a few bright embers, and beside Bappie who had fallen into a restless sleep. Hester was suddenly awakened by the sound of a polite tapping on the front door. At first she thought it was only the wind, but when the tapping became more pronounced, she went to lift the cumbersome cast-iron latch.

"Yes?" she asked, peering thought the gloom and a heavy, swirling fog that was cold, wet, and so thick she could see only a form.

"Is Bappie here?"

"She is, but she's indisposed at the moment."

"I would like to talk to her."

"Who is calling, may I ask?"

"Levi, Levi Buehler."

"Oh, yes. We borrowed your team of horses and wagon last fall."

"Yes." He seemed hesitant, unable to state his purpose, yet unable to leave. He shifted his weight uncomfortably, looking around as if searching for a clear direction somewhere in the dank, swirling fog.

"Can I be of any help?" Hester asked.

"Well, no. Bappie knows my wife well, or used to, before she got so bad. She's not doing so good. I thought maybe Bappie could come sit with her, talk with her, as she often has in the past."

"Bappie is very sick with a cough and fever."

"Oh, is that right? Well, then I'll go."

"There's nothing I can do?"

"No, no." Without another word, Levi turned, made his way down the steps, and disappeared into the vast gloom and fog.

Slowly, Hester closed the door, wincing as the dreaded coughing began in earnest. This was not good, Bappie being so sick in this wet, heavy weather. She had to get something down her throat, or things would only go from bad to worse.

Scabious would be first. This odd-looking plant, with thin, hairy leaves and a long, bare stem holding a blue flower in the time of blossoming, was the best for a cough or any disease of the throat and lungs. The clarified juice, given with plenty of liquid before an infection settled in, was without fail.

She woke Bappie, telling her she must swallow the liquid she would bring. If she refused, she might very well have permanent damage. She must take water and allow Hester to continue with the vinegar compresses, as well as an onion and sugar syrup.

Bappie glared. A grimace changed her features, but it seemed as if all the wind had gone out of her sails, leaving her compliant and rocking lethargically in the waters of her sickness.

For two days and nights neither one had very much rest. The cough persisted and the fever remained high. Finally, on the third day, after a poultice of cooked onions was applied to Bappie's chest, her fever broke; the cough became loose and rattling. Hester gave her a decoction of mallow, an herb that was good for pleurisy. A few hours later, Bappie rolled over, opened one eye, and asked if they had any oat cakes left. Then she pulled herself up, wobbled over to the rocking chair, squinted at the afternoon light, and whooshed out a long expulsion of air.

"I was pretty sick, huh?'

"You were."

"Guess I'm still here for a purpose. God spared me good and proper."

Hester smiled. "I'm glad he did, Bappie."

CHAPTER 5

NOAH RETURNED.

Bappie was still weak, but eating like a horse and drinking copious amounts of steaming spearmint tea laced with honey. Sometimes she added a generous dollop of homemade whiskey, grimaced, sneezed, coughed, and sputtered, but said they always had it down cellar at home. It was good for fevers.

Hester let Noah in through the back door, the brilliant spring sunshine blinding her for a moment. As always, he inquired about her well-being, quickly noticing the dark circles under her eyes, her pinched look of exhaustion.

Without looking into his face, she assured him she was fine as she led the way to the rocking chair beside the stove, where Bappie sat with a quilt around her knees. She held a cup of steaming tea in her hand, her hair a disheveled riot, freed from any moisture, comb, or cap. Her face was peaked with weakness; a certain exhaustion clouded her eyes.

Noah was quick to notice this. "You must have been sick, Barbara," was his way of greeting.

Flushing brightly, Bappie waved it away, his concern like an affront to her pride and determination. "I'm better. It wasn't anything. Bit of a cough."

"Well, I hope you had the doctor out."

"No, of course not. That's costly. I had Hester."

"Hester?"

"You know, all the weeds she bottles. She poured them down my throat. Against my will, mind you." Lifting one long, skinny, finger, she began to shake it, but the weakness in her arms made it droop, so she quickly curled it around her mug of tea.

Noah turned, a light of recognition slowly dawning. "Hester, you . . ." Speechless, he searched her face.

Hester turned away, hiding her face and refusing to meet his eyes.

"I remember the old Indian woman and the book she gave you. I had forgotten all of that."

"She treats a bunch of people. Especially down in the poor section of town. Not too many Amish yet. They're all afraid of witchcraft."

"Well, Barbara, I'm glad you're feeling better. Now that the rain has cleared, I'm ready to begin, if you're well enough to accompany me out there."

"Sure. I'll go. Let me get my shawl and bonnet."

Noah watched Hester's back, the lovely slope of her shoulders, the black apron tied snugly against her soft form, but he decided not to try to engage her further. She had opened the door and glanced at him only for a second before closing the door behind him. But she had

let him in, which meant she must approve of Bappie's
hiring him.

Elation waved its warmth through him as he thought
of this. He still had a chance. No use pushing her or
requiring more than she was ready to give. If she did not
want to talk about her herbs or the use of them, perhaps
she would another day. For there *would* be another day,
and that was all that mattered.

Hester urged Bappie to remain at home, afraid the
damp, spring air would be too much for her delicate
lungs.

Noah pretended not to hear as Bappie told her it was
all right to boss her around while she was sick, but now
that she was well, if she wanted to ride out to the farm
with Noah, she would.

"Put a scarf over your mouth."

"Yes, Mother." Without another word, Bappie pulled
her bonnet over her scraggly hair, pinned the black wool
shawl across her shoulders, and, minus the scarf, left
with Noah in Dan Stoltzfus's top buggy to review the
renovations at the small farmhouse.

Frustrated, Hester wandered through the house picking up vases, pitchers, pin cushions, and small dishes,
and setting them back down. Her mind raced, full of bits
and pieces of her past, including the torment that the
book containing the herbal remedies of the Indian tribes
of Pennsylvania had brought.

Well, she was not going to tell Noah that their stepmother, Annie, had threatened to burn the book. He
didn't need to know all that. Besides the deep wound
of failing William and his parents, she couldn't bear to

go back to the time of Annie's hatred, which had been brought about by Hans's infatuation, or whatever was the right word to call it. Much better to leave that stone unturned. Noah did not have to know anything about her past from the moment she stepped into the woods in Berks County and traveled the vast distance across mountains, fields, creeks, and rivers. If he wouldn't have taken Annie's part, and then come to dislike her and want nothing to do with her, things might have been different.

Hester decided to do the washing. She'd take the covers off the comforters, wash them and the pillowcases, all the muslin clothes and rags, the dresses and socks, washing away all the sickness that had hung about the kitchen like a pall. Hester know the scabious plant had again proved its worth. How amazing that God had provided for humans' diseases in the form of plants of the earth. Now, slowly, people were losing this knowledge.

Only the simple and the ignorant retained it. The red people, the Lenapes, the tribe of Indians whose blood ran in her veins. And yet she knew now that she would never return to them. She was steeped in the culture of the Amish. It was all she knew.

She recalled Noah standing in the warm spring air, the sun at his back. Her heart swelled. She put up a hand to cover it, ashamed of its beating. If she could still it, she wouldn't need to be reminded of how she felt. She could not give in, ever. It was too misleading, this thing called attraction, which tempted her to believe that it would grow into love and marriage. No, no, she couldn't bear a whole new set of deceptions.

She threw kindling underneath the brick oven that held the great copper kettle. She pumped as if her life depended on getting all the water she could to fill the buckets and then slosh them into the kettle before setting fire to the kindling.

A roaring fire took hold, and soon the water was steaming. Using a bucket, she filled the tin tubs with hot water, shaved a portion of the white lye soap into it, and then threw in the covers and pillowcases. Taking up the smooth, well-worn stick, she swirled the items in the steaming, soapy water until it had cooled enough so she could rub them up down across the washboard.

The day was perfect, so she swung open the back door, then bent to wring the covers out, twisting them securely with her strong hands before pegging them onto the sturdy rope washline. Droplets of water were flung from the clean squares as the spring breezes caught and flapped them. Good! They'd be dry by sundown.

She paused on the back steps, inhaling the sweet fragrance of April. Here in town she detected the smell of mud and dirt and squalor from the poor section, but over top was the scent of hay, of new green lumber, of horses, and of whatever else makes up the people and houses that are a living town.

Hester longed to ride in an open buggy out away from the town, if only for a few hours. The garden in spring was like a tonic to her soul, but to live in the little house that Bappie wanted was an idea she could not imagine.

She'd wait and see what Noah accomplished. She had no plans of going out there while he was working. That would only be inviting trouble, the kind that required too much effort to control. Better to stay here and let Noah and Bappie figure things out.

She wondered where Walter and Emma Trout had gone. Their horse and carriage had been away from the shed already. She'd love to sit at their table the way they always used to do, but Emma was unhappy about their plans to move out to the farm. She had never been capable of displaying the good manners of her husband, so there was no use going over there only to be shoved out the door by her disapproval, her face red with it.

Hester ate a molasses cookie, then sat in the rocking chair by the fire. Just enough warmth radiated from the kitchen stove to make her eyelids droop, and sleep overcame her quickly. Her nights of tending to Bappie's needs had taken their toll.

The loud knocking on the door failed to waken her at first. Repeatedly, the sound entered her consciousness until she sat bolt upright, her eyes wide. She heard the sound again, more urgent than ever. Back door? No, definitely the front.

Hurriedly, she walked down the hallway, pulled open the oak plank door, and looked into the wild stare of the same visitor of a few days ago.

"Is Bappie here?"

"No, I'm sorry. She accompanied uh . . . our worker out to the farm."

"I need help. My wife, Martha, is gone. She's disappeared. I have searched every corner of our farm, and I thought perhaps Bappie could understand her ways better than I."

"How long since she's gone?"

"This morning. She was in her bed when I went to do the feeding."

"Have you asked anyone to help? The town constable? What about your hounds?"

"No, I haven't. I wasn't sure if our bishop would approve of having English people searching for my wife. Yes, I used the hounds to find her scent, but . . ."

Here Levi stopped and his voice choked. He lowered his eyes and shook his head, as if he meant to hide a thought that was too fearful to contemplate. Denial seemed best. "Bappie had a way with her."

"But I don't remember Bappie visiting Martha ever."

"She did. More than you know. She was very good for Martha's feeble mind."

"Is there anything I can do?"

"No."

Hester listened. She thought she may have heard the clatter of buggy wheels.

"Come in, Levi. I am going out the back door. I think Bappie may have returned."

Together they hurried through the house and out the back door to find Noah throwing the reins across the sweated horse's back. Bappie had already climbed off the buggy.

Levi pulled his hat down over his head to keep it securely in place. His eyes immediately sought Bappie's face.

"Levi Buehler."

"Hello, Bappie."

"What brings you?"

"My wife is gone missing."

Bappie stopped short, the color leaving her face, her dark eyes wide.

Noah remained in the background, tying the horse to the hitching post, although he glanced at Levi a few times.

"How long?" Bappie asked, curtly.

"This morning, early."

"Did you get help?"

"Not yet."

"Why not? You need to round up a bunch of men. She can't be very far. She's not strong enough."

Levi nodded.

Hester tried to convince Bappie to stay in the house, but she would not hear of it. Martha was her friend. She had been ill in body and mind for far too long, and lately without the aid of a doctor.

On her last visit, Martha had been disoriented. Some of her talking sounded more like a dream, as if she lived in a world of her own creation. Bappie felt caught. If she revealed her worries to Hester, she'd want to try healing through herbs. But the doctor was unable to diagnose her illness as her mind steadily weakened, along with her body.

Martha talked incessantly of the children she had lost as infants, one after another. Sometimes Bappie listened without trying to stop her. At other times she tried to have her think about something else by speaking forcefully, as if chastening a young child.

Martha railed at Levi from her twisted confinement, blaming him for the loss of the babies. Patiently, he absorbed her disgruntled cries like a sponge. He closed his eyes in an effort to squeeze out the bitterness, telling himself she couldn't help it. He fed her, changed her clothes and her bed, and did the washing and most of the housework with the aid of a *maud*, a young Amish girl hired out to help.

Some days she would cry and beg his forgiveness, which he gladly granted, for she was his wife, and he had promised to care for her in sickness and in health.

Bappie thought she must have a cancer growing in her head, which was damaging her brain. She was an innocent victim, beset by a disease, an *unschuldicha mensch*. Bappie's loyalty stood firm. Let people say what they would, she would not bend. She'd told Josiah sei Esther that if she kept on judging poor Martha Buehler, she'd end up worse than Martha if she didn't watch out, which pretty much set Esther on the straight and narrow, what with that Bappie Kinnich's flashing eyes and red hair and her splattering of freckles.

It was a situation in the small Amish community of Lancaster County that few people understood. The doctors called it nervous affections and treated her with different medicines that brought on sleep or stupors, but she always resumed calling out to Levi, her husband. Now she had disappeared.

"Well, here is a horse. Levi, I'll go with you now. Perhaps she's hiding, and when she hears my voice, she'll come. Noah, you and Hester hitch up Silver. Go to the blacksmith shop and spread the word. All able-bodied men will be needed."

Noah nodded and turned to go the small barn. Levi sat in Dan Stoltzfus's buggy like a man in a dream, weary of the tension, the demands placed on him, and now this. Bappie wasted no time in seating herself beside him, picking up the reins, and taking off at a fast trot.

Hester did not want to go. Her first instinct was to run into the house and hide upstairs where Noah could not find her. Let him go by himself. She didn't want to sit beside him in the buggy.

Noah threw the harness across Silver's back, then adjusted the straps quietly and efficiently. Silver's ears pricked forward, then slid back, ready to listen to any command Noah would require.

Hester stood, unsure of herself.

Noah looked up. "Ready?"

She shook her head. "I will need my shawl and bonnet."

"I'll wait."

CHAPTER 6

OVER AND OVER, WHILE SHE PULLED ON HER OUTER CLOTHES, she told herself that this was only Noah, the brother from her childhood. She yanked her hat forward, well past her face as a protection, a wall between her heart and this blond giant.

He helped her into the buggy, a gesture she was unprepared to accept. Amish men did not normally do that, so she became flustered and unsure. But when he stayed on her side of the buggy with his hand extended, she had no choice but to place hers into it, the mistake already done before she could retrieve it and place it beneath her black woolen shawl where it should have stayed in the first place.

Holding his hand, even lightly, was not something she could do ever again. The touch of his hand broke straight through the barrier of her strict resolve. They were at the blacksmith shop, and he had already climbed off the buggy before she could even begin to gather the fragments of the shell she had built around her heart.

Her hat helped. Like blinders on a horse, she could look straight ahead without seeing him. That was good. She had gotten her resolve firmly back in place again. She focused on Silver turning, leaving the blacksmith shop and taking the well-traveled road out of town.

Noah remained quiet, driving with one hand. Hester watched the tip of Silver's ears flicking back and forth. The muddy road stretched before them, and nothing else.

Suddenly, Silver shied away from a groundhog that had popped up from its hiding place, his haunches lowered as his hooves dug into the muck. When he took off running, a large portion of the mud flew out from under his hooves and landed on her face. Hester let out a bewildered sound before reaching up to brush away the offending dirt.

Noah brought Silver under control, then put the reins between his knees, turned, and placed a hand on each side of her hat. His fingers found the strings, untied them, and slid the hat off her head. "There, now maybe I can see your face."

He brought out a square men's handkerchief and wiped the splatters of dirt off her face, smiling directly into her eyes. "Better?"

He returned to his driving without waiting for an answer.

Hester was deeply ashamed and wildly elated as she nearly choked on her beating heart. She wanted to get down off the buggy, tell him she wasn't six years old, and stalk away. She also wanted him to wipe the mud off her face again and smile at her one more time. What she did do was say, "You used to do that a lot."

"Did I?"

"Yes, you did. Remember when I cut my face on that corn-husking knife?"

"It wasn't really your face, was it? More a cut just above your temple. Is there still a scar?"

Hester shrugged and looked sideways at him without meaning to. Certainly without wanting to.

But Noah was intent on his driving, watching for the almost hidden road that was Levi Buehler's lane. By all accounts, he had dismissed Hester in favor of remembering more important things, which was the matter at hand—finding Levi's wife Martha.

"Did you know Martha very well?"

Hester shook her head. "Not at all. I only learned about her when Bappie spoke of her, which wasn't often. I don't believe I've ever seen her."

"It's very sad. Levi has had his share of sorrow."

"Oh, he did. He took to coon hunting with a pack of hounds. He sold his cows. Says he makes more money raising the hounds."

Noah nodded.

They rode side by side, her shoulder jostling against his sturdy arm, both thinking their own thoughts about the sadness that was Levi Buehler's life, as well as Martha's slide into unreality, caused by something so mysterious even doctors could not begin to figure it out.

"Perhaps someday we'll understand diseases better. Or how our brains work," Noah said quietly.

They had to duck their heads to get past the low hanging branches that hung over Levi's drive. When they arrived at the buildings, Hester was surprised to see that things were in order—well-kept doghouses, repaired fences, the garden plowed, harrowed, and planted.

The baying of a dozen hounds brought Hester's hands to her ears, a pained expression on her face. Noah reined in the horse, then climbed off the buggy amid the milling of the dogs, each one wagging its tail, a friendly gesture in spite of the baying.

Levi and Bappie stood by the fence uncertainly, facing this unfortunate nightmare head on, as was Bappie's way.

More buggies clattered in, men throwing the reins, their faces grim.

Bappie stood with Levi as Hester turned to Noah. "I'll go inside, do what I can. I won't be much good searching with the men. It would be unseemly."

Noah's eyes were kind as he found hers.

"Of course. I'll go."

He walked off as she turned to enter the front porch. More women stepped down from the buggies that kept arriving.

Enos Troyer's wife, Mamie, was crying copiously. Great tears slid down her cheeks, lining the folds around her mouth. She held a fresh handkerchief at her nose, which had already swelled to a mammoth size.

"*Oh, mein Gott. Bitte dich, bitte dich,*" she moaned over and over, as she reached out to shake Hester's hand firmly. "*Vie bisht, meine liebchen?*" she choked, which brought forth a fresh burst of tears and a wobbly sob.

"I'm all right, Mamie. As well as we can be on such a sad occasion."

"*Oh, ya, ya. Gewisslich, gewisslich.*"

William's mother, Frances, was the next one to arrive, her tall, thin form propelled by her long feet moving her up to the porch without much of an effort, her walk a study in efficiency. "Mamie, Hester."

A curt nod, a slanted look, and she drew her shawl tightly about her scrawny form and pushed open the door that led to the kitchen. "You may as well come in. Chilly out there."

Bappie walked with Levi, calling and calling. When the men felt they had depleted that plan, they set the hounds on Martha's scent.

The men and dogs disappeared to the swollen waters of the Pequea Creek, where the animals ran constantly back and forth, milling about, whining, their wagging tails whipping with pent-up energy. But that was as far as they would go.

Men and boys from the town took up the search— English, Irish, Lutherans, Catholics, barkeepers, livery men—it made no difference this afternoon, each one having the same goal—to find Levi Buehler's wife.

Henry Esh's wife and daughter, Emma and Katie, brought a roast of beef. Frances brought a pound of butter and one of lard. Mamie, two dried apple pies. Ezra Zug's Elam brought three loaves of freshly baked bread and dried mulberry jam.

The hotel owner, the one who built that new structure on the corner of Queen Street, sent a pot of pork and beans and a pot of sauerkraut.

Evening fell. The sun lost its springtime splendor as it slid close to the farmland and woods of Lancaster

County, casting a shadowy gloom around Levi Buehler's buildings.

"*Ach, du yay,*" said Mamie. "*Ess vort dunkle.*"

Around the circle, the farmers and their wives traded glances discreetly. Each person was afraid to say what the curtain of evening would bring. Or if they said aloud what they were thinking, it might come to pass.

Bappie entered the kitchen, pale and shaken. She went to the hearth, held out her hands, then sank into the small armless rocking chair Hester had vacated. "It's just so hopeless. I can't imagine she could have gone far. I just can't."

"How was she in the past few weeks?" Mamie asked.

Bappie shook her head without speaking.

So they stood, this small knot of Amish women finding comfort in the fact that they were together. Dressed alike in almost every detail, their faces grim with the sense of awaiting disaster, they still believed there was reason to hope, as Mamie said.

The fire burned low, and the light in the windows faded from a sunset of orange and yellow to a dull twilight. Shadows climbed the log walls of Levi Buehler's house as the women moved about dully, speaking in quiet tones, as if any ordinary conversation would be unholy at a time when they all whispered prayers for Martha's deliverance.

When Levi's brother Amos's wife, Rachel, Martha's sister-in-law, came through the softly opened door, she shook hands solemnly, graciously, her eyes wet with unshed tears.

"Bappie." Rachel greeted her with emotion, knowing she had been the one who helped Martha most. Bappie bestowed kindness in her gruff, forthright manner, but she delivered kindness nevertheless. For Bappie took the time to be with her when others turned away or lost patience with her declining health.

As the night wore on, the woman prepared a *schtick*, some simple, handheld food to tide the men over until the morning. Many of them went home to their wives, while a few lit blazing torches and continued the search. Now and then they entered the house exhausted, wet, and puzzled, drained by the tension of not knowing, of wondering that was almost too much to bear.

Late in the afternoon of the third day, almost two miles away from the Buehler homestead, a group of men from town came upon the body of Martha Buehler, carried downstream by the swollen current and caught in a wide eddy beneath the roots of a large sycamore tree. They were ordinary laborers who offered their assistance from the goodness of their hearts and because of their respect for the "black hats."

It was a miracle she had been found, the white of her nightgown the color of the sycamore's bark. God had shown those men where poor Martha had been taken.

When Levi Buehler met the men carrying the form of his ailing wife—when he knew there was no hope— he placed his hands on either side of her poor swollen face and lowered his head. Gentle tears rained down his unshaven cheeks and into his straggly beard.

Each one of the men turned away, their shoulders shaking. Then they laid her gently on the tender green grass where the April sun had warmed it after the rain. They stood, their hats in their work-roughened hands, their heads bowed, as they gave their respects to Levi Buehler and his deceased wife, may she rest in peace.

One of the Irish Catholics from the livery stable crossed himself, while the buggy driver rumpled his hat and whispered his prayer, "Lawd have muhcy." The Lutherans and the Mennonites, the Dunkards and the Baptists, all the groups were united as one in that moment.

Faced with the way of all humankind—the finality of death—every doctrine and disagreement fell away, leaving everyone in awe of mortality. Love sighed in the April afternoon, from the west breezes to the east, and the people stood united in sympathy and in death.

The women up at the house received the news in disbelief, then each stood alone in varying degrees of mourning. Mamie cried, giving herself up to great heaving sobs, with a good supply of white handkerchiefs to soak up her grief. For hadn't that poor Levi suffered enough? Why, the poor man already had an awful rough row to hoe, and now this.

Hester stood by the fireplace, her eyes wide with the tears that would not come easily, not here where the other women would see. She had not known Martha well, only hearing some things from Bappie. She had often longed for the chance to treat her with some of the herbs that may have helped, and yet, she had no way of knowing what caused Martha's mind to worsen. Some things were beyond knowing, and that was that.

In her black dress Hester was more beautiful than Noah had ever seen her. He tried hard to remain in the background and never glance in her direction. Yet he was always aware of exactly where she was.

Many visiting ministers came. Many relatives from Berks County traveled as swiftly as their wagons and horses could bring them. Some chose not to make the trek, sending their sympathy in letters that arrived a few weeks later.

Noah helped care for the horses with the other young men, although there were those who asked why that young man was even in attendance. Wasn't he a Zug from Berks County? Wasn't he the one who ran off and fought in the war? Well, he's dressed Amish enough, some said. Others watched him with suspicious eyes, saying he walked like a *grosfeelicha* soldier and shouldn't be here.

Dan Stoltzfus, his employer, said he was as good as any of the rest of them. "Let him alone. He's not hurting anyone." It was quite a speech for Dan, the man of few words, but it shut them up properly.

The sermon was preached by Ben Kauffman, a brother to Martha. Hester sat on the hard wooden bench, her feet on the fresh, yellow straw that had been spread on the barn floor, her head bowed as the loud chants of the minister settled in her heart.

Death was so real at a funeral. The end of time had come for the individual who lay before them. God had cut the golden thread of Martha's life, and now her bewildered suffering was over. No one would ever know what had happened that fateful evening. Naturally, everyone thought of suicide, the desolation of her poor brain finally taking its toll, but no one knew so no one judged. Let Levi have the benefit of the doubt. He had been so good to her through all the years of her declining health. And so it was not spoken of.

The minister preached *an gute hoffning*, the hope that her soul would be taken to heaven, while tall, gentle Levi bowed his head and nodded it slightly, the hope in his heart in tune with Ben Kauffman's.

The funeral reminded Hester of Kate's, a blur in her memory, the heartbreak almost too much to bear. Even then she had depended on Noah's companionship to get her through the days that followed.

It was Noah who carried the wood, dumping it carefully into the wood box without creating dust or unnecessary splinters on the floor. He spent hours at the chopping block, ensuring that he cut pieces of wood that were not too long or chunky to fit through the round lid of the cookstove.

They talked of Kate's death. At 14 years of age, Hester knew the finality, the separation of body and soul. She believed in heaven, in God and his son, Jesus Christ, who saved believers by his suffering on the cross. *Heilandes blut*, the Savior's blood. And so she could find snatches of joy in the midst of the dark fog of grief, thinking of Kate in heaven with the angels, and of Rebecca, the wee child who died of the dreaded lung fever.

Hester's faith had been like a fledgling sparrow, fed by Kate's love, her kind ways, and her care. After her death, Hester was forced to fly on her own. But now, sitting here in this sad service for Martha, she knew Noah had flown beside her in spirit, shielding her from the worst blows, the responsibilities that seemed too heavy.

He had protected her from Hans's worst days when he lay around the house awash in his grief, unable to accept the fact that the pillar of his life lay beneath the soil in that lonely graveyard. When Hans would shout in frustration at the little ones, Noah would speak kindly to them, getting down on the floor to build a tower of blocks until the children's tears turned into smiles of happiness.

Hester lifted her head and looked around at the benches filled with Amish, her kinfolk, all dressed in the black of mourning. Her people. She was accepted by them as she lived among them, although not all was perfect. There would always be those who were stingy in spirit, giving little and judging harshly, who would never fully approve of *sell Indian maedle*.

But with the Lenape, the people of her blood, would it be different? God-given natures were just that, given by God, and weren't folks much the same? They all aspired to goodness in their own way, some much less than others, but who was to judge but God alone.

A wave of gladness and contentment, an emotion she could hardly define, made her lower her head in gratitude and self-acceptance. Let it be so, Lord. Let me accept the kindness of these, my people. Let me accept myself for who I am. Guide me now that Noah is back in my life. If I need a shell to protect my heart, then help me to keep it in place.

Hester stayed behind at the house with those women of the community who were not relatives or close friends of Martha's. Friends and family joined the procession of carriages to the graveyard for the burial.

She helped with the meal, setting the table with apple butter, bread and butter, kraut, pickles, and cheese, while other women prepared the potatoes and gravy. There was the usual running commentary about the merits of making the smoothest gravy.

Old Suvilla Buehler shook her head, smiling in spite of herself, and beckoned to Hester with one crooked forefinger. "*Komm mol.*"

Quickly Hester obeyed, holding a fistful of knives and forks. Bending low, she looking into Suvilla's lined face, the wrinkles and deep crevices there speaking of years of labor, of sunshine and rain, drought, heat, winds, snow-storms, grief and joy, love and laughter, all etching the map of her countenance.

"Hester, tell me. Did you ever hear the story of the Tower of Babel?"

Hester nodded, smiling.

Suvilla inclined her head toward the black knot of women, all talking at once by the cookstove.

"Right there you have it. They're all talking at the same time, and no one knows what the others are saying."

Hester laughed and lightly smacked the old arm with an affectionate pat of understanding, leaving old Suvilla with the light of shared humor in her eyes, her shoulders shaking with her own cleverness. Hester continued placing the knives and forks on the table, then looked back at Suvilla who gave her a wide grin, the gaps in her teeth a sign of the wisdom of her years.

Hester went to stand at the cookstove, peering through the black-clad shoulders at the large kettle of bubbling broth.

"What do you think, Hester?" asked Butter John sei Lena, a tall, thin woman who held the wooden spoon and was, therefore, the boss.

"About what?"

"Do you mix the *schmutz* with the flour? I know the chicken gravy is best that way, and I thought beef was, too. But they say not. They say beef is too greasy. But how else will you get the rich flavor? Huh?"

Hester shrugged her shoulders. "I'm not good at making gravy. But when I do, I use the fat—chicken, beef, or pork."

Hannah Weaver broke in. "Well, I don't. My man is fat enough without feeding him all that grease. Gravy is good without it. Save the grease to make soap."

Mamie Troyer inserted this put-down with all the ease of an axe: "We don't all have fat men."

Hannah's comeback was just right. "Well, with a little *Schpeck*, my man can work in winter, unlike your Ezra, who looks like a fencepost, his teeth chattering as he sits by the fire on cold days."

From the rocking chair, old Suvilla cackled her glee. "That's right, appreciate your man. When he's gone, you'll miss him so *hesslich*."

Hannah shrugged her shoulders, and Mamie nodded, yes, yes. Lena went right ahead and mixed the beef *schmutz* with the flour and made the gravy her way, with all that rich flavor.

Hannah and Mamie tasted it carefully, pursing their lips and blowing on the large spoon they had filled—they were hungry; it was past the noon hour—then nodded their heads in approval. "*Sell is goot dunkas*," they both declared, handing the gravy-making prize to Lena, who lifted her chin and closed her eyes as she proudly accepted this verbal trophy.

"*Siss gute, gel?*"

Ah, yes, the gravy was good, they all agreed. This recipe should be written in a small book for future reference, they said, eliminating the need for constant bickering over the bubbling broth.

Hester knew the funeral meal would be delicious, the way all big kettles of food cooked by many different hands were.

The big pots of potatoes would be whipped by a few strong young men. Suddenly it dawned on Hester that Noah might offer. Wild-eyed, she glanced around the kitchen, looking to see if the women had put anyone to work. She hoped to watch him hang his hat on a hook and see his bright hair, knowing he was here at this service with her. Ashamed of her thoughts and afraid of the longing, for that is what it was, she turned away, straightening a corner of the snowy white tablecloth. No one could see her thoughts.

She heard him, then, speaking to the women, his voice low and well modulated, as befitted a funeral service.

She heard old Suvilla from the rocking chair. "*Na, do, veya iss deya fremma?*"

No one seemed to know who Noah was. An awkward silence settled over the kitchen, the women at the stove without the answer Suvilla wanted.

"Hester, who is the *unbekannta?*"

There was nothing to do, but turn, face the women, and tell them it was Noah Zug from Berks County.

Noah was busy sitting astride the bench, a large pot of steaming potatoes shielding his vision. Across from him, Levi's Jessie had taken up the second potato masher with his own large kettle of cooking potatoes.

Mamie Troyer stood, fists resting on her hips, a dish towel clutched in one hand, watching Noah with a light of curiosity that would only result in a loudly spoken question: "Noah Zug. Who is your father?"

"Hans. Hans Zug."

"That Hans. Married the second time to Annie Troyer?"

"Yes, that's right."

The cogs on the wheel of Mamie's quick thinking caught, and she blurted out in that resonant voice that carried so well: "Well then, you must know our Hester. Wasn't she *au-gnomma* by that Hans and his first wife? What was her name?"

"Catherine. Kate," Noah supplied.

"Yes, yes. That's right. So you are Hester's brother. Or something."

The "or something" brought quick smiles, but everyone saw how flushed Hester was, so they righted their smiles into deference, displaying the reverence that befitted this solemn occasion, and said no more.

Hannah added the butter and salt, while Mamie Troyer poured the hot milk from the dipper, viewing Noah's blond hair unashamedly and making a few lilting remarks. For here was a *schoena yunga*, and it didn't hurt to get a smile from him, or at least some recognition.

Noah smiled and lifted his head, but only for a quick second as he looked for Hester. She stood behind the cookstove, away from too many knowing eyes. She was watching Noah's wide shoulders, his white shirt too small and tugging at the seams, the too-short sleeves rolled up as he plied the potato masher. It looked like a toy in his hands.

"Oops. Ach, oops. Ooops!" Mamie Troyer stepped back as she dropped the dipper of hot milk. It splattered across the bench, over Noah's and Jessie's pant legs, eventually pooling on the oak boards in a white, steaming puddle.

Hester grabbed a clean cloth, lowered herself, and began mopping up the spilled milk as Mamie clutched her cheeks, apologizing profusely for such a *dummes*.

Hester swabbed the milk—luckily, the dipper had only been half-full—and assured Mamie there was plenty of milk, it would be all right.

As she got to her feet, Noah and Jessie sat back down. Noah met Hester's eyes. "Thank you Hester." Hester nodded, her smile for only a second, her eyes only for him. But they all saw. These women were sharp. They'd raised large families, were in fact still raising them.

A beautiful young widow, the long lost brother, but not a brother at all. They lifted their hands to their mouths, thinking, *Siss yusht.*

Old Suvilla, from her rocking chair, felt the familiar prick of goosebumps up her arms. She rocked a bit to hide her nodding. *Ya, dess gebt hochzich.*

In Gottes zeit. In Gottes zeit.

CHAPTER 7

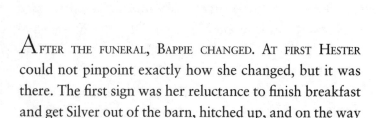

AFTER THE FUNERAL, BAPPIE CHANGED. AT FIRST HESTER could not pinpoint exactly how she changed, but it was there. The first sign was her reluctance to finish breakfast and get Silver out of the barn, hitched up, and on the way to the farm. Noah was close to completing the sturdy oak floor, and he had only a few directions from Bappie.

The house was even more desolate than Hester remembered. She could not see how Bappie could improve very much with only two weeks of Noah's labor, but she didn't say anything until the second week, when Bappie expressed no more enthusiasm or ideas.

They were finishing up a breakfast of fried mush and eggs, with coffee soup, a rare treat. There had been a few coffee beans left over at the funeral, which Bappie asked to take home, mincing no words and offering no apology. She wanted coffee soup for breakfast.

Hester liked it, remembering it as a treat at Christmas, when Doddy Zugs would bring coffee beans. Kate would brew coffee, while they all inhaled the rich, brown fragrance. She would add hot milk and brown sugar to the drink, and they would pour it over toasted bread, enjoying every spoonful of the soggy, sweet, coffee-flavored soup.

Bappie scraped her spoon carefully across the heavy dish, put it in her mouth to savor the last bit of soup, slid down in her chair, yawned, stretched her arms above her head, and whooshed out a breath of air.

Hester eyed her from the opposite end of the table. "Either you're not sleeping well, or you're plain lazy."

Quickly, Bappie sat up. "Oh, no, no. Nothing like that. Come, Hester. Let's get these dishes washed. We need to get out to the house. Noah's probably been there since sunup. Nope, nothing wrong with me, Hester. Why?"

"It just seems as if you've lost interest in fixing the house."

"What? Me? No, never." With that, Bappie jumped up and cleared the table so fast she was like a blur rushing past. She scalded herself with the hot water she dumped into the dishpan. She threw the harness over Silver's back with so much power it almost slid down the other side.

The faithful horse's sides were lathered with sweat by the time they reached the farm, goaded on by Bappie's burst of high spirits. She was like a whirlwind all day.

Noah pushed back his hat and watched her carrying boards. He sat down in the shade of the maple tree in front of the house, opened his lunch bucket, found the cheese, bread, and butter, and began to eat.

Here he was, on the tenth day of the twelve he would be hired, and he had had not one chance to talk to Hester, other than the usual banter or talking about the job, and with Bappie present every time. He thought perhaps she might not show up one of these days, the way she seemed to lack direction or energy after the funeral. But then, he guessed it was because she had lost a friend and she felt defeated.

The addition was well on its way. The walls were up and the rafters set. Now all it needed was the roof, which Bappie had bought from the lumberyard in town, saying they had no time to make their own.

Noah sat against the trunk of the tree, his gaze roaming to the garden where the fine pea stalks climbed up the low fence. He had watched Hester put in stakes close to the roots and then tie hemp rope from stake to stake. With all the good rains, they should have a bumper crop of peas to sell before the middle of June.

He could not imagine a woman being so enterprising, but then he thought, this is a new age, a new generation, and some things do not always stay the same. He was so proud of Hester making her own way. He wished she would talk about her healing with herbs, but she never once mentioned the subject.

He finished the molasses cake, tipped the crockery jug of water, and swallowed gratefully. The sun was overhead, already showing the strength of the sizzling days of July and August.

He was surprised to see Hester walking in his direction, carrying the two-handled lunch basket they filled every day. Her pace slowed as she came near, placing her feet timidly, as if she was afraid she would waken him. Surely she would not sit beside him on the grass beneath this tree. But that is exactly what she did. Settling herself comfortably about a foot away, she lifted the lid of the basket and extracted a slice of bread. She opened a brown paper of cold, cooked bacon, laid a few slices on one side, folded the bread and took a small bite. Still, she said nothing.

He could hear the dull hammering of his heart, a pounding in his ears. His breathing quickened; he hoped she would remain unaware. He prayed for Bappie to stay busy, to stay away.

Hester broke the silence abruptly. "Is Hans . . . are Annie and Hans still alive?"

Noah's heart fluttered, then sank, when he realized that was all she wanted from him.

"Yes, as far as I know. I think the people in Berks County know I am here in the Lancaster settlement."

Hester nodded. "You mean, if they, if one of them would pass away, they would let you know?"

"Yes."

"Are they well? Hans and Annie?"

"I believe they are."

She ate in silence then. "Do you understand why I left?"

His throat constricted with unexpected emotion, closing off the words he wanted to speak. He shook his head from side to side.

"If I tell you, will keep it quiet?"

He nodded, the constriction worsening.

"It was Hans. His love for me should have gone to Annie. She hated me for that reason."

Still he could not speak.

"It was my own fault."

Without thinking, and feeling only rage that pushed back any obstruction in his throat, Noah burst out, "What are you talking about? None of that was your fault."

Hester dropped her head. She bowed her long graceful neck in humility and lowered her eyelids. The profile of her face was unbearably sad.

"Hester, look at me."

Her only answer was a shake of her head.

"You can't mean what you just said."

"But I do."

Suddenly, she raised her head to face him squarely, her chest heaving with the force of her words, her eyes flashing the dark fire of the intensity she felt. "Noah, you don't know what a sinner I have been. I was accosted by my own husband's brother in the cellar at Christmastime. And I was rebellious to William, as well. So how could I blame my life and its trials on others, on men? Things like this occur so often, and, Noah, it is all my own fault. William said so."

Noah took a deep breath to steady himself. He realized his hands were shaking, jarring the lid of his lunch bucket.

"Hester, you must stop thinking this. It is a lie. God gave you your beauty. These . . . those . . . the men, my own father . . ." His voice faded away as the words fell over each other, a stone in his chest replacing the warmth of his beating heart.

Now her hands went up to cover her face as she began to cry, unable to control the years of pent-up fear and self-loathing.

Noah's longing to take her in his arms was so strong that he got to his feet in one swift upward movement and in two long strides, separated himself from Hester. Only now did he begin to grasp the enormity of his undertaking. To win her, to have her, was not possible at this time—and maybe never—with her mind so set on William's accusation, his blaming her.

Of course, Bappie chose to make her appearance just then, waving and striding quickly in their direction. "Where's the basket? I'm hungry. Have you eaten already, Noah? No use rushing off. Stay sitting. Let's have a picnic here under the lovely tree."

Noah smiled and said thanks, but reminded her that he had only one more day, and it would take the rest of the afternoon to finish the one side of the roof. Hester gathered herself together as best she could, partially hiding her face by looking at the fast-growing pea stalks.

Bappie plopped down, opened the lunch basket, wrinkled her nose, and said something in there smelled odd. What had Hester packed?

Hester sniffed, got to her feet, and said if she didn't like what was in that basket, why then she could pack it herself.

Bappie lifted her chin and watched Hester stalk off in one direction and Noah in another. It was too bad, she thought, the way those two simply couldn't hit it off. But then, often that was the way. She'd heard Mamie Troyer talking to Lydia Esh about how *au-gnomma* children often had bad natures, and it didn't work out. Not that Hester wasn't good. You just had to be careful about these things.

That Noah was a looker, though. Made you wonder, the way he seemed to avoid talking to Hester. Bappie guessed they simply didn't like each other too good. Too bad, because they made quite a pair. Well, no romance in the air where those two were concerned, so that was that.

She shrugged her shoulders, bit off a piece of over-cooked bacon, rolled a hard-boiled egg to remove the shell, added a pinch of salt, and popped half of it into her mouth. She chewed contentedly, watched the crows flapping overhead, and thought about living here with Hester. Much better than in town. So much better.

The sun was too hot for the month of May, she observed. These sorry little buds on the trees did nothing to keep the striking light of the sun off her face. Bappie reached for the water jug, wiped her forehead, and thought a storm was likely brewing with this extraordinary heat from the new spring sunshine.

Hester stopped drilling the floorboards, sat back, and looked out the door. Sweat trickled down the middle of her back. Her dress felt too snug; her face was flushed with the heat. It seemed like August when the corn and tomatoes were ripe.

One side of the roof was finished, throwing shadowed light across the yellow plank floor. The opposite side offered only strips of shade, so the heat from the sun was finding its way between the laths Noah had nailed across the rafters.

Hester returned to drilling holes where the wooden pegs would be pounded. This would be a good, solid oak floor that would never wear through. Around and around, her one arm swung the drill, while her other arm pushed down on its top. Oak lumber was hard, the best choice for a floor, but in the heat of this day, Hester was wearing out and her patience was growing thin. It didn't help that the conversation with Noah had gone wrong, veering off into a disagreement.

She had meant to alert him of her inability to be a wife. He had to know. He had to understand that she could not possibly return to her Berks County home.

She could never forgive Hans. That was not possible. She hated him with hatred that ran in her blood. She felt the agonized cries of the Lenape, pushed from their homes and denied their birthright by the white people who moved into Pennsylvania like a swarm of locusts. Like Pharaoh's plague in the Bible. *Diese hoyschrecken.* These grasshoppers.

She know the hatred was wrong. It was so wrong to remember Hans's behavior and to think of Annie's cruelty. It had become much easier to shift the blame onto herself and to set Hans and Annie free from judgment.

Only sometimes on the darkest nights, the tears would seep from her eyes and pool in her ears as she lay staring at the underside of the ceiling, the hewn logs rough and dark, the way her heart felt when she remembered. Yet she longed to return, to feel the safety of the familiar pastures, gardens, and roads of her childhood, to soak up the security of the innocence that was no longer hers.

Yes, God had given her this beauty, but to what end? A curse was all it was, the way the men in her life behaved without being respectful. At least some of them.

If only she had learned to behave in a more careful manner. She had been too free with her smiles, the flash of her dark eyes, allowing herself to enjoy William's company and Johnny's attention.

She had loved Hans and adored him as a child, accompanying him on his horseshoeing forays, becoming the delight of the Amish settlement. Large, swarthy, dark-haired Hans and his astoundingly beautiful little Indian daughter, who handed him his nails and his tools and was never afraid of the spirited horses or the hooves that could strike out with the speed of lightning.

Kate had always been free with her affections, smiling easily, placing a warm hand like a crown of approval on Hester's dark head, softly singing German hymns that Hester absorbed like melting sugar.

She sang boisterously, sometimes, too, her blue eyes laughing, her head nodding in time to the silly words, but only when Hans was safely out of hearing distance.

Her hair is so *schtrubbly* in the wind
Her eyes so big and brown,
I often see her on the road,
When I drive into town.

At the washtub, mostly, she would sing the songs of her youth, when Hans was tall and dark and she was the slim, blue-eyed *schtrubblich maedle*.

The hatred she felt for Hans as she grew older was a canker sore in her soul. If she gave in to it, eventually the canker would burst, poisoning her with its infection and spreading through her whole being with its dark and sinister promise and pushing out God's healing love.

It wasn't possible to harbor hatred and healing love at the same time. They could not coexist. But on some dark nights, fear and remembering would come back. She determined it was far better to blame herself. She wanted Noah to know this, although she wasn't exactly sure why it was important. Well, now he knew. He could disagree if he wanted, but she would never let her guard down.

Late in the afternoon, the water jugs were empty and the sun's heat was like a wet blanket. The air was moist and much too hot after the cold of winter and the bone-chilling breezes of April that had bent the old brown goldenrod and the stubbles of wheat and had matted the grasses in the fields.

Bappie threw herself down along the north side of the house where the damp earth held cool moisture and cold earthworms dug along the base of it. She pulled her skirts up to mid-calf, then untied her sturdy black shoes and kicked them off, each one landing with a thunk in the new grass. She rolled down her heavy socks, then leaned forward and tugged on the toes, slid the itchy garments over her heels, and flung them after the shoes.

She sat back against the log walls, dug her heels into the cool, damp earth, and wiggled each toe, liberating them from the heat of the socks. She closed her eyes, took a deep breath, and let the tension roll off her shoulders and down her back.

The only sound was Noah's steady hammering. She had never seen anyone slap on wooden shingles like that. *An begaubta mensch*, for sure.

Perhaps he'd be like his father, Hans. But then, they said Hans didn't become prosperous till he married

Annie. She was the one that set the gunpowder under Hans's britches and managed like a man. She knew when the moon turned in July and you dug thistles, when to plant corn, which horse could easily work all day and which one should be sold. That's what they said.

Bappie was not the first one to notice the cloud in the northwest. She was sitting in the moist shade, so the fading yellow light went unnoticed by her as she thought about that Annie Troyer wearing the trousers the way she did.

Noah stopped and looked off to where the line of trees met the flat grassland of the meadow. A fast moving line of clouds had already swallowed the sun. Without its heat, the air turned brassy, and a yellow pallor fell over the surrounding fields.

Hester straightened, laid the drill by the wall, rubbed her back, and went to the door, wondering where the light had gone. She lifted her head and sniffed the air. Not a whisper of a breeze. The new leaves on the trees hung as still as lace doilies on a shelf, their pattern constant.

She did not like the brassy atmosphere. There was a storm brewing—ominous, a black panther of the sky stalking the earth below, ready to unleash its power of sizzling lightning and great earsplitting crashes of thunder. This would be a big one.

Her eyes went to the garden and the steady green growth of the pea vines. Healthy tendrils reached toward the top string that Hester had stretched between the wooden stakes. Ah, surely God would spare them. Hard, knife-like sheets of rain, strong winds, and the heavens crashing and rumbling about them would be fearsome, but none of that would have the power to damage like the dreaded hail and its large balls of ice. She took another deep breath. She could smell the rain, the moisture that would fall from that black, boiling bank of clouds.

Bappie came around the corner of the house, her eyes dark, every freckle visible, the blanching of her skin revealing the depth of her fear. "Storm coming, huh?"

"Looks like it."

"Is it bad?"

Hester shrugged. She lifted her eyes to the horizon, watching.

Bappie watched Hester's quiet face. "How bad?" she repeated.

"It's a good-sized storm."

Hester had been born with the uncanny ability to sense the coming of different changes in the weather, an Indian skill and knowledge that had been a part of her since birth. She had no fear of any of nature's forces. She was calm and unhurried in the face of storms and winds.

Noah scrambled off the roof, threw his hat on the ground, and ran his hands through his blond hair, turned dark with the sweat of the day's heat. "Think we should head back?"

Bappie searched Hester's face for reassurance, anything. She swallowed the fear rising in her throat, her breath coming in jagged puffs.

"I wouldn't." Hester spoke quietly, nodding her head toward the black cloud. Noah looked at her dark eyes that were intent, curious, eager. Without a trace of fear. "It's coming fast."

"What about the garden?" Bappie asked, her voice quivering.

In answer, Hester shrugged slightly, her eyes never leaving the clouds.

They stood in front of the house, the small log hut with the unfinished addition, the new shingles a lighter shade than the dark, warped ones on the original roof. The small front porch would give them a bit of shelter when the storm hit, but for now, it was comfortable to stand in the new grass surrounding the house, feeling the air change to a more seasonable temperature as the storm approached.

Noah, looking around, decided to push the buggy into the small barn with Silver, then latch the door securely, as he had always been taught.

The first rumble could soon be heard, even before any lightning was visible, which was unusual. A prickle of apprehension raised the hair on Noah's arms. He crossed them across his chest and absently drew a palm across his forearm. "Let's go inside."

Bappie's teeth were chattering as she sat on the edge of the porch to put on her socks, now a welcome warmth. Noah watched her, seeing that she hated a storm. A quick stab of sympathy softened his eyes, and the lines around his mouth softened, as he thought about how alone she was and how responsible, without a husband, father, or mother to care for her.

Hester lifted her arm, pointing a finger in the direction of the storm. Small, orange streaks, like trailing threads, appeared as a fringe on the fast-moving clouds. As they watched, the streaks' size and color changed until they appeared as white, hot, jagged streaks of lightning, powerful and breathtaking in their fury.

Ahead of the boiling mass of clouds, the blue of the sky had changed to a dirty yellow, as if the hissing clouds had spewed their tepid breath before the onslaught they contained.

Still, the new leaves hung unmoving; not a blade of grass whispered. A large brown spider scuttled across the bare spots, disappearing beneath a wall of grass. In the barn, Silver whinnied, a high, lonely sound, as if the static in the air reminded him that he was in a solitary pen, deep in the surrounding walls of the barn.

"He wants out. He's afraid," Bappie said, quite unexpectedly.

Noah shook his head. "He's better off in the barn."

The first sign that the storm had come closer was a soft rustling of the new leaves, a subtle rearranging of their pattern. The small grasses waved, disturbed by an undercurrent of the winds that were about to sweep through.

Noah rubbed his palms across his forearms as the wind increased, lifting the wet hair from his moist brow. Hester reached behind her back, found the wide, white strings of her muslin cap, and tied them securely beneath her chin.

Bappie whimpered like a child as she watched the heavy pea crop begin to shiver, the tender shoots waving slowly like tiny, slim dancers moving to invisible instruments, the prelude to the approaching storm.

CHAPTER 8

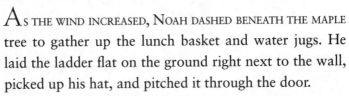

As the wind increased, Noah dashed beneath the maple tree to gather up the lunch basket and water jugs. He laid the ladder flat on the ground right next to the wall, picked up his hat, and pitched it through the door.

The last row of shingles hummed, as if an unseen hand was rifling through them. In a matter of seconds, the wind rose, a wall of power that ripped the tender new leaves off the purple stems and sent them whirling through the thick yellow atmosphere, followed by dead growth from all trees and bushes. Grasses were flattened in a minute. The garden became a mass of undulating movements, the plants twisted and tortured by the power of the storm.

When Hester shouted and pointed, Noah reached her side, then followed the direction of her finger. Where the clouds were darkest, in the middle of the restless, roiling mass, a lashing tail appeared, a dark, terrible tunnel of fury, whipping as if building its strength for the moment it would hit the soft green earth beneath it.

Bappie screamed a sound of rich terror as gigantic hailstones hit the earth in front of them. As one, they turned and raced for the safety of the four log walls. Noah slammed the door, breathing hard, but Hester yanked it open, yelling that being watchful was what they needed to do. She stood at the door, her hands bracing her body, as the wind roared and hailstones sharp as knives whirled onto the porch floor.

The roars and moans reached a shrieking crescendo. Bappie's screams of terror were lost among the intensity of the wind.

Suddenly, Hester turned, flattened herself against the wall of the house, and cried out for Noah and Bappie to do the same. Like three fenceposts, they lay prone against the sturdy log walls. Hester stopped her ears with her fingers, the pressure in her head almost unbearable. Bappie no longer screamed, and if she made any sound at all, it was lost in the roaring and gnashing that were the wind and hail, the torrents of water and ice.

All they knew, then, was a ripping, tearing sound, as if a giant piece of fabric had been torn in two. And then the hail—and cold, wet pain—hit their bodies. Noah yelled as a bough of the maple tree hung on the log wall where the roof had been, toppled, and fell on top of him, the weight of it smashing into his back and taking his breath away.

As he fought to regain it, out of the corner of his eye he saw the opposite wall shudder, then fold out and crumble, the logs falling haphazardly. Dust, thick and brown, was instantly soothed by a biblical deluge from the moaning, roaring sky.

Hester pressed her body to the ground, praying the wall would hold. If the logs came dislodged and rolled, they'd be killed, if even one fell on top of them. She had never known such fear, didn't know it existed. She pressed her face into the cracks of the lowest log and breathed in the splinters and sawdust, dirt and dust of years of neglect in this little old hut they meant to call their home.

She was aware of being soaked through, of being cold and shivering, of being accosted by sharp blades of freezing rain, by the clamoring wind, and by a high keening sound like the howling of a thousand demons left helpless in the storm's wake. Her tears were undetected as her soul cried out for deliverance. She knew only that the grace of God alone could save them all from this untamable fury. She was as helpless as the day she was born.

A great ripping, tearing sound rose higher than the wind. She heard the splintering of some object she could not identify. Sobs rose in her throat, along with the knowledge that they would all surely die.

A great sadness for what might have been welled up in Hester. But suddenly she throbbed with anger at the rip-roaring elements that had turned her into this dirty, wet, sniveling heap. She was not going to die. If a log fell off this wall, the wind could just place it beside them. A cry of deliverance emerged from her throat as she felt, rather than heard, an easing of the shrieking wind. The worst must be over. But better to stay here than risk the deceiving lull in the wind.

Rain still pounded against their bodies. The log wall shivered but held. The wind moaned around it; the clouds boiled like black porridge over their heads. Piles of ice were scattered across the floor of the hut, banked against the tree trunks, and whooshed into the air and flung out of sight by the power of the gale. And yet Hester knew the worst was past. She could sense the storm's weakening, its defeat.

Noah was the first to sit up, painfully, his shirt soaked with blood where the branch had jammed into the muscle of his back. The dark reddish color turned pink where the rain and hail had lashed at the cut. He winced, then put his head in his hands to steady himself as the world tilted and turned black.

Bappie had fainted dead away. Hester leaned over to place a hand on her narrow, sodden back. The heartbeat was there, strong and sure, but she slept on.

Hester rolled over and got to her feet. Quickly, she surveyed this new world. Only two walls of the hut remained standing. The maple tree was twisted off and flung across the garden, a sentry fallen in its prime.

Her throat tightened. The roof was gone. It had simply disappeared, the new one and the old one, like a grandfather and a newborn grandson joining hands and melting into the horizon. The barn was a pile of debris, everything misplaced, the buggy somewhere inside.

Silver. The dread of discovering Bappie's faithful horse injured or dead made her nauseous. Oh, surely not.

She turned to Noah. She was shocked to see his bent head. Dirt, wet, puddles of filthy water, splinters of wood, sodden leaves and dead grasses, branches—destruction was everywhere.

She nudged Bappie, then tried to speak, but only croaked. She cleared her throat, turned to Noah, and reached out to touch his head. "Noah?"

He lifted his head, the pupils of his blue eyes black with pain and shock, his face the color of new muslin.

"Are you hurt?"

"My back." He spoke the words around a block of pain. The effort to speak took his full concentration.

"Can you move?"

In answer, and with heroic effort, he leaned forward, wincing. The muscles in his face worked, but he got to his knees and turned.

Hester remained calm, having seen so much suffering when she treated the poor in the low section of town. The soaked shirt that clung to his pooled blood was not too alarming. So she said nothing at first, quietly bending over Noah's shoulder. Then she asked him to move forward a bit so she could see.

He complied, but sank to the floor, his legs folding beneath him as he fought waves of darkness.

His shirt was torn and mangled, so when Hester lifted it away, she was not surprised to see the massive lacerations. The extent of his wound was beyond her knowledge. She bit her lower lip to extinguish the gasp that rose in her throat.

Bappie moved, whimpering.

Hester straightened and looked around. Noah had lost too much blood and was still losing it, so that made it impossible to move him.

She shouted for Bappie to wake up, nudging her with a wet shoe. "Bappie. Wake up. Come on. Up."

She groaned, opened one eye, rolled over, and covered her face with her hands. "Oh, dear Lord. Dear Lord. What have we done to deserve this, your *tzorn?*"

"Bappie, listen, Noah is hurt, bad."

"Why?" Still dazed and uncomprehending, Bappie lay on her back, as wet and bedraggled as a drowned rat.

And worth about as much, Hester thought. Well, it was off to Levi Buehler's, the closest farm. She'd have to walk. She told Noah to stay there and not to move, ignored Bappie, and headed in Levi's direction, stepping over destruction, trying not to think of Silver somewhere in that heap of lumber that used to be a barn.

When it became evident that the power of the twisting, grinding wind had been a narrow swath, she broke into a steady lope, her feet settling easily on the wet ground, the only hindrance her heavy, sodden skirts that clung to her legs like cold, wet flaps of leather.

Everywhere branches were torn off trees, and broken limbs lay on the ground, leaving yellow wounds in the steady coat of bark that protected the tree. Some of the older, weakened trees were toppled, pulling down more branches of healthy trees, but nowhere was the destruction as bad as at Bappie's small place, the old hut, the small barn, and few surrounding acres.

She slowed and came to a stop, her breathing in short rapid jerks, when she saw an approaching figure. Tall and thin and surrounded by his coonhounds, Levi Buehler was on his way to see how they had fared during the storm.

His hat was floppy, the brim coming loose from its base. One side was higher than the other, giving him the appearance of someone rather pitiful, a poor person needing help. His shirt was clean but old, torn in places and patched, or patched on top of a patch.

His eyes were kind, the laugh lines called crow's feet deep and pronounced from squinting in sunlight, or straining to see through the dark nights when he went coon hunting. His beard was gray and thin, like an afterthought of wispy hair.

"Hester!" He flung up a large, knobby hand, like a fly swatter, a long flat growth on the end of a thin handle.

"Levi."

"I was on my way to make sure you're all right out there. Never saw clouds like that. Figure you had hail."

Hester gave a short, rueful laugh. "A lot more than hail. Listen, Levi, Noah Zug was working on Bappie's roof, and he was hurt. We need a doctor. Can you help us, please?"

Levi had already turned, his hounds like an appendage of himself, and was gone, calling, "Be there as soon as I can."

The desolation was hard to describe. Bappie's small holdings were flattened except for the south and west walls of the hut, the barn was in splinters, the garden ravaged, the crops all lost, and the buggy buried somewhere. Faithful Silver lay beneath the capsized walls, a mound of beautiful silver horseflesh with no life at all. He had gaping wounds on his head and neck; one leg was almost severed, impaled by the beam from the door.

Bappie said it was just as well that he died, because they'd have had to shoot him with that busted leg. She didn't cry, only sniffed and blew her nose, blinked rapidly, lifted her head, and said, "That's how it goes. You never know."

Noah was soon stitched together, bandaged, and taken back to Dan Stoltzfus's, where he lived. The kindly doctor, George Norton, did his work efficiently, giving Noah a healthy dose of whiskey to help with the pain. The flying limb had cut his back so that it looked like great raw chunks.

Only Levi Buehler, Bappie, and Hester remained in the aftermath of the storm. The countryside looked washed clean, in spite of the ruined buildings. The sky rippled with shades of rose, lavender, deep orange, and yellow. The sun had emerged from still grumbling clouds that were neither gray nor white, like dirty sheep's wool before shearing.

Bappie bit her lip as she lifted shreds of ruined pea vines. She kicked the sodden growth, gouged a hole in the mud with the toe of her shoe, and looked at Hester. "You know I have nothing left."

"You have your things. Your furniture and dishes."

"I can't start another garden. I have no money to rebuild. I don't know what I'm going to do."

Levi Buehler stuck his hands in his pockets, leaned back, and eyed Bappie with one eye. The other one was covered by the floppy hat brim. "The church will help. When the men hear about this, they'll be out."

"Who's going to pay for the lumber, Levi?"

"Well, maybe I can."

"With what? Your skinny hounds?"

Levi lifted his face and laughed, a great sound of merriment that he had not made for too long. The wispy gray hairs on his chin waggled, his yellow teeth were in full view like even ears of corn, as he kept up the sound that made even Bappie smile.

"Ach, Bappie, I forgot."

"You forgot what?"

Levi shook his head.

Levi drove them home to Lancaster. Bappie jumped unceremoniously off the buggy, never said a word of appreciation, and disappeared through the back door, a thin stick of a woman, dirty and wet, but efficiently containing all her pride and well-being.

Hester thanked Levi, then turned to follow Bappie. She had already yanked the tub off the wall and was filling the kettle with cold water from the pump, as she barked at Hester to get some kindling made, they needed to wash.

They didn't eat anything, only drank warming cups of tea, holding the heavy mugs in both hands, each one appreciating the warmth, the roof, and the walls that enclosed them.

Walter Trout popped in unannounced with news of storm damage throughout the town. He took the news of Bappie's ruined farm with great soft sighs of sympathy, his swollen fingers entwined over his massive stomach. He pursed his lips and rolled his eyes, dipped his head, and grimaced as they told their story.

Emma stayed home and nursed her solid grudge. She told Walter he could prance over there and make amends, but she wasn't going to. But when she was told of their loss, she threw her hands in the air and cried, "*Ach, du lieva! Du yay! Die arme mäed!*"

She covered her fresh *Ob'l Dunkes Kucha* with a white tea towel and told the boys to stay out of mischief, that Vernon and Richard, the dear ones she'd taken in from the street. They could be a handful, they could.

The scent of the warm applesauce cake followed her, the short, wide woman who rocked from side to side when she walked, the pleated white housecap like a large blossom on top of her head, her beady dark eyes like boiled raisins.

She cried, "*Voss hott Gott getan? Meine arme liebchen!*" She patted their shoulders and kissed their cheeks and said, "No rent, no rent, just stay here with me and Walter," then had to sit down and lay a hand over her heart to still it, to slow it down. "More than a person can imagine. More than these *meine liebchen* can take."

But Walter said the Lord does not give us more than he gives us strength to bear, and he most assuredly had a plan somewhere. Emma nodded so hard her housecap slid forward over one eyebrow, then settled up farther on one side than the other.

Bappie ate three squares of applesauce cake and made another pot of tea, nodding her head in agreement with Walter's words of encouragement. Her eyes had narrowed though, and a new light glinted in them, as if the brown irises had been polished like silver with a damp cloth.

Hester saw this, she knew Bappie so well. Something was churning inside that mind like the dasher on the butter churn—*kalunka, spaloosh*. When she saw Bappie concentrating and chewing her nails, her eyes still holding the same gleam, she became concerned.

They ushered their effusive neighbors out the door with many cries of "*Gute Nacht. Denke, denke.*" Then they went to bed, each to her own room, sleepless, sighing long into the night as they relived the nightmarish event of the day. Never had they seen anything like it.

The following morning Bappie dressed in her Sunday clothes, her black cape and apron, the best muslin cap, and only a sliver of hair combed into submission visible. She told Hester she was going to borrow Walter and Emma's horse and carriage, that she would return right after this errand.

Hester nodded, sleepily frying sliced potatoes and onions in the heavy black skillet, knowing Bappie would eventually inform her of the nature of her morning errand. She'd likely be off to the lumberyard, although she was surprised Bappie had not asked her to accompany her.

Hester spent the forenoon resting, often dozing by the cookstove, attending to the bumps and bruises that kept making an appearance. Her back hurt, and one elbow burned. After viewing it in a mirror, she found a raw-looking scrape, almost like a burn. The back of her head was sore to the touch as well.

When Bappie came home, she opened the back door softly, closing it as if a baby might be awakened. Her face was serene, so peaceful it seemed almost waxen, like a candle.

Hester looked up, her eyebrows lifted in question. When Bappie offered no information, Hester asked what her plans were, how she was going to rebuild.

In answer, Bappie clapped her hands reverently as a rush of color suffused her cheeks, her eyes half-closed with piety. "I won't rebuild."

Hester sat up straight, her eyebrows rising in shock. "Why not, Bappie?"

"I just asked Levi Buehler to marry me."

Hester gazed at Bappie, speechless.

Immediately, Bappie found her voice. "Hester, it's not what you think, really it isn't. I just did what made sense. Levi has not had a wife for a very long time. He is a sad and lonely man. We have known each other for years. I did things for Martha. I tried to help them, but I realized now why I did it.

"The storm, the loss of everything I worked so hard to build, left me without pride. So I did what I thought made sense. I asked Levi if he wanted me for his wife. I told him I could just be like a *maud*, you know, not a real wife. I would clean the house, the garden, and yard. Did you ever see his garden? *Siss unfaschtendich.*

"I could have my room upstairs. We would get cows, raise pigs, have a nice flock of chickens. The hounds must go. But of course, I didn't tell him all this. I just drove up to the fence, tied the horse, knocked on the door, and asked him. I think I said '*Guten Morgen*' or something about the weather. I don't know. Can't rightly remember.

"He never said much. Didn't bat an eye. Just cleared his throat and said that sounded like a good idea. But he said he didn't want any of this *maud* business. He wanted me for a real wife, that he had planned on asking me but not till fall. Any earlier would be unseemly.

"So if people ask why I'm not building, tell them we're not raising produce anymore. That's all they need to know. See, I didn't want to spend money to get those few acres in shape if I'm not going to need the buildings."

Bappie paused for breath. "What's for breakfast? I'm about ready to collapse from hunger."

While they ate, Bappie told Hester she could stay with them, help around the house or teach school, perhaps further her studies of the herbs.

Hester listened, nodding, catching the hopeful tone in Bappie's words, knowing she wanted rid of her, and soon. She cut the pancake on her plate with the side of her fork, her eyes downcast, her shoulders slumped forward, as if it made her weary to lift them.

Slowly, she began to shake her head from side to side. "You won't want me, Bappie. I'd be like a third hand you didn't need. I'll stay here and find some place of employment. Something will work out."

"You should charge the people you treat. Make them pay."

"They don't have anything, Bappie."

"You've treated rich people."

"I know. But they all return to the doctor. They have more faith in him than my jumble of herbs and tinctures."

Bappie nodded. "At any rate, we need to find employment for the summer. I must sew my wedding dress, make tablecloths, and crochet doilies and embroider pillowcases. I know Martha had all that, but I want my own stuff.

"I am getting married, Hester! I'm no longer going to be skinny, red-haired, single old Bappie Kinnich. I am going to be called '*da Levi sei Bappie.*' Think about it. A place to be, close by Levi's side. And he is not wearing that hat. It's *schrecklich mit,* that hat."

She laughed, a sound that welled up from the triumph in her lonely, middle-aged heart. "I'll be a good wife. Just think how I'll keep house and the garden. The barn, I'll help him, show him what it takes to have a nice herd of cows that *faschpritz* with milk. My father was a good herdsman. I learned it all from him."

Hester nodded, smiling. She could see this. That Buehler place would be the picture of good management, now that Levi had the ambitious helpmeet he needed, the push to get him going. After years of having Martha to care for, how must he feel, looking forward to a new beginning?

After wondering what God had done, venting his anger in allowing that storm to lay desolation to Bappie's small buildings, here, like a phoenix from the ashes, arose a brand new life for Bappie. She only had to get rid of her pride.

Of course, in years to come, Bappie and Levi's story would be told and retold, how the old maid became desperate and asked the widower. Embellishment, that added-on packet of spice, would provide entertainment around tables, knee-slapping hilarity, all in good fun. Among the Amish, although the story was true, the telling of it met with open-mouthed disbelief, generation after generation.

CHAPTER 9

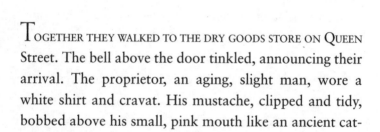

TOGETHER THEY WALKED TO THE DRY GOODS STORE ON QUEEN Street. The bell above the door tinkled, announcing their arrival. The proprietor, an aging, slight man, wore a white shirt and cravat. His mustache, clipped and tidy, bobbed above his small, pink mouth like an ancient caterpillar, or one dropped in lye.

The shop was empty. "Everyone's cleaning up after the storm," he said. They asked to see the blues first. The royal blue was so beautiful, the color of the indigo bunting.

Hester was not expecting the desolation she felt, the need to gather every ounce of strength to be happy for Bappie when she held the color to her face and twirled a bit, jubilation following her every move.

"Do you think it will suit me?" Her brown eyes in the narrow, freckled face were so eager, so anxious.

Quickly, Hester pushed back the thought that she looked like a horse, her face so long and narrow. She felt so wretched inside she turned away, grabbing moments to compose herself. "I think it's perfect. We're allowed blue and purple for weddings, so purple would probably be a bit bright with your auburn hair."

"You think?"

The caterpillar spread out, elongating as the clerk bowed and dipped with pleasure. It was a big sale of very expensive fabric. Hester could not believe the price, but said nothing when Bappie produced the cash from the deep pocket in her skirt.

"What do you think, Hester? Would I be too fancy if I bought black velvet ribbon to sew on the bottom of the sleeves? It looks so nice, the way the young girls do."

Hester nodded, urging her on quickly before Bappie would see the shadow that darkened her eyes. She remembered William's disapproval the time she had purchased a yard of black velvet to sew on the deep purple sleeves of a new Sunday dress. No woman of his would be seen with such finery, for shame. What would Mother say? If this is how she was becoming, then she needed to stay out of that worldly dry goods store. The peddler would be around, and he knew what Amish housewives needed.

Her eyes bright with the anger that infused her, she had said levelly, "The peddler has black velvet ribbon. Your mother bought some for Suvilla."

"Enough!" thundered William.

Lowering his voice, he brought his face close to hers and quoted a verse from Proverbs, about how a woman cloaked herself with righteousness. How could she even aspire to be a woman worthy of the King family and their Amish heritage if she lusted after strange, worldly objects?

Hester had slunk away from him, threw a shoe at the door he passed through, then sank into the armless rocker and cried her frustration at never being allowed to be heard. *Just once let him see that I am capable of making choices, even small ones. Let him acknowledge I am a person with a mind of my own who thinks like other people.*

Bappie paid for the velvet, then fairly danced out of the store and down the street. She waved to passersby, folks she knew who bought her fresh spring onions and small green peas.

"Not this year," she told Hester. "Someone else will have to take my place at market. Someone else will fill my shoes. I have to sew. I'm getting married."

She walked sedately, but her spirit skipped and hopped and danced, visible only by the quick darting of her eyes, the flashing smile, the greetings she called so loudly and easily. Hester had never suspected this of Bappie, her all-encompassing joy at having a man of her own.

She told Hester she had never had a date. No one had ever come to court her. Now she was going to be Levi's wife, and still she had never been courted.

"Whoo-ee!" And on and on, the whole way home.

Bappie spread the richly hued fabric out on the kitchen table, dug out the paper pattern she would need, then fetched the big scissors from the cupboard drawer. This dress would have to be perfect, so she could not make a wrong cut. She hovered over the table, breathing heavily, talking nonstop, cutting slowly, a brick weighing down the pattern.

Hester wandered outside, sat on the back stoop, lifted her burning elbow, and grimaced. She wondered how

Noah was doing. She felt bumped and bruised, sore and aching in every joint. In a way, the storm had been good. She had never looked forward to moving out there, unsure exactly why she wasn't excited about it. And now she wouldn't need to.

Well, one thing was certain. She would not live with Levi and Bappie. She would not intrude into their happiness. Perhaps Walter and Emma would allow her to stay here without paying the rent she could not afford.

The atmosphere was clean, newly washed, and fresh since the storm had cleared the air. Spring breezes wafted around her like an elusive scent she could not name, bringing a longing she could not define or understand. The sweetness and fullness of life was found in God, and in him alone, of this she was sure.

Unlike Bappie, she had been married and failed. God did not give second chances to those who acted as miserably rebellious as she had. She wished her friend a long and happy life, but fervently hoped that Levi was as good as his word. How could Bappie go about making all these plans without consulting him? Thinking of Levi and his kindness to Martha, his love of the people around him, yes, Bappie had a good chance at happiness, she believed.

As if God knew Hester needed a distraction, a vicious cloud of influenza settled over the town of Lancaster and its surrounding areas. Without the cautionary hand-washing, or even the frequent washing of their bodies, people suffered the dreaded virus that spread like a plague, which is what a few of the doctors named it.

"A curse," cried the devout. "God has cursed us with this plague."

Superstition prevailed in many of the homes and neighborhoods where a rich jumble of cultures all came together. Many immigrants were from the German-speaking areas of central Europe, from Switzerland, Germany itself, and the old Austrian Empire. Many of them carried the old fears of a "hex," a word pertaining to witches or witchcraft.

Some were deeply embroiled in the practice of *braucha*, certain rituals for eliminating diseases, because they believed that every sickness was a sign that witches had played their mischief. *Hexerei* was frequently heard, as the old covered their heads with their hands, repenting and declaring themselves unworthy of God's mercy.

Entire families took to their beds, their intestines cramping with pain. A clamping nausea emptied stomachs. And when there was little the doctors could accomplish, they sent for Hester.

The first request came with a firm knock, just when Hester had set a pot of potatoes to boil for the evening meal. Bappie opened the door, alarmed to find a neighbor man, pale and shaking, as if he had encountered a terrible fright. His hair was unkempt, a week's growth of unshaven hair like a scattering of dark, prickly splinters stood out from his cheeks, the ashen color beneath them signaling that he could fall in a heap on their doorstep.

"I beg your pardon. I hear this is the house where the Indian woman abides."

Bappie nodded, thinking *"abides"*?

"We need help. My family is all abed with the sickness."

Bappie stepped back, the sour smell from his mouth assailing her from the distance between them. Turning, she called, "I'll get her for you," and closed the door with a decided clunk of the latch.

Going to the kitchen with swift steps, Bappie focused her eyes on Hester's, then jerked her thumb in the direction of the door, and mouthed, "Go."

Hester slid the pot of potatoes to the back of the stove, wiped her hands on her apron, and went quickly, lifting the latch and opening the door cautiously.

Her practiced eye took in the pallor, the weak, rheumy eyes, the steady tremor of his hands, the chapped lips, and knew this man was indeed very sick.

"Where do you live?" Hester asked, immediately taking stock of the situation, knowing words of advice were useless.

"On Water Street. The second house. Stone. A white door."

"Very well. I'll be on my way. Will you be able to go back on your own?"

"Yes."

Not waiting to see how he fared, Hester was already closing the door. A sense of purpose swelled in her veins, as though her calling was singing her on, to lay her hands on suffering, fevered brows, to find good, cold water.

Going to the cupboard containing the bottled tinctures, she took down different ones, pursing her lips in concentration. Plantain and almond water. Red poppy syrup made with molasses. Bran, flaxseed infused with beer as a poultice for stomach pain. Oil of chamomile.

Her mind churned as she dropped the fruits of her gathering into a basket. Her labor of love filled her hours with wading in swamps, the watery mud sucking at her bare feet like a strong catfish's mouth. Sunny meadows were her favorite place—dry and clean, with easy access to dozens of plants and the herbs she knew so well, although learning their properties was a constant challenge. The origins of her treatments were all written in the old pages of the Indian woman's book. There was the priceless wisdom about the application of poultices for external use, the herbs to be gathered, dried, and then mixed with liquor, although whiskeys and brandies were so hard to obtain for these internal remedies.

At first, after her move to Lancaster, her friend Walter Trout had been able to purchase them for her at one of the many taverns that were sprinkled throughout the town. "Like rotting boils on healthy skin," Emma Feree had said, in clipped, judgmental sentences, hating even the thought of the devil's brew in her pure house.

But the liquor was a necessity, Hester had pleaded. Emma never allowed it after poor Walter came home, stuttering half-lies to cover his mission of procuring the *opp schtellt* liquid for her. So there was nothing left for Hester to do but bargain with the tavern owners herself. She would dress in her most rigid clothing, pull her large hat forward well past her face, and drape a woolen black shawl across her shoulders, obscuring all of her womanly charms.

She had entered through the back door that first time, slipping into a dank and steaming kitchen, filled with an immense cook wielding a wooden spoon the size of a pitchfork, her face red and perspiring. She rushed from dough table to oven, squawking orders at rebellious handmaidens who shrugged their shoulders in resistance, bringing a hard cuff to the offending rebels.

Hester almost turned and went back the way she had come, willing to enlist the service of some young man. But the thought of suffering children kept her from it.

Trying to get the attention of one of the maids, Hester extended an arm from her black shawl and called out a greeting. The girl spied Hester from the corner of her eye, shrieked, and dropped a bowl of boiling hot gravy on the brick floor, shattering it into tiny pieces of crockery that floated in the thickened, greasy puddle like sharp fangs.

She pointed a shaking finger, her mouth covered with her other hand, bringing the cook with the wooden spoon, now turned into a weapon of defense. Quickly, Hester removed her bonnet, bringing into view the white of her cap, flattened beneath the hat.

"Hello. I beg your pardon." She spoke in a well-modulated voice, addressing the woman courteously, the features in Hester's lovely face revealed by the flickering coal oil lamps on the shelves.

Slowly, the cook lowered the spoon, her dark eyes alert, cautious. "State your business, young lady."

"May I speak to the owner of the tavern, please?"

The cook turned and barked an order at one of the girls, who replied with bald insolence, "Get him yersel'."

The cook screeched a volley of words while powerfully waving the wooden spoon, which soon had the girl scuttling through the thick swinging doors that opened to a dark and cluttered area. Smells of leather, sweat, horses, grease, and food wafted into the room after the opened doors closed after the girl.

Hester shuddered, knowing she could not enter the tavern itself, the front room where the men lounged, ate, and drank their bitter ale. She waited, shifting her weight uneasily, fingering the fringes of her black shawl.

There was more shouting from the enormous cook, bringing a thin boy, who darted past her like a trout in a cloudy stream, and who took down a black dust brush and began to clean up the broken bowl, goaded into hurried movement by more threats and scoldings.

The maid returned through the swinging doors without the owner. Hester followed her movements hopefully. She was eager to return to the streets outside and into the purity of moving air.

"He'll be back." The girl spoke in Hester's direction, her sullen eyes sliding away without meeting her gaze, her lips pouting as she turned away. She almost stumbled over the thin boy who was bent over, swiping the dust brush through the mess, the broken crockery jangling into the bucket he had brought. She landed a kick in his ribs, rolling him across the floor, with no more thought than if he would have been a hungry dog lapping at the gravy.

Hester gasped as the boy leaped to his feet and brought the heavy dust brush across the girl's legs, leaving a thick splatter of grease on her skirt. Whirling, she caught him by the ear, her face grimacing with the strength of the twist she put on the appendage, bringing a howl that sounded like the high wail of a wounded cat.

They were both sent scuttling by threats from the cook, followed by the appearance of the tavern's owner, a tall and stately man with the bearing of a gentleman.

Hester breathed a sigh, relieved to find someone who seemed completely accessible. "Good afternoon, sir."

Immediately, the tavern owner's hands began to flutter, two white birds flapping, ludicrous in their movement. Hester took two steps backward, feeling the cold, hard door latch through her shawl.

"My lovely lady. And what, pray, may I do for you?" His face was level with hers, his mouth red and fleshy like the carp that hid beneath tree roots in shallow water. His whiskers were thick and black, so much like William's, his eyes dark and greedy and glittering.

Hester kept her poise, telling him levelly, and, she hoped, coldly, what she needed and why. Instantly, the owner of the tavern changed his approach, becoming the perfect gentleman in every way. He sold her two jugs, one of whiskey and one of brandy, took her money and promised to fill them whenever there was a necessity, wishing her godspeed and blessings in her venture.

From that day forward, he kept his word, recognizing her as the Amish medicine frau. She was always treated with respect and kindness, by the tavern owner, anyway.

Hester told Bappie where she was going, bringing only a nod and the waggling of one finger as she bent over her pattern.

She walked down the street clutching her black satchel, her purple dress offset by the black of her apron. Her long, easy stride, the tilt of her head, the elegance of her graceful neck, made more than one passerby turn for a second look, of which she was completely unaware.

Because it was a lovely day and she had a mission to accomplish, thoughts of her troubling future evaporated like thin smoke. A sense of well-being rode lightly on her shoulders. She smiled and waved as Walter Trout's nephew, Jacob, rode by on his brown horse, cutting a striking figure. Vaguely, Hester wondered if he would ever become as large a man as his uncle.

She arrived at the second house on Water Street, a narrow stone dwelling with a white door, a brass knocker centered in its middle. She grasped it and rapped strongly, eager to begin.

When there was no answer from within, she rapped again and was rewarded by the door opening only a foot, with one pale, tousle-haired little boy staring bleary-eyed into her face.

"May I come in? I am Hester Zug."

There was no answer, only the pulling back of the heavy, whitewashed door.

The odor was stifling, the room she entered in disarray. There was the distinct sound of retching coming from the recesses of a hallway, followed by a groan of misery. The room was dimly lit, so at first she was unaware of the piles of blankets and children strewn across the floor like afterthoughts. As her eyes adjusted to the light, she counted six piles of bedding, the pillows all containing varied sizes of dark-haired children. Some were sleeping fitfully, others lay awake, and a few had thrown up on the floor the watery, yellow bile that comes after the stomach has been emptied of its contents.

Hester jumped when the shadowy figure of the father emerged from the darkened hallway.

"You are here."

"Yes."

"My wife is sickest. I believe she has swooned. The baby is lying very still."

Immediately, Hester brushed past him to the hot, suffocating bedroom. She found his wife hanging over the side of the bed, her face like a waxen doll, her arms like white rags draping to the floor.

Going to her side, Hester placed a hand on her forehead, not surprised to find it burning hot. When she found the white chamber pot, she saw the fullness of it, lifted it and held it sideways to the light. As she had feared, dysentery might be present. Were they all drinking well water? Was there a communal well? If so, this outbreak was not influenza as the doctors thought.

She lifted cold hands to her burning cheeks. But who am I? Oh, who am I to overstep my bounds?

Well, she would do what she knew worked—have everyone who was sick swallow walnut oil, the extraction of the walnut, beaten together with rose water; then fast for two hours; then drink a bowl of boiled milk with salt. It was always a quick relief. Quickly, efficiently, she found the two bottles, stepped over the sleeping children, and located a spoon in the drawer of the blue cupboard by the dry sink.

She went to the woman's side, shook her, called her, all to no avail. Going to the baby's cradle, she bent to touch the child's head. It was cool to the touch, the baby asleep and breathing normally, but the stench of soiled diapers spoke of long neglect.

Nothing to do about that now. She resumed her efforts, finally waking the man's wife, who rolled back on the bed, her head flopping like a rag doll, before she began gagging and heaving violently. The husband made clicking sounds of sympathy before turning to the chamber pot and heaving silently himself.

There was a loud cry from the front room, so Hester hurried out to find a small child rolling in agony, clutching his stomach, grasping and desperately scratching with his small white fingers.

Hester stooped and gathered him into her arms, soothing him by rubbing his back. He laid his head against her breast and wept bitterly, as an older child began to vomit with such force it took her breath away.

Carefully she spooned the mixture of walnut oil and rosewater into the child's mouth, crooning to him as she did so.

One by one, she helped all the children, in varying stages of distress, to sit up. She gave the same medicine to the parents in larger amounts, saying if they couldn't keep it down, she had more.

When the baby awoke screaming, and three of the children vomited, crying out with the misery of it, Hester knew she had to have help. She spoke a few curt words to the father, then walked as fast as possible, without running, up the street to their house. She burst through the door, calling out for Bappie, who accompanied her to Water Street with strident complaints. Her stiff-legged gait gave away the reluctance she was determined to convey.

"I'm getting married, Hester. A houseful of vomiting people is about the limit. I don't know how you stand it. How am I going to get my sewing done if you keep this up?"

Hester stopped, grabbed Bappie's arm, yanked her back, and thrust her face close to her freckled one.

"You stop whining, Barbara King. You are selfish, thinking only of yourself and Levi Buehler. How can you have a blessing in your life when you act like that? Huh?"

"You stop acting so self-righteous, Hester. When you grab that black bag, it's like you think you're God. Or at least his right-hand helper." Bappie stamped her foot for emphasis, like a cow protecting her newborn calf, then stomped off, her arms held stiffly away from her body, her hands rolled into stubby fists.

Hester scuttled after her, so furious that tears welled in her eyes. But when they entered the house, both women forgot the angry words and got down to work. Bappie heated large quantities of water, added yellow lye soap, rolled the beds on the floor out of the way, and began scrubbing.

Hester kept shoveling in the walnut oil with rosewater, the children grimacing, even crying, but she remained resolute.

After they had all been dosed once, she took up the baby, holding him away from her body while Bappie, her mouth a grim line and a clothespin propped firmly on her thin nose, peeled away the soiled diaper that had been on the sick child far too long.

They lowered the howling baby into a tin of warm water and bathed him well, wrapped him in a clean towel, applied a tincture of lobelia to his poor body, then spooned in a small amount of medicine. When his crying resumed, they boiled milk, added salt, and offered him a portion in a bottle.

They replenished the candleholders, trimmed the wicks of the coal oil lamps, and lit them.

Darkness came suddenly, as the sun disappeared behind the buildings, and still they labored. When someone couldn't tolerate the medicine, the heaving began anew. Hester waited, then spooned in another small amount.

Bappie swiped viciously at the soiled floors and carried the chamber pots to the privy out back, her eyebrows lowered, her upper lip slightly lifted with distaste, her smallest finger extended, holding the pot gingerly as if it was red hot. In passing, she muttered, "I guess you know we're not all created the same, Hester."

Hester answered, "That's right," and kept on going. By one-half hour past midnight, the vomiting and heaving had stopped. There was deep breathing from the bedroom as the parents finally found rest from the torturous, heaving pains that had roiled their stomachs like boiling water. The children remained restless, some of them sitting up and crying out, the fear of pain stabbing at them like unseen claws.

Hester was always there, talking softly, giving them more medicine. Bappie, however, stopped in her tracks, fell on a blanket, rolled over, and began snoring almost at once. She was tired, so she slept.

Hester laughed softly to herself. In Berks County, Hans Zug owned a horse that reminded her of Bappie. He was a good worker and pulled the plow, or the wagon of hay, for hours, but once he was finished for the day, there was no use trying to rouse him. He would not budge. It was as if his huge hooves were nailed to the floor of his pen. He was done.

Hester sat and rocked the hungry baby, gave him watered milk from a rag, burped him, and sang softly. As her eyelids fell lower and lower, the rocking chair eased to a standstill and she laid her head gently on the baby's.

A deep ache of remembering filled her then, a slow trickling of longings coupled with despair, as she recalled those days of unfulfillment, of never being able to give William what he wanted most. Children. Heirs to the farm. Generation after generation, carrying the seed of William King, just the way God had promised Abraham in the *Heilige Schrift*.

It never occurred to William that he may not have had the blessing. He had found favor in God's eyes, he felt sure. He was honest in all his dealings, kept the *Ordnung* to the letter, worked hard, rose early to read God's word, and prayed and prayed for Hester, who, it was plain to see, was the one who erred.

Oh, she knew, she knew his thoughts. She asked him one night in the intimacy of the bedroom, "What if neither of us has sinned?" She quoted the verses from the New Testament, where the people asked Jesus who had sinned because a child was blind, and he answered, "No one. Now the glory of God can be revealed." And hadn't it been?

The glory of God was here, too, when she was left alone. God's ways were so mysterious, but his glory so perfect. For would she have even been allowed to think that she could practice this medicine, these forgotten Indian remedies, if she was a widow with many little ones to care for?

CHAPTER 10

A ND SO HER THOUGHTS WHIRLED, AN ENDLESS VORTEX OF wondering with no definite answers, always just bits and pieces she would never understand.

She stroked the baby's back and thought she didn't need to know. To understand everything was not exercising faith, the faith of her culture, the faith of her people, the Amish. She knew her faith was firmly rooted, and she deeply appreciated it as she grew older. She was certain the Almighty was watching over her like the brightest star, guiding her into the future.

Hester's eyes snapped open, sensing a figure standing close by. It was the mother, dressed in a clean gown, her hair held away from her face by a freshly tied ribbon.

"I'll take him," she whispered, her white hands reaching for him in the semidarkness

"How are you?" Hester whispered back.

"Thirsty."

Hester shook her head. "Do you mind drinking left-over milk? When morning comes, I'd like to bring water from a different well. I'm afraid this well may be causing the sickness."

Quickly she added, "Though I don't know."

Weakly, the mother nodded her head. "I'll do anything you want. I have never been so sick, even when I was with child."

Even before the day arrived, Hester was on her way, Bappie in tow, chilly and grumbling, attacking her back with darts of threatening words. "Hester, I'm hungry. Now you can't expect me to eat anything in *sell cutsich haus*. I'm not eating a bite. I'm skinny as a pole, so I can't take much sickness. I have to eat. I didn't eat yesterday. Well, last night you know those potatoes on the stove got ruined. What a waste."

And so she railed against Hester, who walked swiftly to their pump in the backyard and pumped two buckets full to the brim without speaking.

"Help me carry these to Water Street, then you can come straight home and start frying mush," she said, the words as hard as pebbles.

"Use a yoke."

"All right."

Bappie ran to the stoop, got the wooden yoke, settled it on Hester's shoulders, attached the buckets, and shooed her away.

She was going to make soft-boiled eggs and, if she was still hungry, *Schnitzel Eier Kuchen*, with the old bacon hung in the rafters and new eggs that the chickens laid this morning. If she felt like it, she would make *panne kuchen*, too. With maple syrup.

Hester threw up a hand and was on her way, balancing both wooden buckets with her hands, striding easily. She swallowed more than once, thinking of bacon, eggs, and pancakes.

As it turned out, her work had just begun.

The first family she helped, the Lewises, were able to be on their own that afternoon. They pressed a few coins into Hester's hands and thanked her with genuine sincerity, over and over, as the large-eyed children sat up and watched her, still feeling weak but rid of the clawing nausea.

She had closed the door behind her softly and was on her way home, her head spinning from lack of sleep, grateful to be able to put one foot in front of the other. She heard footsteps, then.

"Ma'am? Beg pardon, Ma'am."

Turning, she looked into the eyes of a child, a boy with a thatch of whitish-blond hair, eyes like saucers, his chest heaving.

"Were you at the Lewises'?"

"Yes."

"Would you come? My mum's sickern I ever saw her."

"Lead the way."

Only a few houses from the Lewises' stood a wood-sided house, its door well built, with two fairly large windows facing the street, heavy curtains draped on each side.

Wearily, Hester climbed the stone steps and entered the house, surprised to find her feet cushioned on soft rugs, and a low reclining chair, unlike anything Hester had ever seen, placed below the windows. Luxurious pillows, stitched with a rose pattern, were set along its back. Various pieces of ornate furniture sat tastefully along the walls with brilliantly hooked rugs scattered in front of them, as if each one had its own little flower patch. *Ein English haus*, she thought, as she followed the boy to the bedroom.

An exact replica of the Lewises' illness sent Hester's heart plummeting. The husband, moaning feverishly from the high sleigh bed, the wife like a plump porcelain doll sunk into voluptuous pillows, the telltale acrid smell of sickness—it was all there.

Quickly, Hester checked the room for a cradle, a trundle bed. Turning to the small boy, she asked, "Do you have sisters or brothers?"

"Yes. Four."

"Where are they?"

"My grandmother came to get them. They weren't sick."

"Where does your grandmother live?"

"Just down the street."

With a sinking heart, the weight like a stone in her stomach, Hester realized she could not handle this alone if it was dysentery from the well water. She needed to talk to a doctor, someone who would support her theory, her speculation.

She bent over the people in the bed, touching their foreheads as they groaned in pain. She asked for cool water, which the boy brought gladly, then wiped their faces with a cool cloth. She spoke to the man when he awakened and asked him and his wife to swallow the bitter herbal tincture.

After deciding this situation was not as grave as the Lewises had been, she asked the boy if he knew where Doctor Porter's office was.

He shook his head.

"Are you feeling sick?"

"No."

"Have you already been sick?"

"No, ma'am. Just my mother and father."

"Do you drink the water there?"

Hester pointed to the bucket, the one on the kitchen dry sink.

"No. I never do. I drink milk. That water is yellow and tastes like sand. I drink coffee though. And tea."

Hester could feel the excitement rumbling along her veins. Was her guess the correct one?

She had no time to think as the front door burst open and a large, wild-eyed apparition barreled into the room with the force of a runaway bull.

"Ah needs help!" The poor Negro woman was clearly alarmed, her hand going to her huge heaving dressfront, the whites of her eyes like little half-moons on each side of her dark irises. Her mouth opened and closed as she struggled to gain her breath.

"De little 'uns, is sickern' calves. Like little babies, dey spit up, dey cryin'. De missus too old for dis."

"Did you call Doctor Porter?"

"Yes'm. Ah done sent ma man a few minutes back."

"Good."

Hester accompanied the heaving figure back out the door, down the street, and into another house, almost identical to the one she had left. An older woman rose to greet them, her bearing regal, stiff, and condescending.

"An *Amish*? Royal, I didn't know the woman was *Amish*." She said the word as if it tasted bitter on her tongue. Hester stood tall, unbending, too sleep-deprived to care.

"Yes, 'm, she Amish, I black, you white and English. S' far as de Lawd go, we look zactly alike." Royal was in no mood to take any airs from her mistress, who had puffed up like Bappie's hens, ready to strike out.

"Well, I beg your pardon, but I don't believe an Amish girl . . . woman will have enough knowledge to know what to do with these children being ill all at once."

The piteous sound of gagging and retching, the high, thin wail of a terrified child, and Royal moved out of the room like a large ship, her skirts riding the floorboards efficiently.

Hester was left facing the taut face of the older woman. Up went the chin, the nostrils dilated, the lids of the eyes slid lower. She crossed her arms at the waist, drew a deep breath, and spoke, the words like scalding steam. "I would ask you to leave. No Amish is going to minister to my grandchildren. Your people have no idea about sickness or health. No schooling, no knowledge. You are a fraud. Do you hear me? A fraud."

The last sentence was spat in Hester's face.

"You will not enter my son's house again. Leave. Now."

Hester drew up her chin, bent to pick up her black bag, and spoke slowly, "As you wish, ma'am." She let herself out, walked up the street heavily, the weight in her legs from exhaustion, but also from defeat. So be it. Perhaps she was a fraud.

Hot tears welled up in her eyes as she walked past the Lewises, past houses where others would become sick, or were already gripped by the stomach pain and nausea. She went past the round, brick well in the small courtyard without seeing any children pulling up buckets of tainted water.

What had the Indian woman said? If the spring runoff produces an ill stomach, it must be boiled to sweeten it. Now the illness was called dysentery.

Well, it was up to the doctors to figure it out. She would go home to Bappie, get some much needed rest, and see what occurred in the following days.

She stumbled into the house, her face pinched and drawn, slammed her black bag against the wall in the hallway, and grumbled to herself, ill humor escaping her mouth.

"Bappie!"

"What?"

"Can't you ever get this rug straight inside the door? I always stumble over it when I use the door from the street."

When there was no answer, she walked into the kitchen. Noah was seated at the table, watching her face with his blue eyes squinting in delight. Hester did not see him at first, her vision clouded with the mist of exhaustion, her temper short because of it.

When she looked up, her eyes widened. She became flustered, but desperate to hide the mixture of feelings, she hung up her shawl, straightened her windblown cap, and tucked an imaginary stray hair behind her ear.

"Hello, Hester."

She nodded, short and curt, without meeting Noah's eyes. Still, his eyes twinkled with good humor and something more. "Rough night? Bappie tells me you think there might be an outbreak of dysentery."

Whirling, her fists clenched, Hester faced him, her eyes like polished black stones. "Bappie has no right to tell you anything. I don't know what's wrong with the people who have been taken ill."

She turned, yanked open the narrow door that led to the small, twisted stairway, and disappeared, her feet sounding dully on the stairs, the floorboards creaking in her room.

Bappie watched, raised her eyebrows, and pursed her lips. "Whatever brought that on?"

Noah shook his head, the light of humor replaced by a dark brooding, an unfathomable shadow in the depth of his eyes.

"It's all right, Bappie. You forget I spent my childhood in her company. I know her much better than you have any idea. She'll tell you what's bothering her, then you can let me know. I have a hunch she was put down pretty badly by someone."

Bappie looked up, puzzled. "You think?"

He nodded, then got up to leave. "I'll be back."

Before Bappie could protest, he had slipped silently out the door, leaving her shaking her head. Like a puzzle with most of the pieces missing, those two.

Noah had collected his pay from Bappie, although he cut the amount to less than half. He smiled at her announcement that she would not rebuild, a very good move, as he had seen Levi Buehler and figured there would be a public announcement when the time was right.

The storm had been an act of God, yes. There was a time when he wasn't sure he believed in God, and certainly had no faith at all in the goodness of the Christian faith when it was carried in a pious manner behind a veil of deception that hid a hornet's nest of sins. It had shaken him to the core when he discovered that folks around him were not always what they professed, but he learned to shrug his shoulders and judge no one unduly, knowing it was a part of life.

When Hester left, disappearing into the forest one golden evening, every suspicion he had tried to dispel came roaring back, setting him back on his heels. He had helplessly watched Hans thrash through the surrounding woods in a fever of agitation, driven by a passion he could not understand. At first.

He had been forced to search for her with Isaac and his father, torn by the wild hope that she would escape the cruelty that dogged her life—Annie's jealousy of her a rampant misery—and the unbearable fear that he would never see her again.

He had lived the ensuing weeks in bouts of utter emptiness. Joining the cavalry became a way to escape the loss of his faith—not only in God, but in his father and his stepmother, Annie, too, whose wrongs multiplied by the hour. But he had come to realize that he, too, had chosen to betray her. By trying to keep the peace, he had ignored the depth of Annie's cruelty to Hester.

Yet he carried an all-consuming love for Hester like a torch held aloft, the flame burning with an endless supply of oil like the vessel in the Bible. Hidden away in his heart, it burned steadily.

Riding with the men of war astride a powerful horse, he cared nothing for his life. Like a rotting log, his life was crumbling and bitter, without foundation, his hatred of his father corrupting his own soul. He rode into battle recklessly and without fear, not caring whether he lived or died. He forgot Kate, his gentle mother, along with her love and her upbringing, his mind clouded with the untrustworthy deeds of his father.

The only thing he knew for sure was the torch he carried for Hester. Images of her put him to sleep on cold, rocky stretches of earth. She walked softly through his dreams and was there in his thoughts when he awoke. He wasn't sure if it was real love, or if he had an obsession with the child of his boyhood. He just knew she was the only thing that mattered, and since she left and he would never see her again, he saw no use in living without her.

And so he rode, shot his rifle, marched along, steadily losing sight of the person he had been. Isaac, his brother, followed him, as devoted as he was when they were children. They had two years of being in the war, two years of unbelievable sights and sounds, experiences they would never fully forget.

Then Isaac was killed. Hans and Annie gave him a decent burial at home in the graveyard among the pines. That loss broke Hans completely, aging him in years as well as wisdom. He believed it must have been his own personal atonement, a payment to God for his wrong fascination with his adopted daughter, Hester, his downfall. In spiritual sackcloth and ashes, he sat for days as tears of remorse cleaned his soul, washing away the dust and the dirt he had been unable to overcome by himself.

Hans wept unashamedly over Isaac's coffin, gathered his children round and loved them, making amends for the past. He had come to love Annie, whose palsied hands worsened. Tenderly, he cared for her, helping her with household chores. He kissed her cheek and squeezed her shoulder affectionately when yet another pitcher or serving bowl crashed to the floor, her poor afflicted hands shaking and fluttering.

And then Noah decided to go home.

Slowly, his faith was being restored. God came to him in a dream one dark and weary night when his body and soul knew no rest. He blamed himself for Isaac's death. Isaac had been the younger brother, following his older brother's footsteps straight into the devastation of war, and he could not forgive himself.

He dreamed the sun rose, blackened by sin, and made an arc across a blood red sky, all the way to the western horizon where it hung without sinking. There was no power in him to change this, and he knew he was doomed. Then God spoke and reminded him that though his sins were dark and heavy, God's mercy is as sure and present as the sun rising in the east and setting in the west. Noah saw the red sky change with a swipe of a dazzling white hand, bigger than he would be able to grasp and larger than the universe, and wash the landscape clean. Whiter than snow, as pure as the angels.

He awoke, sobbing, flattened into his bed by the force of God's love. He was nothing, an empty shell, and only God could give him life. His faith was restored, his soul fed by the knowledge of God's mercy and the sacrifice of Jesus for him, for his sinful, empty soul.

When word came from Bucks County about the chance to make quick and plentiful wages as a builder in and around the town of Lancaster, he left almost immediately, thinking of the money he would need to buy his own acreage.

While there, he heard of the Indian woman named Hester, plunging him back into the world of his first love. Despite all he had known and experienced, had he ever really lost that love?

Wryly, he shook his head as he rode home from Bappie's house. He was sure he'd made some progress with Hester, but about the time he thought she would speak to him, and resume a childhood friendship at the least, she became abrupt, aloof, and so alien she may as well have not even been an acquaintance. It was like trying to tame a deer.

He knew she had been with sick people, and of her ability to heal with the plants she bottled and dried. He believed in her talent, but she could get herself into situations where holding those unconventional truths about healing would be risky. Hester hated being put down. It stemmed from her own low account of herself, being an Indian in a white Amish world.

Teased mercilessly in school, she had never joined the group of youth during the time of *rumspringa*—for hymn singings, for buggy rides home through the darkened forests, furtively holding hands, or going for dates during weekends.

Noah winced, the pain in his back irritated by his horse's movement. He thanked God for sparing his life through the storm. He dared to hope he was here for a purpose—mostly being Hester's husband—a thought that brought a wide grin to his face as he lifted his hat and whistled back at the crazy mockingbird on Levi Stoltzfus's fencepost.

Hester slept till the sun cast a wide band of light across her face, then got up, dressed, and went downstairs. She washed her face at the dry sink, combed her hair, pinned on her muslin cap, and marched resolutely to the black bag she had dumped in the hallway. She grabbed it, took it outside to the outhouse, and began uncorking bottles as fast as she could.

With the bottles lined up on the wooden seat, she grabbed them, one by one, and emptied them down the hole, the glugging and splashing satisfying. No more of this. She replaced the corks, pitched all the bottles into the bag, then walked back to the house, her mouth set in a stubborn slash across her face.

She emptied the tea kettle of hot water into the dishpan, added a generous sliver of lye soap, swished her hand back and forth till the suds appeared, and began to wash the offending glass bottles, now emptied of her failure.

Fraud, the woman had said. Fraud meant a deceiver, a cheat, a fake. Well, that was one thing she would never be. Hans was a fraud. But she was not. So there, you English lady, you just get the doctor to fix your problem. I will not spend one minute of time wasting these herbs on people who think I'm a liar.

Her anger was like brute strength, and a sharp pain shot through her thumb. Quickly she lifted her hand from the water, already dripping with blood, the gash deep but clean.

Hester snorted with frustration. Now who would wash the bottles? Where was Bappie? Annoyed, she tore clean muslin into strips and went to the cupboard for dried comfrey. Without thinking, she laid the leaf in a small bowl of hot water, then lifted it, patted it dry and draped it across her thumb, winding strips of cloth around it. She'd keep some comfrey for cuts.

She was sweeping bottles of tinctures off the shelf when Bappie returned from Walter Trout's house, where she had gone to borrow a cup of rye flour.

She stopped inside the back door, watching Hester with suspicious, dark eyes, her eyebrows lowered. "What are you doing?"

"What does it look like?"

"You're not emptying those bottles, are you?"

"I sure am."

Two giant steps of her large, bare feet, and Bappie thrust her outraged face into Hester's surprised one. "You're not getting away with this. Whatever are you thinking?" Bappie spread her hands, palms up. "You can't let those sick people fall like flies down there on Water Street. I'm sure you're right, that it's the well water."

In answer, Hester swooped all the remaining bottles
of medicine up in her arms and carried them to the sink.
"The doctors can figure it out." Then she pulled the cork
from one bottle and upended it above a wooden bucket.
Bappie grabbed her hand, shouting at her to stop this
silliness. "What in the world has crawled over you?"

Hester drew back, the backs of her hands on her hips,
her fingers curled into fists. "She said I was a fraud, Bappie. That's one thing I will never be."

CHAPTER 11

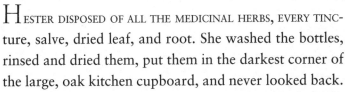

HESTER DISPOSED OF ALL THE MEDICINAL HERBS, EVERY TINC-
ture, salve, dried leaf, and root. She washed the bottles,
rinsed and dried them, put them in the darkest corner of
the large, oak kitchen cupboard, and never looked back.

Not once did she inquire about the well-being of the
people who lived on Water Street. If there was a funeral,
she did not know it, figuring the doctors could decide
what to do. If the well water was unclean, so be it. For
the last time, she had been called a liar.

Bappie shook her head, paid the rent, and prepared
for her upcoming nuptials. She suggested many different
types of employment to Hester, even buying swatches of
muslin and embroidery thread, putting down a pattern
and tracing an intricate design for Hester to work, but
she would have none of it.

Hester cleaned the house, did the washing, tended the
small garden in the backyard, and avoided Noah and
Levi Buehler—and every other man—going about her
days in silence, an injured ghost.

Bappie shrugged her shoulders, made small talk, and ate the meals Hester cooked. But she spent most of her time out at Levi's farm, cleaning, washing the walls, the floors, the blankets and quilts, avoiding the hounds as best she could, tagging after Levi, and making bold statements where the management of the farm was concerned.

Levi indulged the peppery Bappie with slow humor. Ripples of laughter rumbled deep in his chest, but Bappie never heard them as she spread her thin arms, gesturing to make a point. Levi nodded, his eyes twinkling and dancing with unaccustomed amusement, so gratified was he by the spirited woman who had promised to become his wife.

It was the evening he asked her to go coon hunting with him, that he kissed her—a slow, gentle expression of his love, his admiration, and the wish that she should know this. Bappie was taken completely by surprise, the gentle kiss knocking all the speech out of her as thoroughly as a faint. She put two fingers to her lips and would not look at Levi the remainder of the evening. She went home with a silent demeanor and an unusually humble, "*Gute Nacht.*"

She sat at the breakfast table with Hester the following morning, her brown eyes large and limpid, saying nothing, eating very little. Hester eyed her friend discreetly, finally asking what was wrong, she was so silent.

Bappie lifted shamed eyes to Hester. "Levi kissed my mouth. Now I'll have to make my *socha* in church." Hester looked at Bappie and her shoulders began to shake. She laughed clear, delicious merriment that welled up from her stomach, worked its way through her chest, and was finally thrown into the air like visible music notes, bouncing and jostling against the ceiling where they sparked the day with pleasure.

"Ach, Bappie, no. No. It's very much a part of his love for you. I'm surprised he waited this long."

Bappie's eyes turned from dark suspicion to shame to acceptance to ribald humor, flavored with relief and capped by gratitude. "You mean, it's not wrong?"

"For some, maybe, but it's up to you."

Bappie clasped her hands reverently just beneath her chin, let her eyelids fall as demurely as a blushing bride, and sighed with pure contentment. "I'm glad I'm getting married," she whispered.

They went coon hunting. It was a warm evening when the sky was moonless, and only a scattering of stars, like pinpricks in the dark sky, was barely visible through the thick canopy of trees.

Bappie was prepared, wearing sturdy, black, leather shoes. Hester wore only the soft moccasins she used around the house.

They drove to the farm with Walter Trout's horse, the brown mare they borrowed frequently after Silver had died in the storm.

Hester was alarmed, then dismayed, to find Noah standing in the barnyard, the coonhounds roiling around him and Levi like a current of dogs. Her breath quickened and her head spun with dizziness, as she clutched the handle of the buggy with whitened knuckles to lower herself to the ground. Angry at the rush of anxiety that sped up her senses, she helped Bappie unhitch the brown mare without glancing at either man, who walked over to offer assistance.

Bappie blushed furiously but met Levi Buehler's gaze with open appreciation, the twilight a kindness to her reddened complexion.

Hester stayed behind the horse, her head bent, unclasping the britching as slowly as possible. She felt exposed when the brown mare was led out of the shafts of the buggy and taken away by Levi, with Bappie walking beside him to put the horse in the barn.

Noah stood on one side of the shafts, Hester on the other. If the twilight was kind to Bappie, it made Hester look enchanting. Like a vision, she stood, her head bent, her eyes lowered.

Noah could tell by the droop of her shoulders that she struggled with failure inside her, the feeling that she was nothing, an outcast, and now, a liar, a sham, and worth less than nothing. Bappie had told him what happened.

A love welled up in his chest, unrivaled by anything he had ever felt for her. This lovely, lovely woman, so battered by life, by experiences that drained the small amount of self-worth she did have, threw her gift away like a used shell, broken into a thousand pieces.

One high step, and he was across the shafts. Up went both hands to her shoulders, which he gently clasped, and then drew slightly toward himself. He could find no words to express what he felt, so he applied a bit more pressure. His chest exploded when she came willingly. A stifled sound of defeat emerged from her lips, a small, entreating sound of pain, a gentle begging.

Noah had never held Hester. Only in his dreams did he allow himself the thought of perhaps, someday, being able to take the liberty. Far beyond his imagining was the feel of her, and the thought that she allowed herself to stand in the circle of his arms, if only for a moment.

Hester laid her head on his firm, rounded shoulder, closed her eyes, and let the delicious encounter with the broad chest close over her like a warmed quilt on a cold winter night.

They stepped apart, Noah relinquishing her to the wide space that was the remainder of the world, the great atmosphere that now seemed an eternity, a million miles between them.

He gathered his senses, called in his thoughts. "I'm sorry to hear of your . . ." Almost, he said, "refusal to practice the use of your herbs," but he caught himself and said, "loss of the herbs."

Hester nodded, a slight movement of her head, but the large eyes, fringed by the beauty of her lashes, stayed on his. She wondered how he knew and what he thought, yet she wasn't ready to ask and risk hearing his opinion. She pulled away and lowered her eyelids, the thick dark lashes sweeping her cheeks like the delicacy of a bird's wingtips.

Out of the corner of his eye, he saw Levi and Bappie return, so he said quickly, "Hester, it was one woman. One opinion. You are not a liar."

"How do you know? Who told you?"

"Bappie."

Again she inclined her head, with only the whisper of acknowledgment.

Levi was jubilant and in his glory. This night was his chance to show his Bappie the thing he loved most. On a dark night like this, the marauding raccoons that inhabit the fields and streams of southern Pennsylvania became unaccountably bold and daring, breaking into henhouses, eating eggs, chickens, and hatchlings, plus corn from the fields, pulling down ear after ear. They'd eat a small amount, then leave the year's profits to waste in the frozen mud of autumn.

For once he hoped to display the reason he kept all these lean dogs, unattractive perhaps, but worth their weight in redeemed corn and the contents of henhouses. Simply put, they were his passion. Now they set off, the men shouldering their guns, the rifles thick and heavy, as deadly as Hester remembered of Hans and the boys bringing in wild game in winter.

Down the small incline behind the barn they went, the creek next to it gurgling full and glinting in the starlight where the ripples roiled over the boulders hidden beneath.

Levi lifted the kerosene lantern, telling Bappie where to put her feet, pointing out the three smooth rocks placed at proper distances to step across the stream, proud that he had so much forethought. Bappie, on the other hand, was thinking, *Here's something else that needs attention—building a decent footbridge going to the cornfields.* How did he think she was going to bring him dinner, or a cold drink of ginger tea on a hot day, if she had to leap across from stone to stone?

A bit huffy now, she started across, becoming distracted by the splashing, surging hounds. She slipped, stumbled, and remained upright, but she was in the water up to her knees now, her long skirt dragging in the dark creek.

Levi gasped, laughed, and kept on laughing as she clambered up the other side, her fury evident in the shrieks, grunts, and volley of grumbles that came out of her.

"You all right, Bappie?" he shouted, after he saw her reach the opposite side.

In answer, she plopped down on the bank, lifted her sodden, dripping skirts, shook them, and yelled, "Levi Buehler, now what am I supposed to do?"

A whoop from Levi, a bent-over figure slapping his knee, and his hilarity sparked a shout of anger from the bedraggled figure on the bank.

Bappie took off first one shoe, then the other, dumped the creek water out, and pulled her socks off as if shedding a second skin, all the while mumbling about coon hunts and creek stones. She wiggled her slippery toes and glared at Hester, who came bounding across, her arms outstretched for balance, the toes of her moccasins curling around the stones. Noah followed, striding across easily, a bit of mud on his boots the only evidence he had been close to water.

Levi dried his eyes, made his way across, sniffed, then stood above Bappie, asking if she wanted to go back and dry her feet. But Bappie regained her pride, grabbed hold of her shoelaces, stood up, and stalked off. Levi stumbled after her with the lantern bobbing like a misplaced moon, the smirk still not completely wiped off his face.

Noah looked at Hester. She lifted her chin, and they started off. Noah reached for her hand, but only in spirit, restraining himself, unsure of the outcome if he touched her. In silence, they followed the bobbing light, Hester as light and quick on her feet as she had always been, like a fawn, her footsteps effortless and easy.

The silence was not uncomfortable, yet it was there like a garment unneeded but tolerated, a bit too snug, a slight tension between them.

Hester wanted to ask him why he had come, if he planned more of these forays, and if he was here in Lancaster County as a permanent resident. A thousand questions, quenched by her pride.

The need to break the silence was eclipsed by the unearthly howl from one dog, and then the eerie baying joined by ten more voices, as each dog took up the scent.

"Coon! Co-oo-n!" roared Levi, immediately bounding after the dogs. Bappie dug her toes into her sodden leather shoes and hustled after him.

Laughing, Noah reached for Hester's hand. He wasn't thinking when he did it. He just wanted to be sure she wouldn't stumble and could keep up. She placed her hand in his, as natural as breathing. Together they hurried after the leading lantern and the baying, yipping, frenzied pack of dogs.

They plunged through the dark woods on spongy moss and wet earth, through puddles, tripping over tree roots, righting themselves, and resuming the dash to keep up. Ahead, the trail dipped down a steep incline. Noah gripped her hand tighter, his breathing fast.

"You all right, Hester?"

She nodded, then remembering the dark, said, "Yes."

They slipped and slid. When Hester's feet lurched out from under her, she sat down hard, her hand yanked loose from Noah's. He stopped immediately as Hester's laugh rang out.

"Like a mule, Noah!"

He laughed.

She got to her feet, the bobbing lantern below them, the hounds setting up an unearthly ruckus. Hester had never heard anything like it.

"Co-oon!" Levi yelled, in a high crazy pitch.

They reached the giant tree on the banks of a wide, still creek bed. Levi bent over backward, his hat tilted up on his head as he searched for the elusive raccoon, the dogs leaping, falling back, howling like banshees.

Bappie stood staunchly, the coonhounds knocking against her bedraggled skirts. She took no notice of them, her head tilted at the same angle as Levi's as she stepped in one direction, then another, helping Levi find the raccoon.

Hester and Noah reached the melee but chose to stay back, observing how this was done.

"There he is!" screeched Bappie, her voice only snatches between the sound of agitated dogs.

Immediately, Levi was by her side, his long neck stretching out of his shirt collar, the wispy gray beard like old moss. Lifting his rifle to his shoulder, he pointed it at a ridiculous angle, squinted, and fired off a deafening shot. Hester heard the rustling of leaves as the heavy body of the raccoon tottered, then fell down through the branches, snapping off small ones, loosening twigs and leaves, till a dull splat sounded and the animal was on the ground.

Amazingly, the hounds stayed back. Their baying ceased almost instantly, but not quite. One young dog had not been taken on a hunt more than a few times, the yipping sound from her a testimony to her inexperience. Levi bounded over, cuffed her sharply, and shouted, "No. No." The small hound lowered herself to her stomach, as another smart blow landed across her nose.

"You listen to me, Baby. When that coon is down, you hush up." Bappie watched as Levi picked up the fat raccoon, rolled it onto its back, and made a swift incision down his stomach. A few flicks of the curved knife, an order for the dogs, and a pelt hung on his pack. The remainder of the coon was torn apart by the snarling, fighting pack of hungry dogs.

"Onward, ho!" Levi shouted. The hounds took the cue to resume howling, their noses to the ground, first in one direction, then another, tumbling over each other and snapping, as quarrelsome as tired children.

Another coon, and Bappie sat down on the floor of the forest, her legs straight out in front of her, propped up by the angle of her arms. "That's it, Levi. My feet are soaked inside these shoes, and I have at least a dozen blisters."

"You sure, Bappie? We can get another, maybe two."

"Well, you just go right ahead. I'm staying here."

Undecided, Levi hesitated. He had never taken a girl coon-hunting and certainly never his wife, so he guessed if Bappie was tired, it would be the honorable thing to take her home.

He cleared his throat, then scratched his head by tilting his hat back over his head. In the light of the lantern, Hester saw his eyes soften as he watched Bappie yank off a sodden shoe and rub her toes, grimacing with the pain of the raw blisters that had formed there.

"We'll have to carry you home, I guess, won't we?" he said, gently. Bappie became so frustrated she put her shoe on again, got to her feet, lifted her chin, and set off, calling back, "Of course not. I can get home. What makes you think I can't? It's not that bad."

Noah smiled and turned to follow with Hester behind him. Levi brought up the rear, the lantern bobbing as he hurried to catch up to his indignant bride-to-be.

Back at the house, they were amazed to find it was past midnight. Levi stirred up the fire and put a kettle on, while Bappie threw off the offending shoes, yanked off her socks, and turned her head to hide the pain of the raw blisters.

Hester saw them. If only she had chickweed, comfrey, perhaps a burdock leaf. But she stashed that idea away and didn't say a word. She would not go back to that, ever.

Every ounce of her pride intact, Bappie got to her feet, padded lightly to the table, then hid her poor, injured feet in the safety of the shadows beneath it.

Noah sat in the lamplight, wide and solid, his white shirt open at the throat, his blond hair a halo of light that reflected the yellow flame from the lamp. His blue eyes were lined at the corners, his mouth wide with the kindness he carried in his features, a soft revelation of his feelings. His eyes left Hester's face only occasionally when he was brought back to the present by a spoken word from Levi or Bappie.

Bappie got to her feet, moving cautiously, the blisters a riot of pain. Levi noticed, gently took her shoulders in his large, gnarly hands, and stopped her.

"Sit down, Bappie. I'll get the tea."

Bappie looked at him, opened her mouth to resist, closed it, let herself be guided to a chair, then sat down heavily, her face flaming.

Forgetting Hester's purging of her medicines, Noah said, "Don't you have something for her feet, Hester?"

She hesitated, keeping her eyes lowered. Pouting only a bit, she shook her head.

That exchange twisted a knife in Bappie's ill-concealed humiliation; she so hated being the weak one. "Puh!" she spat.

Levi turned, watching her.

"You need a mother to tell you to get off your pitiful self and stop acting so childish, Hester," Bappie ground out.

Hester's eyes widened with surprise. She felt the heat rise in her face and was glad for the color of her skin. "Yes, well, my mother is dead, the only mother I knew. She would not have said that to me."

"Well, she should have. Stubborn girl."

Noah interjected, unable to watch Hester miss Kate. "She was hurt too many times, Bappie. It would be hard to practice medicinal plants if people made fun of your ability."

Bappie snorted, "Oh, get over it, Noah. Which one of us sitting here at this table has not had their ears clipped by negative words? Huh? Who hasn't been told where they're wrong? It's weak to throw out a lifetime of knowledge. It's stiff and proud and self-centered. Think of others, Hester, not yourself and how you are a poor martyr, persecuted by awful people. Fight back. The only thing that will prove your worth is the bedrock of the whole idea—people who get well after all the different illnesses you've worked with. Sores and fevers and poxes and rashes."

She pulled her feet out from under the table, lifted one, spread the toes, and winced painfully. "And these blisters."

Noah looked at Hester for only a second before he looked away. Hester's face registered pain and the fury of emptying all those bottles, but there was something else. Bewilderment? He didn't know and he didn't try guessing.

After that, a somber mood hung over the room. No matter how many lighthearted remarks Levi attempted to dispel it, the atmosphere didn't change.

Noah hitched up his horse, and Bappie and Hester climbed into the buggy. They left Bappie's borrowed brown horse till another day, allowing Noah to transport them since they had no lights on their buggy.

When they reached their backyard, Bappie clambered off the buggy, mumbled a word of farewell, and hobbled into the house, bent over by the blisters, stepping gingerly as if walking on pins.

When Hester got out to follow, Noah stopped her with a hand on her arm. "Will you wait and listen to something I have to say?" In the light of the flickering kerosene lamps attached to the buggy, her luminous eyes were dark with a polished sheen of yellow, a reflection from the flames mirrored there.

He turned to look at her, losing himself in her eyes. "Hester, I know you're having a bad time with the herbs and all. But I do believe you need to reconsider. It's a shame to throw all that wisdom, or whatever you call it— the knowhow—to throw all that away." Hester sat quietly listening, the only sound the dull whacking of her pulse.

"Summer and its heat will soon be here. So I'm asking if you'd consider going with me to a few places I found on the Dan Stoltzfus farm. I want to show you something."

"What?"

"It's a secret."

Hester smiled, a small lifting of the corners of her mouth. "We used do to it all the time."

"What?"

"Roam the woods and fields. Snare rabbits, find birds' nests.

"Remember my slingshot?" Hester asked. "I still have it."

Noah laughed, a deep sound that shook the shoulder resting against hers. "You were a dead shot."

"I still am."

"Take it when we go."

"I haven't said yes."

"No, that's right. You haven't. But please come with me. Just a day out as old friends."

He could not bring himself to say "brother and sister." He was afraid that was all he would ever be to her. A big brother. Never a man.

"I have no need of plants, herbs." She spoke the words quietly, without conviction.

"You do, Hester. Don't let one woman's opinion . . ."

He was cut off by her passionate words. From her side of the buggy, the sound of her voice was surprising. "More than one. Often, over the years, there were those who made fun of me, our own people, as well. They think I am *behauft mit hexerei*. Even some children hold their hands sideways over their mouths, lean in, and whisper, rolling their eyes. 'An Indian,' they say. 'Mixing her weeds with whiskey.' They may as well spit in my face, it hurts the same. It will never amount to anything, this healing. The doctors know more. Every day they are learning, making pills and medicines with plants that are grown in foreign countries, better cures."

"But among our people, Hester, surely you can practice what you know among those who love you and know who you are."

"Sometimes, they're the worst."

"Who? Name one."

Hester refused, crossing her arms and leaning back against the seat, the flame from the lantern flickering and losing her.

Suddenly, Noah said, "If we were small the way we used to be, I'd pull you out of this buggy and beat you up good and proper."

There was a small sputter from the recesses of the buggy, then a sound of merriment and a whoosh, followed by a genuine laugh. But something like a sob stopped the laughter, a choking sound, and Hester was crying, muffling the sound with the handkerchief she fumbled to produce.

Frightened and unable to stop it, Noah sat, his hands drooping helplessly, thinking he had said something terrible. He had never heard Hester cry. And he certainly didn't know how to stop her.

He spoke miserably, his voice edged in pain. "Don't cry, Hester. I'm sorry."

"It wasn't you."

Noah didn't know what to say. He felt big and dumb and completely at a loss.

She shuddered and blew her nose so delicately, he wasn't sure if that was the sound he heard. Then she said, "Sometimes I wish we could go back and be children, when life was good, carefree, easy."

She took a deep breath, as if clearing the air between them. "All right, Noah, I'll go. You can come with your horse and buggy, but don't ask me yet if I'll gather plants. I have not decided if I'll go back to herbs and medicines."

She placed a hand on his arm. "I'll make molasses crinkles. Our mother used to make them all the time because you and I loved them so much."

CHAPTER 12

Bappie MADE A SAMPLER OF BEAUTIFUL WORK DRAWN ON stiff muslin—delicate flower stems with blossoms, entwined in vines, filled the borders. She stenciled on her full name, "Barbara King," and also "Levi Buehler," the date of their wedding and the year. She asked Hester to help her find a suitable Bible verse to stencil along the bottom.

Hester was in the cellar sprouting the old, wrinkled potatoes that had been gathered the previous August and stored in the potato bin since then. Now some of the sprouts were two or three inches long, like waxen white worms. Hester snapped them off, threw them in one bucket and the potatoes in another.

"My wedding sampler says, 'What God has joined together, let no man put asunder,'" she called up the stairs.

"Perfect," Bappie said.

Hester repeated the verse, and Bappie set to work. She would keep the sampler in a small basket with the embroidery thread, needle, and a wooden hoop that would stretch the fabric for better sewing, and take this with her when they went *yung kyat psucha*.

After their wedding, the bride and groom were expected to visit every invited guest, sometimes for a meal, other times for just a call to collect their wedding gift for the *haus schtier*, the start of housekeeping. It was a time-honored tradition; newlyweds were held in high esteem. How Bappie looked forward to this time, when she could enter the homes of her friends, now married with a husband, able to feel like one of them and not just Bappie Kinnich alone.

Oh, she'd always been able to converse, keep up a good argument, serve food in high spirits, to be the perfect hostess welcoming the newlyweds and giving them useful gifts. Never once had anyone imagined how she ached to be a newlywed herself. Unflappable, no one had ever seen beneath the facade, her mask of energetic happiness.

Now she could sit with Levi and partake of all the special dishes made for the *yung kyaty*. There were no common dishes for visiting newlyweds. No brown flour soup or potato cakes. There were butter *Semmels*, *Krum Kuchen*, German bread, soft gingerbread with whipped cream, beef brisket with sauerkraut and dumplings, sweet and sour tongue, and stuffed beef heart. The flavorful, traditional dishes were spread on the company table fit for a king.

She would feel like a queen. She was a queen. Humming the old wedding song, Bappie burst into song, a loud rendition of the plainsong, the slow chant sung at each wedding. Bent over her work, she tapped her foot in time, nodding her head slightly with each word.

"*Schicket euch, ihr lieben gäschte.*" Thump, thump, nod, nod. "*Zu des lammes hochzeit fest.*" Thump, thump, thump. At the third line, Bappie's voice rose to a shrieking pitch, "*Schmücket euch aufs allerbeste.*" Thump, thump.

She bet anything Enos Troyer sei Mamie would make her three-layer hazelnut cake with boiled icing when she and Levi, the *yung kyaty*, would come to visit.

She started in again, singing raucously, tapping her foot with all the grace of a wooden pestle.

"Hey!" Hester shouted.

"What?"

"I'm down here, you know. You're loosening the whitewash and cobwebs. Stop your stomping on the floor."

"All right."

The singing resumed, louder than ever, and jerkier, but the thumping stopped. There were footsteps overhead; the cellar door squeaked open.

"Did they sing that one at your wedding?"

"I'm sure they did."

"Brings back memories, huh? Good ones, though, on your wedding day, huh?"

"Yes." Hester acknowledged this, mostly to get rid of Bappie's questions. She had been in love, she supposed. And yes, happy to become William's wife. She wondered vaguely if the sense of doom that hovered around the edges of her conscious thoughts had all been her own unwillingness to surrender to William's stringent rules even then.

He had spoken of this the week before the wedding. He had asked if she knew the verses in the Bible about giving over her will to him, and she had said yes, she knew. This was expected.

But was she ready? he had asked, digging for straight-forward answers of complete obedience. So total, he had swallowed her own life or may as well have.

May he rest in peace. William was gone, and there was no use gathering senseless memories that only served up fear of the future like a plate of unappetizing, moldy bread.

Her senseless feelings of agitation when she was with Noah would only dissipate with time. Noah, too, would expect that life-sucking submission, the authority over her so complete it was like a hood, stifling, allowing one to cling to life by short half-breaths, just enough to stay alive.

What had he done last night? Tried to tell her to start over with the herbs. That was very likely only the beginning.

No, she could not trust him. She could not begin to imagine that any form of friendship, and especially mar-riage, would be safe. It would be like stepping off a cliff, never being able to tell the outcome. She would be either dead, half-dead, or somewhat alive.

She had to stop thinking about Noah. She could not continue to harbor any thoughts of love or even attrac-tion. Nothing. His touch, the way he smiled and looked at her, the sheer force of him as he sat at a table, drove a buggy, walked away or toward her; eventually she would be able to banish any feeling of wonder or amazement. If she stayed aloof, the thrill would fade.

If only she had done that with William, she would not have had to endure the marriage, the death, and all the hideous ghosts of self-blame that still haunted her at night.

Yes, good for Bappie, her dear friend. Levi was captivated by his ginger-haired sweetheart, the secret of their friendship only making it more precious, more sacred. But Levi had suffered in his life, had shown he was willing to give his life for his beloved, even if she was given to him with a weakness of the nerves. And who could have foretold the dying of the dear babies?

Bappie's raucous singing continued as Hester snapped the sprouts off the potatoes and threw them in the bucket. She had found only a few very small wrinkled ones in the corner of the bin.

She was conscious of Bappie's footsteps, and then heard the back door hinges squeak. Someone had entered the house.

A man's voice.

Bappie's voice. Her footsteps, quick, light.

"Hester?"

"Yes?"

"Someone to see you."

Hester straightened, dusted her skirt with the corner of her apron, and climbed the steep stairway to the kitchen.

A man of medium height, a youth, stood inside the back door, framed by the blinding spring sunshine at his back. Hester walked toward him, puzzled.

Dressed in the ordinary street clothes of the English, he looked like dozens of young men milling about on the streets of Lancaster. His face was pleasant, vaguely familiar, but she had to admit, she had never seen him. Until he removed his hat.

All the red hair, that copper-hued thatch as thick as a bird's nest, came tumbling down about his ears and over his forehead. An impish grin followed, and Hester's hands went to her mouth.

"Billy!"

"Yep!"

"Billy Feree."

"Sure am."

They shook hands, Billy's face turning as red as his hair.

"Oh my," Hester breathed. "Look at you. All grown up."

The light from the back door was darkened as a beaming Emma, with Walter in tow, entered the room, the pride in her son so evident. It was unbelievable, the way Emma's face seemed youthful, even radiant. Walter dipped and bowed, smiled at everything Emma said, and ushered little Vernon and Richard into the room where they stood, gazing up at Billy with amazement.

Bappie rushed around, produced more chairs, and put the kettle on, while Hester explained Billy to Bappie, if she held still long enough to listen.

When Hester was taken from the Indians, that dark and fearful night, and left for dead in the livery stable, it was Billy, Emma Ferree's adopted son, who had found her. He loaded her on his sack wagon and brought her home to Emma, who nursed her back to health.

Then, when Hester married, he ran off and joined the war. It was just an awful blow to his mother, who meanwhile, had married her neighbor, Walter Trout. Now here he was, a youth, hardened and seasoned by the terrors of one battle that led to another, a senseless clashing of bayonets and rifles. But he'd stayed and was only released when he lost a leg.

Proudly, he rolled up the cuff of his trousers. The women gasped to see a wooden peg where his shoe should have been. "Ain't much wrong with me now. I strap this thing on and away I go."

His grin was crossed by delicate shadows of remembering though. The pain of it clouded the exuberance of his eyes, too, but only Hester saw that.

Bappie produced a plate of cinnamon cookies and *smear Kase* with new brown bread, hard-crusted and filled with whole grains of wheat and oats. She set out a pat of butter, a glass jar of plum conserve, and a large, heavy bowl filled to the brim with pickled pears.

A stack of plates, a few knives, forks, and spoons, and the midmorning *schtick* was spread.

Walter pulled up his chair, happiness creasing his cheeks, which pushed up against his eyes and squashed them flat, the prospect of a snack so pleasurable, there was no hiding it.

Emma said, "Now, Walter, we just ate our breakfast."

"Ah, my good wife, I agree, certainly, and good porridge. It was the best. But porridge speaks of a lightness to the meal, unlike scrapple and ponhaus or puddins.

Although, Emma, I do acknowledge, porridge is so much better for the constitution, is it not?"

Emma raised her eyebrows. Frowning prettily and patting his arm, she told him they were in the presence of ladies, and perhaps that was more information than they needed to know.

Billy laughed outright and said it was good to be home. When Emma smiled indulgently, Walter took this as a good sign, spread an enormous chunk of the butter on the thickest slice of bread, and chewed, enjoying the delicious flavor with his eyes closed.

Emma handed each of the boys a cookie. They each murmured their "thank you" and ran outside to play next to the henhouse, where they terrorized the chickens so badly, they declined in their egg-laying.

Billy told them many stories of his years away from home, peppered with his quick grin and infectious laugh, the Billy they remembered so well. If the years had taken their toll, his good humor and frank outlook were still intact, which was so good to see.

Hester found herself caught up in his stories, listening with rapt attention, her large eyes never leaving his face. Indeed, he had met some interesting characters and seen so many new places, including plenty of things he had no wish to speak of.

"There were these two brothers, though, that stand out to me. I rode with them for awhile and I'll never forget them. The oldest, Noah, was magnificent. Ain't no other way to describe him. Can't forget a name like that, huh? Straight off the ark. Oh, he was a sight. He rode with the colonel. He was put up in the ranks, the way some of 'em are. Never saw anyone ride like that. That build, that hair. He had wildness about him. Didn't care if he lived or died, that one. He saved my life, but he couldn't save his brother. Forget his name."

"Isaac," Hester whispered before she could stop herself.

Billy snapped his fingers and sat up straight. "You knew him?"

"I did."

"How?"

"They are my brothers from Berks County."

"That's right! You told us that. You mean, these guys are . . . you were raised with them?"

His face fell, folding in on itself as memories attacked him. "You know Isaac's dead."

Hester nodded.

"It was vicious cold that winter, so cold our breath froze to our mustaches. Tears froze on our faces. It was Noah, Isaac, me, and maybe a few dozen others ridin' into camp, mindin' our own business, when one of the younger men—those often don't think, just act—shot into this bunch of whacked Injuns to scare them off. Stupid little skirmish, nothing any commander knew about, just some Injuns drunk on some kinda poison someone sold them, must be.

"It was terrible. Savages didn't seem human. Painted faces, half-starved, their minds half gone with the slop they were drinking, acting out of revenge, knowing they was being chased outa Pennsylvania.

"Isaac took an arrow through the chest. He died in the snow, with Noah holding him like a baby. Just sat in the snow and cradled him. He was talking in Dutch, I guess, or German. Singing. Noah was singing. He laid Isaac down, real gentle-like, then tended to me, with an arrow through my shin, bone splintered like a chunk of wood. He packed me to camp like a bedroll, where he took care of me till the doctor could take off my leg. The infection I got after a few weeks couldn't be stopped. That's how come they had to take it off.

"Noah sang sometimes. Hummed, whistled, kept talking about his sister back home in Berks County. Said she was something. Could shoot a slingshot better than anyone he knew or ever heard of. Said she was good with the children. I forget everything he said, but he sure thought a lot about his sister. So that musta been you, Hester. He never mentioned your name. Didn't say you was Indian."

Hester was blinking back the tears that pricked her eyelashes and trying to swallow the lump that rose in her throat. "He probably meant Lissie."

"No, he talked of her, too. Said she was a loudmouth."

Hester said nothing, clearly ashamed of this, afraid what Bappie would say.

Walter cleared his throat and looked around for a napkin. He would never get used to these Pennsylvania Dutch and their eating habits. How was he supposed to wipe his mouth if they did not supply a good cloth napkin? He wiped a finger across his buttery mouth, quickly slid it beneath the table cover, and rolled it back and forth a bit. There, much better.

He raised his head, tilted it back a few inches, and lowered his eyes to view his shirt front. As he had feared, it was scattered with crumbs, an embarrassing plop of plum conserve, and a wet spot at another place, no doubt a splash of pickled pear juice. This was annoying. He had tried and tried to impart to his dear wife the importance of a napkin, but she waved him away like an irritating mosquito, saying it made too much wash. This, when he so gladly built the fire, heated the water, even shaved the soap.

Quite in despair he sat, the plum conserve and pear juice glistening on his shirt front, his face heated with consternation, his stomach only half full, the loaf of bread sliced and so inviting.

"Walter, would you like to have a napkin?" Oh, the redemption in Bappie's voice!

"Why, yes, dear girl, if there is one available, I would be enormously grateful."

Billy watched as Bappie brought a stack of snowy white cloths embroidered on one corner with the letter B and crocheted delicately on the same corner. She was blushing all the way to her ears, the high forehead the same color as her hair.

"There you go," she said, her voice thick, her face flaming. Emma smiled up at Bappie and put her hand on the long, thin forearm. "How nice of you, Bappie. I know napkins make so much wash. Did you embroider and crochet these? B for Barbara, lovely. These napkins are lovely."

Hester said quickly, her eyes dancing. "The B is for Buehler."

"Buehler? But her name is King, I thought." Emma was confused, sitting in the sun-filled kitchen, her round, wrinkled face glistening with the excitement of Billy's arrival and too many cinnamon cookies dipped in her steaming, heavily sugared tea.

"It will be Buehler in November," Hester said, enjoying the mystery.

"Buehler? But how?" Emma was completely flummoxed, till Billy's grin gave him away and he whooped and pointed. Walter looked up from tucking in the blessed napkin and smiled, his eyes closing in delight.

"You are betrothed, Bappie!"

Bappie reveled in the moment, floating in the delighted stares, luxuriating in the drama that spread across the table, as her guests swooped up their hands in disbelief, full of pure happiness for her.

"I am marrying the widower, Levi Buehler. He asked me, and I have consented to be his wife."

Hester slanted a look at Bappie and pinched her leg at the white lie. Bappie grabbed Hester's thumb and twisted until her mouth went slack with pain. Bappie's shoulders shook, but she steadied them quickly.

Congratulatory words, pats on shoulders, hand-wringing, even a few maudlin tears from Emma, brought a festive air to the kitchen that forenoon in the early summer, when the sun-kissed room held so much joy.

After that, Bappie held forth like a royal monarch raising her scepter, with tales of Levi and his long-suffering wife, the farm that languished, raising no profit, his coon hunting, the dogs, everything.

Emma was amazed, so Walter figured if she was occupied in this manner, he may as well take advantage of it and proceed with the bread and butter, seeing as it was almost the noon hour.

Billy and Hester wandered to the back stoop, allowing Bappie her time with Walter and Emma. They sat side by side talking about old times, about how short a time it actually was.

Hester told him about her marriage to William, the grief, the loneliness, but hesitated about telling him more.

"No kids? I mean, children. You had no children?"

Hester shook her head.

"Well, good you didn't. They wouldn't have a father."

"I know."

After awhile, Billy shook his head. "He must of thought an awful lot of you."

"Who?"

"That Noah."

Hester didn't know what to say to this, so she said nothing. She lifted the hem of her apron and twisted it into a roll across her legs, over and over, while Billy looked out across the cramped space of the backyard. He squinted, his little boy's face turned into the square-jawed, undimpled face of a man. He was clean-shaven, with too-long hair tumbling in untamed strands over his forehead and down his back.

Not unattractive, Billy had a strong face with good humor lurking beneath the surface. Hester watched him sideways without his being aware of it.

"He wanted to write to you. Said you'd left. Never said why. Just that you'd left. I don't think many evenings went by without his talking about you, mentioning things."

"Like what?" Hester clasped and unclasped her knees.

"Oh, just stuff. You know, the kinda stuff you do with your sister. Shuck corn, make hay. He said you could drive a team of horses like a man. He said you used to chew on clover and then eat the whole stalk, even the purple blossoms. Stuff like that. To me, seemed as if he loved you a whole lot more than most brothers, but then, he ain't your real brother.

"In fact, I think he loves you the way grown folks do, not some kinda brotherly thing that he tried to make me think it was. But then, Hester, *I* always wanted to marry you. Remember? So maybe I shouldn't tell you all this."

Hester laughed. "Is this a proposal? You still want to marry me, Billy?"

He turned to look at her with the frank good humor of the eleven-year-old he was when he had saved her life.

"Yeah, I do. The only thing is, you're Amish, and I don't like them big caps you all wear."

Hester tilted back her head and laughed. It felt good to be with Billy who had not changed so terribly much. Bless his heart. She would have hugged him, but that would never have been proper, so she leaned her shoulder against his, and said, "Dear Billy. I would have you, although I'm at least nine or ten years older than you."

"That's not too old. You're still a beauty. Never saw anyone prettier, I don't think."

"You don't think! Oh, come on. There've been quite a few."

Billy shook his head, resolute in his spoken declaration. "Nah, I'll have to see if I can find that Noah. What was his last name?"

"Zug."

"Oh, yeah, funny name. But guess that's yours, too, ain't it?"

"Yes."

Then, because she felt like a traitor, she told Billy that Noah had found her, that they were friends, and that he'd come back to the Amish again.

"Noah's Amish? I don't believe it."

"Yes, he is."

"He wasn't Amish when I knew him."

"No, he wasn't."

"So what's going to happen now?"

Hester remained quiet for some time, then shook her head. "I don't know."

She told Billy more about having been married to William. She described it as less than perfect, trying to avoid the issue that stayed with her, the lack of restraint on her part.

Billy looked at her. "But I guess you of all people— you know, bein' Amish and all, you know, taught to be good and righteous and all that stuff—should know that marriage goes well if you're good people, don't it?"

His words, the wisdom in them, were a blow, a hard whack below the ribs that took her breath away.

There it was. The whole thing. Placed in her lap in all its monstrosity. She shuddered and clasped her hands tightly in her lap, interlocking her fingers until the knuckles turned white from the pressure she applied.

"William was good. It was me. I was rebellious toward him. I have suffered remorse. Wished it would have been otherwise."

"I can see that."

There it was again. Billy could see it, and he knew her well. The upcoming event, this going with Noah on a picnic or an adventure, a secret, he had said, would have to be stopped. Her mind churned, her thoughts of the future caterwauling about, unsettling every semblance of peace she may ever have held.

They got up, speaking their goodbyes. Walter and Emma gathered up the boys and went home to their own house.

Hester let herself in the back door, numb and reeling with the words Billy had spoken. She found Bappie jubilant, glowing, and fairly walking on her tiptoes, caught up in the heartfelt congratulations Walter and Emma had strewn about the room like confetti.

"Walter loved my napkins," she sang out.

"Good."

Hester pushed past Bappie, clomped up the steps, and sat on her bed, staring dead ahead, not seeing anything. Her hands hung loosely from her knees, her feet thrust in front of her.

She felt like a desert, dry, unforgiven, without life. First, the vegetable garden was taken, then the farm, and next the herbs, her lifelong passion thrown into a bucket and dumped in the outhouse. And now Bappie was going.

There were no tears; she felt no emotion. Only an emptiness, a lifeless landscape of sand and cold wind, a barren place in her soul.

It had all started, all her misery, when Hans behaved unseemly. That's all it was. It was Hans. Unsure about how she could ever forgive him, she set her lips and planned the remainder of her life without Noah's or any other man's help.

CHAPTER 13

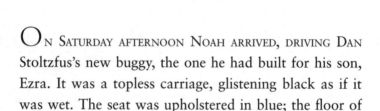

ON SATURDAY AFTERNOON NOAH ARRIVED, DRIVING DAN Stoltzfus's new buggy, the one he had built for his son, Ezra. It was a topless carriage, glistening black as if it was wet. The seat was upholstered in blue; the floor of the buggy was carpeted as well.

The black gelding horse had lots of fire, his neck arched proudly, his tail flowing in a graceful arc.

The harness was new by all appearances, without a trace of dust or grease. Because it belonged to an unmarried young man, a few silver rings and other splashes of fanciness popped up here and there.

Hester had become completely undone as she bathed, washed her hair, and put on the clean, freshly ironed blue dress. Its indigo color matched the spring buntings, those elusive little birds that appeared too infrequently, singing their hearts out from high places.

If only her head could convince her heart to quit slamming around in her chest. Her anticipation of seeing Noah had driven away all the resolve she had shored up against him, like sandbags along a flooded creek, placed there to save the low-lying village that was her life, her future.

Then there was the remorse about her marriage to William, and hatred—yes, a raw word, but it seethed in her veins now—for Hans, and nothing better for her spindly cruel stepmother Annie, or her sister Lissie who was always favored.

When she had put on her black apron and slipped her feet into the brown moccasins, her face was still not calm. Agitation played across her features, darkening her eyes and turning her mouth into a hard slash, as she thought of telling Noah that she had no plans to ever become any man's wife again, if that was what he was after. She would be his friend, but nothing more. As far as those herbs, she guessed that was her business as well and none of his.

Luckily, Bappie was out at Levi's farm whitewashing and cleaning. Walter and Emma had taken Billy to visit aunts and uncles, so Noah's grand entrance caused no fuss among Hester's acquaintances.

He stood beside the buggy as imposing as a general, his bearing almost regal. He was well over six feet tall and built like a workhorse, this Hester could not help but acknowledge. When he watched her walk toward him, he smiled, the kindness so like Kate's that Hester felt the beginning of a lump in her throat, a breach in the dam of her resolve.

Oh, Heavenly Father, stay with me. The prayer was like armor. She had to stay strong to resist this giant of a man who was not her brother at all. Not at all.

"Good afternoon, Hester. I hope you are well."

She acknowledged his kindness with a curt nod and averted eyes, her mouth dry with the acceleration of her heart and her senses.

Noah's heart sank. So this was the way it would be today. He took her hand lightly, helping her into the buggy. He leaped in after her as the horse lunged. Noah grasped tightly at the black leather reins, hauling back while the horse reared, shaking his head and trying to rid himself of the unwanted restraint.

Hester watched as the horse rose, up, up, his back long and black and powerful. She thought he would surely topple over backward, crushing them, but then he lunged forward, turned right, and came down running, hard. Dogs scattered and a child in a wagon watched them with awe as Noah struggled with the reins. The town required a lot of a driver, with other teams and pedestrians everywhere, and a horse that was clearly uncontrollable.

Once they reached the open road, Noah let him run, slowly releasing the reins through his hands until the wind tore at Hester's muslin cap and pried loose the black strands of hair she had so carefully combed with water and a fine-toothed comb.

They did not speak. Noah knew this was not the time or the place to make small talk. The day seemed to be unraveling before him, his anticipation and hope of reintroducing Hester to her medicinal herbs darkened by her lowered brows, her mouth a thin line, her face a map of her stubborn mind.

Today there was something else about her, an aura of rigidness in the way she shrank away from him, as if he was too big, too real, too loathsome. By the time they reached the Dan Stoltzfus farm, the black gelding was shining with sweat. There was no white lather, however, which meant Noah had been careful to wash him before throwing the harness on his back. That was good.

Noah drew back on the reins, and the horse came to a standstill. Noah leaped down, tied the reins to the ring on the side, then came around to Hester's side, extending his hand, his eyes searching her face. She barely touched his hand, landing lightly on her feet. She averted her eyes again, and stepped a dozen paces away, holding her hands stiffly by her sides.

Noah unhitched the horse and rubbed him down, then turned him out with the rest of the horses in the green pasture that led to a line of thick trees.

Hester turned to survey the new barn. She had been careful to avoid looking at it before, not wanting Noah to start an enthusiastic tour of it before she told him what was on her mind. It was the most magnificent building she had ever seen, including the stores and hotels in Berksville or Lancaster. Built into the side of a hill, the front of the barn was immense, as high as two houses built on top of one another. No, it was higher. The stonework was amazing, the grayish-brown stones cut to size, exquisite in their handiwork.

Six heavy doors, with the longest black hinges she had ever seen, were built into this stone wall, rectangles of perfection.

Above this first floor rose a sheer wall of boards, attached vertically to the massive oak beams with hand-hewn wooden pegs. The boards were still yellow, the new lumber retaining its original color before the elements, the sun and wind, the rain and snow, turned the boards a dark gray.

Above the doors in the stone wall, on the next story, were five shorter doors that could be swung open at haymaking time. Intricate arches, the wood shaped into half-moons above these doors, made Hester wonder what builder would put that kind of workmanship on the second story of a barn. She felt Noah approach.

She lifted her eyes to the third story, which was probably the fourth or fifth story on the other side of the barn, and saw windows on top of that, with half-moons of trim above them. The eaves from the roof were deep and wide, casting shadows on the window glass. Without thinking, she said, "What a wonderful barn!"

When Noah said nothing, she turned sideways, afraid of what her blanket of silence had done. Perhaps she'd overdone it.

She saw him lift his shoulders, then drop them.

"About a year's work."

"Who did it?"

"Dan and I. You want to see the inside?"

"Of course."

He led her through a side door and into a wide bay where harnesses hung on long pegs and water troughs lined the walls. The stables were so well-built and so clean that Hester was amazed.

The interior of the barn was dark and cool, the air hazy and thick with smells of corn and oats, cured hay, and glistening yellow straw. The acrid undertone of manure was a sweetness to Hester. Her sharp pang of remembering felt almost physical as she recalled the barn in Berks County where she had learned to milk cows, clean stables and harnesses, sweep the walls of cobwebs, and bring baby lambs from the cold windblown pastures of early spring, when the air was still raw and unforgiving to the shivering little white bundles.

She wanted to tell Noah this, but how could she, with the job she had chosen for today? She must not waver.

Noah let her breathe in the smells and run her fingers over the water trough and the pegs that held the harnesses. She went to the stable doors, bending over them to talk to the piglets and calves. She found a baby colt, lying in the straw alone.

"Why isn't he with his mother in the pasture?" she asked.

"Dan and Rachel went away today to her sister's house. They have a frolic to build a springhouse."

Another memory was suddenly upon her—the springhouse Hans had built for Kate, the rocks dripping moisture, the water smelling like dew in the morning, the crocks of cheese and new butter, the lard and peppermint tea they stored there. She saw Kate's pleasure like the sun through the storm clouds' aftermath, her round face beaming with the inner light she always carried, magnified now, as she praised Hans.

Hester turned to Noah. "I'm ready to go."

They left the barn with the memories that threatened her resolve and went back to the buggy, where Noah lifted out the basket of food Hester had prepared. He held the gate for her, and she walked through without meeting his gaze. Silently they walked across the pasture, her strides matching his, the basket between them.

The sun was already well past noon, throwing their shadows into chubby caricatures of themselves behind them. They climbed a fence where the flat meadow turned downward into a much lower level. The thick border of trees was beyond this low pasture. The closer they came to the trees, the more spongy the ground became. A familiar smell, a woodsy, decaying odor rose from the low ground.

It was not a swamp like the one Hester would wade in with water up to her knees, collecting skunk cabbage and bulrushes. She'd gather bits of mosses, too, that were good to pack around other plants, keeping them wet till she replanted them in Bappie's garden.

"You'll have to walk behind me now, please. There's a narrow trail here that leads into the woods."

Hester stepped back, letting Noah lead the way. She knew there were no plants growing in that dense forest. What was he thinking? But he'd said he wanted to show her something, so she would see what it was in spite of her mistrust.

"Careful." Noah held aside blackberry brambles, branches of wild roses and thistles, holly bushes, and nettles. They walked swiftly, their long strides covering the distance easily. The woods turned darker, the trees overhead a roof of leaves, shutting out the sun's light. In shafts, light broke through, pinpoints of dust-filled light that created an otherworldly atmosphere. Rotting leaves, new growth, moldy logs, crumbling bark—the familiar smells of the forest rose and filled her senses with another form of remembering, the woods her only home after she left the Berks County farm.

She swallowed and lowered her face as quick tears rose to the surface. Instantly, she bit her lip and kept her eyes on Noah's back, refusing to give in to the scents, the dank, heady odors around her.

Suddenly, without warning, even before she could sense the changing of the light, they broke out of the dense woods into a sun-dappled circular ring without a single tree in its midst.

The grass was brilliantly green, the new grass the color of premature peas, the older grass like just-cooked broccoli, a beautiful deep green. Peppered among the glorious green, in a profusion of delicate color, grew small flowers in pink, soft dainty yellow, and white. Bluebells nodded over the smaller flowers. The most amazing thing was the fact that this profusion of beauty grew in a perfect ring.

Hester's hands came slowly to her mouth as her eyes widened. She leaned forward a bit, as if her spirit was being led to its home. She dared to breathe, but only softly, for fear this vision was only that, a mirage that would disappear.

Noah watched her face from a polite distance, putting his hands firmly in his pockets. She walked swiftly then to her right, fell to her knees, her hands reaching out to touch but not to gather.

There was an abundance of spearmint, lush and heavy, a growth of the wonderful tea unlike anything she had ever seen. Leeks, wood sorrel, lily of the valley, mullen, so many plants, all growing in abundance, a patch of nature's gift to mankind, unspoiled, pristine.

Murmuring, she got to her feet, only to bend back and exclaim softly, as she stroked the spikenard that some called petimoral. It was so good for the elderly who had aches and pains of the joints, and for anyone with unhealthy kidneys.

Her thoughts went to the victims of nausea, how they would need fresh water and tea made of herbs. Without sufficient drinking water, the bladder and kidneys would ache.

A hand went to her heart, a painful sorrow for the sick children pulsing there. When she had denied this and left them to the doctor's care, she felt nothing. The sadness vanished, leaving her cold and dead inside.

As she walked among the wondrous profusion of plants, Noah remained silent. He watched her bend to caress the healthy plants and followed the movement of her lips. He saw the inward battle. He knew how determined she could be, how impossible to persuade. And so he said nothing.

The sun slanted through the trees, casting a rosy glow across the flower-gathered clearing, making it appear almost heavenly. Like a paradise on earth, in a way you could feel more than see.

Finally Hester stood, her hands crossed at her chest. She took a deep, painful breath.

Noah waited, observing her face.

When she lifted her large eyes to his, they were like dark wells of torture, filled with the suffering of her inward struggle.

He met her gaze with the only thing he was capable of, his long and undeclared love which he had carried within himself as long as he could remember. It was a flame, tended by the angels themselves, after he had accepted that it would never go away. It shone blue from the depth of eyes, so much like Kate's, a love that was the strongest emotion, the most powerful force on earth. It broke barriers, crashed down defensive walls, a glorious Roman gladiator of the soul.

The gaze held as their two spirits clashed, sword against sword. Hester panicked when she felt his power, the love in those blue eyes. Turning, she cried out, a soft, strangled cry of defeat, and took off running across the flower-filled clearing.

It wasn't that Noah even thought about a choice, he only knew he had to keep her. Lunging after her with a dozen quick strides, he caught her shoulders before she reached the thicket of trees.

She wrenched free, crying out for him to let her go. He held her in his powerful hands and turned her toward himself. He felt her resistance weaken as sobs, thick and deep, rose in her throat. He thought she was choking, strangling, and so held her away, searching her face.

Her eyes were closed, her mouth open, anguish written in bold letters in the way her eyebrows were drawn down. It was as if the pain in her soul would render her unable to breathe or to live.

"Hester, please don't."

With a groan, he brought her into the circle of his arms. He held her so powerfully, it was hopeless for her to resist.

She wasn't sure if she wanted to. His arms tightened slightly, and her own crept up slowly, hesitantly, until they were placed about his waist. She told herself this was only for comfort. Like a child she stayed there, afraid to breathe.

Then she felt a quietness, not a void, just a silent place of rest where there was nothing. A place of pure peace where no thoughts could enter. William King, the herbs, Hans and Annie, her Indian heritage, the pain, nothing, not one semblance of her past, had the power to enter this place.

Noah remained still, neither asking her to speak nor speaking himself. He simply held her, allowing her to tell him when she was ready.

Hester sighed but had no idea that she did. When the rest became so calming, and all the railing of troubled thoughts were banished, she sank forward and laid her head against the thickness of his chest. The sobs rose, quietly then, the anguish melting away by the flow of her tears. He pulled her closer, closer still, as she cried. And still they spoke no words.

When her tears soaked through the homespun fabric of his shirt, he felt as if he was anointed. Hope welled in his chest.

Vaguely, calmly, Hester thought Noah might release her, then lift her chin to kiss her the way William used to do. How would this be different with Noah?

Suddenly she was overcome by a longing that Noah would kiss her. That he would gently lower his mouth to seek hers, an affirmation of his caring, his wanting.

When he loosened his arms, it was all she could do not to clutch at his waist, a needy child who searched for safety. The haven of Noah's arms was a known place now. She knew there was rest there, and she could never not want it.

He released her.

She was jolted to bare, stark reality. He handed her a clean square of white linen, saying something she failed to hear.

They stepped apart, each one stranded now, knowing they were alone, when moments before they had not known this.

Noah said, "Would you like to share the picnic lunch? I am suddenly quite hungry." He laughed softly when he looked at her. "It's all right, Hester."

That was all he said. She knew what he meant.

He used to say that when she missed a target or the cow kicked over a bucket of milk that they had to have, or when some other unfortunate episode happened. He had always used those words to help her set her life right. So she followed the pattern of her childhood, believing it *was* all right, including the tears and her love of the plants in this hidden glade. It was all right.

They ate ravenously, the cloth spread on the brilliant carpet of green. The sandwiches were filled with the best roast chicken and with spring lettuce from the tiny backyard plot they called a garden. The molasses cookies were crinkled with rivulets where they separated in the heat of baking, then sprinkled liberally with white sugar. They ate, their eyes like magnets now, finding each other, knowing that they could return to this place just with a glance.

Ordinary food had never tasted like this. The cold peppermint tea was like ambrosia, liquid stars in their mouths.

Noah smiled and asked if she wanted to gather any plants, perhaps fill the picnic basket? He spoke easily, ready to accept a No, or an unwillingness to bend or to allow herself freedom from her wounded pride. She bowed her head, slowly moving it from side to side.

"You don't want anything?"

"No."

Then, "Noah, this place is magical. If I would believe in fairies, I would have to say I saw a real fairy ring. These thousands of little flowers are like stardust, sprinkled over the grass by the tips of the fairies' wands. You know, Kate used to tell me stories about elves and fairies and Saint Nicholas, always telling me first that none of it was true, but her stories always took me places. I imagined these things. Then she would hold her finger to her lips and say it was our secret, that I was not to tell anyone, especially not my friends in school. The other Amish mothers would be shocked, such *unwort*."

Noah laughed. "Yes, our mother was a bit adventurous with her songs and poems and the stories from the old country. I often wondered about her parents, our grandparents, and if they were truly Amish. Did they belong to the church?"

"She never said."

"I know. But Mother was different; not as exacting as Father."

"Don't you call them *Dat* and *Mam*, the way you used to?"

"Sometimes, Hester, I don't know who they are." A note of bitterness crept in his voice.

"After our mam died, a part of me died with her. I loved my mother so completely. Dat was different. He never cared much for Isaac and me. We were his hired help. If we didn't do our work to his expectations, we were whipped with the buggy whip. I can still feel the burning welts. It drove us to do our best, but so often the best was not good enough. By the time we were teenagers, after 14 years of age, we were worked far beyond anyone can imagine.

"I remember felling trees at a young age, well before others our age did. I tried to spare Isaac. He was smaller and lighter, and he used to weep with weariness."

Noah's smile was gone, his kindness absent, now replaced by a harsh light, his mouth set by the anger in his remembering.

"But that physical part, the hard work, the endless labor, was nothing compared to the time after our mother passed away. That was when . . ." He stopped, emotions washing over his face like churning storm clouds.

"That was when I had to face what I tried hardest to deny. Hans loved you more than as a daughter. We were insanely jealous, Isaac and I. To hide his feelings, Hans became rigid in discipline, forbidding you everything, the horses, the rides to town. You remember."

Hester nodded, hanging on to Noah's words like a drowning man thrown some form of hope.

"As I grew taller, stronger, Hans, Dat, Father—all the same, but sometimes I am unsure of who he really was— carried a certain fear of me. I'm not sure when it actually happened. I just know it did.

"He saw the trees I felled with an axe, the amount of hard labor Isaac and I accomplished, and he knew his days of whipping us were over. Annie was a bitter disappointment, which created fear as well. He was consumed, then swept away, by his obsession of you, Hester.

"Why did I stay? I don't really know. Perhaps the whip had driven undivided obedience into me. Fear of disobeying must have been stronger than my will to turn against him. At any rate, I stayed, watching the way Annie treated you, knowing there was no way out.

"If you will forgive me for telling the truth, my love for you was destroying me. I had two choices—to stand against my father to protect you, or to get rid of any feelings I ever had, any fondness for sure, to try to destroy the love I imagined I had. I was unsure, ashamed, and feeling it was as wrong for me to love you as it was for Hans. I drove you out of my mind, my conscience, and my heart. I became a dead, empty shell, a living, walking, breathing person who was left with no emotion, no love, no fear, no anxiety, and, as I practiced daily, no caring."

He watched Hester's face, the drop of her bent head, the long dark lashes that lay so close to the golden, burnished cheek.

"I was just inside the house, listening to you and Hans on the porch that evening. I heard his speech."

Here, Hester's eyes raked his face, widening in disbelief. She watched his cheeks contract, the muscles turning his mouth grim and taut as he fought with remembered outrages.

"When you spoke, my heart swelled, my tears ran freely. Goosebumps raced up and down my spine, the hair on my arms stood straight up with the thrill of the truth you pounded into him.

"'My Hester,' I thought, 'you keep going. Please tell him all of it.' I was shaking, alone as I listened. My bones turned to water; I think I prayed. I remember that God felt closer than he has ever been. I was sure this was the end, and perhaps we could leave together. And then you were gone.

"Hans became like a person demented. We had to follow you, but I went only because I could not bear the parting, knowing that you were gone forever. I was not afraid of your ability to survive; I knew you would do it. But to think of the years stretching ahead without you, even to see your face from a distance, was more than I could bear."

He stopped, quieted now, and looked off into the distance.

"At war, the outward world around me was in real chaos, but there was a spiritual war just like it in my mind, my heart, my whole being. The only way I knew to survive was to spend all my energy riding, building forts, digging ditches, not caring if I lived or died. Through all of it, including the worst times, I carried one of the smooth stones from your slingshot in my breast pocket. It was like my image of you, the only real thing in my life."

CHAPTER 14

THE SUN WAS SLIDING TOWARD THE EVENING SHADOWS, THE rosy glow turning deeper. As they remained seated side by side, the sounds of the forest became a symphony, the glade of fairy flowers their theater.

Hester's eyes were filled with emotion as she listened to the voice beside her, bringing back all the events she had tried to dispel, or blame herself for, which was easier. But now it was clear that neither one had worked.

She watched the antics of two black and orange monarch butterflies, flitting in their dizzying, uncharted spirals, drunk on the nectar of so many flowers, so much color and profusion.

Noah breathed in, a deep cleansing of his emotion, then let the breath out with a quavery sigh, as if the beating of his heart had interrupted the clean breath.

Hester said, soft and low, "I had no idea. I thought you hated me. Along with Annie, with everyone."

"No Hester, never. It wasn't possible. I loved you. I just felt it was wrong, somehow, and did what I had to do to survive."

The Indian blood in her veins held her silent as Hester pondered deeply every word he had spoken.

Finally, she ventured, "You did love me back then. But now it's different for you. Isn't that what you're saying?"

"Look at me, Hester."

She would not turn to him, so great was her fear.

"I have never given up the love for you that I carry within. I never will. But I know you are like a trapped bird, caged by your past, your own sense of failure."

Hester nodded. Then she turned, her eyes soft with gratefulness. "Thank you, Noah. You do understand. If I would not have married William . . ." Her voice drifted off.

Noah let her have all the time she needed to think how to say what was on her mind.

Finally, she said, "I am not a good wife."

Noah let this sentence hover between them before he attempted a reply.

"Why do you say that?"

"In so many different ways I failed William. His mother, too. My cooking, my rebellion. Sometimes, I hated him. As I might come to hate any man I marry. That exacting obedience, that rigid control, Noah. It takes away your mind, your thoughts, until you don't know who you are. It's like a giant leech that drains away your life. And still, you keep up a perfect outward appearance, looking as if you're happily obeying so that the community around you keeps up their admiration for William and Hester King."

She flung the last words into the idyllic little forest clearing, destroying the holiness of God's handwork, the venom rising in her throat.

Noah nodded, choking when he tried to speak, so he let her continue.

"I believe in God's Word, Noah. I believe in submission, a woman's place, giving up her will to obey her husband. And this is right and good. God ordained it. But the husband is to love his wife, giving his life as Christ gave his for the church, so is that really any different from what a wife is to do? Doesn't that mean William had no right to insist on everything he wanted, to say anything, no matter how hurtful? No matter what I did, Noah, it wasn't good enough. But I wasn't holy."

Her voice rose. "Do you have any idea the crushing weight of being unable to produce a son? Barren, Noah. I am barren. I was told repeatedly that the Lord could not bless my womb because I was rebellious. I believe this is true. Please forgive me for speaking boldly, but I know no other way to let you know who I really am—an unfit person, someone who should never marry again."

"Hester, stop. Those two things are not related— whether you are rebellious or not able to have children. There is a love that transcends that, overlooks it, or doesn't see it at all. I knew you since you were a child. Do you think I should not love you because you are not perfect?"

"Yes."

"But that's not how it is. We love all the imperfections in each other. It is who we truly are."

"That's just the English way of thinking. We're Old Order Amish, Noah, you and I. Frances and William have beaten every aspect of the marriage vows into my head, believe me."

Noah decided, then, to end the conversation, seeing how Hester was clutching with determination her own shortcomings and that she would not relinquish them. She was like that. As bullheaded as a mule, once she decided something. His eyes twinkled, shining very blue, as he thought about how angry she would be if she knew his thoughts just now. She'd likely take off her shoe and throw it, the way she used to do when he and Isaac threw a wet, slimy frog at her.

No, he would not push her. He had the rest of his life. In spite of himself, he burst out laughing. He tossed back his head, opened his mouth, and laughed until he was finished.

Hester turned to him, glaring, her eyes black with misunderstanding. "What?" she asked.

"Oh, you! I can just imagine. I bet you took off your shoe and threw it at your poor husband." Again, great ripples of movement sounded through the meadow.

Hester leaned over and hit his arm solidly with her fists. "You can't laugh, Noah. It's not funny."

He caught her hands, held them firmly, looked into her eyes, and said he would love to have a wife that threw shoes at him.

And then, because of the feeling that rose in his chest, and because of how much he wanted her, he released her hands and bent to gather the remains of the picnic lunch, leaving her standing alone again.

Noah drove her home in silence, thanked her for accompanying him, and drove off as she stood in the backyard. The town's buildings rose up around her, tall and dank and suffocating. She felt trapped, or as if she was wandering aimlessly. She wasn't sure which. She only knew that Bappie irritated her and that the streets were dirty and filled with far too many people, carts, and filthy old farmers' wagons with slovenly drivers.

Often, she wondered about Noah's injury and how it had healed. She wondered if she should have inquired about it, but that seemed too personal so she had let it go. She had noticed him grimace, and observed a stiffness in the way he had carried himself across the pasture. It seemed his back was still bothering him somewhat.

If he thought he could show her all the lovely plants and persuade her to change her mind, he would discover otherwise. This time she meant it. There would be no medicinal herbs in her house. She would never make tinctures again. As time went on, doctors would find many more plants in other countries, hire men to explore those places, and cultivate and gather many more growing things than Hester could ever begin to name. Even now, there were many more cures available from companies called pharmaceuticals. Walter Trout had read to her from the *Intelligencer Journal* about this booming industry.

So what was puny little wisdom from the old Indian woman really worth? Very likely next to nothing, as medical wisdom grew by leaps, and highly educated men who went to colleges learned about the body and about plants they could turn into pills to heal it. And so her thoughts swirled about, filling her mind with the noxious fumes of defeat.

One morning, however, she had had enough. The sun rose red with pulsing heat at eight o'clock. She threw out the dishwater, rinsed the tubs, swept the kitchen carefully, went to the mirror and smoothed back her hair, set her muslin cap straight, walked out the door, and did not stop till she came to the biggest house on Duke Street. It was immense, with white pillars cast on either side of the massive doorway, the door itself so large and ornate, Hester had a moment of indecision.

The walls of the house were built of quarried limestone, smooth and blue-gray, and laid to perfection by the finest mason the town could find, the mortar thin and straight without chinks. The windows were tall with numerous small panes, and heavily draped, with ornate moulding at the top. Set back from the street far enough to allow the growth of a few cultivated hedges, trimmed conifers and holly, it was the home of someone who was wealthy, the group known as the "gentry."

Hester had made up her mind to seek employment in the only way she knew—going door to door, asking if those who lived there needed servants in the kitchen, the laundry, or with housecleaning. She knew it was not allowed by the Amish church, this employment outside of the home, but she was becoming desperate with Bappie getting married and her savings dwindling. She needed some source of income.

Lifting the brass knocker, she let it fall repeatedly, with no answer. The door remained closed. She had just turned to go back down the steps, when the door was opened from the inside.

"Yes?" The voice was level with Hester's face, the interior shadows making it difficult to see the person framed in the doorway. When the door opened wider, Hester saw a large woman, her hair tied into a white cloth, a white apron covering her dress front, immaculate in her appearance.

"Hello. My name is Hester Zug. I am seeking employment as a cook or housekeeper."

Before she could finish, the woman rolled her eyes, shook her head from side to side, and closed the door with a whoosh, a clunk, and the decided snap of the heavy latch.

Hester wiped her face gently with the palm of her hand as the sun climbed the midmorning sky. She had walked far, she was thirsty, and could only do one thing—keep knocking on doors.

The neighboring house was made of stone like the first. The only difference was a deep porch on two sides of the house, setting the side windows and doors into a cool shaded area. A strip of cut green grass bordered the steps, and some coneflowers and iris nodded in the sun's heat as she made her way up to the front door.

She knocked, lifting the brass ring and letting it fall. Immediately, Hester looked up into the haughtiest face she had ever seen—the butler, she guessed, wild-eyed.

"My name is Hester Zug. I am seeking employment." Before she could finish, the butler spoke in clipped, icy tones: "The house is fully staffed. Good day." The door creaked and banged, the latch fell, and that was the end of that. Hester felt like knocking again to tell him the door needed to be oiled, and perhaps they could use a door oiler, but she went back down the steps, her pride intact, and kept on trying.

From house to house, always asking the same thing, Hester met with varying degrees of politeness, but she was always refused.

Discouraged, hungry, and thirsty, her feet throbbing in her black shoes and stockings, Hester couldn't stop thinking of Bappie's garden out on the farm, the ruined, storm-ravaged garden, her place of previous employment. Digging in the good earth with her hoe, pulling weeds, harvesting vegetables—she had never appreciated the job enough, those sun-filled days with Bappie, even that pest Johnny King, who finally realized they simply didn't want his company.

That was all gone now. Her bottled tinctures, along with her dreams of helping people, healing, and curing— which she believed in strongly, along with the wisdom of the Indians—had been thrown into the outhouse in the small Lancaster backyard.

She stopped in the shade of a deep eave on the north side of a brick building. She needed only a moment to get out of the sun, to wipe her face with the edge of her apron, then she'd continue home.

There was no use trying to find a job. These homes were all filled with Negro servants. Hester was curious if they were slaves or free. Likely they were free, working in those grand houses, perhaps having relatives in the South who were in bondage. It made her shiver. At any rate, these well-to-do landowners' houses were fully equipped with capable people, so that avenue to employment had just been closed off.

She bent over to tie a loose shoelace, then continued on her way, stepping smartly, her mind on the cool mint

tea down cellar, along with bread and cheese and perhaps a slice of apple pie waiting for her at home.

The sun was merciless, straight overhead, the tall
buildings on either side shutting out the faintest whisper
of a breeze. But she marched toward home, resolving to
forget this forenoon and to never try such a foolish thing
again. If all else failed, she could always move in with
Levi and Bappie.

She heard a horse approaching from behind and
wondered vaguely who would be in such a hurry in
the downtown. It was foolish, besides being downright
dangerous.

She turned and froze. Noah sat astride an impressive
horse. He was a commanding presence with his way of
sitting on the saddle and looked completely in control.
For years he had ridden in that position on a horse the
cavalry provided.

Time stopped for Hester. The heat of the sun, the
teams passing by, the sparrow's chittering music, everything slid out of her senses. Only Noah filled her world.

He reined in the magnificent animal, who tossed his
head and fought the bit, slewing his head from side to side.
Then he rose on his hind legs as his front ones pawed the
air. Hester remained beside the street but shrank away,
afraid the animal's hooves would flail in her direction.

"Hey, whoa, whoa, there," Noah called, his teeth
flashing white in his face, his eyes squinting beneath the
brim of his straw hat. His white shirt was splattered with
mud and splotched with grease, along with his trousers
and boots. The horse danced, stepped sideways, snorted.
When Noah spoke again, the animal's ears flicked back

and forth, but the whites of his eyes did not show, speaking of a quiet temperament. He was merely too full of energy to behave.

"Good day, Hester!" Noah said, tipping the brim of his hat as his smile spread wider. The blue of his eyes reflected the blue midday sky.

"Hello." The word was choked, her happiness at seeing him an obstruction in her throat.

"I was on my way home from the blacksmith. This horse needed new shoes, and it appears he needs a good long run on them now!"

Hester smiled up at him openly, her eyes alight. "He's beautiful."

"I have two. A matched pair."

"Both black?"

"Yes. They're part Percheron, a cross. Bred for hard work and endurance. I should put them in the plow, but part of me doesn't want to make regular work horses out of them."

"I can't say I blame you."

Noah's eyes held hers. "What are you doing out and about in this heat?"

"I was on a fruitless search for employment." Hester lifted her shoulders, spread her hands, palms up, to show Noah the defeat she felt after the responses from behind the grand doors she had knocked on.

Noah acknowledged this with a disbelieving stare. "You were what?"

Hester felt the color rise in her cheeks. "Looking for work." She spoke quietly, the humiliation suppressing her words.

"Why?"

"Noah, why do you think?" she burst out. "I'm a woman alone, now that Levi and Bappie will be married."

With that, she turned on her heel and walked stiffly away, bouncing a bit by the pace she set for herself, getting away from Noah as quickly as possible.

She kept walking rigidly, her arms pumping as her long strides covered the heated dust of the street. She heard the hoofbeats, heard his call, "Hester, wait!"

She increased her speed, turned the corner, and ran, where there was no one to see her lift her skirts, allowing her leather-clad feet to pummel the street. Her breath soon came in hard jerks, and perspiration dripped from the end of her nose, making glistening rivulets of salted liquid down the side of her face. Still she ran, not stopping until she reached the doorstep of their house, let herself in through the front door, and collapsed on a kitchen chair, her chest heaving.

She did not cry. The only emotion she felt was the fierce pride that caused her to run. He was not going to sit on that horse and look down his regal nose at her, making her feel like the beggar she was. She may as well have been sitting by the gate of the orphanage with her tin cup when he rode by in all his finery. She wished she could take back the words she had spoken, unashamedly telling him what she had been doing. A fine example, she was, of speaking before thinking.

Ah well, the deed was done. Luckily, he didn't follow her. And Bappie was nowhere around, inserting her nosy questions like pesky starlings fighting over potato peelings.

Bappie was a bit too full of herself these days, Hester mused, as she wet a clean rag in cool water and mopped her face. She drank a glass of tepid water, longed for the cool springhouse in Berks County, considered buying ice from the ice house on Strawberry Street, then thought better of it. Much better to keep the small amount of cash she had in the carved wooden box on her dresser upstairs.

When Bappie returned, her face was glowing, every freckle darkened by her exposure to the midsummer sunlight. The crow's feet at the corners of her eyes gathered a few freckles and pinched them in the folds when she smiled and laughed, which she alternated with words. She strung her sentences together with fervent enthusiasm, punctuated by exclamations of a future so bright she could hold nothing back.

Levi was digging the foundation for a tobacco shed. She had helped him haul limestones up from the low fields by the creek. Did Hester have any idea how lucrative tobacco was? Buyers would come from the north; they'd even get orders from overseas, Levi said, like the gentry from England. There were some problems with tariffs and laws, whatever in the world Levi meant by that, but yessir, Hester, we'll be rich.

Acres and acres of tobacco. They would make ten times the amount of money that little truck patch brought in. They would have to hire help in the summer. Cows were out. They didn't need to get up early and have their lives ruled by five o'clock milkings. Sheep. They'd graze sheep in the pastures, raise coonhounds and tobacco, and keep the barn for the sheep.

On and on she went, as she built a small fire to heat some potato soup, peppering it with a heavy hand. She brought out the apple pie, bread, and elderberry jam, stopping midsentence to ask why Hester hadn't thought to make lunch.

Hester mopped her face and glared, halfway through thinking that the coonhounds might eat the sheep, and there would always be drought or hailstorms or flooding to take care of the tobacco and all the future wealth Bappie envisioned. She was warm and without any hope of a future even a portion as amazing as Bappie's, and she wasn't about to sit here and goad her on with exclamations of wonder. Bappie had plenty of wonder gathered and stored.

"I was too hot to think of eating. Why do you need to built a fire for soup on the hottest day of the year?" she asked testily.

Undeterred, Bappie informed her it would taste good and she was hungry, then launched into a ribald account of hers and Levi's plans, their conversation on the wagon, how pitiful his straw hat was, and how she just had to get that thing off his head somehow. And on and on and on.

It wasn't until the sun burned the edge of the sky red, losing its power as it slid below the Lancaster County fields and woods, that Hester washed in cool water, dressed in an old, thin, cotton dress, leaving off the black apron and white muslin cap, and sat on the black stoop as the twilight spread its promise of comfort across the backyard. The maple leaves looked spent, drooping with retained heat, the waxen grass like melted candles below.

The chickens lay in low corners of their dusty chicken yard, their wings spread out, trying to find a bit of cool, damp earth to relieve themselves from the heat of the day. The rooster strutted around, his thick, red comb wagging in a princely fashion, the clucks' low, homey sounds like backyard music as he bent to pick at a stray ant or bug.

She could hear the distant, muffled clopping of hooves, a child's cry, a door swinging shut, the deep barking of a large dog.

She felt a contentment settle around her, chasing off the anxieties of the day. Lancaster was her home; this is where she would stay. Some form of employment would show up somewhere.

One of the barn cats, the large gray one, came out from beneath the steps and rubbed along Hester's bare toes, emitting a long, healthy purr. Hester reached down to stroke its back, then laid her cheek on her knees, talking softly to the animal, telling her what a pretty creature she was, what a fine mouser, and that when Bappie left, she could stay with her.

She heard footsteps come close, figured it was Bappie, and stayed in that position. When she heard a deep voice above her, she sat up so fast the cat bolted, streaking across the yard and disappearing underneath the wooden fence that separated their property from Walter Trout's.

Yes. It was him, and here she was with no covering on her head, wearing no apron, her feet bare.

"Noah!"

"Just me once more," he grinned.

"How did you get here?"

"I walked."

"All that way?"

"It's probably less than five miles."

Hester didn't know what to say to that, as clearly he was right, and, clearly that distance was likely soon covered with his long, powerful strides.

"Beautiful evening," he said. She heard the kind smile in his voice, his way of speaking that was tender yet careful, as if each word was meant to portray goodwill toward the world.

Hester blinked and pulled the hem of her skirt down as far as she could to cover her feet. That task accomplished, she didn't know what to do with her hands or her eyes, so she clasped her fingers tightly and leaned over them, as if this movement would help with the part about meeting the blueness of his eyes.

Noah tried again. "Really warm today."

When no response was forthcoming, he took stock of the situation, noticed the bare step beside her, and sat down, the length of him brushing against her as he did so.

"I think, Hester, that there is a very real possibility that the cat got your tongue."

He didn't know for sure whether she had heard this stab at conversation, until he saw her shoulders become more rounded, then begin shaking as she started laughing.

She sat up then, and turned to face him. Unprepared, his closeness undid her battered pride and broke down her self-applied tower of resistance. The scattering of her thoughts, and the need to lay her head on his shoulder and weep like a child with a skinned knee, made her turn away so quickly, that Noah sighed.

And then he spoke, his words thrown out into the mild summer evening, without fear or caution. They were merely a question. "Hester, would you consider accompanying me to Berks County? Annie is not well. I have a team of horses that would benefit from that long trek. I think that before we step further into the future, that we need to step back into our past. Will you do that with me?"

Chapter 15

His words were astounding.

Oh, she wanted to go. As the crow flies, her spirit had soared countless times, far above the trees, the patches of corn, the barns and roads and gardens. Over the mountains that lay between them, the rivers and creeks and puddles of water, over every tiny thing and every large thing that kept her from seeing her home one more time.

But to go with Noah?

To retrace her footsteps by herself, her memories wrapped around her head like a turban, would be effortless compared to sitting beside him on a wagon, to be in his company every day. It was too hard work to keep the barrier up, protecting herself from the dizzying encounters with the blueness of his eyes. She always started out firm, serious, steadfast, but after a few hours she would fall away, forgetting to guard the feeling of severity, of distance, and there she'd be, as helpless as a newborn lamb.

No, she could not go. She told him so.

He did not say anything for a long while. When he spoke, his words were raw and devoid of kindness. "Listen, Hester. Why don't you try, just this once, to forget about your foolish pride? You know you want to see your home."

She nodded. "I do."

"Well, then."

"What would people say?"

"We're brother and sister."

"Like Abraham lied about Sarah, entering that town, huh?"

Noah looked at her and was met only by the tops of her lowered lids. He turned away, sighing. "I'd like to leave in a week or so. It will be a bit warm for the horses, but I figure it will be better to spend the night, in case we need to camp somewhere."

"Camp?" Hester breathed, the thought alarming.

"There are inns along the way, but they're not always a place for an Amish woman who's been sheltered from many things."

When Hester had nothing to say to this, he got to his feet and stood over her. He took in her black hair, darker than the surrounding twilight, the part in the middle the divide between a raven's two wings. She looked small and childlike. But underneath he knew there lurked a will of iron, a stubborn mind of honed steel. Neither made him change his mind. They only presented a challenge, an obstacle he would enjoy, given enough time.

"I look forward to seeing the Berks County mountains," he said. "Hopefully, you'll be willing to accompany me."

With that, he was off, his long strides covering the backyard in a few seconds, leaving Hester with one hand extended, her mouth open, the call for him to come back balanced on the brink of her voice, then pushed back and swallowed by the force of her pride.

So great was her turmoil, she slept only a few hours that night, flipping from side to side, punching and rearranging her pillow, angry, sometimes mellow, and crying, praying into the blackness of the night, unsure if God heard her or not, wondering why he withheld answers when she so desperately needed them.

In the morning, Bappie was off to the farm. Hester knew that according to tradition, it was highly unusual for a single woman to be spending full days with a widower. Hester told Bappie so, waking into the gray morning with a temper so short, Bappie stayed out of her way.

"Yeah, well, tradition is fine in its place, but Levi needs me out there. Nobody sees me going so early in the morning, and if they do, it's no business of theirs, so that's that."

Hester made porridge but left it uneaten to congeal on the dry sink, deciding to see if they would hire her at the dry-goods store. Perhaps the milliner might. She smiled to herself, thinking of an Amish woman fashioning the outrageous hats and bonnets of the wealthy women who sailed the streets of Lancaster on Sunday. Their hoopskirts swayed, their fans swished, their arms firmly tucked in the stalwart, richly clad, top-hatted gentlemen's, who walked slowly to accommodate the showboats beside them.

Sometimes Hester wondered if her best answer would be to leave the plain, restricted life of the Amish, the life where humility and hard work, fear of God and the denial of all frivolous things were the bedrock of their faith.

Oh, she knew, Jesus Christ was the cornerstone of the plain people. This fact she never doubted, hearing the ministers speak of it every two weeks. And it was true.

She could always hear the words of Ben Kauffman, his visage dark with effort, his long white beard wagging with the vehemence of his words. The commitment to deny oneself all worldly pleasures, along with the sins they brought, to take up the cross of self-denial and follow our Lord, was serious.

Sitting on the hard wooden bench, Hester had bowed her head with shame and guilt as she remembered her marriage. Ben's words pressed against her heart, weighing against her breathing like a stone.

On good days, when the sun shone and life stretched before her with all its uncertainties, she was glad for her faith, glad for the belief that one's happiness lies in serving others—Jesus first, yourself last, as her mother Kate would say.

It was good to be afraid of sin and good to seek humility, but when Kate spoke of it, she seemed to fulfill the law the way Jesus said he had come to do. It was not hard, not an insurmountable chore, not something that felt like repression. Kate had truly found joy and happiness in the life she led—in simplicity, in a homey kitchen filled with praise and laughter and new babies, a fresh blueberry pie cooling on the windowsill and a pot of stew bubbling on its hook above low coals, sending out an invitation to contentment.

The world and its ways meant nothing to her. Every stray cat or dog was fed and cared for, every bird and butterfly adored. She explained to Hester the reason for plain clothes: not to be superior to worldly fashions, not to appear self-righteous, but to be clothed with humility and obedience to the laws of the church, which would benefit the soul throughout life.

Hester was filled with a longing so great she felt it physically in the region of her heart. She clasped both hands there, her eyes swimming with quick tears, blinding her for an instant. Ah, Kate, if only you were here.

She thought again of Noah. So much like his mother, was he God's way of leaving Kate in the world through her son? This oldest son of Kate received so little from her husband, except reprimands and stinging slaps at the supper table. Kate would wince, and a certain shadow played across her face.

Hester wondered if she should go with Noah. She wanted to so fiercely. In fact, she had not longed for anything ever quite like this. But was it her own will, or God's? How could a person know?

Ah, but she knew. She knew. Ben Kauffman had explained it clearly. If we sacrifice ourselves to God, we can discern the will of God. If we empty ourselves and give up our own will, then we will know.

She wanted to go. She wanted Noah. She wanted to marry him, to be his wife, and live in Berks County among the beloved hills and forests, next to the streams that played clear music as the water rushed over the rocks, then eddied in deep pools where the tree roots hung low above the dark brown water, covered with moss and sprouting with lichens. The smell of the damp, muddy creek bank was ambrosia, a heavenly perfume in her nostrils.

She wanted to watch Noah build a small house, a log one, with a barn just the way she remembered. A sturdy fence would surround the barn, making a yard where the cows would wait to be milked, the barn cats would purr and stretch around the posts, and violets and wild irises would nod and play in the breeze.

To have Noah, to have and to hold him, to live among the beauty of the hills of Berks County, the home of her childhood and his, was a dream, a mirage, shimmering on the horizon, conjured by her imagination. It was not to be. How could it be meant for her if she deserved nothing, not even a small portion of such happiness?

No, she would remain firm, resisting her selfish desires. Once she had been attracted to William King's dark, good looks and swayed by his confession of great love.

And now this. This blond giant who was her brother. So great were the differences between them, so unbelievable, so far beyond her imagination. Even the lights in their eyes couldn't have been more opposite, one as dark and forbidding as the other was light and pure.

Hester stood by the kitchen table, her hand lightly on a chair back, staring through the narrow, wooden-paned window. She saw nothing as these thoughts ran through her mind, all connected one to another in sequence, as if the order of her mind had been freshly cleaned and organized. She had questions, too many of them, but they could not all be answered now. She would remain on course, deny herself the pleasure of going with Noah, and see what each day would bring.

She had just dropped her hand from the kitchen chair and turned to go to the backyard to gather the eggs, when the front door burst open, followed immediately by "*Eppa do?*"

Hester hurried through the short hallway leading to the front door and found an Amish man standing inside, the sweat on his hatband grayer than the darkened old straw of his well-worn everyday hat, his beard long and black, the hair hanging in greasy tendrils. His clothes were slick with dirt and grease as well. An unwashed aroma hung in the small hallway.

Without thinking, Hester's hand went to her mouth and two fingers covered her nose. A short cough followed.

"*Ya, ich bin* Amos Stoltzfus."

"Hello."

"*Doo bisht* Hester King?"

"*Ya.*"

"*Die vitfrau?*"

"*Ya.*"

"Well, I came to ask for a *maud*. Our girl fell from the hay wagon and broke her back, we think. My Frau had a *bupply*. She is in bed. We have now 13 children, and no one to do the wash. The peas are overripe. The beans are coming on, and there is no one to hoe corn or potatoes."

Hester nodded, wide-eyed. So here stood God's answer in all its soiled form. She had never in her life smelled anything like this man, except perhaps in the houses in the poor section of town when she still occasionally practiced with medicinal herbs. She glanced at his feet, then swallowed when she saw the telltale stain of liquid cow manure spread up between his knobby bare toes.

She nodded again, swallowing quickly as she looked away from his toes.

"How soon can you come?"

"Well, I need to tell Bappie, do some washing, pack my things. Can you come back tomorrow morning for me?"

"Ah, I don't know. I was hoping you'd ride back with me."

"Well, do you have any business in town?"

"I was going to buy my wife a new copper pot, for the washing."

"Go ahead. Give me about an hour to get my things and leave Bappie a note."

"*Goot. Goot. Sell suit mich.*" Clapping his filthy hat on his head, he let himself out. Hester stepped up to the door quickly, caught the latch, and peered out at his form of traveling.

As she had figured, a two-wheeled cart was pulled by a pot-bellied mule, every rib showing above the distended stomach, the blinders on the harness wobbling outward, revealing the eyes of the animal, half-closed in laziness. The cart was splattered repeatedly with untold layers of mud.

Hester shut the door quietly, sagged against it, laid her head against the moulding and closed her eyes. She let out a long, slow breath of acceptance. "Here I am,

Lord. Truly, here I am. Completely given up to do your will. This family needs me, and I am willing to go. Just provide strength for every day, every hour."

She leaned away from the door and sprang into action. Her movements were fluid and quick. She ran upstairs and grabbed her two extra work dresses, the oldest gray aprons to tie over them, and a fresh cap. She decided against shoes. Summer was here, so there was no need. She'd come back every two weeks to attend church.

She sat at the kitchen table with a square of brown paper, an inkwell, and quill pen. Slowly, she dipped the pen into the ink, spread the palm of her hand across the paper to smooth it, and bent her head to the task.

Dear Bappie,

Amos Stoltzfus came for me. His daughter is ill, and his wife is in bed after childbirth. I will be back to go to church.

My regards,

Hester

That was all. No indication of her whereabouts, or how long before she'd write again, or any more information. When Bappie found the note, her face turned as red as her freckles. She crumpled the paper and threw it on the floor.

There she went in all her righteous martyrdom, very likely without telling Noah what she was doing or where she was. Sometimes Hester made Bappie so mad she saw red. If she could only move past that Hans and William once and for all, instead of nearly throttling herself on her rope of grudges. She took better care of her self-pity about her past then she did of the chickens.

Bappie often wondered what that Billy Ferree told Hester. It seemed to give Hester a fresh hold on some past wrong. Oh, well, so be it. She'll come to her senses soon enough, if it's the Amos Stoltzfus Bappie thought it was.

Hester sat beside her newfound employer, perched on the edge of a hard wooden seat that slanted backward, her bare feet planted firmly on layers of dried mud and dust, bits of twine, pieces of hay, and something that looked very much like a snakeskin.

The mule's flapping haunches seemed to be only a few feet from her knees, the cart bobbing and wobbling along behind it. The wheels seemed to be strangely oblong, coming around each time with a thump and a sideways shift of the cart, leaving Hester scrambling for a steadying grip, so as not to be thrown against the less than clean Amos.

The cart was so low, and the mule so huge and loose and flappy, Hester sincerely hoped they'd make it to the farm before nature called for the mule and they were splattered.

Amos rode in silence, his beard and face a stark profile. He looked like Daniel in the lion's den, so serious was he. The picture in Kate's Bible storybook of the unfortunate prophet looked so much the same, with a long black beard, a square cut of bangs on his forehead, and hair so unwashed it hung in sections over his protruding ears, smashed flat here by a discolored hat.

She turned her head wistfully to view the low-lying meadow, that patch of swampy ground with an abundance of herbs and plants all lush and green, ripe for drying or boiling into healing tinctures.

She looked away.

From his trouser pocket, Amos produced a grubby, homemade pipe made of corncobs. He tamped down the half-smoked bowl of blackened tobacco, lit it with a match, then sucked away on it until the bowl glowed red and tiny sparks rained over his shoulder, plumes of smoke decorating the air between them.

Hester's mouth was a grim line. He had a match, those expensive little wonders that even Bappie refused to buy. She bet his wife had no matches for her cookstove.

When the mule slowed to a tired walk, Amos hit him across his skinny haunches with both reins, accompanied by a loud yell of, "Come on, *du alta essel*. Git up there."

When that endeavor brought no change, Amos bent low and scrabbled under the seat, searching for a whip. Amos brought that down with a vicious crack on the bony back, and the mule lunged forward, throwing Hester back with a hard jerk. Fortunately, she had driven carts and wagons and was prepared, tucking her legs beneath the seat and hanging onto the edge of the seat with both hands as the mule broke into a run, the cart bobbing and swaying behind him.

Hester noticed the absence of a copper pot and was just about to ask Amos about it, but then thought better of it. She was a new *maud* so it wouldn't have been proper to ask.

The sun shone down, spreading heat across Hester's black hat, its power felt along her shoulders and down her back. The mule's haunches were stained dark with sweat, and a thin band of white foam appeared on his legs where the harness jostled along the back of his legs.

Amos lifted his hat, the pipe clenched in his yellowed teeth, and let the breeze blow through his hair, which did not move at all, so hardened by weeks of not being washed. Hester swallowed and looked away.

It was no surprise, when the road shifted downhill, to find a farm nestled along a forest, the ground low and uneven around it, dotted with rotting stumps. Trees had been felled and the wood cut and taken away, but the stumps were still there, sentries to Amos and his dreaminess, his unwillingness to finish a job he started.

As they approached, the mule, with a final burst of speed, sensed the presence of home. Hester was appalled to discover an Amish farm quite like this one. She had not known it was possible, or even godly, to live in such squalor. The farm lay in another church district, a natural border dividing it from her own church, perhaps a creek, a road, or a band of trees, so she had never met or known about this family.

The house was built of lumber and had grayed to a nondescript color since the once-new boards had been allowed to face the elements without the usual coat of whitewash. There was no porch, only the square, unadorned two-story house with only one window on each side, small ones with even smaller panes.

The barn was small as well, surrounded by a split-rail fence in varying stages of disrepair. The vegetable patch was a growth of solid green, the weeds as high as the potato plants, the beans and yellowing pea vines barely visible among the thistles and crabgrass, burdock and red root.

As they approached, a small group of children, each barefoot with clothes torn and filthy, their hair uncombed, came around the corner of the house. They stopped and stared, the youngest sucking on thumbs, their knobby little knees showing through the holes in their trousers.

Stiff, yellowish-brown diapers, tablecloths, and towels had been thrown across the decaying yard fence to dry in the sun. Without a washline, that was suitable, Hester supposed.

The weeds and clumps of dry grass that was the yard around the house contained firewood, broken wheels, bits of cloth, buckets upended or lying on their sides, cats as thin as pieces of slate, and red-eyed chickens with all their tail feathers missing, pecking belligerently at any remaining bits of food or bugs not eaten by the whole hungry flock.

Washtubs and a scrubbing board stood close to the door, the bare earth around them wet and gray from being sloshed repeatedly by the water containing lye soap and dirt.

"Here we are, Mrs. Stoltzfus!" Amos sang out.

Hester felt her mouth widen into a polite semblance of a smile, an acknowledgment, before she stepped down from the cart, lifted the valise containing her clean clothes, then picked her way gingerly between the broken pottery and angry chickens to the front door. The wide-eyed children stayed rooted in place, nothing moving except for the soft motion of their mouths, drawing comfort from the thumbs inside them.

Taking a deep breath, Hester knocked at the faded gray door, noticing the broken board where the thin shadowy cats had easy access to the interior of the house.

"*Komm rye!*"

The voice came from what Hester supposed was the bedroom. As her eyes adjusted to the dim light, she saw a pallet made with graying covers in the corner beside the blackened fireplace. A slim form lay inert, the small face turned to the wall as motionless as a doll. This must be the injured daughter.

It was the smell that stopped her from going into the bedroom. Thick and cloying, the rancid stench colored the air around her with images of unwashed diapers, overfull chamber pots, spoiled food, unswept floors, unwashed beds and bodies. Hester almost turned and fled.

She imagined herself running, her feet skimming the earth as she flew down the hot, dusty road, finally reaching the shade of a heavy forest, and never stopping until she reached her home in the town of Lancaster.

From the hearth, a teenaged daughter glared at her. She was holding the newborn infant wrapped in a gray blanket, her eyes petulant and unwelcoming. Hester directed a faltering smile in the vicinity of the fireplace, swallowed, and made herself enter the bedroom.

A low bed stood against the opposite wall. The only light came from an uncurtained window that was stark and yellow, trapping sunshine and shimmering heat. A woman was propped up by two pillows, both stained and brown. A light quilt was thrown across her legs. Her face was large and square, the jaw as prominent as a man's, but her eyes were kind, in spite of being so small they appeared to be two black dots in the big face.

"So you are the *maud*."

Not a question, no inquiry about her well-being, not even a request for her name. Only a recognition that the *maud* was here, which, Hester supposed, was a lifeline thrown to a drowning person.

"Fannie is hurt, we don't know yet how bad. Amos thinks her back will heal."

Her voice became strident, then, impatient with what Hester supposed was her lot in life. "I know it's *shreck-lich*. We didn't start out this way. I'm going to ask you to just take ahold, do whatever you see needs to be done, which is everything. I've been in bed for six days, so I have four more to go, I'm afraid. I'll get milk fever if I get out too soon. Had it last time. Put the girls to work. They don't always listen to me. Amos is so easygoing with the children."

Here she paused.

"I'm awful hungry," she soon said. "Dinnertime is past, but it seems Rachel didn't know what to make."

Grimly, Hester set her lips, glanced at the valise clutched in her white-knuckled hands, and asked where she would sleep so she could put her things away.

"Oh, upstairs somewhere. We supposed you could sleep with Rachel since Fannie hurt her back."

Turning, Hester made her way upstairs and into the acrid smell of stifling rooms filled with sheets used by a horde of little bedwetters. She had no way of knowing which bed was Rachel's, so she set the valise down and made her way downstairs.

Looking around, she took stock of the situation. The hearth was unswept. Rachel and the baby sat rocking on gray ashes and bits of burnt wood. The long trestle table was piled with unwashed dishes and bits of leftover food, all on top of a tablecloth that appeared to be stuck to the table in its own grease.

A cupboard on the opposite wall contained more dishes, so Hester piled all the soiled ones on the dry sink against the other wall. When she tugged at the tablecloth to remove it, she found it stuck so tightly, she had to unearth a knife to scrape at the substance that held it to the tabletop.

Rachel sneered, "Leave it on."

Hester pretended not to hear and kept right on scraping until she lifted it off, stiff with weeks of food and mold. Holding it away from her body, she flung it out the door close to the washtubs, then turned to go back in, determined to get food on the table somehow.

Slowly, the small kitchen filled up with children trickling in through the doors. They were wide-eyed and silent, filthy and painfully thin, with sores around their eyes, mosquito bites, and angry-looking rashes, their hair stiff with dirt and the lack of a comb.

This home was no different than those in the poorest section of Lancaster. Perhaps worse. How could they live like this, having been brought up in the hard-working expectations of Amish culture? Hadn't they arrived from spotless farms in the Rhine Valley in Switzerland? Weren't they successful landowners in Germany?

Quite clearly, something had gone awry. Maybe it was a rebellion against a harsh parent or simplemind-edness, marrying a girl who didn't know any better or who had given birth to such an overwhelming number of children in so short a space of time that she had given up and gradually, without noticing, had succumbed to hopelessness.

CHAPTER 16

HESTER DID GET DINNER ON THE TABLE, BUT NOT WITHOUT snapping at the insolent Rachel, telling her to give the infant to her mother, then sending her to the garden for beans, scattering the other children with orders to help their sister.

There was no bread or cheese, so Hester stirred up a panful of biscuits. By raking the coals, she unearthed a few red embers, so she could set the biscuits to bake after bits of kindling flared into a fire.

She found a cloth, spread it on the soiled table, and covered it with dishes, including using some tumblers that were half-clean. Since there was no meat to be found, she boiled a pot of cornmeal, then took Rachel's beans, which she handed over disdainfully, and set them to boil as well. She used only salt to flavor them since she was unable to find even a bit of salt pork or bacon.

Amos was fetched, and the children scrambled to their assigned places. Five boys appeared from the barn, in varying stages of adolescence, pimply-faced, sullen, and as thin as rails. They watched Hester with small, narrowed eyes, like trapped ferrets.

At the sight of the enormous pan of biscuits, the vast pot of cornmeal mush, plenty of milk, and enough green beans to go around, their eyes glittered with hunger and something close to happiness. They smiled tight smiles, jostled one another, poked stick-thin elbows into prominent ribs, and whispered, "*S, gukt vie blenty.*"

There was plenty, and they ate ravenously like starving wolves. Amos grinned, smacked his lips, and ladled large portions out for the children. Hester took a plateful to his wife, inquiring now about her name, which was Salina. She seemed to be embarrassed to pronounce her own name, blushing pink and blinking her eyes rapidly. Hester felt a stab of pity in spite of the nauseating stench surrounding her, which made it impossible for her to eat. She tucked a cold biscuit into the pocket of her skirt, knowing she would need her strength later.

That whole day remained a blur of motion as she barked orders and pushed the angry Rachel and her sister Sallie to the dry sink with orders to wash and to keep washing until every dish was clean.

Behind her back, they stuck out their tongues, giggling, but they set to work while Hester emptied pots, swept, scrubbed, and built a roaring fire in the yard. Then she scrubbed and washed and boiled clothes and bedsheets and towels some more until it was time to prepare yet another huge meal.

She threw open the door and the windows, preferring flies to the smell that seemed to cling to the walls of the house, to live in the floors, and to dangle from the ceiling like cobwebs.

Rachel grudgingly offered that there were potatoes and salt pork down cellar, and some turnips and carrots if Hester wanted them, but she refused to go down the ladder to get them.

"There's a black snake down there. I know it," she said forcefully.

Hester growled, "Well, then, I guess we won't eat."

"I'm going to tell Mam how you talk to us."

With that, she did, followed by the whining voice of Salina asking Hester to go down cellar, that Rachel was very afraid of snakes.

Hester grabbed a reed basket, backed down the ladder into total darkness, and groped her way to the potato bin. She reached into sprouts and decayed matter, the nauseous mushiness of spoiling turnips, spiderwebs, and finally, the greasy barrel of salted pork. She guessed if there were snakes down here, they'd likely slither away with all the banging and scraping she was doing, partly because she was so angry and partly to do just that, scare the snakes.

She was greeted at the top of the stairs by Rachel's triumphant eyes alive with mockery, knowing full well she could get away with anything she chose, fortified by her mother's sympathy. Twelve-year-old Sallie, it seemed, had a whole other relationship with her mother. Salina snapped at her from the bedroom for the slightest misdemeanor.

Hester lowered her head, refusing to acknowledge Rachel's superiority, and set to scraping carrots, peeling potatoes and turnips, adding more beans to the mix, and then setting the immense pot over the fire, sweat trickling into her eyes as she turned to making more biscuits. While they baked, she fried thin slices of salt pork and then made a milk gravy, thick and smooth and filling.

With that meal, she won the heart of each thin and hungry boy around the table, their empty stomachs a way of life. Now filled and sated, they were comfortable, their moods and energy given a boost they didn't know was possible. Shyly, with eyes averted, thumbs hooked in trouser pockets, and shoulders squared for courage, they said, "*Sell vowa so goot. Denke.*"

Hester blinked the wetness from her eyes, smiled, and said, "*Gyan schöena.*" They were so welcome. It was a joy to fill those stomachs.

A low moan from the pallet alerted Hester to Fannie's needs. She had had no time before this to check on her. Rachel had fed her. And between them, Amos and Rachel had helped her to the outdoor toilet, Fannie's face a mask of pain and suffering.

Hester went to Fannie's pallet, sank to her knees, and asked what was wrong.

"It hurts."

"Has the doctor been here?"

"No."

"Where does it hurt, Fannie?"

"Low in my back."

"Can you roll on your side?"

"I believe I can."

Despite Rachel's disapproval, Hester helped her, easing her gently as Fannie took a deep breath, then began crying softly. Quickly, before Rachel went to her mother with tales of more martyrdom, Hester opened the back of the soiled nightgown. Feeling along the painfully thin spine, she found a bulge of grossly swollen vertebrae and peered closely at the discoloration, the blue fading to red, the sickening yellow and green.

Hester's soft hands explored lightly and tenderly. When she felt the heat and inflammation, she knew what to do. Nettles and plantain leaves, cooked with wood ashes and white wine, would act as a liniment.

She stopped, straightened, and focused her mind as Fannie's soft crying continued. She would not give in. She had vowed, making a silent pact with herself, that she would no longer practice using medicinal herbs. Instead, she put a pillow against Fannie's back to ease her suffering, filled the wooden tubs with warm water, and proceeded to wash the children's heads with loads of shaved lye soap. Amid plenty of rebellious yells, threats, and grimaces, she sloshed and splashed, showing no mercy as she scrubbed, then parted clean hair to check for lice or fleas from those bilious-looking cats that slunk in and out like an evil vapor.

When darkness fell, nature's curtain of privacy, she built another fire, heated more water, and bathed every one of the little ones. She gave orders to the boys, who promptly informed her that they bathed in the creek every month or so, and the month wasn't up yet. Whereupon she informed them they should be bathing every week, with a bit of hysteria injected into the word "week." She sent them off with a chunk of soap and a bundle of clean clothes and told them not to come back till everyone was thoroughly washed and had clean clothes on, as well, *Denke schöen.*

Rachel and Sallie staged a rebellion, which Hester quelled in a hurry. She was close to total exhaustion and her patience was in short supply. She longed to lie down anywhere, even on the bare floor, and close her eyes.

Hester lowered her face into Rachel's and gripped her shoulders, her eyes exuding the black fire of her outrage. She told her that she was an Indian, and if she wouldn't do what Hester wanted, Hester was not afraid to call the *schpence* of her Indian heritage. Old ghosts of the past, she said.

Hester's shoulders shook with laughter as the girls disappeared, casting wide-eyed glances over their shoulders as they went. Maybe it was not the best form of discipline, but it worked on Rachel.

Far into the night after the children were in bed, lying on straw ticks without sheets, their bodies washed, their hair clean, Hester stayed up, retrieving clean laundry from every fence and bush available. She would wash the ticks tomorrow and ask Amos for clean straw. She would address the bedwetting as well.

From her corner, Fannie cried softly, her cries turning to moans, then back to sighs. Her small, soft sobs wrapped themselves so tightly around Hester's heart, she felt as if she could not go on living or breathing.

Finally, when the washing was folded in neat stacks on the table, she heard Fannie pray in the only way she knew how.

"Ich bin Klein,
Mine heartz macht rein,

Lest niemand drinn vonnen
Aus Jesus alein."

A great and terrible conviction gripped Hester's soul, and she could not stand against its righteousness. All that firmness she had built around herself would have to melt away. She would forget all this focus on self and think only of poor, suffering Fannie in the way that Jesus healed the suffering, knowing full well not everyone approved of what he did.

She stopped, shaken to the core, with this new understanding. Well, she wasn't Jesus, not even close, but if she could spare this suffering, she would.

She didn't feel very holy, when she told Rachel she'd send her Indian ghosts on her, that was sure.

Quickly, her exhaustion forgotten, she took down the oil lantern, lifted the chimney, and lit it with an ember. Where were Amos's matches? Likely filched away somewhere, handily brought out to light his odorous pipe. She heard his snores, and Salina's soft ones, as she let herself out the door. No need to stir up another cauldron of protest or chunks of unbelief.

The night was dark with only a sliver of white light from the moon. The stars blinked from their dark space, little pinpricks of soft, white, midsummer light. Crickets chirped an occasional goodnight tiredly. The more gutsy katydids filled in with their energetic tempo.

The grass was already wet with dew. Hester's bare feet felt washed by the coolness as her long strides took her to the fencerow at the end of the winding uphill lane. Her muscles ached, but in a good way. She would sleep well in spite of the dirt and the smell in the house.

The flickering yellow light from the lantern cast a comforting arc around her, catching the winking dew on the tips of grasses. She had no problem finding nettles, as she knew she wouldn't, but the broad-leafed plantain was harder to locate. She finally climbed an unsteady rail fence, hoping there were no bad-tempered cows or a bull to chase her off. She settled for a dry hilltop where the cows had eaten most of the grass. But they had left piles of dung in the almost bare pastureland, and thick grass grew around them, including the plantain, which bovines don't eat.

She grabbed two tough leaves, then beat a hasty retreat when she heard the lowing of a cow, answered by the high bleating of a calf. Sometimes a mother cow protecting her offspring was as bad as an ill-tempered bull, or worse.

Almost running now, the lantern light bobbing up and down with her rapid footsteps, Hester hurried to the house, the pure clean smells of the summer's night giving way to the scent of filthy living. As she entered the house, she knew she would never become accustomed to the wall of pungence that enveloped her.

She boiled water, then added the plants, letting them steep like good tea. Lifting the lantern, she slid noiselessly backward into the cellar. She searched among the half-rotten vegetables for wine or vinegar, but found only dusty bottles of aged whiskey, which would have to do.

She found an empty, small glass jar and returned to the kitchen, washing it quickly. Then she bottled the whiskey, the extract of the plantain leaves, and the nettles and shook the mixture vigorously. She liberally soaked a half-clean rag with the warm liquid. Then she spoke softly to Fannie, who was lying wide-eyed in the semidarkness, her hands crossed on her chest, silent tears sliding down the sides of her face and pooling into wet spots on her pillow.

Gently, she lay Fannie on her side, then applied the cloth so softly Fannie hardly knew Hester had touched her. On top of the cloth she laid the wet plantain leaf, put another cloth on top, and then let her roll gently back, lying against the poultice. Fannie sighed and turned her head to the wall.

Hester slept on the floor rather than sleep with the belligerent Rachel. She fell into a deep sleep without dreams, her head resting on her outstretched arm, the air warm and acrid around her.

When she heard Amos call the boys to do the milking, she pulled herself up into a sitting position, her muscles sore and stiff.

Why wasn't Rachel expected to help milk? Spoiled child.

Hester had been too taken up with last evening's tasks to think of the morning meal. She suddenly knew her first job was to find some sort of food for breakfast. First, she bent over Fannie's pallet, alarmed to find only a slight rise in the quilt and fearing she wasn't there. So slight, so terribly thin, these children.

She resolved to talk with Amos and Salina about finding more and better food for their growing offspring, and with special concern for the new babies which they added with such regularity. Well, if they didn't cooperate, she would do what Bappie did—march right over to John Kauffman, the bishop, and alert the church to this family's needs. If something was not done soon, the church would have to place these children in other, more capable homes. This was done at times, Hester knew well.

Fannie opened her eyes. A new sensation dawned in her eyes, and they opened wider. A small, shadowed smile clung to the corners of her too-wide mouth, a slash in the pale, peaked face.

"How do you feel, Fannie?" Hester whispered.

"It's not so bad."

"Isn't it?"

Fannie shook her head. Then, "I'm so hungry."

Hester patted the thin shoulder. "I'll hurry up with breakfast."

She found only ten eggs, hidden under pieces of unused lumber, wheels, and a broken wagon. She took a garden rake and swung it fiercely if one of the red-eyed chickens came close. She beat the eggs, added milk, salt, and plenty of flour and baking powder, making an *egg kuchen* of sorts. She stirred up more biscuits and put a big pitcher of milk on the table. That was breakfast. It had to be. There was nothing else, unless some new potatoes could be salvaged from that vast sea of solid weeds called a garden.

As usual, Amos was jovial, his good spirits infectious, lighting the sleepy eyes of the little ones and making the boys smile shyly. Salina ate all her breakfast in bed, thanked Hester, and went back to cuddling the wee bundle, who had not been bathed at all. Hester planned to do that as soon as possible.

She told Amos she needed the boys that day to clean the vegetable patch, or they would not have anything to put down cellar for winter. Amos nodded agreeably, saying he had to go to *schtettle* anyway.

Hester said if he went to town, she had a list of things for him to buy. When he frowned, she told him in firm, clipped tones that if he was going to be too tight-fisted to see that his family was fed, then she was going to see the bishop, John Kauffman, and not the less decisive Rufus King.

Amos blushed a furious red, put on his sweat-streaked hat, and let himself out the door, closing it none too gently behind him.

Instantly, the boys spoke as one. "Would you? Are you going to? What would he say? Is someone coming to talk to Dat and Mam?"

Questions pelted Hester like a hailstorm and were every bit as painful. Could it be true that these boys actually lived in deprivation, leading lives of hunger and repression? Hester came to believe it as the boys kept asking questions.

Of course there was the matter of Fannie, too, told to lie on her pile of blankets in the corner, without sending for the doctor. The monstrosity of the situation was like a multi-layered disaster. You took off one layer, only to keep discovering other layers underneath.

Hester said nothing. She wrote the shopping list, then ran to the barn and handed it to Amos. She reminded him that the house contained very little to eat, and if he wanted to avoid public shaming in the church, he would need to bring back everything on that note. *Everything.* Coffee would be nice, too. Oh, Amos said, that was far too expensive. Hester quickly told him then, that he needed to stop buying tobacco and matches, too.

Afterward, Hester found she was shaking, although she felt empowered and alive in a good way. A mountain of work lay ahead of her, but adrenaline flowed through her veins, fueled by her newfound purpose in setting things right. She hadn't once thought of Noah or his invitation to travel to Berks County. Not for at least two hours anyway.

She set Rachel to churning butter, Sallie to washing dishes. She accompanied the boys to the vegetable patch and instructed them in the proper technique of pulling weeds and cultivating the soil with a hoe. They picked the overripe peas; they'd be all right cooked with sliced carrots in a cream sauce. Rachel and Sallie joined them later, setting to work at picking the green beans. They harvested the late radishes and the wilted lettuce. Nothing went to waste, not even the tops of the red beets.

Hester left the children to their work and went to take care of Fannie. She was softly crying, but only because she had accidentally soiled the bed. Hester crooned to her, assured her it was all right and that she should have come sooner.

When she changed the bed, boiled and washed the bedding, then bathed the thin body, the great angry bruise on the girl's lower back felt like a vise around Hester's heart. Fannie said she would like to try walking now.

First, a fresh poultice needed to be applied and tied in place. Then Hester lifted her gently, her hands cupped beneath the bony hollows of the child's underarms. Fannie grimaced, then gasped, but Hester held her steadily, smoothly lowering her weight onto her feet when she was ready.

Fannie took two very small steps as she rested her hands on Hester's extended forearms and leaned into the smiling encouragement on Hester's face.

"My back is not broken, is it?" she whispered.

"No. Oh, no. Only bruised very badly."

"It will heal?"

"Yes. I believe it will. Do you want to show your mam?"

"She probably won't want to see me. When she has a new baby, she doesn't want us for a while."

"Oh, she will. Come."

Hester refused to believe Fannie's statement, knowing Salina would be so comforted by the sight of her daughter standing upright.

"Salina? Are you awake?" Hester called softly.

"Oh, yes," came the soft reply.

"Look!" Beaming with excitement, Hester led Fannie to the doorway. Intent on the face of her newborn, Salina afforded Fannie only a short glance, saying, "I figured it wasn't broken," and went back to the baby.

Fannie remained stoic as she followed Hester out to her pallet where she was willingly lowered, a sheen of perspiration along her upper lip, testimony to the pain still present in her lower back.

"You're a brave girl, Fannie. You really are."

Hester smoothed back the hair on her forehead, then caressed the thin, pale cheek, softly stroking her face, before bending to kiss her.

Fannie's brown eyes opened wide, sparkling with amazement. "I often wondered how a kiss would be," she said, smiling fully for the first time.

What an astoundingly pretty face, Hester thought, like an underfed little fairy. A feeling of so much love that she could barely contain it swept over Hester like a life-giving rain to a parched and barren desert. She had never imagined such a sweetness of love and life and living, that had little to do with her personal desires and didn't begin by serving her own selfish happiness. She was suddenly exploring the unending possibilities of life, triggered by a wellspring of something she could not explain. She felt privileged to care for this broken-down little soul who was living in the corner of a room on a pile of blankets, whispering a child's German prayer through her tears.

Hester laid the palm of her hand against Fannie's cheek, so tiny and pale, for what she guessed was an eight-year-old.

"How old are you, Fannie?"

"I'm eleven. Sallie is twelve."

With that pronouncement, Hester knew without a smidgen of doubt she would be going to see John Kauffman before the week was up.

In the meantime, Hester cooked and baked, washed endless tubfuls of dirty clothes, scoured and scrubbed, lectured, and taught the children how to be useful, to care about the appearance of the yard, to pen up the chickens, to build nests where they could lay their eggs.

Amos remained agreeable and good-humored to a fault. He even bathed in the creek one evening, although he then dressed himself in the same clothes he had worn for almost a week.

Salina left her bed, dressed, combed her greasy hair filled with flakes of white dandruff, put on a limp, whitish-gray kerchief, and settled herself into the hickory rocker by the hearth.

The little ones climbed on her lap, clamoring for attention. She ladled it out sparingly, but it was there. Salina remarked on the house's order, the freshly baked bread, the good butter. Rachel told her almost shyly that she had done all the churning. But when that brought no praise, the hooded, sullen look replaced her hope of a few words of praise from her mother.

Hester was quick to notice. She touched Rachel's shoulder, telling her she could not have done it without her, with all the washing and cleaning she had to do. Rachel's eyes flashed a quick grasp of Hester's thanks, but then turned away just as quickly, before Hester would see her tears.

That evening Hester boiled the last of the sweet potatoes she found down cellar, made a brown sugar sauce for topping them, cooked beets with sugar and vinegar, and split a ham into two pieces before boiling one part in a pot on the hearth. Then she instructed Rachel about how to make a sponge cake and set Sallie to bring in the washing and fold it, while eight-year-old Eva set the table.

Salina took this all in, observing the way Hester put these girls to work, and her small, black eyes filled with hope. Was that the way other women got their work done, when she never could? Aloud, she said, "If I had a cookstove, I could make better meals."

"Ask Amos," Hester remarked.

"Oh, he doesn't like to part with his money." She lifted the baby to her shoulder, patting the tiny little back, the baby's legs scrooched in under his stomach like a baby squirrel.

She watched as Rachel whipped the cake batter, her strong, young arms never tiring of the effort.

At the supper table, the family ate and ate, enjoying every spoonful of the good, wholesome food. By now, the row of older boys almost worshipped Hester, the saving grace sent into their lives in the form of a *maud* to help out for awhile.

Hester looked at Amos and told him his wife needed a cookstove, and a good one, now that they had 13 children, and it wouldn't be a bad idea to build her a washhouse either. No wonder the clothes didn't get washed if she had to do it out in the cold of winter and heat of summer. And did he ever think of putting up a washline?

"Oh, this stuff costs money!" he exclaimed. "*An lot gelt.*"

"You have money, people say," she replied quickly, knowing nothing about it but hoping it would bring the desired response.

Amos lifted his shoulders and inhaled, clearly enjoying the thought of other people thinking he had money. "Well, I have some put away."

Startled, Salina looked at her husband. She could clearly not believe the words from his mouth. "You need to buy these things. Take a bit of pride in this place. The boys can paint."

Amos narrowed his eyes and looked at his row of sons, who were already losing the furtive, hungry look that ruined their faces so much of the time. His gaze went to his daughters, slim, capable young girls, who were so unaccustomed to attention from their father that they all blushed deeply, lowered their faces to their plates, and kept them there.

One thing kept the family together, sparing them the pain of being separated, with some of the older ones being put into other homes to be raised—Amos's good humor. He was too unconcerned to be harsh; he just didn't think. It had never occurred to him that they needed more money for staples like flour and sugar and oatmeal, or a cookstove and a washline. He thought a fireplace and a fence was just all right for Salina, and she was too simple or too afraid to ask.

Hester still couldn't understand her. What woman would be so taken with yet another baby, leaving an eleven-year-old crying silently in pain?

How Kate would have gathered little Fannie to her immense bosom, crying freely with her! Immediately, a new thought formed. Would Noah, like Kate, love Fannie, too?

CHAPTER 17

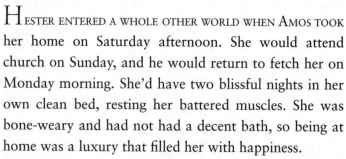

HESTER ENTERED A WHOLE OTHER WORLD WHEN AMOS TOOK her home on Saturday afternoon. She would attend church on Sunday, and he would return to fetch her on Monday morning. She'd have two blissful nights in her own clean bed, resting her battered muscles. She was bone-weary and had not had a decent bath, so being at home was a luxury that filled her with happiness.

The house was cool, orderly, and so clean. Hester ran a hand along the scrubbed oak table, the gleaming cookstove, the dishpans turned upside down in the dry sink. Even the glass-paned doors on the cupboard seemed to beam and wink with cleanliness. And the smell! The scent of soap and spices, of warm air flavored with growing things, the summer sun, even dust from the street, all of it seemed pure and sweet and unsullied.

Bappie was gone as usual, so the first thing Hester did was spread all the food on the table that she could find, pour a glass of cool buttermilk, and begin to eat. She had brown wheat bread, the crust hard and chewy, spread with good butter from Emma Ferree, plum preserves, dried venison, hard white cheese, new strawberries, a slice of custard pie, then another one, and more bread and butter.

She built a fire in the washhouse and filled the large iron kettle with water from the pump so she could wash her clothes first, followed by a good, long, Saturday-evening soak behind the curtain in the corner of the kitchen. Then she would visit Walter and Emma.

Hester was humming, her spirits revived by the waves of joy that broke over her, swelled around her senses, and filled her heart. The week was over. She was here now.

She sang as she scrubbed her clothes, wrung them dry, and hung them reservedly in a corner of the washhouse. No good housewife, or old maid or widow, would hang clothes in the backyard on a Saturday evening.

She filled the iron kettle again, upended the large tub, pulled the curtain out on its string, and was shaving the good scented soap into a bottle, when the door was pushed open, followed by a raucous cry from the ebullient Bappie.

"You're back!" she yelled, her hands clasped to her skinny chest.

"I am! Oh, I truly am!" Hester sang out.

"Well, it's good to see you, Hester. Leaving a note on the table and being whisked away by some Amos Stoltzfus was pure nonsense. What in the world, Hester?"

"I knew you wouldn't understand. This man had a wife in bed with a new baby, thirteen children, and a daughter with a broken back. Or so he thought. It isn't broken, only bruised."

Bappie's eyes narrowed. "How do you know?"

"I checked."

"You gathered herbs."

Hester's eyes twinkled, a dimple appearing on one cheek when she smiled only slightly. "I did. But, oh, Bappie! You have no idea. I hardened my heart and turned away, determined not to give in, but she cried so softly and is so painfully thin and repeated '*Ich bin Klein*,' the children's prayer, over and over, until I just lit a lantern and went to gather nettles and plantain."

"That is a good thing. God's ways aren't so mysterious sometimes, now are they? What about Noah?"

"What about him?"

Hester looked straight at Bappie, the twinkle in her eye erased, the dimple flattened by the grim line of her mouth.

"Does he know about you being out at Amos's?"

"Of course not. Why would he?"

Bappie turned without another word and let herself out the back door, slamming it harder than necessary on her way out. Hester shrugged her shoulders and began the ritual of her Saturday night bath.

Later she was welcomed and fussed over, with questions popping from Walter's and Emma's mouths. They made her sit down and have a glass of grape juice, cool and sweet from the cellar.

Walter said the butcher had a new product called Lebanon bologna, which was a tad spicy, heavy on black pepper especially, but if you ate it in small quantities, accompanied by buttered toast, it was exquisite. In spite of the heat remaining in the kitchen at this hour of the evening, he lit the kindling in the cookstove, brought out a cast-iron skillet, and proceeded to fry slabs of Emma's good bread in copious amounts of melting butter. He sprinkled the fried bread with bits of thyme and rosemary before serving the crispy slices with round, thinly sliced portions of the new bologna.

Richard and Vernon had gone to the neighbors, Mr. and Mrs. Amesly, to play with their children in the back alley, returning as the light in the windows began to fade and Emma got up to light the coal oil lamps. Richard had grown into a strong-limbed, towheaded little boy, his face round with cheeks like apples, gleaming with good health. Vernon was taller and thinner, but like Richard, the picture of health and contentment.

Hester's throat constricted as she watched Vernon grasp Emma's heavy upper arm in both hands, smiling up into her round, dimpled face before laying his head on her plump shoulder, her arm bringing him close to her side.

Richard grunted, the effort of pulling himself into Walter's lap turning his face dark with his maneuvering. Walter, so intent on placing a slice of bologna exactly in the center of the buttered toast, failed to discern this.

"Walter," Emma said, sharply.

"Oh, oh, goodness, Richard, goodness."

He quickly placed the eagerly awaited food on the plate, licked his heavy red fingers, and bent to help Richard onto his lap.

Hester smiled to herself, wondering what had become of the English napkins. Or was he slowly being converted to the more relaxed style of the Pennsylvania Dutch?

She watched as he bent sideways to cut the delicacy in half and handed one section to Richard before finally closing his mouth around his own portion, closing his eyes in appreciation.

It was so good to be home here with Walter and Emma, to have good food, and to relax in the luxury of being clean and rested and well fed.

Already, Sunday was almost here, and so soon it would be over.

Church services were held in the home of Danny and Lydia Miller, who had a prosperous farm east of Lancaster, only two miles from the town.

Hester dressed in a blue shortgown and pinned the traditional black cape and apron over it. The many layers of fabric were designed to disguise the womanly charms of her figure. Plentiful gathers in her black apron discreetly hid the curve of her hips. The hem of her long, full skirt fell to her shoe tops. The cape hung slightly over her shoulders and was pinned loosely down the front. She tucked the ends beneath the thin band that was the belt of her apron. The sleeves were long, all the way to her wrists, and loose without adornment. She tied her muslin cap beneath her chin. The cap was large and shielded most of her hair and her ears.

In spite of the austere dress code, there was no hiding Hester's grace and beauty. Even from a distance, her gait was lithe and fluid, her steps easy, befitting the Indian princess she was. Her face was small, oval, and well proportioned, her big, dark eyes pools of light and dusk, twilight and night. Womanly thoughts and secrets were stored away in their depths.

As Hester aged, her beauty increased from winsome girl to a woman who had suffered, having experienced life and its imperfections. Her spirit was like the gold that can emerge from refining, when bitter dross is burned away. She believed that a greater being was in control of her destiny, which lent her an aura of restfulness, of quiet contentment.

Beside her, Bappie strode along with her choppy gait bobbing her up and down, her arms swinging vigorously. She was shorter, but the brown dress she wore covered her identically, including the heavy black cape and apron, the large cap, black shoes, and serviceable stockings.

Her hair was like tamed fire, combed severely for now. Her brown eyes danced and the freckles traveled along. They had been stamped on her fair skin the day she was born. The summer sun always deepened their color, even as it heated the skin beneath to an alarming pink that would turn into an attractive copper hue as the summer waned.

Bappie's sheer happiness could easily be accounted as beauty, or at least radiance. She was betrothed, promised, wanted by the one man she had both pitied and admired. Now, given free rein, her love was like a tropical flower, lush, watered, a thing beautiful to behold.

At the Miller farm, a few buggies were parked along the barnyard fence. The horses had been led into the cool interior of the barn, given a cool drink at the trough, then tied to a stall to wait till church services were over. The barn itself was similar to Dan Stoltzfus's barn, the one Noah had worked on for almost a year.

Painted white, it had louvered windows on the gable ends and fancy trim along the front, where glass windows gleamed in the hot morning sun.

Freshly painted board fencing outlined the rectangular garden, a showcase of beautiful vegetables. The dark earth between the rows had been loosened with a hoe, a testimony to hours of labor. Already, the sweet corn was higher than a person of medium height. The potato plants were dotted with white, star-shaped blooms, the harbinger of large, brown-skinned potatoes growing underneath.

The beans and beets looked lush. The wide bare spot where the pea vines had been pulled was now tilled and planted with lima beans or late corn. Along the garden fence, the huge, red-veined leaves of rhubarb plants thrived; the frilly tops of the carrots showed off like a decoration of lace.

Bappie said this was what her garden would look like after she and Levi were married. She had serious *zeitlang* to work in such a garden. Looked like Lydia didn't grow turnips, which was something Bappie would not do either. The sheep would eat them.

Hester saw Levi Buehler drive past, his buggy grayish, splattered with bits of mud, and coated with dust, his horse a bit ungainly. He held his neck out at a tired angle, not high with a spirited stance, the way some horses did. It was just the way Levi was—relaxed and happy, never competitive, nor trying to make a show of his own good management. If the buggy was less than clean, well, no one would notice or care.

Unfortunately, Bappie did.

First she said, "There goes Levi."

Then she followed it with, "He should have washed his buggy."

Followed by, "After we're married, I'm getting rid of that horse. He runs like a cow."

Hester smiled. Levi climbed down from his buggy, caught sight of his future bride, and beamed like a ray of sunlight before turning away quickly, busying himself with the reins. But it was enough for Bappie, who had caught Levi's shining look of happiness, which seemed to take away her dissatisfaction with the less than clean buggy and cow-like horse.

Hester smiled wider but lowered her face before someone caught her being bold or brazen on a Sunday morning. It was bad enough that Bappie had persuaded her not to wear a hat that day. A hat was a Sunday requirement. Large enough to cover all of one's hair and the sides of one's head when it was pulled front, a hat did its part to obscure a face, so that a woman's appearance was mostly a shapeless, black figure, the rustling of skirts on shoe tops the only distraction from the severity.

Bappie refused to wear the thing on hot summer days, stating briefly that if someone didn't like it, they could come talk to her. She had once gone barefoot to church, which was met by drawn eyebrows and mouths turned down like upended bowls of disapproval. Whispers and head-wagging were of course followed by a visit from the deacon, Abner Esh, from south of town.

Bappie wouldn't admit it to Hester, but she was plenty shook up by the visit, ashamed, humiliated, and even a wee bit sorry after being rebuked in Abner's loving, godly manner. Her face was white as a clean pillowcase when she came back into the house, after he had spoken to her on the back stoop. She wouldn't say much to Hester, but she didn't need to, as her face flamed and her eyes blinked rapidly and she told Hester she didn't care what anyone thought, she wasn't going to wear shoes to church in this humidity. But she did care. She was ashamed of her own boldness, and she wore her shoes and stockings to church from that day on.

In the Millers' house, the furniture had all been put in the bench wagon or stacked against the back wall of the bedroom to make way for long lines of wooden benches. Copies of the thick, chunky *Ausbund*, the black hymnal filled with German hymns that had been written centuries before by prisoners who languished in the cells of a Swiss castle for their faith, were scattered over the benches.

Some women stood in the kitchen, all dressed similarly in modest clothes, their arms crossed, talking, smiling, and greeting one another with firm handshakes and holy kisses, as they believed the Bible instructed.

Little girls were in blue, purple, or green, with plain and unadorned white pinafores. Their small muslin caps were tied beneath their chins with wide strings; their bare feet peeped out beneath the hems of their dresses.

As always, Hester was glad to see all the members of the church, especially the women she met regularly every two weeks. She knew them all, their names, their children and husbands, where they lived, who would be having a new addition to the family, and many other facts about their lives. When there was a barnraising, she was there, cooking and sharing community news, trying not to gossip but enjoying a few hair-raising bits of it. When a child died, or an elderly person, she was there, helping with the food, cleaning, and cooking some more.

Weddings, funerals, accidents, barnraisings—each was a calling to pitch in, to willingly give what she could, even if it was just a few loaves of bread or a pie, babysitting or cleaning the house, raking the yard or quickly sewing black dresses. It was all about being part of a body of people, cultivating bonds of love and belonging.

And yet she longed to return to Berks County, at least out of curiosity, as she wondered about the welfare of her people beyond her family—Theodore Crane and Lissie, her friend Amanda—all of the folks she could picture so clearly in those times when she felt the tugging at her heart.

But first she would finish at Amos Stoltzfus's, delaying until they were in a better situation. She would wait.

And so it seemed right, this waiting, as the first lines of the song rose and fell around her. She felt a settling of her spirit, a sense of balance as she was finding her way. She could help with the singing, her throat swelling with an emotion that felt good, the words tumbling over her parted lips like a clear brook of sound. Doing the right thing was no longer a burden. It would materialize out of life. All she had to do was wait.

Noah was not in church. She had not seen his bright hair among the darker colors but figured he might only be late. She felt a sense of depletion, a vague uneasiness. Had he been to Bappie's house, only to find her gone with no explanation? She found it unlikely. With a jolt, she wondered if he may have gone to Berks County alone. The thought brought a sense of failure so sharp it took her breath away, leaving her with only short, shallow breaths of panic.

Where had all the rightness gone? One minute peace wrapped itself around her; in the next, Noah had destroyed it the way he always did. Well, she hoped he did go to Berks County without her. It would be better if he went by himself and stayed there, and she stayed in Lancaster, always. He scattered her senses, raced through her mind, churned it all up, and confused her. Just like now.

But the voices of the preachers were comforting. They delivered their sermons in a kind of traditional chant carried over from the Catholic church where the priests would elevate their voices, the Latin rising and falling, a singsong way of speaking that was both comforting and regular, like the sun's rising or clouds giving way to summer rain or birdsong in spring.

Under the sound of the Amish minister's German words going up, then down, her choppy and distorted thoughts quieted, rested, and slowly absorbed words from Scripture. She heard admonishments, encouragement, and sometimes a story from the Old Testament, simplified in Pennsylvania Dutch for the children's benefit. As the voice droned on, Hester's eyes and thoughts roamed around the room. She wondered why Noah had not come to church.

Thinking about the upcoming week, the endless hard labor, planning and cooking of large meals, and with only a limited amount of food available, drained her energy and her spirit of joy and contentment if she dwelt on it. Better to let it go, if only for this afternoon.

It was when she was helping to serve the dinner that she caught sight of Noah's well-groomed blond hair, sitting in the row of single men and boys. Hester's stomach roiled one hard lurch, her breathing became quick and short, and the room spun sideways before righting itself. She almost dropped the dish of sweet pickles she was carrying. Quickly, she set it down on the farthest end of the table, turned, and exited the suddenly stifling room.

She wanted to talk to him. She wanted to walk beside him and tell him she would accompany him to her home in Berks County. She wanted to go now worse than ever. It was raging in her breast, this desire to return, if only to be seated beside Noah for two whole days, or three, however long he chose.

She did not want to go back to Amos Stoltzfus's, back to the smell, the beds that needed to be washed of their acrid odor, the children clamoring for only a shred of attention from the preoccupied Salina, to Fannie with her injured back and her lack of love, so gamely accepting the fact that her mother was done with her now that she wasn't needed because she had a new baby, that her brothers and sisters were all she had.

But were they?

She was on her way to find Bappie. Her head hurt. She wanted to go home and lie down in the coolness of the living room just for an hour, until her headache went away.

From the corner of her eye, a shadow came near. She turned. Noah whispered, "I'm coming to talk to you this evening." He had merely walked by, so casually and so quickly no one would have noticed. It was simply not acceptable, a single man speaking to a widowed woman in broad daylight.

It wasn't a question that he asked. It was a telling, the stating of a fact.

Hester bowed her head and walked away quickly. She found Bappie, and together they walked out the lane in the hot afternoon sun.

The heat was a shimmering, white cloak cast over the land in midsummer. But Hester noticed only the blue of the sky, the wild rosebushes, the white columbine growing in profusion along the road, the butterflies and meadowlarks, the song of the mockingbird that hopped along beside them like a raucous escort, trilling one mocking note after another.

The dust puffed up, coating their black shoes and the hems of their skirts, the hot winds tugged at their caps and riffled the edges of their capes. Hester talked, spreading her hands in emphasis. She laughed, trying to keep from skipping and throwing her arms wide, to restrain herself from lifting her face to the sun and saying, "Thank you, thank you."

Bappie eyed her sideways. "Sermon must have done you good."

"Oh, it did, it did."

Bappie let out a wee remnant of a snort, which Hester failed to hear. She knew it wasn't the sermon, but as skittish as Hester was about any mention of Noah, she chose, wisely, to keep her mouth closed, if only for this once.

They spent the afternoon sitting in the backyard, a bowl of popcorn and glasses of peppermint tea between them, talking.

Bappie sensed a new willingness in Hester to share her life, so she listened, only occasionally nodding or opening her eyes wide in acknowledgement of Hester's words.

She spoke of the mysterious Salina, of Amos and his lackadaisical view of the world, his farm, all those children, multiplying each year.

"Bunch a rabbits," Bappie said, straightforward.

"But, Bappie, I honestly think that is his pride and joy—to have a house overflowing with children. I imagine he sees all those hired hands and *mauda* out earning money which they'll bring home to him, the time when he can sit at the blacksmith shop in town and smoke that nasty old pipe to his heart's content."

"Well, maybe he is inclined to believe the Bible and is just so happy to have his quiver full. Just as Proverbs says, you know."

Hester nodded. "At any rate, I'm going back tomorrow morning to work all week, and probably several weeks after. If I could only get Salina motivated to teach Rachel and her sister to work. Can you believe, after every meal I still have to tell them to do the dishes? Then they slop around in lukewarm water with hardly any soap. They simply aren't taught."

"Do you dread going back?" Bappie turned her head, upended her glass of tea, and dumped the contents with a splash beside the steps.

Hester's shoulder shrug went unnoticed as the two women sat in the comfort of each other's company, not speaking. The quiet clucking and pecking of the chickens was a homey sound, as was the distant yell of a child, followed by the deep barking of a dog. Heat hung over the town. The shade of the maple tree, the occasional restless movement of its leaves, stirred by a muggy puff of air, did nothing to relieve the cloying warmth.

Bappie picked up her skirt and flapped it madly, her knobby white knees like startled white birds. "It's uncomfortably hot."

"It usually is, midsummer."

Bappie grinned, punching Hester's forearm. "Is Noah going?"

"Going where?"

"To Berks County?"

Hester's irritation showed by the flicker of fire in her dark eyes. Now how did she know anything about this? Eavesdropping, likely. She faced Bappie, squarely. "How do you know?"

"Oh, the birds were singing about it."

"Don't add a white lie on top of your other trespasses, namely, hiding somewhere and listening to Noah talking. You do that, you know."

"Do I? Nah, not me. No, never would, never will."

Hester glared at her till Bappie's words cut her off. "Well, miss secretive lady, let me tell you something. We choose to be happy, we choose to be miserable. But when unexpected love comes along, we don't brush it off. We grab it and thank our Heavenly Father.

"We take it, Hester, because it enriches our lives. Yes, you think, what does she want with that odd-looking Levi Buehler? You know, there was a time when I probably wouldn't have chosen him, and he wouldn't have wanted me either. I'm older now, a bit baggy and wrinkled, but then so is he. And if God wants us to enjoy the rest of our days together, well, then, so be it.

"I'll always cherish these years with you, Hester. Your friendship has made me into a better person, and I'll always carry that in my heart like a fulfillment. If you do go with Noah and you don't come back, let's never forget each other. You must write to me always. And Levi and I will visit."

Hester sat very still. Then she whispered, "That is so sweet, Bappie, my friend."

They sat together, the moment a lovely comfort of feelings.

"I'm so frightened of Noah, of marriage," Hester whispered finally, a sort of clutching, choking sound overriding her words.

"I guess you have reason to be, Hester. I can't make fun of your fears. But maybe, just maybe, you've suffered enough, and God knows you deserve better. Maybe he has a great, big, happy surprise for you, and you won't open that wonderful gift because of your fear. You're always looking back over your shoulder, hanging on to past mistakes, carrying them around like a sack of horse feed."

"You think?" Hester asked.

"I know."

They both stopped speaking as Noah's tall form rounded the corner of the barn, his bright hair tousled, his straw hat in his hand, relaxed, smiling, genuinely happy to see them both.

CHAPTER 18

THEY CONVERSED TOGETHER AS THE HOT SUMMER SUN SLID below the horizon and the light began to fade, casting shadows across the small barn, the henhouse, and the maple tree. The heat evaporated slowly, grudgingly giving up its hold on the sweltering town as the twilight settled softly, bringing unexpected breezes of cool air and comfort.

Bappie yawned and stretched, saying she was going to bed since she had to be up early to go to the farm. "Sheep fence," she said, in a voice anything but humble, wanting to convey to Noah her anticipated prosperity. Sheep would need a large pasture, good water, and a solid fence, so she planned to help Levi with the acreage and the planning.

Hester knew Bappie would plan and Levi would follow, but she said nothing, hiding her grin in the dusky evening light.

After the door closed behind Bappie, a silence settled, an uncomfortable stillness. Hester felt the urge to say something, anything, to rid the air of prickliness.

She cleared her throat, picked a blade of grass, and wrapped it around her thumb, pulling it tight before breaking it.

Finally Noah spoke, inquiring about her week. Startled, Hester groped for the correct word. He didn't know she had gone to be a *maud* to the Amos Stoltzfuses.

"I wasn't here, you know."

"Oh, Amos Stoltzfus from east of here, close to Bird-in-Hand, needed a *maud*, so he came to see me."

"And?"

"I went."

"How was that?"

"All right, I guess."

"Hester, why did you go?"

"They needed me."

"There are plenty of single women around. The countryside is full of large families with girls loaned out for hire."

"I wanted to go."

Noah didn't reply. When he finally did speak, the kindness had returned, his voice softened by it. "I don't mean to be critical of your choices, but it has to be terribly hard work. Terribly. I know the Amos Stoltzfus family. The church is often called to help them out with food donations, labor, or handing over money from the collected alms to fish him out of yet another fiasco he got himself into. I know you meant well, Hester, and I'm sure you were great for that family, but I wish you would not go back."

"I need to go."

"Why?"

"Salina is not recovered from childbirth, Noah, and Fannie is hurt."

"Fannie?"

"The third daughter. She's eleven years old. She fell and hurt her back." Like the beginning of a slide down a snow-covered hill, Hester's halting first sentence gained momentum until she described in rich pathos the feel of that too-thin spine, the skeletal little body lying on a heap of filthy quilts, crying softly to herself when the pain became unbearable. She told him of her plant-gathering at night, all of it. Salina and her disconcerting way of looking up from her newborn, and Fannie's innocent acceptance of the fact that her mother didn't need her or much want her, now that she had another baby to care for.

"Hester, you surely know what will happen to her, don't you?"

"Well, I know some destitute families give their children to more well-to-do families to raise, don't they?"

"Yes, they do."

"Really *give*, to keep forever?" Hester whispered.

"It's a fact of life, Hester. It's sad, but when a father like Amos does his best and is not able to feed so many mouths, some actually do give their children to another household."

"I can see Salina doing that."

"Amos, too."

"He's always good-humored, though. He doesn't seem cruel. He says he has some money put by. It just never occurred to him that Salina might want a new cookstove or a washline."

"He has money?"

"That's what he says."

Noah sighed, "At any rate, you are not responsible to keep that household running smoothly. They have older children to carry on without you."

"But I need to go back. What will happen to Fannie? They'll put her with another family, and she won't be loved. Noah, please listen to me. She's so painfully thin, so disarmingly accepting of the few crumbs of caring she does receive, so content, asking nothing more from life but a bit to wear, a bit to eat. All her life, people will take advantage of her goodness. She'll be a slave, a white Amish slave, no better."

Hester's words rose with the passion she felt. Noah remained quiet, his legs stretched in front of him on the cool grass, the darkness now hiding his features. Only the lightness of his face and hair were visible. Down by the henhouse fence, a katydid began its clamoring call, the unsettling rhythm, the urgent squawk of its cadence. The answering call of another katydid rose high and sure, a beckoning. Still Noah did not speak.

She heard him get to his feet, felt, rather than saw, him bend in front of her, his thick arm and hand extended.

"Come, Hester, let's walk for a while. The fresh air and change of scenery will make us appreciate the coolness of evening."

She hesitated, then placed her hand in his. He never let go of it after that.

Hand in hand, they walked out of the short drive, the back alley, down Mulberry Street past the Lutheran church, then on to Vine Street, past the haberdashery, the wheelwright, and out of town, without speaking at all.

The silence was no longer prickly, but a kind of soothing quiet. A million white stars blinked above them. A half-moon allowed shadowy light, the merest whitewash of silver bathing them in the midsummer night's glow, spraying pearls of luminescence.

Noah's hand was wrapped firmly around her own, claiming her hand. When he dropped it suddenly, Hester did not understand, feeling cut off. It was as if the hand was an extra unwanted appendage, and she had no knowledge of what to do with it. She put it behind her back where it was safe without his hand.

When Noah spoke, his voice was garbled, as though coming from underwater or from a distance. "One more time, Hester, I will ask you. One more time I will lay everything at your feet. I know you hold my future in those perfect dark hands."

Hester's breathing stopped but her heart beat on, dull thuds of life suspended between her own desire for Noah and what she felt was God's will for her, a confusing mixture she could never quite understand.

"I will tell you again one more time. I love you, Hester. I love you. I always have loved you, and my love only grows with the passing of time. Will you accompany me to Berks County, our home, to make peace with our father and his wife?"

Suddenly Hester was tired. She was drained emotionally from building her fortress of pride and mistrust. It was too much effort. The wall would not stay. Repeatedly she built it higher and stronger, only to have it crash around her, leaving her standing exposed in a heap of rubble, smoking debris, and dust that shut off her vision.

It was dangerous business to bare her soul, to tell Noah what she felt. How horribly awry things could go afterward. She wanted to warn him that they could both be stranded high and dry with nothing to sustain themselves except bitterness and self-loathing, that they could each feel stupid and unable to acquire the Lord's blessing. She had experienced being dry and barren, never able to meet requirements, never being enough.

When she started talking, her words were whispers caught on short, soft sobs, like hiccups. Noah had to bend his head to hear, and then he was able to understand only a portion.

She wanted to go with him. She wanted to see her old home. But what if she did? The future was not safe. It was like crossing a frozen lake, never knowing when the ice would cave in. How could she know if her desire was God's as well?

Did he fold her in his arms, or did she wrap herself around him? In the starry night, with the insufficient light of the half-moon, they found the comfort of each other, the melding of two bodies that drew together, instinctively seeking comfort and assurance, needing trust. They stood, one taking comfort from the solid form of the other, and it was enough. More than enough.

Noah bent his head and whispered, "Does this mean you want to go? You said you have a desire to go, so may I assume you mean just that?"

In answer, Hester released him and stepped back.

"Noah, there is nothing on earth I want more. I want to be with you. I want to go home."

"Then why are you stalling? Why go to Amos's?"

"I don't know if it's God's will or just my own."

"You are afraid."

"Yes."

"Of what?"

"The future. You say you love me, but will you always? What is love?"

That last plea was Noah's undoing. That cry from the depth of her wounded heart had come from years of living with a man who was capable of cruelty. She had shared the marriage bed and could still ask that pitiable question. He wanted to have Hester believe that his love for her was like a pure jewel which he wanted to give to her tenderly.

His strong arms drew her close, closer. With a sigh, a groan, a sound coming only from the gentle kindness of an overflowing love, his hand touched her chin and brought the beautiful beloved face to his. He bent his head, his cool, perfect lips sought hers, found them, and stayed there until her arms went around his neck. She pressed him closer to her loneliness, her sadness of a past gone wrong.

In this brief space of time, she understood the meaning of God's will. God's will was one with the purity of a person's own will, after that person bowed to God supreme as Lord and King. It wasn't something other, it did not require a martyrdom or an act of deprivation to obtain it. It was not harsh and brutal.

It was this: God's love of people, of man and woman for each other. It was all true love. A blessing beyond all understanding. A love that was not earned.

When they finally moved apart, they were both crying. Tears like healing rain wet both of their faces. Noah gathered her back into the haven of his arms, kissing the tears on her cheeks as they mingled with his own.

"I love you so much," he whispered.

He waited, holding his breath.

When her words came, rich and full of meaning, he was filled with indescribable joy. Floodgates long closed, opened, allowing his love to flow.

"I love you, Noah."

He could not speak.

When she said, "But I didn't always. You and Isaac were mean to me sometimes," he let out a great whoop of laughter and held her so close she struggled to breathe.

"My precious, adorable Hester. I have a hard time believing this night is real. That you are here, and that this is not all a dream and I must wake up to my usual life without you."

Hester smiled, softly parting her lips. She knew this was different. This was not a dream.

Far into the night, they talked, sitting on the back stoop in the sleeping, quiet town of Lancaster. Even the hens did not make a peep. The summer's night was soft and warm as a newborn lamb, the air mellow, caressing them with the newfound expression of their love.

Hester went back to Amos Stoltzfus's in the morning, transported in the same rickety cart pulled by the same pot-bellied mule.

Amos was in high spirits, the gray smoke trailing behind him in regulated puffs, as if the mule and cart were partially run by the power of the tobacco. He said the boys were cutting hay, Fannie was in the garden, and

Rachel was helping with the baby. Everything was going great, he said. Salina was gaining her strength.

Hester scowled. Fannie in the garden? What was Fannie doing in that hopeless patch? She compressed her lips and shoved her anger into silence.

When she entered the house, an acrid stench almost made her gasp. As it was, her hand went to her mouth and she struggled to breathe. As her eyes adjusted to the dimly lit kitchen, she saw a half-dressed, uncombed Salina sprawled in the rocking chair by the blackened remains of the fire on the hearth, gray ashes mixed with charred wood scattered all the way to the creaking rocker. Her feet were bare, her dress front soiled, stiff with grease and remnants of dried milk from the baby held across one shoulder. She had on the large white sleeping cap she had worn to bed, which was faded to a cloudy gray and torn across the ears, one pink lobe protruding out the side.

Salina was smiling, glad to see the capable Hester again.

"*Goota mya*, Hester!" she sang out, in a strong voice.

"Good morning," Hester replied, then swallowed quickly as the nausea rose in her chest.

"Did you have a good Sunday at home?"

"Oh, yes."

How insignificant that answer. She could not begin to tell Salina of the wonders of Noah's love, which he had offered and she had taken, two hearts melted together, searching and insecurity things of the past.

"Well, that's good. Now you're back. I'll let you begin with the washing. I think the cloth on the cradle needs attention; perhaps our bedding as well. And, oh, you might want to empty the pot in the bedroom and the slops on the table. Rachel saw a maggot this morning. The flies seem to be extra plentiful this year. Seems as soon as a bit of food stays on the table, the flies are laying eggs on it."

"Where are Rachel and Sallie?"

Salina gazed absently at Hester. "Around here somewhere."

Hester eyed the piles of dirty dishes, the food congealed in puddles of grease, the black houseflies droning above it, the greenish bodies of the blowflies settled quietly to deposit the eggs that would produce the loathsome maggots.

"Why did no one attend to yesterday's dishes?" Hester ground out, her thinly veiled disgust unnoticed completely by the slovenly Salina.

"I have an awful time with Rachel. She doesn't like to do dishes, and sometimes I just don't have the strength to keep telling her. It seems Sallie takes after Rachel. I don't know how to handle them, I suppose."

"What about Fannie?"

"Oh, she's in the garden. She is supposed to be picking beans. Amos said the beans are overripe, so we need to get them."

"Why is Fannie picking beans alone with her back injury?"

Salina waved the question away with a flopping wave of her large white hand. "She's better. She always was so childish, so *bupplich*, with aches and other trivial pains."

"The way she hurt her back is not a trivial pain."

"She'll be all right."

With that, Salina lumbered to her feet and came over to the table, where she lifted a piece of cold fried mush amid a flurry of disturbed flies and stuffed it into her mouth.

Hester turned away, sickened by the gulps as well as her dismissal of Fannie's injury. She pumped water with energy generated by her anger, dumped it into the copper kettle, and built a roaring fire underneath. Then she marched off to look for Rachel and Sallie. She didn't care if it was dinner-time till she got the washing started.

The lone figure of Fannie, sitting in the long rows of green beans, her thin body twisted sideways to find and pick the endless clusters of beans, fueled her anger even more.

When she finally located the two older girls by the corncrib, absentmindedly shelling corn and throwing it across the loose rails of the fence to the horses, Hester had no hesitancy or fear within her. She walked up to them with solid steps, grabbed one arm of each girl in a grip that did not convey gentleness or goodwill. "Get up," she hissed.

Startled, Sallie stumbled clumsily to her feet, her eyes wide with alarm. Rachel swung her head in Hester's direction, her eyes hooded with insolence, and she tried yanking her well-muscled arm out of Hester's grip.

The years of hoeing, mulching, and hauling manure for the huge vegetable patch, along with the strong muscles of her Indian lineage, had honed Hester's arms and hands into solid strength, her grip like a man's. When Rachel saw she would not be able to free herself, she got to her feet, pulled back one leg, and placed a solid kick on Hester's shin. Pain shot through her, but she chose to ignore it, increasing her hold on both girls until their mouths opened with howls of frustration.

"Let me go!' Rachel bellowed.

"I will not. You come with me, both of you. You ought to be ashamed of yourselves. Why have you left the dishes unwashed till there are maggots crawling on the table?"

"Mam doesn't mind a few maggots."

"Well, I do. And as long as I am the *maud* here, you will wash dishes, or I will tell your father."

"Dat? Puh! What does he care?"

"If he doesn't, then I'll have the ministers pay you a visit, and I can guarantee that some of you children will be given to other families to raise."

"Dat and Mam wouldn't let that happen," Rachel said petulantly. "Let go my arm. You're hurting me."

Sallie began crying, opening her mouth wide, her yellow teeth protruding as wet sobs and wails rose from her throat.

"Now look what you did. You made Sallie cry."

Rachel's own face had taken on a quality of surprise, a mixture of disbelief and fear upheld by a fading brashness.

"I don't want to be given to someone else," Sallie wailed, gulping and hiccupping, a thin stream of mucus trickling down her nose.

"Be quiet. You'll scare Fannie with that howling. Stop it now."

"What do we care about Fannie? Mam doesn't like her. She's *bupplich*," Rachel sneered.

When Hester entered the house with the two girls in
her grip, Salina glanced up, then as quickly looked at the
girls' faces, the traces of Sallie's tears and Rachel's white-
faced rebellion.

"Hester! My goodness. You made Sallie cry!"

"I did, yes. These girls need to be disciplined if you
are expected to live in a decent manner."

"Oh, but they would have washed the dishes without
hauling them in that way."

Rachel's sneer of triumph told Hester what the actual
situation was here in this hovel, this decrepit caricature
of an Amish household. Others were brought up to
believe that cleanliness was next to godliness. The children were expected to obey, to learn a solid work ethic
as they grew up in a family that was organized, to hold
good morals and develop a strong Christian foundation.

How could Hester hope to achieve her goal of getting this family on a solid footing, teaching the children
to pick up and pull their share, if their mother frowned
about any discomfort experienced by her older daughters, the ones who could carry the bulk of the workload?
She dared not think of Fannie, faithfully picking the
green beans, very likely humming the children's tunes in
German to herself.

As she scrubbed the soiled bedding and diapers, the
dresses and shirts and trousers, repeatedly changing the
dirty, gray water with fresh clean hot water, stirring and
scrubbing, rinsing and wringing every article of clothing out by firm twists of her capable, brown hands, her
anger was replaced by a daring plan: she would ask for
Fannie, to have this small, unloved child.

Hester's heart beat swiftly and strongly. Her veins sang with the beauty of it. To give one small, injured soul a new kind of life—wasn't that what Hans and Kate had done for her? Without *their* love, for, yes, there had been that from both of them, in spite of Hans's feelings gone awry—where would she be? She would have died there at the spring. There were times when she wished she could have perished as an infant, but not now. Oh, no. Her whole life had not been in vain.

She had not lived or suffered without a reason. She had never been alone or forgotten or unloved, in spite of it seeming so at times. A thread of purpose had been woven into every event—with the birth of Noah, Kate's death, her own leaving, finding William and Bappie, everyone—all of it.

Her whole life led to the perfection of Noah's love, an undeserved but richly abundant gift straight from the throne of God. To relinquish her hold on the castle of resistance she had built and to release her fear, the deep, dark moat around it, were gifts as well. She knew that Noah's and her love was only a beginning, that a draw-bridge back into the castle of fear was easily available if she chose.

But now with the beauty of having Noah in her life, wouldn't it be richer, indeed, to include Fannie? The knowledge of her barrenness, that dry place that knew only suffering, was something she needed to recognize. Thank God she had told Noah in her outburst of soul agony.

He had accepted her in spite of it. He said it didn't make a difference in his love for her. Hester's heart overflowed in salty tears that ran down her cheeks and pooled in the corners of her lips, her hands busy scrubbing and wringing the clothes in the steaming water.

She would spend the week cooking, cleaning, and tackling the endless cycle of hard work, till Amos took her home. She would try her best with Rachel and Sallie. Then she would propose her plan to Noah.

Somehow he should meet Fannie before actually giving his consent. The thought of little Fannie, so thin and undernourished, seated between them on the way to Berks County, her brown eyes taking in the wonders of another world outside the squalor of her own, was so inspiring it brought a song to Hester's lips.

"Mein Gott ich bitt
Ich bitt durich Chrischte blut,
Mach's nur mit meinem
Ende Gute."

Over and over she sang the chorus of the German hymn till she had the washing all strung on the line, pegged firmly with wooden clothespins. It flapped and danced in the summer breeze, the noon sun already high overhead.

When Amos and the boys came in at lunchtime, they were disappointed to see the fire was out, the kitchen soaked with strong lye soap, every dish washed and put away, but without a smidgen of food to be seen anywhere.

"Voss gebt?" Levi asked, his good humor intact.

Salina shrugged and lightly slapped the gurgling baby, letting the milk he had spit up settle into the fabric of the dress she wore, already stiff with previous milk, hiccups, and burps.

"I guess Hester thinks cleaning is more important than eating."

Hester turned, her eyebrows lowered, her face dark with effort and the heat of the day. "We can't eat if we don't have dishes to eat from," she said, her words clipped and sharp.

"*Ach, ya, ya.*" Amos nodded, smiled his benevolent smile, reached for the sour-smelling baby, and settled him contentedly in the crook of his elbow. He lowered his face, clucked and crooned, coaxing a small smile out of the alert little newborn, so well cared for and cuddled.

The older boys crowded around, eager to catch sight of that fleeting little smile. Reuben reached for the tiny fist, waiting till the perfectly formed, pale, little fingers wrapped themselves instinctively around his forefinger.

And out in the garden, in the blazing heat of midday, little eleven-year-old Fannie continued her bean-picking, waiting until someone called her for dinner and a glass of cold water.

CHAPTER 19

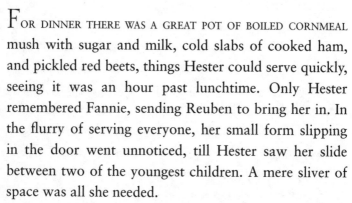

For dinner there was a great pot of boiled cornmeal mush with sugar and milk, cold slabs of cooked ham, and pickled red beets, things Hester could serve quickly, seeing it was an hour past lunchtime. Only Hester remembered Fannie, sending Reuben to bring her in. In the flurry of serving everyone, her small form slipping in the door went unnoticed, till Hester saw her slide between two of the youngest children. A mere sliver of space was all she needed.

Fannie reached for her water glass first, drained it completely, then looked around for the tin pitcher of water. When she was unable to find it, she didn't ask, merely waited till her bowl was filled with mush and milk.

The children bent their heads, then lifted spoons of dripping mush to their mouths without speaking, intent on filling their cavernous stomachs, which hadn't been fed well for breakfast or the night before.

Two of the smallest boys, their mouths ringed with dirt, squabbled for the last two red beets. The smallest one set up a howling after being roundly smacked by his peer. Amos looked over, said, "Here, here," then resumed shoveling mush and milk into his mouth. Salina never noticed, tearing at the tough, stringy ham with her teeth, chewing contentedly, glad to find her family so well fed with a minimum of effort on her part.

Hester ate a bowl of mush but chose to forego the ham, unable to forget the flies and eggs she had seen laid in leftover food. Again and again her eyes went to Fannie, watching her eat, taking in the sweet way she conversed softly with Ammon, the six-year-old boy, not asking or seeming to want anything. She took only what she was given and asked for nothing more.

By all accounts, with a meal on the table and clean laundry on the line, this was an ordinary family, raised with Amish values, but Hester knew that the minute she would leave, chaos would resume in a few hours' time. This she acknowledged—that there would be no change, no permanent turn for the better. She could scrub and clean till her hands were raw, cook and bake and sew, but what she did was only temporary, a quick fix that would disappear the minute she walked out the door.

As in all things, there was some good with the bad, and this Hester easily recognized. There was companionship, caring, and a family structure, and if a few of the children were haphazardly neglected along the way, that was not overly alarming to anyone. If Fannie was a bit poorly and went unnoticed much of the time, it was simply the way of it.

Hester watched, narrowing her eyes and biding her time. She joined Fannie in the garden after putting Rachel and Sallie to the dishes, so she could include her fully in her plans. She talked about many things with Fannie—her back, school, her parents, anything she could think of, trying to draw this little closed person closer.

Fannie sat on the weed-choked earth, her dress carefully pulled to well below her knees, her thin, blue veined legs straight out, the soles of her feet brown with dirt, bits of earth clinging to her toes. Her hair was brown, her eyes set wide apart in a small, pointed face, as brown as old honey, almost golden, but darker. She was so thin and narrow, Hester could hardly find the shape of her body in the loose, ill-fitting dress she wore, also brown, mended many times with dark colored patches of various nondescript colors.

She reached out her thin arms and pulled the beanstalks as close as possible to grasp handfuls of thick succulent beans, way past their prime but edible. These would be nourishment for the family in winter after they were put in jars and sealed by boiling them in a hot water bath, usually the same pot that was used to heat water for the washing.

Hester watched as Fannie became sleepy, her eyelids drooping, her hands slowing in their constant scrabble for beans.

"Fannie, what would you say if I asked you to go away with me for a while?" Hester asked, very softly.

Fannie watched Hester's face curiously without a trace of fear, ready to accept anything Hester might say.

She shrugged her thin shoulders, causing the neckline of the too-large dress to slide to the right, exposing a painfully thin, blue-veined shoulder. "I don't care."

She caught Hester's eyes and smiled, a small lifting of the corners of her mouth.

"Would you miss your family very much, if we went away for awhile?"

"Where would we go?"

"To a place called Berks County, where lots of Amish people live."

Again, a small shrug, an even smaller smile. With one hand she pulled her dress back into place. "I guess I could go. If my mam and dat said I could."

"Do you want me to ask?"

"I don't care."

"Only if you want to, Fannie."

"I don't have good dresses and only one Sunday apron and no shoes."

"That's all right. We'll sew for you before we go."

"Will you bring me back?"

"Do you want to come back?"

Like a quizzical little bird, she tilted her head sideways, put one finger to her chin, and pondered this question, all the wisdom of her eleven years weighing the question.

Finally, she said, very soft and low, "I guess they don't need me much now that Mam has a baby to play with. Once, I was a baby; then Mam liked me, too."

Hester quickly assured her that her mother loved her now, too. Fannie nodded, her eyes alight.

"When she has time."

That evening, without the usual amount of dishes to wash, having served only cold fruit soup, Hester approached Amos and Salina, telling them she would only finish the week. They needed to find another *maud*. The reason was her trip to Berks County, and would they consider allowing Fannie to accompany her?

Salina agreed immediately, stating as fact that with fifteen mouths to feed—thirteen children and two parents—with Fannie so puny and all, she certainly wasn't worth much as far as the work went.

Amos cleared his throat a few times and swallowed, a pained expression crossing his face more than once. He glanced at his wife, as if her decision would help him decide as well.

"But, Salina, she's ours," he finally said.

"I know, Amos, but we have thirteen now. My Uncle Ezras gave their Samuel and Jonas to his brother Joe. Not that the boys had an easy life after that, Joe was so hard on Jonas, but I guess it didn't hurt."

"Oh, I would never mistreat Fannie," Hester said hurriedly. "I'm only asking her to accompany Noah Zug and me to Berks County to visit family. I think it would be a good thing to heal her back, maybe have her get some rest."

"Who is Noah Zug?"

As quick as the darting of a butterfly, and as subtle, Hester's answer was true but void of much content.

"He is my brother."

"You were a Zug?"

"Yes, before my marriage to William King."

"Oh, yes, that's right." Nodding easily, Amos remembered her as Isaac King's William's wife. Salina looked pleasantly blank, her face as smooth and untroubled as the moon when it was full.

"*Ya, vell don.* I guess you may take her along and see how everything goes," Amos said finally.

"I think she'll be just fine. She's so easy to have. Doesn't say much, won't cost hardly anything to keep."

And so it was decided.

The week was filled with work, hard work that made Hester's muscles ache at night and put dirt under her fingernails and toenails. Her hair was filled with the dust that never quite settled on the beaten paths surrounding the house, where children's feet stomped down any weed or plant that tried to raise its head and flourish.

She butchered those red-eyed chickens. With Amos's permission, she caught them early in the morning on their roosts, using a long wire hook. Then she grabbed them by their feet and hauled them squawking and screeching with that doomed sound captive chickens will make. That was fine with Hester, who hated those ill-tempered chickens only slightly less than the family's slovenly lifestyle.

She laid each chicken so its neck was positioned between two nails. Hanging onto both feet with one hand, she brought the hatchet down with a solid whop with the other, severing the head cleanly. The chicken felt no pain, it was so quick.

While their bodies flopped around headless in the dirt, she carried buckets of scalding water and set them close by. When the blood-soaked carcasses stopped their carrying on, she grasped the feet again and dipped the bodies in the scalding water to loosen the feathers. Then she set about plucking them, grasping handfuls of soaking wet feathers and yanking them out until each chicken wore only its skin, sprawling on a board in all its unadorned baldness.

Hester summoned Rachel and Sallie to help clean the pin feathers, those annoying little growths that needed to be pulled out with a knife blade. They groaned and grimaced simultaneously, then made a great show of pretending to throw up, while Hester glared at them between lowered brows, perspiration dripping off the end of her nose.

Finally, every last one of those hateful chickens was cleaned, cut up, put to cool in cold water, stuffed in a glass jar, cold-packed in the iron kettle, and put down cellar with the beans.

Salina mourned the loss of the eggs, saying she wanted eggs more than she wanted all that chicken meat, so Amos brought home twenty poults, half-grown peeps that ran around the yard on legs that seemed much too long for their bodies, with feet splayed like turkey feet, pecking wildly at anything within reach. Cats, worms, frogs, children, any moving object was easy prey. Hawks circled overhead, waiting to zoom down and grab a tasty lunch, but the poults remained safe, probably saved by the many children and toddlers that ran around among them.

Hester cleaned the cellar, carrying up decomposing potatoes and half-rotten bacon. She coughed when she wiped green mold from the vinegar barrel and rolled the crock of salt pork to the cellar's doorway to check for spoilage, then rolled it back. She carried out rotting boards and sour carrots, turnips bloated with decay like wet sponges. She swept and scrubbed while Rachel carried buckets of hot water, grumbling and making nasty remarks, which Hester chose to ignore.

Finally, when Rachel could get no response from Hester, she asked her outright why she was named that different name, "Hester." It wasn't in the Bible, she said, lifting her brows piously.

Hester chose not to answer, feeling guilty for the anger that rose up in her over a question as harmlessly spoken as that.

"See, you don't know," Rachel goaded.

Hester was carrying a heavy crock filled with spoiled turnips and in no mood to put up with Rachel's craziness, so she said she was found by a spring as an unwanted baby, and the lady that found her named her Hester.

"Was she Amish?"

"Yes."

"I bet."

Hester shrugged her shoulders. *Believe whatever you want*, she thought.

"She wasn't, was she?"

"Yes, she was. Her name was Kate."

"That's not an Amish name."

"Catherine."

"Oh."

Then, still determined to get the better of her, Rachel kept going. "Where is she now?"

"Buried in the graveyard in Berks County."

"Why? What happened to her?"

"A bear mauled her. She died later of infection."

"You're making that up."

That was the communication she had with Rachel, with Sallie nearby like a shadowed twin, placing an emphasis on every word. The girls were not endowed with their father's good humor. Their mother's lack of caring or discipline or love, or perhaps a combination of all three, left these girls without social skills.

They whitewashed the cellar, then pulled the carrots and dug the potatoes in the garden. They carried the root vegetables down cellar and placed them carefully in clean bins. Amos was grateful, chortling over his good fortune. Finding a *maud* like Hester had sure set him free of the responsibility of managing the cellar. Salina said it was all right, either way, but would Hester make a few cakes yet before she left? She was hungry for black walnut cake, and Amos had brought eggs from Abner Hershbergers.

So much for her appreciating a clean cellar. That lack of recognition solidified Hester's decision not to return the following week. She had baked the cakes, done the washing, cleaned the house, scythed and raked the yard, and had harvested and canned all that was possible. Now it was time to go.

Fannie was ready—bathed, with her hair rolled, braided, and twisted into a coil on the back of her head. She had no valise or haversack; only one change of dress, a blue one faded to a splotchy gray, and one black apron. No comb or brush, no shoes or stockings, and no underwear.

When Amos handed Hester two five-dollar bills, her wages for two weeks, she thanked him, feeling well and fairly paid. She pocketed the money, smoothed her hair, and said as soon as he was ready, they could go.

Salina was on the rocking chair, the baby flung across her lap face down, like a bundle of blankets if you didn't know any better. She watched Fannie with an expression Hester could not discern. A blank look, but not exactly a scowl, more of an acceptance, a lack of caring.

Did Salina know she was overwhelmed and, like a mother pig, a sow with a large litter, realize that the smallest, hungriest in the litter, the runt, might not survive? Pushed back, without proper nutrition, would Fannie fall easy prey to childhood diseases that crept up on her in the cold of winter when the house was full of sniffling siblings? Salina may have known this—a primal wisdom, the way of nature—when the babies kept coming and there was never enough energy to feed and clothe and nurture them all.

Hester placed Fannie's small bundle of clothing in her own valise, then straightened and caught Salina's eye. She stepped across the room, extended her hand in a formal handshake, and said, "Thank you for everything, Salina. I'm glad I had the opportunity to be your *maud*." More a formality than truth, but there it was.

Salina smiled widely and said she'd miss her, but she guessed Rachel and Sallie could *fasark* things. Amos's mother would come on Wednesday, but she couldn't wash, the way her hip was hurting.

Finally she asked Fannie to come over. She complied, standing close to her mother, her wide eyes searching her face, an eagerness about her as if she was aware this moment was special. Now she would know how much her mother wanted her to stay, how much she was loved.

But Salina pushed her back with a palm flat on her shoulder, said, "*Ge bacht.* Don't touch the baby."

Quickly, Fannie stepped back, her hands knotted behind her back, an expression of shame and bewilderment erasing the eagerness.

"Now don't you be a bother to Hester. Bye." Salina lifted a large white hand in dismissal, her face as bland and expressionless as a large wheel of cheese.

"Bye," Fannie said, the word coming out hoarsely. Embarrassed, she cleared her throat and tried again. "Bye."

Salina nodded, bending her head to the baby.

Hester looked at Fannie, a fragile, almost lifeless sparrow, then reached for her hand, encircling her thin fingers.

They walked out the door without looking back.

Amos smoked his pipe with a vengeance without speaking. The day was hot, the heat suffocating and shimmering above the dry pastures. The trees stood stiff and unbending, their leaves lifeless as the heat withheld even the comfort of one stirring breeze.

The afternoon was waning, bringing the promise of evening and its cooler air, a luxury that made the heat bearable. The mule walked tired and discouraged, so Amos reached under the seat for the usual whip to slash across the thin rump. A good thwack, a lurch, and they lumbered uphill and down, the cart rattling and heaving in its craziness.

Fannie was stuck between them like a wedge, and yet there was barely room for her. She showed no emotion, simply sitting quietly, her hands in her lap, even when they approached the town with all the buildings, the horses and carriages, the many pedestrians. It must have caused her at least a bit of surprise or bewilderment, but her face remained impassive, inscrutable.

When the mule heaved to an ungainly stop, Amos crawled out over the wheel, tapped his pipe on the steel rim of the buggy, and said, "Well."

"Thank you for the ride home," Hester said, going around to shake hands with Amos, a formal parting.

"*Gyan schöena.*"

Amos became quite agitated, shifting from one foot to the other, his eyes going to his daughter, only eleven years old, but leaving home.

"Fannie." Awkwardly, he extended a hand.

Fannie took it, and he shook the limp white hand once. She tucked it behind her back, keeping it there.

Amos blinked. His face worked. He swallowed, once, twice. When he cleared his throat, his mouth twitched downward, as if emotion was dangerously close to having the upper hand.

He looked at Hester. "It shouldn't be like this. She was always *schpindlich*. Salina had a hard time."

He shrugged his shoulders. "Bye, Fannie," he said quietly.

"Bye," Fannie said, obediently.

"You'll be back," he said.

Fannie looked at Hester, a question in her eyes.

"We'll see how things go."

"*Ya, vell.*" Amos turned to go, climbed into the cart, lifted the reins, and chirruped. When there was no response, he brought the reins down across the mule's loose-skinned haunches. That brought up the ears, then the ungainly head, and a half-hearted pull on the traces. Amos waddled off on the rickety old cart.

Fannie watched her father go without a word. The only sign that Hester noticed was her hands clasping and unclasping behind her back. Her thin shoulders were almost square, her eyes expressionless.

Hester looked down at her and smiled. Only the beginning of a smile teased the corners of Fannie's mouth, but her eyes were alive with wonder.

"So, here we are, Fannie."

Hester grasped the valise in one hand and Fannie's hand in the other. Together they made their way through the back door to find an eager Bappie, her eyes quick and bright, her curiosity sizzling, waiting to meet this child Hester had brought home.

"Well, hello, Fannie!"

Fannie looked steadily at Bappie with no response.

"Fannie, this is Bappie. Her name is Barbara King. She lives here with me."

Fannie nodded, but said nothing.

"Did you have supper?"

"No, we are both starving, aren't we?"

Fannie nodded.

"I fried chicken and made mashed potatoes."

Fannie looked at Hester, checking her response. When she saw Hester's smile of approval, she smiled widely.

Bappie watched Fannie's face, then wiped her eyes with the back of her hand, her only response to the child's lack of certainty.

They sat down to their meal, bowing their heads in silence, as was their custom. Fannie, taught to fold her hands beneath the table, waited reverently till Bappie lifted her head, the signal to begin serving the food.

When a crispy portion of chicken was placed on her plate, Fannie had no idea what to do with it, so she ate her mashed potatoes and gravy, then placed her spoon quietly beside her plate and waited.

Hester leaned over and asked if she didn't like the chicken.

Fannie's mouth trembled as her eyes filled with tears. She whispered, "I don't know what it is."

Bappie and Hester exchanged further looks.

"It is chicken, fried. You can use your hands. Here." Hester showed the child the procedure, biting into her own.

Fannie shook her head.

When Noah arrived, he greeted Fannie warmly, bending over the hesitant child and telling her he was glad to be able to take her with them to Berks County. He let her know in his kind voice that he was Hester's brother.

Fannie watched him warily, her eyes turning dark with some unnamed emotion that puzzled Hester. When Levi arrived a few minutes later, she disappeared into the front room where the fading light of evening obscured her, giving her a measure of safety.

Bappie's eyebrows went up and she mouthed a rapid question, followed by a hiss of "*Voss iss lets mitt sie?*"

Hester shrugged her shoulders, spread her hands with palms upward, and shook her head.

They moved to the backyard where the air was turning cooler, sitting on chairs they brought from the shed. Levi said the child was only frightened, likely never having been away from home. She'd come around. He had heard of the Amos Stoltzfus family, had helped them shuck corn in the fall.

"Amos is a real nice man. Not much ambition, but I am not sure about the wife. She seems a bit slow."

"They are nice, as far as that goes. I don't think the children are treated unkindly. The parents just don't have much insight as far as the children's needs, never giving the ordinary attention and caring most families are accustomed to showing. Fannie is so quiet, so used to going about life unnoticed, that going away and meeting strangers is too much for her tonight," Hester said.

"So what are your plans?" Levi asked.

Noah looked at Hester, his eyes questioning. Finding the joy he sought in the warmth of her eyes, he told them of the upcoming journey to the home of their youth, the hope of keeping Fannie with them.

Bappie, as sharp as a blade, connected the dots saying loudly, "With you? With both of you? Or just with Hester? How is this now? You're traveling together as brother and sister, but when you get there, who is going to live with whom? Huh? I mean you're not getting married or anything, the way Levi and I are, are you?"

With this, she reached over and grabbed Levi's hand proudly, possessively, her face radiating happy ownership. Levi's face shone in the twilight as he reached over with his other hand, covering Bappie's with both of his own.

Completely at ease, Noah responded. "Oh no, we have no plans. We are brother and sister, so I'm sure our parents will welcome us and allow us to stay as long as we want."

Hester got to her feet, saying she was checking on Fannie. There was nothing to do or say to this, out of respect for the Amish tradition of not announcing a wedding until just a few weeks in advance, in spite of Bappie's unladylike snorts of disbelief.

A romance was always kept well hidden, even if the truth was stretched by small white lies at times in order to keep it a secret. Courting was done in the late hours of a Sunday evening, after the traditional hymn-singing that usually ended an hour or so before midnight. The secret was well kept by both sets of parents, too. Typically, a young man accompanied a girl into her house, well hidden from her parents, who had already gone to bed. In fact, it was not unusual for a young man to court a young woman for a few years without actually speaking to either of her parents until he asked to marry her.

Only after the engagement was announced publicly in church did the young man show his face at the home of the bride-to-be, freely coming and going in broad daylight. At that point he became an honored *hochzeita*, a prospective groom, a son-in-law-to-be, already welcomed warmly into the family.

Noah pulled it off seamlessly. Levi was completely clueless, or if he wasn't, he respectfully didn't show it.

Chapter 20

And so on Monday morning, Hester packed her clothes into a small wooden trunk, along with some of her most cherished possessions—a few linens she had embroidered, the set of fine china William had gotten for her, the figurine Emma had given her as a Christmas gift.

When Noah pulled up to the backyard with his team of pawing black horses and a canvas stretched securely on bands that arced above the sturdy spring wagon, Hester's heart beat crazily in her chest. A myriad of emotions overcame her, fluttering butterflies of every color that confused her, magnified by the sheer number of them.

How to describe how she felt? Anticipation, wonder, fear, trepidation, sadness, a sense of loss. But also a great swell of love and adoration for Noah, now released and allowed to flow unfettered, her wall of refusal a faint and dimming memory. This love overrode all others like a leader, a giant who strode forth with an impenetrable armor.

When Walter, Emma, and the boys appeared, a lump rose in Hester's throat and quick tears blurred her vision. Emma. The rotund little woman with a heart of gold. She was the angel of mercy, the one who had nursed her back to health after the white men's destruction of the Indian village on the banks of the Conestoga Creek. In her memory, Emma would always shine with a pure light. And Walter. Dear man, so devoted to his food, his impeccable English manners, and his wife. Richard and Vernon, the homeless waifs, would grow up to be good, solid citizens under their tutelage.

Billy had not returned yet, which saddened Hester, the longing to see him before she left surprisingly real.

Hester stood, clothed in a shortgown of summery blue, her black cape and apron pinned over it, her muslin cap strings tied beneath her chin, her black shoes and stockings worn according to the *Ordnung*, but a cumbersome bother. Her feet were already uncomfortable, longing to be free from the stiff leather.

Fannie stood beside her watching warily, taking in the pawing horses and the strange people with the small boys. She was dressed in her one presentable shortgown, a gray color that may have been purple or blue at one time, covered with her black Sunday apron, pinafore-style and buttoned with two black buttons down the back. Her feet were bare, which was acceptable in summer, even for Sunday services, to spare the use of shoes, which were expensive.

Noah loaded the trunk, then stood politely as Hester said her goodbyes. She was enveloped in long, hard hugs by both Emma and Walter as tears flowed unashamedly, their bodies as soft as pillows and as comforting.

Hugs were unaccustomed among the Amish, a show that was much too physical, but Walter and Emma were English and displayed their love freely.

When it was Bappie's turn, she and Hester simply stood facing each other, their eyes speaking what their throats would not allow, lumps of emotion cutting off any words that formed in their hearts.

"Good-bye, Bappie," Hester whispered, a strangled sound that was met by a sob. Bappie threw her long, skinny arms around Hester, two bands of love as sturdy as leather straps on a harness.

"I'm going to miss you terrible," Bappie sobbed.

Hester's eyes were closed but her cheeks were wet with tears that squeezed from beneath her heavy lids. "Thank you, Bappie, for everything. I'll write," she choked.

"You have to come back for my wedding in November."

"I will."

"You mean, *we* will."

They stepped back, both of them fumbling in the pockets sewn to their skirts, lifting their black aprons, blowing their noses, then beginning to laugh through their tears.

Noah lifted Fannie first, seating her on the cushioned seat. Then he gave Hester a hand, looking gently into her streaming eyes, his touch a reassurance of his love, his caring so great he could not fully convey it.

From her perch on the wagon seat, Hester waved and called out her good-byes, promising to return in November. She turned in her seat to continue waving as the horses pranced off, pulling the wagon behind them.

"Good-bye, good-bye," the small knot of friends called in unison as the buggy rumbled out of sight.

The air was thick and sultry, the sun's intensity cloaked with a veil of haze. The air that moved past them as the horses trotted along was wet and stale, as if it had smoldered over the town all night.

The trees were limp and discouraged-looking, as if they knew their heyday was in the past and fall was imminent. The cornstalks were heavy and green, the ears of corn weighing them down, brown streaks along the stalks speaking of the end of the growing season. Soon would come the crisp, cool air of autumn, when the fields surrounding Lancaster would ring with the cries of the cornhuskers as wagons moved slowly through the fields of rustling brown corn, and the hard, yellow ears were ripped from the stalks and thrown on the wagons.

Most of this bountiful crop would be stored in corn cribs and then fed to the livestock. Some of it would be ground into cornmeal at the mill, then cooked with salt and water, a staple of many Amish families' diets. Fried mush, mush and milk, cornpone, cornbread. Virtually free, these corn-based dishes were nutritious and filling, fueling the children as they ran off to school.

Meadowlarks opened their beaks like scissors, lifted their heads, and trilled their country song, singing from fenceposts and stone fences.

Crows wheeled overhead. A convoy of blackbirds circled through the sky, scrabbling hurriedly through the air on busy wings as if they were late to an important meeting. A bluebird flitted ahead of them, its wings beating frantically.

Noah didn't speak, his attention on the eager horses, allowing Hester time to dry her eyes and remember her friends.

Fannie didn't move a muscle. Only her eyes showed her interest as she watched oncoming teams and the road opening to the countryside.

Hester squeezed her shoulder. "Are you all right, Fannie?"

Fannie looked up, nodded, then added a small smile like an afterthought.

"You'll be all right with leaving your home? If you're afraid of *zeitlang*, we can always take you back if you want to go."

Fannie's silence made Hester feel uneasy. What if the poor child would want to return? In spite of the squalid conditions, it was her home, after all. Who was she to think Fannie's life would improve with her and Noah?

When Fannie spoke, Hester had to bend low to hear the words.

"Maybe I will get *zeitlang* for Ammon, but they won't miss me. Not my mam."

"Oh, she will miss you, Fannie. She'll think about it that you're gone."

"I don't think so."

She spoke breathlessly with a wisdom beyond her years, so Hester did not try to correct her. She merely slipped an arm around the slim figure and pulled her close.

"It's all right, Fannie. What would Noah and I do without you?"

Fannie tilted her small face upward, looked into Noah's face, then Hester's, as the slow light of understanding crept across her features, bringing up the corners of her mouth. "That's right, isn't it? You don't have any other brothers or sisters, do you?"

"We do, but they are all in Berks County. At home. But none of them is you. They don't have a Fannie among them."

"They don't?"

"No."

Fannie pondered this for some time, then opened her mouth as if to speak. But she closed it again, choosing instead to lay her head against Hester's arm and breathe deeply.

The two horses trotting together formed a sort of rhythm that made its way into Hester's senses, a cadence not unlike the night sounds of insects. Sometimes the hoofbeats were synchronized in perfect unison; other times there was a mishmash of off-beat thumps until they gradually returned to the same orderly beat.

The harnesses flapped on the glistening backs of the horses. The traces pulled taut on the upgrade, then flopped loosely going downhill when the britchment surrounding the haunches drew tight, holding back the covered buggy they rode on.

The horses' black manes rippled and shone, streaming with every footstep. Their tails arched proudly, the long black hair spreading evenly behind them. They held their heads high, their ears pricked forward, flicking back occasionally in response to a command or an instruction from their driver.

The sun had unwrapped itself from the fog, its red, blazing light shimmering across the backs of the horses. A thin, white band of sweat appeared around the britchment on each animal. The hairs along their backs turned slick with it. One of them, the horse on the right, slowed visibly, lifting his mouth until the bit rattled the reins, then letting it fall. Over and over he did this, till Noah looked at Hester and said he believed Comet was tiring. They'd pull off at the next shady spot.

"Comet?" Hester inquired.

"Comet and Star."

She smiled. Finding his eyes, their gazes held.

"Good names for these beautiful horses."

"Yes, I am fortunate to have them. However, they aren't nearly as beautiful as my most prized possession."

Puzzled, Hester asked, "You have more horses?"

"Oh no, she's not a horse."

When Hester met his eyes, she blushed furiously and wished she had a hat to yank forward over her heated face. As it was, she turned her head to the left until her cheeks cooled.

She said, "I am not your possession."

"Almost. Someday soon."

"Does a man possess his wife?" asked a small voice between them.

They had forgotten Fannie. Hester gasped.

Noah lifted his face and laughed aloud, a great freeing sound without embarrassment, just the joy of finding something extremely funny.

Hester fumbled for words, made a few very bad starts, gave up, and stared ahead without speaking. Noah took the situation in hand, saying Hester was not his sister, except in name, and they hoped to be married someday, although he had not yet asked her. That would all come later, after they visited their parents, Hans and Annie Zug.

Very firmly the words came, put into the atmosphere with meaning, an expression containing so much wisdom for a child of eleven, it took Hester's breath away.

"I didn't think Noah was your brother. His hair is almost white. Yours is very black. But Abraham said that about Sarah, his wife, and since you are traveling like they were, well, it's almost the same thing."

This speech coming from the timid Fannie left Hester speechless. Noah began humming and turned his face to the right, away from Hester's unease. There was only the sound of the buggy wheels on the wide dirt road, the dull hitting of iron clad hooves on packed earth, the jingle of buckles and straps, the flapping of leather against the horses' wet legs.

Evidently Fannie was not uncomfortable with her speech left unanswered. She sat against Hester, her eyes bright and alert, watching the ever changing landscape.

When the road led downhill to a clump of trees, an appendage of a large tract of thick forest, Noah reined in the tired horses and pulled off to the side of the road. Unsure what was expected of her, Hester remained seated till Noah asked if she wanted to unhook the traces for Star and lead him to the creek with him and Comet.

The horses lowered their heads, snorting and snuf-
fling, blowing out their breaths on the surface of the
water till thirst overcame their distrust and they lowered
their mouths and drank.

Noah watched Hester's face as she looked at Star
drinking from the tepid little creek. She felt his eyes on
her face, looked up, and smiled.

"They are good horses," she said.

"They sure are. I got a bargain when I bought these
from Dan."

"Are you planning to hitch them to the plow?"

"Oh, my, no. It would ruin them. They're far too
highstrung to wear them down in the plow. That's for
draft horses or mules."

Hester nodded.

"Will you be buying a farm?"

This question startled Noah. He was surprised Hester
asked him, because she was so shy about many other
things.

"I am hoping to persuade Hans to let me have about
half the acreage he owns. I don't want to live close to
them. First, I need to see how things are, how Annie is,
the children, just everything. We need to be very careful,
Hester, with the way things were in the past."

"Oh, I am not implying anything. I am just going for
a visit. Not that I have any concern as far as your buying
a farm."

Hester ran her hand through the heavy, tangled hair
in Star's mane, keeping her eyes averted, her face taking
on a deeper, darker hue.

Noah said, "Look at me."

She would not, finding the safety she needed in the horse's mane, as if the most important task in the world had presented itself to her.

Noah clipped a snap from Comet's harness to Star's, came around to Hester, and put his hands around her waist, hidden from Fannie's bright gaze. He stood behind her and spoke soft and low.

"We have spoken of our love for one another, my darling Hester. You are the love of my life. Hopefully God has many years planned for us together. But first we need to take care of this business with Hans and Annie, my parents and yours."

"Hans is not my parent, and neither is she."

Hester flung the words into the air, her language portraying her long-remembered hatred and the grudge she carried within herself. This was the one thing Noah was afraid of, the reason he had not yet formally asked her hand in marriage, coupled with the fact that he was unsure how he felt about Hans and Annie himself. That was the reason for this all-important trip.

Hester's words were like a dagger in his back, as painful and as dangerous. He knew forgiveness would not come easily for her, if ever.

He also knew they could not step into a holy union as husband and wife, while still carrying the baggage of past hurts and unforgiveness. Even if their love was a thing of brilliant splendor now, with time, it would tarnish if these past ruptures were not dealt with. Noah felt it was important to forgive and honor their parents. Only then could they be blessed with a real and lasting love that came from God alone.

He believed he loved Hester enough to carry both of them through any trial that came into their lives, his need to have her for his wife sometimes overpowering his solid common sense. He longed to tell Hester that she needed to forgive but figured it would do no good.

All he could do was take her to these two aging people, watch her reaction, and wait to see what occurred. If God had a plan for their lives together, it would all fall into place like pieces in a child's wooden puzzle.

They ate in the shade of enormous oak and sycamore trees, nestling in the grass by the side of the road. Noah allowed the horses a long tether so they could graze, biting off the lush green grass and chewing contentedly.

Fannie was confused when Hester handed her a sandwich. She finally took it, then lifted the top slice of bread and ate it dry before grasping the cold, baked ham and eating it separately as well. She drank the water obediently, then got to her feet, wandering among the blue bells and white columbines, humming softly to herself, her small face alight with happiness.

Noah lay back in the grass, his hands beneath his head, his knees bent, his shirt unbuttoned at the neck. His blond hair was in disarray from passing his fingers through it, his eyes closed, the heavy lashes sweeping his tanned cheeks.

Watching him, Hester thought his face looked lined, perhaps even older than his years. Had the war taken its toll on him, or had some hardship in his life chiseled the features, like storm winds on a rock or a cliff face, wearing away the perfect symmetry after years of time?

Noah could not have had a carefree childhood without the ease and acceptance found between most fathers
and sons. Hester's mind retained vivid pictures of growing up in the little log house in Berks County when Kate
was still alive.

The heavy plank table, Noah's and Isaac's chins barely
reaching to the table top, being cuffed on their shoulders
as Hans's great red hands came down in punishment for
something as insignificant as a giggle or a forbidden burst
of laughter at the table, where children were to be seen
and not heard. Once Noah had spilled a half-tumbler
of water, resulting in a ringing smack across one cheek,
then the other, his head spinning in both directions.

He never made a sound. Always it was the same.
Noah's eyes would be a brilliant blue, the color enhanced
by unshed tears. His mouth would tremble once, slightly,
and that was all. Hester always winced, feeling the slap
on her own cheek. But she had learned to squelch her
pity, folding it away where no one would see.

Now, thinking of Salina, she suddenly wondered.
Had Kate been a bit simple? Overwhelmed? Or was she
only obedient to her husband's wishes, honoring him to
the point that she had no will of her own, leaving the
discipline of the children to him?

That Kate had loved her husband was without doubt.
She had loved him, made him laugh, helped him through
his anxiety and fits of depression. And Hans had been
good to her, the way most husbands were.

Watching Noah's face, the craggy, chiseled planes
of his features so striking, Hester remembered him as a
baby, a toddler. Much larger than most babies, his head

was big and almost bald till he was well past a year old. His wide mouth was almost alarming when he cried, which seemed to be his favorite thing to do.

Did some fathers find themselves having a secret aversion to a newborn son? Hester only knew that Hans had often been unfair, even cruel to the two sons, born so quickly after they brought her home from the spring and nursed her back to health with goat's milk.

All her life Hans had been good to her, as well as to Kate. She had been favored even above Kate, but she had been too young to know. She had found security and happiness in Hans, the perfect attentive father.

Until he wasn't.

Then her privileges were taken away and she was forbidden to ride horses, as Hans became harsh in his expectations of how she should follow the *Ordnung*. He was strict and unyielding where her clothes were concerned. After Kate's death, he married thin and frigid Annie, who was merciless in her contempt for Hester. She treated her, the adopted Indian girl, with a coarseness that sprang from dislike, fueled by her jealousy.

With a groan, Hester turned away. The unfairness of it, the patience of Noah and Isaac, the shame of Hans's unrighteousness. She loathed Hans. She felt a deep and abiding humiliation, the knife edge of the wrong Hans had harbored in his ill-concealed heart.

Why, then, did she feel as if she herself was tainted, soiled by the knowledge of his fatherly love and affection gone wrong? How could she hope to find even the smallest measure of peace by returning? How would she face him, the robust, swarthy man who had been her father, a figure of security? As she grew, she had been the *dumkopf*, the simple girl in school. But she skipped through her days with innocence, until Kate died and Hans married Annie, followed by the sense that something had gone very wrong. She could relive the intense glittering of Hans's eyes, but how was she to know how wrong it was, never having encountered anything of that nature?

She sat beside Noah, her arms wrapped around her bent knees, and let the misery overtake her. How could she have been so naïve, so uncomprehending, when so much was at stake? She could not go on, blindly riding into the Amish settlement and being among so many acquaintances after all she had gone through in the years since she left.

How was she to know Noah would be any different than Hans? Here she was, taking Fannie, her pity for the thin, neglected girl overriding her common sense, perhaps into the same trap she herself had been caught in.

A soft movement caught Hester's attention. A whisper, "Here."

A bunch of white columbine, mixed with lacy ferns and waxy bluebells, was thrust into her lap.

Hester looked up into Fannie's face, her white cheeks flushed with embarrassment.

"Fannie! These look just like a garden. I can't believe you arranged these flowers to look so natural. It's amazing. How did you do it?"

Fannie lowered her eyes, blushed deeper, and shrugged her thin shoulders. "I don't know."

"Thank you. I love these flowers. I think it's the nicest bouquet anyone ever gave to me."

"Oh."

Noah awoke, sat up, and smiled immediately, as if kindness slept and woke with him. Fannie watched him warily as Hester showed him the flowers and laughed when he shook his head in disbelief, banishing Hester's dark thoughts like a sunrise on night waters.

They traveled steadily through the afternoon, the two black horses trotting faithfully, sometimes walking, the canvas top flapping in the breezes, Fannie content to sit between them.

Noah observed the gathering clouds like dirty sheep's wool rolling into dark colored bundles. He did not like the stillness in the air or the oppressive heat. He chose to say nothing, so when Hester questioned him about the approaching clouds, he simply nodded his head, taking in the surroundings, his gaze sweeping left, then right.

They passed farms dotting the countryside, homes of the Amish, Mennonites, and the more liberal English, all dwelling side by side, forming neighborhoods of diversity and, for the most part, enjoying a life of peace, if not exactly spiritual unity. That part was accepted and acknowledged, as each family traveled to their respective house of worship on Sunday mornings, passing each other with friendly waves.

The Mennonites had their meetinghouses, while the Amish met in homes. The English attended massive stone or brick churches scattered through the towns. Each chose to worship the same God in many different ways, following the Scripture according to their own understanding, love, and tradition. These were the ties that bound each one to family and congregation, the strong-holds of their own individual faiths.

Noah had spoken of his desire to stay in Lancaster. He thought it was the only sensible thing to do. With the soil so fertile, the crop yields were higher than anywhere he had ever been. But the land was costly, three times the amount per acre than it was in Berks County. He could purchase a tract of land without borrowing very much, if any, if he chose to buy in his homeland.

Hester had been too shy to ask or to add to the conversation, certainly not wanting him to feel as if she had any part in his future.

In her heart, she couldn't imagine a future without Noah, but perhaps she was only being irrational and not thinking clearly.

She also recognized that she had never cared for William the way she did for Noah. As each day passed, each week an eternity if she was not with Noah, her growing understanding of what love actually encompassed was staggering.

Why had she married William? Did everything have a reason? Had it all been in God's plan? If this is what real love is like, then perhaps she shouldn't blame herself for her lack of obedience or her fiery rebellion.

Her thoughts were unsettling, her spirit tumultuous, as she sat in the deep grass beside Noah. She glanced at the approaching clouds, wondering if a coming storm was causing her mind to produce all these endless, senseless thoughts.

Noah suddenly suggested they hitch up and try to make it to an inn by nightfall. He got to his feet and reached for her hands, drawing her up with him. He would not let go of her hands, looking into her eyes until her vision blurred and her head swam. Wise little Fannie looked over her bouquet of flowers and nodded once to herself, then sighed softly.

CHAPTER 21

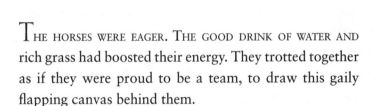

THE HORSES WERE EAGER. THE GOOD DRINK OF WATER AND rich grass had boosted their energy. They trotted together as if they were proud to be a team, to draw this gaily flapping canvas behind them.

The road made a few turns, dipped down once, then steadied into a gradual incline up to a higher level. A steep ridge lay ahead, and then a small mountain.

The clouds moved in steadily from the northwest, a low bank that seemed caught above the line of hills. The sun shone hot and brilliant, turning the backs of the sweating horses into polished glass.

Noah said he remembered an inn at Black Creek at the foot of the ridge, which was a line of small mountains called Eagle Rock.

Hester said they would be fine beneath this canvas, that she was afraid it was simply too expensive to stay at an inn. A waste of money.

In answer, Noah pointed to the approaching storm, shaking his head.

Toward evening, the light turned gray with a cast of yellow-orange.

They passed a barn so new the lumber shone golden in the haze of the approaching bad weather. The house had been painted white and shone like a beacon of solid workmanship, the white sheets and towels and tablecloths dancing on their clothespins. A buxom woman clad in purple came hurrying out of the house, a wicker clothes basket balanced on one hip, glancing at the dark clouds. The hammering of nails reverberated from the barn. Children dotted the yard, colorful little characters running and tumbling about like birds.

They waved when the woman set down her basket, stopped, and raised a hand to her forehead like a salute. Shading her eyes from the glare of the sun, she lifted her hand in a wave immediately.

The wind was getting up, stirring the summer's old leaves, rustling the dry grass by the side of the road. It lifted the horses' manes, riffling through the thick hair. The breeze felt refreshing as it blew a few of Fannie's *schtrubles* across her face.

Far away, they heard a low muffled sound of thunder. Noah peered through the trees as they approached the ridge, muttering under his breath.

"Don't worry about an inn, please. When I traveled alone from Berks County, I slept in the rain more than once. If we get wet, we'll dry out."

Noah smiled at her, flicking the reins across the horse's back, goading them forward a bit faster as another low muffled sound came from the distance.

The road wound in and out of the forest, the trees giving way to cleared land repeatedly, but always on a steady incline. The horses were tiring, their steps flagging, the neck reins stretched taut as their heads went lower, no longer held quite as high by their own accord.

The distant rumblings were no longer muffled but a solid, rolling sound, followed by thin, jagged appearances of bluish-white light. These were powerful storm clouds that could send balls of fire through buildings and light barns with their ferocity, a thing feared but not understood. Lightning was the power of God on full display.

The first raindrops that hit their faces were carried by powerful winds that swelled the canvas, whipped green leaves from thrashing tree branches, tossed the dusty roadside grasses, and flung the horses' manes and tails to the right.

The inn was nestled against a high bank of trees, built of solid gray limestone that had been carved and set, creating a building that would withstand the elements. The door was wide and thick, its boards painted a dark blue. The shutters beside each many-paned window looked like solid sentries, guarding the patrons within.

Noah pulled up to the door, leaped off the wagon, and went to the horses' heads without offering assistance to Hester or Fannie.

"Get inside. I will be in," was all he said.

Hester walked up to the inn, lifted the heavy, cast-iron latch, drew back the massive door, and stepped inside, her eyes lowered and her face averted as she kept a steady grip on Fannie's frail hand.

The interior was dim, cool, and smelled of strong drink and burned food. The odor was thick and stale, clinging to Hester like a sticky vapor, a cloying scent she could not dispel. She stood uncertainly, gasping slightly as her senses became accustomed to the stale air.

Immediately, a man came from behind the counter, a white dish towel tucked into the belt of his apron. He was about Hester's height, thick and muscular, with a mustache and a full beard covering most of his face, his small black eyes like two dark beetles.

"Yes, ma'am?"

"We're waiting for my brother. He's seeing to the horses."

"Oh, indeed. Indeed. Welcome. Welcome. You may be seated at any of these tables while you wait. May I bring you sustenance?"

Hester shook her head. "We'll wait."

Bowing deeply, the dishcloth lurching forward, he straightened and moved quickly behind the counter.

Curious stares directed their way made Hester uneasy. She longed for her big hat which she could pull forward, obscuring her face. She felt exposed since her muslin cap did nothing to hide her features, so she lowered her eyes, keeping her gaze directed on the tips of her shoes and the floor beyond.

Slowly the hush lessened, voices rose in their usual crescendo, and conversations resumed as the inn's customers lost interest. Hester was relieved when Noah appeared, his eyes sweeping the room with a practiced gaze before he dropped into a chair.

Blue lightning flashed against the windowpanes, followed by lashing rain and deep but muted growls of thunder. Candles were lit by long matches, the flames large and unsteady till they gained the full wick. Then they burned steadily, throwing a homey light across the greasy, smoke-filled room.

The bearded man hurried over, the two dark beetles glistening, his eyes small and close to his nose. But a friendly smile showed his teeth somewhere in the recesses of all his facial hair. "Yessir. How do you do, sir? I welcome you to Black Creek Inn. How may I be of service?"

Hester thought of Walter Trout, and a lump formed in her throat.

"We'd like two rooms for the night, please. And an evening meal as well." Noah had risen, extending a hand, a towering blond giant but given to a gentle demeanor, an air of kindness about him. He viewed the innkeeper with the same charity as he held for all the rest of the human race. Hester's breath caught, a sensation of love and admiration quickening her heart.

Of course, Noah held the innkeeper in high esteem. Condescension was not an attitude Noah practiced. He clearly thought well of the stranger and received his welcome with sincerity.

"Two rooms indeed, sir. And just in time, the weather affording you no welcome," the innkeeper said, indicating the violence of the storm with a wave of his hand.

Their food was brought by a comely young woman dressed in a manner that made Hester blush, her eyes on Noah as she served their supper. He remained as polite and kind as he had been to the innkeeper.

The heavy plates were heaped with roasted sausages, mounds of boiled potatoes and turnips, slices of summer squash and chunks of tomatoes and parsley. She brought glasses of dark frothy beer, which Noah asked to have replaced with hot tea and tumblers of water.

Fannie's eyes became big and round in the flickering candlelight as she eyed the mountain of food. Her cheeks were pink, her brown eyes full of light, as she dipped her head and put a hand to her mouth, trying to suppress a giggle.

Hester caught Noah's eyes, smiled, and leaned over. "Just eat what you can, Fannie."

And she did. She enjoyed a large portion of the potatoes and turnips, but only tasted the sausage delicately.

Hester found the food delicious. The sausages were browned to perfection, the potatoes creamy, the tomatoes rich and satisfying. The shoofly pie that followed the meal was heavy with the rich brown sugar and molasses concoction that made up the two-layered filling, all baked in a thick, flaky pie crust.

Noah ate two platefuls and three slices of pie with his tea. Hester finished her serving of food but felt overfull and uncomfortable after eating her piece of pie.

Outside the storm continued, a summer thunderstorm that would cleanse the whole countryside of the cloying heat and humidity. The inn seemed a haven now, a warm, dry place to be, the horses stabled and fed, the wagon pushed into a wide bay on the top floor of the bank barn.

Hester had never been served food at an inn. She had no idea how to go about ordering a meal or paying for it afterward. She had certainly never slept in an inn. She hoped the night would prove restful, imagining the misery of riding on the high seat of the spring wagon while sleepily clinging to the side of the seat.

"Would you like to retire to your rooms?" Noah asked after draining his tea.

"It's still early, isn't it?" Hester wondered.

"I'd say nightfall is only a few minutes away, although it's hard to tell on account of the storm."

"At any rate, I am tired, and I'm sure Fannie will be willing to lie down after the long ride."

Noah went to make arrangements, brought the valise from the wagon, and led the way up a steep narrow stairs that opened to a long hallway with closed doors along each side. Towards the back of the hall, he opened a door to the right, gave the candleholder to Hester, set the valise on the floor, and asked if she and Fannie needed anything else.

The wide, white bed shone like a beacon of rest; the washstand beside it held a large pitcher and bowl, along with clean white towels. Hester had all she needed. Weariness crept over her, a numbing sensation as she nodded, telling Noah that everything looked more than sufficient, and she was extremely grateful for these luxurious accommodations.

For a brief instant his eyes stayed on hers, containing all his love, his longing as well as restraint. In his kindness, he bid her a good night's rest before bending to take Fannie's hand in his and putting a hand to Hester's shoulder. Then he was gone, the door closing behind him with a soft click of the latch.

Hester and Fannie both fell sound asleep almost the minute their heads touched the pillows, the distant hum of the activity in the tavern below only a minor distraction.

The rain beat steadily on the good, sturdy roof as the storm stayed above the ridges and hills bordering Berks County. The moisture seeped into the soil, boosting the corn and hay crops, the gardens, and surrounding creeks and ponds. Frogs chugged in the bulrushes, the voice of the crickets stilled on this rainy night. When the storm passed, a thin half-moon shone weakly through the clouds, its silver light illuminating the darkness of the quiet inn tucked beneath the trees.

Hester was awakened by a soft mewling sound, piercing her senses with the force of a scream. At first she thought a kitten may have found its way into the room. She got fully awake when she realized that Fannie was crying soft, muffled sobs, restrained by a hand across her mouth. She had drawn her knees up to her chin, a thin coil of humanity, obviously suffering some pain or loss, and perhaps both.

Hester rolled over and gathered Fannie into her arms, holding her as she smoothed her hands down the back of her linen nightgown.

"Fannie, please don't cry. What is wrong? Shh. Don't cry." The sobs increased until the small body shook so violently, that her teeth chattered.

"Can you tell me?" Hester urged.

When no words came, Hester began to hum, keeping up the soft stroking. Almost immediately the shaking subsided and the sobbing slowed, then stopped. An occasional sniff, a whimper, and then Fannie's deep breathing continued. Her coiled body relaxed as sleep overcame her, as if nothing had happened.

Hester released her, sighed, burrowed into the pillow, and fell into the sleep of a child, untroubled, resting completely.

In the morning, Fannie was bright-eyed, fully awake, eager to get on with the day.

When Hester inquired about her misery during the night, Fannie's large brown eyes met hers, deadpan, owllike. She spoke with the same wisdom she had displayed before. "I was crying because thinking of Ammon gave me an ache in my throat. He would have liked to have one of my sausages."

Quickly, Hester was at her side, hunkered down, looking into her eyes as Fannie sat on a stool, tying her apron. "Fannie, we want you to be truthful. If you want to return, we'll take you back. You know that."

Fannie held very still, her head tilted to one side. "No, I can't go back. There's no room for me there. They don't always have enough to eat."

She stopped and spread her hands, palms up. "And my mam doesn't care for me much."

Instantly, Hester assured her of her mother's love, but was stopped halfway by Fannie's quiet, "Stop that. You know it's not true. I'm eleven years old. I should know by now."

Then she paused, before deciding to continue. "What would be the difference, do you think? A mother finding you at a spring, or a *maud* asking to have a half-grown girl?"

"Oh, Fannie," Hester cried, throwing her arms around the small frame and holding her close. "None. There is no difference. If you want me to be your mother, then that is exactly who I will be. I will take you as my own foundling, just as Kate took me."

Fannie sighed, then pulled back to look into Hester's eyes with a direct gaze. "Well, then. Now I will never cry at night again."

But Hester cried then, while she combed her hair and braided Fannie's. A fountain of tears welled up and ran over, a seemingly unstoppable flow, like an artesian well of more minute volume. Quietly she wiped them away, and quietly they continued to fall.

Noah was alarmed at the emotional display of tears, but Hester whispered to him on tiptoe, close to his ear, that she was quite all right and that she would tell him the reason for her tears when they were alone. His arm gathered her close for a stolen instant and he left, satisfied with her answer.

Hester decided that morning that Fannie was sent into their lives for a purpose. Perhaps it was for a small reason, if providing a home, love, stability were small things. God directed lives for a reason, and here was the miracle of Kate's large heart, with her never-ending kindness passed to her son, the love of her little foundling's life, and now a haven for one unwanted little girl. Love was the chain that threaded through the generations.

Each link added was a golden one, enriching the lives of families like a beautiful gem, passed on to the next generation.

The morning was what Hester imagined a portion of paradise to be. The air was achingly clear. Freshly washed grasses and leaves held drops of diamonds glittering on their backs. The woods were alive with a choir of birds, trilling the jubilance of the morning, glad to welcome the arrival of a brand new day.

In the early evening, Hester had recognized landmarks, forests, the rolling of the land. In the golden light, they entered the Amish settlement by way of Berksville. They passed the school and then Amos Ebersole's farm.

Hester gripped the seat. Her throat worked.

The horses trotted gaily, the harnesses tapping out a rhythm. Every hoofbeat was the echo of her heartbeat, timing the minutes. She had forgotten the blue of the mountain, the vibrant green of the ridges, how rolling and magnificent the undulating landscape.

There was the grove of birch trees. There, the great white sycamore. The ache of coming home was a weight in her chest. She put up a hand to still the tumult there, as if she could quiet the emotion that threatened to spill over.

Noah watched her face. "Another mile and we'll be home."

Hester nodded as her throat constricted.

The road had been packed down, graded, and widened, becoming a good serviceable one. Hester noted the new fields, where someone—maybe Hans?—had cleared more of the forest.

And then the farm itself came into view as they rounded the final bend.

The house had not changed, the stone still as she remembered it. The barn, however, was painted white, with a new addition, judging by the still-yellow lumber. There was a new corncrib and a wagon shed.

The pasture was dotted with black and white Holsteins, the cows she could remember milking. The fences were in good repair, the maple trees, one on each side of the house, trimmed and healthy. So Hans and Annie had continued to prosper. The children who remained at home were taught well in the ways of farm management.

This was home, Hester thought. This farm is my home. Why, then, did the surrounding hills and forests bring more emotion than this homestead? Too many thoughts fought for control. Too many bad memories suppressed what she might have felt—true happiness upon returning to this childhood home.

When the horses came to a stop, real fear pervaded her soul. She was rooted to the seat, her eyes wild with the rush of all she recalled.

Noah's eyes questioned her. "Would you rather go with me to the barn first?" he asked.

Hester nodded. It was all she could do to keep her teeth from clacking against each other. She folded her hands in her lap to still their trembling.

"No one seems to be home," he stated.

She searched his face for signs of the anxiety she was experiencing, but if he felt any, he did not give himself away. He merely sat solidly, his eyes searching for signs of life from within before telling the horses to go, heading them to the barn.

They came to a stop at the forebay, the wide empty area containing the stone trough and harness racks. Noah leaped down, threw the reins across the horses' backs, and was turning to help Hester down, when a door banged open. Footsteps pounded across the yard, and a grown man, whom Hester could not name, came running, out of breath, his face wreathed in welcoming smiles, clearly delighted to see his big brother Noah.

"Noah!"

"Solomon! Sollie, old boy!"

Hester grimaced as she watched the energetic pumping of their handshake.

"How are you, old chap? *Eye due lieva, mon*, you're riding in style." Solomon gave a low whistle as he circled the black horses, his practiced eye taking in the horses' deep chests, their long muscular legs, the fact that they were barely out of breath after their long run.

"Let me help you wash them down."

He noticed Hester and Fannie then, and stopped in his tracks, a comical expression crossing his face.

"Who do you have with you? Are you? Wait a minute. It's Hester. Hester, is it really you?"

Noah helped her down and Hester stood, her knees so weak she was afraid she would crumble onto the hard packed dirt.

"It's me," was all she was capable of saying.

Solomon came to Hester, his eyes as blue as Noah's, and bent over her hand, shaking it warmly in the old traditional manner. "Welcome home, Hester, welcome back to Berks County. But I don't understand. How did Noah find you? And who is this?"

Hester introduced Fannie Stoltzfus, an *au-gnomma Kind.*

Solomon nodded, then reached up to help her down. Fannie came to Hester's side immediately, shrinking against her when Hester reached to draw her close.

"How is Dat? And Annie?" Noah asked.

"Oh, they are both poorly. You heard, didn't you? Isn't that why you came?"

"We know nothing about our parents."

"You don't? I find that rather hard to believe."

Solomon kept talking as he helped Noah unhitch, telling them of Hans losing his strength, his weight plummeting, his being wracked by constant stomach pain. Annie was stronger but a victim of the palsy, the only thing the doctors could find to explain her constant shaking.

"Where is everyone?"

"Oh, they don't live here. My wife, Magdalena, and I and our two children have taken over the farm."

"Where are our parents?"

"They live about half a mile out the road. Only Barbara, Menno, and Emma are at home. Daniel is newly married and moved to his wife's brother's farm, and John, well, John ran off with an *Englischer.* He was always the wild one. Lissie's married."

"And what's Emma doing?" Hester asked.

"She's at home and going to school."

"What about Theodore and Lissie?" she asked.

"They're both well. Still living in Lissie's house and tutoring pupils. She quilts, helping out whenever there's a need, but she's aging. They're both a great influence on the community with their unselfish ways."

The horses were stabled and fed a good portion of oats and hay. Noah put his hand on Hester's elbow, and together they went to the house, where they were greeted by a tall, thin, young woman with a friendly smile of welcome, her face round and pleasant, with interested brown eyes that held no suspicion or animosity.

Hester held her hand warmly, glad to meet her first sister-in-law. She followed Magdalena through the house, guided by her memories, the house so much the way she remembered and yet so different.

The kitchen was the same, large and pleasant, the crackling fire on the hearth absent, the fireplace cleaned, brushed, and scrubbed, waiting for the cool nights of autumn. Most of the cooking was done on the stove now, although in summer they'd sometimes build a quick fire just for mealtimes.

Magdalena's furniture took the place of Hans and Annie's well-built cupboards and rocking chairs, making the place appear new. The walls had been whitewashed recently. There were new curtains in the windows. Rag rugs in brilliant colors added sunshine to the otherwise dull floors.

It was a good, substantial house, the house Hans, Noah, and Isaac had built, the product of months of back-breaking labor. It was a monument of hard work, good management, planning, and forethought—the closets, the wall space with hidden nooks that were used for storage, the root cellar, the well-built fireplace that rose all the way through the second story to the roof, with an enclave that housed red-hot coals to help heat the upstairs bedrooms in winter.

As Hester moved through the rooms of the house, she was wrapped snugly in nostalgia, a warmth of memories that flooded her soul. Here was where they sat to eat as a family, such as it was, after Kate's death. But it was home, and here is where she had felt secure, if not always loved. Home was a haven with a repetition of comforting daily duties, the days measured by their required tasks.

She suddenly recalled the routine of milking cows, the creamy milk directed into the tin pail, the froth building up the sides as the pail was filled, the handkerchief tied firmly across her forehead as she rested it on the cow's flank.

Breakfast was served on old homespun tablecloths of various hues. The menu was porridge, fried mush, and eggs in spring when they were plentiful. There was always good hot tea, freshly churned butter and bread, the family gathered together, their heads bowed in silent prayer, both before and after the meal.

Washing, bread-making, butter-churning, scouring, scrubbing, and cleaning filled the days. But there was always time to stop and soak up the birdsong, allowing it to elevate your spirits while pegging white sheets and tablecloths, and grabbing toddling little Menno by his suspenders and sitting him in the clothes basket made of reeds that Kate had woven together.

In the afternoon, when the weather was fine and Hans allowed it, Noah, Isaac, and Hester would race pell-mell to the creek with their homemade fishing poles and a can of fat, juicy earthworms they dug from the base of the manure pile. Yelling, racing each other, and sliding down the steep bank at the edges of the water, they'd dig around, come up with a round, wriggling worm, impale it on the cruel hook, then fling it out into the water, knowing where the fat, sleepy bass lay under a fallen log or tree root.

Hester could smell the filet of bass rolled in egg and cornmeal, then fried in sizzling lard in the two cast-iron skillets, sprinkled with salt, and fried to a golden crispy goodness. Hans always praised their ability to supply these wonderful portions for the dinner table. Or, he mostly praised Hester, the boys turning their faces to him, eager to absorb a few crumbs that might fall from the loaf he shared with his eyes on Hester's face. That was simply the way it was.

She had to give herself a mental shake, now, to pay attention to Magdalena's words as they moved from room to room. She had been nodding absently, her eyes taking in what she was showing her, but her thoughts lagged ten years behind.

"So, that's it," Magdalena was saying. "Oh, and you can just call me Lena. Everyone does."

She bent to pick up the baby from the large oak cradle, who yawned and stretched contentedly, his pink cheeks like patches of cherry blossoms.

"This is Hans," she said proudly.

"Oh, you've given him a namesake. That's nice."

"Yes, it is. He was pleased. That was one thing I told Solomon we should do, as it doesn't appear as if he will be gaining in health."

"Really?"

"He's not well. I'm afraid you will hardly recognize him."

Hester said nothing, her stomach immediately in knots of anxiety. She could not tell this loving woman about the fear that lay in her stomach like bile, the sour taste Hans brought to her mouth, the plague that sickened her soul. Tomorrow she would have to face him, look into his eyes, and wish him well.

Magdalena watched Hester's face with curiosity and benevolence, but no suspicion. How would she even understand? She could not know anything about the past, the unforgiven, the unforgivable sins of the fathers.

Hester froze when Magdalena said, unexpectedly, "Solomon told me about your leaving. He remembers the argument. He remembers Annie being cruel and threatening to burn your book. He told me much about your life here, Hester."

Hester kept her back turned as she fought to control her anger. She felt a soft hand on her shoulder and heard the words Magdalena said. They were kind words, encouraging ones, but they rained about her head with all the consolation of fiery darts.

Hester whirled and faced her sister-in-law, her eyes black with fury. Magdalena stepped back, clutching her baby tightly to her chest, her eyes wide with alarm.

"Yes, well, it's good of you to say all the right things. It's good of you to give Hans a namesake. But you didn't live through any of his slimy deceit, his lies. You were never splattered with the mud of his hypocrisy. You have no idea what I have to face tomorrow, so don't give me a package of smooth words," she hissed. Then, with a strangled cry, she disappeared through the back door of the kitchen, moving like a wraith across the backyard and into the woods.

Chapter 22

THE HEAT OF THE DAY CLUNG TO THE PALLID LEAVES, THE briars sagged with the weight of their own untrimmed growth, the earth was damp and verdant. Hester's steps were hampered by loose soil and the clawing of the thorns on the raspberry stems.

She swung her hands beside her skirt, raking back the briars, sliding back one step for every several steps she went forward. She had no idea where she was going; she was simply filled with the blind urge to get away from prying eyes and people who knew and remembered.

How could he? How could Solomon have told his wife? How many people had *she* told? Hester had always thought that her past, that pit of despair, the smudge of shame that lay on her face like a birthmark, was hers only. Not even Noah knew who he should blame nor could he comprehend her feeling of having been sullied, even if she never was physically.

Sobbing harsh sounds that ripped from her throat as she climbed up the ridges, her breath came in ragged gasps. She knew nothing but an urge to hide, to remain hidden. She could not face tomorrow.

The cliff was too high. Her strength to scale it was gone, taken away by remembering Hans.

Crowding out her sudden weakness was her desperate recognition that she had allowed herself to fall in love with Noah, when she should have known it could only turn out badly. He would forgive his father out of reverence for him. Noah was so good. He was kind like Kate. And here she was, born an Indian, with the proud blood of the Lenapes flowing through her veins. She would not bow to that man Hans, even if he was on his deathbed.

Here it was again. All her life she had tried to fit in, to be a white Amish woman, when all she was, all she ever would be, was an Indian, a red-skinned person of the earth who belonged to an entirely different culture.

She felt herself slip, then let go and fell to the ground, heaving sobs tearing from her throat, dry and hoarse, until she was spent.

She sat up when the light through the woods turned rosy, a covering of beauty she couldn't notice as her eyes swelled with the pain of her tears. She caught sight of the outcropping of limestone, her girlhood place of worship. Tears ran unchecked down her face as she rose and fought her way upward to the place of her youth.

When she finally reached the flat surface of rock, she saw, through streaming eyes, a heavenly vista before her—the late summer sunset a blaze of glory, painting the sky in magnificent shades of red, fiery orange, and yellow, fading into the restful hues of lavender and blue.

Berks County, her home, spread out before her, a land of rippling green, shades of blue, rivulets of black, sparkling with yellows and lighter greens. Below her lay the Amish settlement, the people she loved, remembered, and cherished.

But it wasn't enough. She could not forget the blood-red stain of Hans. She would have to give up and release Noah, release her love. It would never work.

With a groan, she flung herself down, shutting out the beauty of the evening. She closed her eyes, willing herself to keep them closed. She felt the need of prayer, of joining her thoughts to God.

God? Did she believe he cared about her at all? Here she was in this last hour, her life of happiness stretched before her, and she could not close the gap, she could not cross the bridge of forgiveness. Maybe, just maybe, she could try talking to the Great Spirit, the god of the Indians, her foreparents. Did he care?

Here on this rock she had found God. She had found him in the eagle's flight. She had taken God into her heart and fully realized that he was one with her own self. She would wait on him, she would renew her strength, she would run and not walk, she would rise up on the wings of an eagle.

But now she could not pray, so great was her inner battle. She lay face down and became quiet; deep in her soul, she became still and waited.

Her tears ceased and her heart slowed, as the warm breezes played with the high branches of the sycamore trees and spun the pine needles, wafting the sharp, gummy scent across her spent face. A chipmunk dashed across the edge of the rock, disappearing beneath a few brown weeds, their swaying the only sign he had been there.

When Hester heard the bird's cry, she waited, tensed, straining to hear. Surely it could not be. She sat up, held a hand to her forehead, straining her sight, searching. The sky was empty, a panorama of heavenly brilliance. She heard it once more. Twisting her back, she let her swollen eyes rake the sky.

Like a mirage to a man dying of thirst in a desert, the silhouette of an eagle, his wingspan magnificent, his white head visible, soared across the sky, followed immediately by his mate. Together they sailed their vast empire, the evening sky, floating on unseen pockets of air, swirling currents that carried them on the evening, slowly away from her and into the beauty of the sunset.

Hester stood then, tears coursing down her face. She lifted her arms, flinging them to the sun and the beauty of the pair of eagles. She called aloud, "Here I am, oh, my Father, my God."

He had sent not one, but two eagles, her symbol of strength.

She remained in that position until the eagles disappeared into the sunset. She slowly folded herself onto her knees as the sun slid behind the Berks County mountains.

Then, like the softest whisper, a mere stirring of her senses, she recognized her own lack of power. On her own strength, she was helpless to forgive, to forget, to love, to live triumphantly. She could not do it. But with God, the white Amish version of God or the Indian version of the Great Spirit, the God who created everything—the earth and its inhabitants—with him and in him, it was possible.

Unexpectedly, Hans became very small, a dot that was disintegrating fast, where before he had been a huge stain that kept her focused on her own self-loathing. Life before her was imperfect, filled with trials and troubles, but God within her was perfectly capable of renewing her strength each morning, every morning fresh and new.

And so she stayed on the rock, her tears slowing, her body and spirit both entering a place of tranquility.

In the sun's afterglow, in the golden evening light the shape of a white cross appeared, shimmered for a few seconds, and disappeared.

Had she imagined the cross? No, she couldn't have. It was the way of the cross that would lead her home. She was learning not to make herself the center of the world. Jesus would be her model, giving the ultimate sacrifice as he did.

"*Mein Yesu*," she murmured.

She heard the cracking of brush and tensed, remembering the youth who had slipped through the trees, watching her. The shadows were deepening and the woods were becoming dark, and still the cracking sound continued. Someone was coming up the ridge. She remained seated, listening, watching the treetops in the direction of the breaking brush and the scuffled leaves.

In the fading light, his blond head hatless, his eyes round with fear, Noah stood just below the rock, his face lifted, searching.

Ashamed, Hester remained seated, huddled in the safety of her own personal chapel. On he came, until he stepped to the base of the rock and caught sight of her. With a glad cry he moved swiftly. He stretched out his arms, but with a question in his eyes.

"Hester! I was sick with worry."

She gave him her hands, and he drew her to her feet. His eyes searched her face, taking in the swollen eyes, the tear stains, the emotional havoc on a face so beautiful. And yet fear kept him from taking her in his arms.

"What is it, Hester?"

She lowered her eyes, feeling guilty.

He put his hands on her shoulders and gave her a gentle shake. "Please tell me. Is it just too much, this returning to your home?"

Hester drew in a deep breath, then turned her head to look away from the searching eyes. "You'll think I'm *kindish*. Out of my mind."

"Never."

With a small cry, she flung herself into his arms, into the solid warmth of the man she loved. She wrapped her arms around him, clung to him, and buried her face in his chest. "I love you so much, Noah. I love you, I love you."

With a muffled cry he kissed her swollen eyes, the tearstained cheeks, her trembling mouth. He held her as he had never held her before with a newfound possession, gladness in having her, so afraid of this great love gone wrong.

Finally he let her go, searching her face in the fast ebbing twilight and asking if she was ready to tell him. Side by side, his arm around her waist, they sat as she talked in low words of her struggle.

He listened, rapt, as she spoke from the depth of her shame about feeling tainted, in spite of Hans never having touched her.

Noah's jaw tightened, the muscles in his cheeks moving rigidly. He nodded, mutely understanding, absorbing her misery.

She told him of the eagles and of God's message to her heart.

"Hester, do you believe God wants us to be together as man and wife?"

Suddenly Hester's shoulders began to shake. Thinking he had made her cry again, he quickly took back the question, stammering some nonsense about not meaning it.

But Hester was laughing. Great cleansing waves of merriment. "You never asked me," she chortled.

So he did. There, on Hester's rock, on the stone floor of her personal outdoor chapel, he asked her to be his wife, to walk beside him all the days of his life. He knew he was not worthy of her, but he hoped to love her and care for her as long as God gave each of them the breath of life.

Hester could only bow her head to absorb the beauty of his words.

Then she whispered, "Yes, Noah, I will marry you. With joy."

When they reached the house, Solomon and Lena showed their relief, visibly able to relax now that they had returned. Lena apologized effusively for having said the wrong thing and for hurting her feelings.

Fannie's eyes were large and so afraid that Hester went to her immediately, took her in her arms, and held her there, explaining that she needed to take care of some unfinished business in a place she had to go to. That seemed to be sufficient. She helped Fannie put on her nightgown and led her upstairs, tucked her into their bed, and said she'd be up soon.

"Poor little Fannie," she crooned, smoothing back the fine, brown hair. "I'm so sorry I left you like that."

But Fannie smiled and sighed, adjusting her head on the thick, goose-down pillow, already fading into the land of a child's dreams. "If I cry during the night, it's your fault, you know," she whispered.

Hester kissed her cheek, and tiptoed quietly down the stairs.

They told Solomon and Lena about their engagement, knowing the secret was safe with them.

Solomon whooped and shouted, saying he figured there was something going on, coming back like this out of the blue without telling anyone ahead of time. Lena smiled widely and congratulated them sincerely.

She served hot tea with sugar and milk, slabs of cold cornbread with honey, a bowl of purple grapes from the vines beside the garden, and slices of cheese with a bold, nutty flavor, the thick slices full of holes. Solomon said it was Swiss cheese from Ohio, made here in America now.

Far into the night, they talked of farms and land, the price of an acre here versus in Lancaster County, which was where so many were migrating and paying crazy high prices for smaller plots of land.

But the yield there is tremendous, Noah argued, although he couldn't imagine that the Amish could last very long in Lancaster. How could they keep their conservative ways while living so close to the worldly people—that whole hodgepodge of Irish and Lutherans and Dunkards and Germans—a vegetable soup of people.

"So why don't you buy land there?" Solomon asked.

"I like these ridges."

"It's my home. Our home," Hester said.

Solomon nodded. "Such as it was after Kate died. My mother. She was the best."

Noah nodded. "Remember how mad she used to get when we teased you, me and Isaac?"

"Your fault. You showed no mercy."

Noah's eyes became soft with the memory of Isaac. They talked of his death, of the fruitlessness of war. Noah thought that if life and love were somehow different, wars could be eliminated. But he supposed that as long as people had natures of greed, hate, and jealousy, there would be war. That led to a long discussion of whether there was ever a war that was right in God's eyes. Or should everyone be nonresistant, like the Amish and Mennonites?

"Isaac was nonresistant in his heart. He was much too gentle in his spirit to be a soldier. He should never have followed me. Or rather, I should not have gone in the first place. And yet it was a good experience. I learned and lived so much more than I would have, had I stayed home."

"Why did you go, anyway?" Solomon asked.

"Hans. And Hester leaving. Dat made me mad. I was wild inside. Rebellious. I didn't care if I lived or not. Reckless."

"Do you blame Dat still for Hester leaving?"

Silence hung over the kitchen, the only sound the ticking of the clock on the wall, the sleepy sounds of tired crickets, the shrill screech of cicadas.

"I did for a long time, but how can I still, if I say I have forgiven him for what he did?" Noah finally said.

"Things were never right between him and Annie, right?"

Noah shook his head. Hester lowered her eyes, keeping her gaze on her hands. Solomon and Lena exchanged meaningful glances.

Noah saved the conversation by saying, "She was plenty bossy, for someone accustomed to Kate."

Solomon nodded. "That's about right."

When morning came, with its special, sun-dappled light filtering in between the maple leaves, Hester was dressed and ready to go when Noah called for her at the doorway.

Her hair was combed neatly, the muslin cap pinned over it, the green of her dress bringing out the olive tones of her skin. Her eyes were still slightly puffy but clear, containing a new confidence. She held her head higher, she straightened her shoulders with new purpose.

Fannie wanted to stay with Lena and the babies, having taken to the toddler, Levi, immediately. Her natural love of infants and her sweet, unassuming ways captivated Lena, who was happy to have Fannie till Noah and Hester returned.

Noah looked at Hester and told her he had never seen her more beautiful. The green of her dress made her seem like a princess of the forest, stepping out from the trees.

Hester held his gaze, returning his love without a spoken word.

Every step of their walk was the old path to school, down past the barn, a left turn onto the road, through the woods, and past Amos Fisher's to school.

The morning was clear and already warm, the dust swirling at their feet. Dry, dusty grass waved in the summer air. A box turtle ambled across the road, heard their footsteps, and pulled himself into his shell.

Hester bent down the way she had always done, picked up the turtle, and carried him to safety by the side of the road.

Noah smiled. "He'll crawl right back, likely."

"No, he knows better."

They laughed, walking on until they came to a small clearing where a wood-sided house had been built by the side of the road, along with a barn and a few outbuildings. "This must be it," Noah said softly.

Hester's heart beat thickly in her ears, the blood pounding as she took a steadying breath, then another.

"You all right?" Noah asked, searching her face.

"Just frightened. Scared terrible," she whispered.

"Shall we turn back?"

"No."

A wide porch was built along the front. Firewood was stacked on one side of the door; a chair sat on the

other side. A rain barrel caught the water from the edge
of the porch. The house was small but substantial, built
by Hans, and sturdy. Each window was encased in heavy
trimwork, the door thick and solid. The yard was scythed
and raked, the fence around the garden well maintained.

Hester noticed the chicken coop, with the chickens contained inside the fencing, and thought of Amos
Stoltzfus's vicious hens.

She gripped Noah's hand for one last shoring up of
strength, then tilted her chin up, her eyes holding his.

Noah lifted his hand and knocked firmly.

After the second knock, the door was opened slowly
by a young woman, her eyes as blue as Noah's, her hair
streaked with blond, her face round and sweet—so like
Kate that Hester's breath caught in her throat.

"Hello. *Kommet rye.*"

She stepped back to allow them to enter.

"Emma?" Hester asked.

"Yes, I am Emma. But I don't know you."

"Hester. Remember your older sister?"

Emma shook her head, bewildered. She looked up at
Noah without recognition. Then she gasped and pointed
at him, saying, "Noah?"

Noah laughed and gripped her hand.

Emma led them to the right into a sitting room,
lighted well by two large windows. Hester immediately
recognized the rugs, the oak sideboard, and the armless
rocking chair, before she noticed the person lying on the
bed in the corner.

He was only a thin rail beneath a small blanket that
covered him from the waist down. A muslin nightshirt

was draped over his skeletal frame, his hair gray and matted to his head, the thick black beard now turned gray as well.

His face was white as parchment, his once full, robust cheeks hollow and sunken below prominent cheekbones, the full, protruding nose thin and beaklike. His eyes were closed, his bony hands resting on the top of the blanket.

"Dat is not doing good, as you can see. He sleeps a lot. The doctors have done all they can."

Hester was aware of someone at the doorway and turned to face her stepmother, the thin, cruel Annie of her past. She was thinner, even, than before, her dress hanging as if on a rack, the black apron circling her waist loosely, the gathers below the belt the only thing that kept her appearance from resembling a pole. Her face was drawn downward, as if the pull of gravity enabled her normal expression to appear more sullen than ever.

"Mam, Noah has come back!" Emma announced. But Annie had not heard. One hand went to the doorframe, another to her mouth. Her thin, claw-like fingers shook violently, her eyes wide, now, with fear. She pointed one unsteady finger at Hester. "You!" she spat.

Hester stood facing her stepmother squarely without alarm or shrinking. "Yes, it's me, Annie—Hester."

"What do you want here? Have you come to worry me with your Indian ways and your *hexarei*?"

"No."

Noah stepped forward.

"Annie, we have come to see our dat. We didn't know he was ill until Solomon and Lena told us."

"What do you care now? You left us to fend for ourselves. Why bother coming back now when he is too
weak to know you?"

"Mam," came the whisper from the bed. Then,
louder, "Mam."

Quickly Annie went to him, bending over her husband to catch every word. Her hands shook so violently
she could not lift the blanket to cover his hands. But
Hans had seen the two visitors. His black eyes, sunken
deep into his face, were large, alight, keen with interest
as he struggled to see them clearly.

"*Henn ma psuch*, Mam?" he whispered.

Annie nodded.

Noah stepped forward, went to his father's bedside,
and placed a strong hand on the shriveled, weak ones of
his father.

"It is me, Noah," he said.

Hester shrank back, the room spinning with her dizziness. From the bed, the dark eyes searched the face of
his son before Hans opened his mouth, trying to speak.
But the only sound was a dry, hacking sob, one harsh
intake of breath followed by another.

Hester had often heard Hans cry. He had cried loudly,
sobbing in despair when Kate passed away and crying
at little Rebecca's death, but never like this. It was the
crying of a man who was almost too weak to breathe, a
sound so pitiful it brought quick tears to Hester's eyes.

Hans lifted a thin hand. Noah took it, held it.

"Noah, *unser* Noah. Kate's and my Noah," he whispered. "*Ich bin so frowah.*"

That Hans was glad to see Noah was pitifully evident. He clung to his oldest son, his eyes alight with pleasure. He asked for more pillows, which Annie provided, putting him in a semi-seated position. His eyes found Hester. He blinked, then blinked again.

He relinquished his hold on Noah's hand and waved the hand weakly in Hester's direction. "Have you brought a wife, Noah?"

Hester stepped forward, buoyed by a calm that was not her own. "I am Hester."

Again, Hans's mouth opened, but he was soon wracked by fresh dry sobs, his eyes closing by the force of his sorrow. Over and over he raised his hand as if to speak, but the rasping sound continued.

Noah came to stand close to her, wanting to support her in the only way he could here in this room, with Annie like a specter of disapproval. Finally, Hans gathered some weakened control over himself.

"Ach, Hester, Hester, Hester. *Komm mol.*"

He waved a feeble hand. Hester caught it and held the hand as light as air.

"How I have prayed!" Hans gasped for breath. Annie rushed over, saying it was too much.

"No, no," Hans shook his head.

"God heard the prayers of a sick man. Over and over I prayed that you would come. Ach, my Hester. My *liebchen maedle.*"

He stopped and asked for water, which Annie supplied from the kitchen, holding the tumbler to his cracked, dry lips gently, as if for a child.

"*Danke*, Mam," Hans whispered.

As if the water revived him, Hans seemed to gather strength. "First of all, I owe you an apology. I am sorry, Hester. I was a man possessed by you. I allowed the natural affection of a father to turn into something that nearly destroyed me, my faith, you, and many more members of the family. You have suffered on my account, Hester. Annie has suffered. Noah. And my Isaac, gone to his eternal rest. Oh, how I hope he remembered his teaching."

Noah broke in. "He did Dat. He was saved at the end."

"*Preist Gott*. We are not worthy of such grace."

Hester lifted the black apron to find the white lawn handkerchief in her pocket, blew her nose gently, and dabbed at quiet tears.

"As I was saying, my unnatural affection, the lust of my heart, caused great hardship, and I have reaped many times over what I have sown. Isaac's death, your disappearance, Noah going to war, but worst of all, the ferment of my own conscience. I begged God to forgive me day and night, yet I found no peace. I felt I had to make it right with you, my dear Hester. I know I am lower than the worms that burrow below the earth's surface and do not deserve to be forgiven. If anyone ever deserves to burn in hell for all eternity, I do. Will you try, at least sometime in your life, if not now, to forgive me? I know I'm asking for more than you can ever grant me."

By now Hester was crying freely, her lower lip caught between her teeth, the lawn handkerchief catching the tears that welled up and spilled over. It was the pure, jeweled releasing of a festering sore, finally opened and beginning to heal by the miraculous hand that healed so many people before.

She stepped up and bent over his hands as she caught them in both of hers. She spoke clearly in her low voice. "I forgive you, Dat."

For a long time the only sound in the room was the awful, dry sobs, the sound of a broken man, crushed to bits by his own failure, completely repentant, honest, and finished. Annie blinked repeatedly, pursed her lips, scowled, and made all manner of strange faces to keep her tears hidden. Emma merely stood at the foot of her father's bed, sniffed occasionally, and wiped her eyes with the back of her hand. She was a child and could not grasp the full impact of her father's confession.

When the sound of his crying ceased, he drew a deep, ragged breath and spoke again. "I won't be here long, so let me say this. To make restitution, Noah, you shall have two hundred acres to the south. It is all surveyed and posted. I am leaving you five thousand dollars to build on the land. That is my wish. Solomon has the home farm. Daniel and John will also inherit land."

Suddenly, he smiled. "But Menno, I'm afraid, won't require land. He has inherited my love of horseshoeing. So be it."

Instantly Hester was at his bedside again. "Oh, Dat, I have many good memories of going with you on the spring wagon, shoeing horses. Those were the best years of my life. I do thank you for allowing me to go."

Those words brought another smile and a new light in his eyes. But he was tired out, completely exhausted by the force of his confession. Before anyone could say anything more, he was asleep, breathing slowly but deeply.

Noah turned to Hester, took her hands, and held them, as Annie watched with disapproving eyes, scowling, and pinching her lips.

"How do you feel, Hester?"

"As light as a feather. And very hungry."

Annie erased the scowl, led the way to the kitchen, and said stiffly, "Well, you should have said something."

"Oh, no. You shouldn't go to any trouble."

That was the way of tradition, the polite answer, but in truth, Hester was ravenous and unreasonably happy, her great burden lifted. She suddenly remembered Annie's baking, especially her molasses cakes, the oversized sugar cookies sprinkled with brown sugar, the huckleberry pie and butterscotch pudding drizzled with clabbered cream.

Annie spread snow-white tablecloths on the plank tabletop, turned, and said, "I just made a fresh molasses cake."

She scowled immediately after saying that as her hands shook fiercely. She made two or three attempts at placing the tablecloth, but so much had happened. At least she had made a molasses cake.

CHAPTER 23

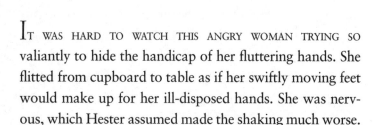

I<small>T</small> <small>WAS HARD TO WATCH THIS ANGRY WOMAN TRYING SO</small>
valiantly to hide the handicap of her fluttering hands. She
flitted from cupboard to table as if her swiftly moving feet
would make up for her ill-disposed hands. She was nervous, which Hester assumed made the shaking much worse.

The knife wobbled as she sliced through the perfect
layer cake. The tumblers clacked wildly as she brought
them to the table. She asked Emma to pour cold buttermilk, and Hester could easily see why. Annie would not
have been capable. Now, more than ever, Hester would
so have liked to try the Indian remedy for palsy of the
hands, but she chose not to speak of it.

While they were seated, there was a clatter on the
back porch and two more children burst through the
door, their faces red from exertion, their hair plastered
to their foreheads, perspiring freely.

"Barbara. Menno," Annie said sternly.

They stopped, two adolescents, the picture of good
health and vitality, smiles fading from their faces as they

struggled to recognize these people who were seated at the table.

Barbara's voice burst out, "Noah! Hester!"

Noah beamed, hugging his sister and then his brother. Hester gathered them into her arms immediately, laughing, teasing them, and saying they certainly hadn't grown up much at all.

They were both dark-haired and dark-eyed like Hans. They exuded the same ambition, the lust for life, the boundless energy, never quite able to sit still for any length of time. They were clearly delighted to have Noah and Hester here at the house and were soon swapping tales of childhood shenanigans.

"They're probably pretty much the same way we were, Hester," Noah laughed, punching Menno on his upper arm.

"I can't shoot a slingshot the way you could, Hester," Barbara said. "You killed the rooster once."

"Did I? Oh, I remember. I guess I did. Well, don't blame me. He had it coming. Roosters can't go through life flogging people!"

Noah laughed heartily. "That's not the only thing you shot. I still remember that rumor about the ghost in the hollow. I think you climbed a tree and shot Obadiah's hat off one morning on our way to school."

Hester's eyes danced. "You will never know, will you?"

Through all this banter Annie moved stiffly. She seemed determined to hide any show of interest in Hester and Noah, intent on heating water in the polished kettle, sweeping up a few crumbs, straightening the curtain by the dry sink. Hester watched, wishing there was a way of getting to know her better, a way of understanding her.

Annie moved fast, checking on Hans, going to the back door to pull the latch, and back to the stove. Then she was again at the dry sink, always with her mouth pulled down in a perpetual scowl, a sort of repressed, upside-down smile.

Was her life a bitter potion? After Hester left, had Hans loved her? Had he been good to her?

A sudden pity welled up in Hester. Surely Annie had some reason to be so hard-hearted. The cruelty Hester remembered had bordered on uncontrollable surges of anger. Only after she had demeaned Hester to a mere scrap heap would she let go of her taunting.

Now that all this time had passed without Hester in her life, had she, too, felt badly, perhaps remembering the unfairness of her hatred? Or was this woman simply not aware of having done anything wrong?

It was when Annie dropped the butter dish that Hester's pity became real and deep. She determined within herself to find some way of tunneling into her good graces, if any such thing existed.

She watched Annie bend to retrieve the broken butter dish piece by piece, her hands shaking so badly Hester felt sure she would cut herself. When she offered to help, getting down on her knees, she was elbowed aside so rudely she was almost knocked on her backside.

Embarrassed, she straightened and went back to her chair. Noah caught her eye and winked, smiling widely. *Some things never change*, he mouthed.

Hester sat up to the table, aware of the flush stealing across her face. As Noah kept up a lively conversation with his siblings, Hester remained quiet, watching Annie's determination to hide any form of disability, her mouth drawn in concentration. She set her shoulders and worked stiffly and persistently, as if she, all by herself, could exert control over her shaking hands.

Hester got up, went over to the dry sink, asked Annie for a clean tea towel, and began to wipe dishes without saying anything further. Instantly Annie became terribly ill at ease. Her nose twitched, her mouth worked, her movements became so jerky that water from the dishpan splashed on the floor. She fought the tremors, but eventually, after repeatedly attempting to lift a heavy white plate from the slippery water, she clutched the edge of the sink and stood still until they passed. Then she turned, her tortured eyes sparking with animosity.

"I guess you came to dry dishes so you could see my *aylend*." Her words were quick, harsh, and as dry and scaly as a rattlesnake crawling over a rock at midday.

Hester felt herself shrink, an involuntary need to get away from the words that brought back memories of her overwhelming anger, the tongue-lashings she experienced as a girl. But now she was a woman. A person in her own right, who had been married, loved, and rejected, who worked among people in the world and knew a few things about life in general.

So she said, "That is not why I came to help you, Annie. I think you are managing very well with your difficulty."

"No, you don't."

Hester watched her ailing stepmother, saying nothing.

Annie clenched her hands as she stared out the window. Her words tumbled thick and fast, like quiet hisses from a swarm of angry wasps attacking Hester.

"You think you're so much better than me. You sailed through our house like some queen, swinging your hips at my Hans, you did. Your big eyes are so bold, and here he lies dying, apologizing for something you brought on yourself, you Indian. You never were anything, and you still aren't. I was glad when you left, glad."

Hester absorbed the viciousness of her words quietly. They were merely words, flung out by her mouth from the dark recesses of her heart.

Then Hester spoke. "Annie, you know as well as I do, that you are not speaking words of *wahrheit*. I did nothing to get any of this attention from my father."

Here Annie broke in. "He's not your father."

Hester turned to look at her stepmother, hoping to meet her eyes, to convey some sort of feeling. Annie presented her profile like a brick wall, and as impenetrable.

From the corner of her eye, Hester saw Noah herd his younger siblings out the door and thanked him silently.

"You are right, Annie. He is not my father. If he were, none of this would have happened."

"Yes, it would. You brought it on yourself."

Hester sighed. She polished a glass tumbler until her towel became stuck, then continued to twist it round and round, buying time, desperately seeking a response that was not an argument, a continued clash of senseless word-dueling.

"Annie, I don't believe I ever tried anything intentionally. Hans was a good father to me. I adored him as a child, as he loved and adored his wife. I had no idea there was anything amiss, growing up."

Here Annie snorted, a derisive, mocking assault. "You were dumb. Indians are. He married me merely to cover up his feeling for you. I saw it the first week of our marriage."

This silenced Hester. All too well, she remembered the tight-lipped Annie, the tension between Hans and his new bride, Annie's refusal to meet his eyes, her angry movements like a puppet on a string when she served him at the table. Yes, Hester had seen it, believing that their newlywed bliss had gone far wrong. But never once had she thought of herself as the cause.

Extending the olive branch of peace, Hester bowed to Annie the way Abraham of old bowed to his brother Lot, offering him the choice of the much better land. Hester conceded, allowing Annie her valued opinion.

"Yes, I was dumb, innocent, naive. All of that. Whether it was because I'm an Indian, I'm not sure. Perhaps it's just me being me. I never did very well at numbers and letters in school.

"But, Annie, you must believe me when I say I never did anything to intentionally come between you and Hans. I wanted a mother, someone like Kate."

When Annie turned her head, Hester met her eyes, completely unprepared for the raw pain and the bottomless vulnerability in this thin, spare woman. She saw only for a moment. Then Annie drew the curtain of anger, sparking a dangerous round.

"I'm not Kate," she spat.

Hester remained quiet, set down the polished glass, then picked up a fork and dried it.

Annie launched herself away from the dry sink with quick, staccato steps, marched through the kitchen, her shoulders stiff, her arms like pokers at her thin hips, and disappeared into the sick room to check on her husband.

When she returned, she sat at the table, her hands clenched in front of her, her head bent over them. "Come sit with me," she ground out.

Hester sat.

"All my life my father was cruel. Not just to me, but to everyone. The sting of the whip across my legs was nothing unusual. I needed it. I did most things wrong. I was the small, spindly one, the runt."

Here, Hester thought of Fannie.

"My father always had money. Our farm was well managed. Yet he gave me away to a family who needed a *maud*. A maid.

"Rebecca was a good enough stepmother, but I was not her child. I was on the outside looking in. She held the other children, kissed them. But she never touched me. My heart often hurt, but I found strength in anger. In not caring. I decided it wouldn't hurt me. I became strong. I never complained, I did my share of the work. I had it nice, really. *Ich hab es shay Kott.* Plenty to eat, clothes to wear.

"About five years after I entered *rumspringa*, I realized that I would likely not be chosen to marry. My face was plain. I was thin and already angry most of the time. I lacked charm. It was the other girls who smiled, laughed, spoke clearly, and won the attention of the boys at the hymn singings. One by one, my friends were all courting. And one by one, they were married."

Annie reached into her pocket, produced a spotless square of white linen, wiped her nose with a few swipes, sniffed, and returned it to her pocket. "When Hans asked for my hand at the age of thirty-nine, I was overcome with gratitude. I had returned to my family as a house-keeper, and since I was an adult, Dat could no longer ply that whip. So he used words, as hurtful as the slash of the leather thongs.

"Never once did I imagine I would become like my father. I had always imagined that I would be kind and loving to my children. I would never stoop so low as to lash out with words or a whip. So why did I?"

The kitchen was bright with the late morning sun-shine streaming through the windows, dust motes hover-ing on shafts of it, the polished floor gleaming where the light fell. The ornately carved clock on the wall ticked loudly. Somewhere, the pinging of heated and cooled metal sounded.

"Why did I?" Annie repeated.

Hester opened her mouth to answer, to tell her it was all right, to make her feel better in an urge to convey sympathy.

"I became my father."

Again, Hester took a breath, a soothing reply on her lips. Annie held up her hand.

"Don't. Let me finish. I married Hans with complete happiness. I loved him and looked forward to the time when I would be his wife in every sense of the word."

A long silence ensued, after which Annie lifted her head and met Hester's eyes, revealing another painful glimpse of those tortured eyes.

"He never touched me, Hester," she whispered, a ragged sound so pitiful, it shredded every ounce of painful memories in Hester.

"We lived under the same roof, sharing our meals and our bed as brother and sister. You are the only one who knows. Can you understand my frustration? Although I had no right. As I was treated cruelly, so I treated others. You especially. I hated you. I wanted you gone, out of my life. Away from Hans.

"When you left, he blamed me. He became like a man possessed. It was terrible to see. But life went on. Outwardly, we prospered. We acquired acreage. The crops did well. The children worked alongside us. Hans developed a distant fondness for me, his second wife. If it was all the love I would ever receive, it was enough. I stayed strong, bolstered by work and the harsh words that gave me my strength.

"Then, Hans's strength began to fail. Last July he began losing weight. The doctors tried everything. Bloodletting. Laudanum. All to no avail. He asked about you often, wondering if there was no word as to your whereabouts. These questions were always a dagger to my feelings, robbing me of the tiny smidgen of love I could glean from my husband.

"As he weakened, he became kind. He wanted me by his side. He often held my hand, caressing the back of it with his thumb as he spoke words of praise to me. He thanked me often for being a mother to his children, for being the good worker that I was. It filled my empty heart, this outpouring of his love, for that is what it was, a cup of sweet ambrosia to my scalded self."

Annie became quiet, her fluttering fingers placed in her lap. Once there was a derisive sound of laughter, a mocking note forged with the always present anger.

Suddenly she held up her hands like freckled claws, thin and bony, calloused by the hard labor that had always been her lot, the days of her life spent performing the menial tasks that kept the wheel of farm life smoothly oiled. "They look like the hands of a man."

Tentatively, her fingers went to her mouth.

"My thin, homely face has never been kissed, never." She shrugged, straightened her shoulders, and remarked, "It doesn't matter. It won't hurt me. Never did, never will."

Hester sat in her chair dumbfounded, stunned. In all her life, she had never seen such an example of lonely courage. How could she have known this hateful, cruel woman's deep well of unfulfilled love?

Hester stood, hesitated, then bent slowly to the thin, freckled face. Just before her lips touched the dry, papery skin, she whispered, "Now you have been kissed."

She folded the thin form gently against her breast, one hand stroking the cheek on the opposite side. "Annie, you have been in my life for a purpose. If I would not have left, I would never have met all the people I did, wouldn't have married William or been through so much of what God has given me."

When Annie's thin shoulders began to shake, warm, wet tears coursing down on her fingers, Hester's sob caught in her own throat. Oh, the pity of it.

Annie cried quietly. Then whispered, "*Ich vill au halta fa fagebniss.*"

Hester's throat was so constricted she could not speak for a moment, so she gathered Annie into another warm embrace and said softly, "I do forgive you, Annie. I do. I mean it with all my heart."

"*Denke.*"

The sun shone into the kitchen just as it always had. But now the walls, the floor, the oak table, everything seemed warmed by the presence of angels hovering just out of sight, hosts to the king of forgiveness, the one who gave his life for all of humankind's ills and iniquities. These angels sang the same chorus they always sing when there is redemption and forgiveness. On this day, two women, one so beautiful, the other so unattractive, both designed and created by God, and loved with the same love sent down through the ages, forgave each other.

Again, Annie said, "*Denke*, Hester."

Words were meaningless, unnecessary, with the aura of God's presence so near.

The comfortable silence was broken when Annie asked if there was anything between her and Noah. Hester blushed a deep, charming shade of red. She nodded.

"I thought there might be. Has he asked you yet?"

Hester nodded again.

Annie placed a hand on Hester's knee. "Could we have the wedding here?"

"Oh, Annie," Hester sighed, "That would be a dream come true. I would never be worthy. It would be wonderful, but you know, we have to wait till Noah sets a time."

"Yes, that is true. And we have to see how many days God will allow Hans to be with us."

As it was, Hans slipped away faster after finding peace in Hester's forgiveness. He shook his head, refusing food or water on the second day after their arrival. Often his weak, quavery voice could be heard breaking into an old German hymn, the words barely audible, the frail humming a continued version of the song in his heart.

It rained on the fourth day, a Saturday, a warm summer rain without thunder or lightning. A bank of clouds from the east had been ushered in by strong afternoon winds the day before. Hester woke to the sound of steady rain on the shake shingles, accompanied by a constant drip from the eaves. Low clouds scudded across the sky. Moisture in the form of warm raindrops replenished the good brown soil.

Noah said a rain like this so late in the summer was priceless. Menno looked up from his plate of fried eggs and toast and asked what that word meant.

"Without price. Worth a lot," Noah answered, taking a long drink from his teacup.

When Menno said he'd have a hard time bottling the stuff if he wanted to sell it, Noah choked on his tea, spluttered, and coughed, and carried on until Annie smiled along with everyone's laughter.

Till late afternoon, the rain was still coming down steadily, water splashing from the roof and ripping across the yard. Two white ducks waddled through the grass by the front porch, quacking happily, the short white feathers on their tails wagging with energy, their flat webbed feet slopping along from side to side.

Hester was shucking corn on the front porch, her strong brown hands ripping off the outer husks in two deft twists before breaking off the short stalk and chucking all of it in a reed basket. Her fingers brushed the silk absently, her mind wandering across the unbelievable events of the week.

She whispered a short prayer for wisdom and understanding, asking that she never judge anyone harshly, especially without knowing their upbringing. She looked up when Annie called her name softly.

"Hans is calling for Lissie and Solomon. You had best find Noah." Hester got up, brushing the corn silk from her apron, a question in her eyes. "Is he worse?"

Annie's lips quivered, but she only nodded.

Hester splashed through the rain down to the barn, the barn of her childhood, now enlarged with two different wings. The original cow stable and a small barnyard fence had been taken away and replaced by a larger stable. She found Noah brushing the workhorses, oiled harnesses on a heap beside him.

"Annie says Hans is calling for the children," she said quietly.

Lissie's arrival raised quite a stir, her being as noisy and opinionated as ever. Hester would not have recognized the round young woman had it not been for her strident voice and the take-charge way with which she burst into the house, followed by a passel of toddlers and little children.

Her husband, Elam, entered later, a beanpole of a man with a quiet, good nature, a patient man, happy to let his effusive wife be the center of everyone's attention.

Soloman and Lena arrived soon afterward, followed by Daniel and his new wife, a blond, trim beauty, with eyes so blue Hester found herself staring.

They all gathered by the bedside of their father who was slipping into eternity, drawn by the bands that tie us to the Heavenly Father, whose final call of death is feared by all mortals, but is sweet rest for those weary of life and suffering.

And Hans was weary. His dry, parched lips moved as he asked for Annie who sat by his side, his hand in both of hers. "Mam?" he whispered.

She bent low.

"I love you."

She nodded, pursing her lips in the old way to keep emotion in check.

"Noah?"

Quickly Noah went to his father.

"Ich segne dihr."

"Thank you for the blessing, Dat." Noah spoke thickly, as if he had to push the words past an obstruction.

Hans's breathing was so soft, so faint, that it was hard to tell if he was still with them. When he seemed to gather strength, his breathing becoming stronger, he raised one hand partway, only to let it fall. He sighed deeply and never breathed again.

Each member of the family mourned in their own way—with quiet reverence, a few audible sobs, and tears coursing down grieving faces. They placed his hands on his chest, closed his eyes and his mouth, then left Annie at his side as they filed into the large room to make plans for his funeral service, the burial, and whatever else needed to be attended to.

Neighbors, church members, and all other available members of the family showed up within a few hours. Some cleaned; many brought food, preparing for the days of mourning and burial. The women wore black short-gowns, capes, and aprons. They took over the kitchen, making meals for the family in mourning. Kindness and sympathy flowed freely through soft handshakes and shoulders gripped in empathy, all of it a wonderful way of uniting each person in the bonds of love.

When the rain stopped, the air felt fresh and new. Sunlight speckled the buggies, drawn by all the different horses as they trotted obediently in the funeral procession, driving through the woods to the fenced-in graveyard on the hill.

There, Hans was laid to rest beside Kate and little Rebecca in the soft moist soil of Berks County. The large group of family and friends was dressed all in black, their heads bent, softly weeping as the minister read the *lied*. When the prayer was said, the men held their wide-brimmed hats in their hands, their uncovered heads bent in reverence.

Later, after the graveside service, Noah stood with Hester, their heads bowed as silent tears flowed down their cheeks, at Kate's grave, the small, plain headstone of Catherine Zug, their dearly beloved mother. In blood for one; in spirit for the other. It was a moment Hester would cherish forever, this unspoken bond birthed by the single most loving person she and Noah had ever known. Her memory and the goodness of her spirit had helped Hester through countless times in her life when despair had threatened to sink her.

The rolling green hills of Berks County were still the same—gentle and lovely, a vibrant green refreshed by the rain. This was the place they had spent time together as children, dotted with homes and farms of the Amish. The forest continued to be tamed into submission, giving way to fields and roads, which crisscrossed the ridges and swamps. Here in this land of Pennsylvania with Noah by her side, Hester's life contained a sense of new promise, the possibility of a life fulfilled, until death would part them.

CHAPTER 24

IN EARLY NOVEMBER OF THAT YEAR, THE LEAVES WERE ALMOST all blown off their trees by the autumn blast that accompanied the changing temperatures. A few hardy brown ones still clung to the bare branches of the white oak trees. But most of the yellow, orange, and red of the brilliant fall foliage lay on the floor of the forest, curling and turning brown, compost for the thick bark to thrive on for yet another winter.

Chipmunks scurried frantically, gathering seeds and nuts. Their larger counterparts, the gray squirrels, chirred at them from their perches high in the branches. Raucous crows teetered on boughs too thin for their claws, their beaks open and giving vent to their haunting cries. Red-headed woodpeckers tapped busily at the bark of trees, their tongue slivers darting to catch the grubs and insects inside.

The bashful fawns still trailed along with their larger mothers, coming to the edge of the fields at twilight, their large sensitive ears held forward to catch every available sound.

Along the border of such a field two figures strolled hand in hand, the muslin cap on the woman's head in stark relief against the surrounding trees. The man wore a yellow straw hat, his white shirt front visible between the black coat front on either side. The woman's shawl was pinned securely, its corners waving in the evening breeze.

Noah stopped, held both arms out pointing east and west, his eyebrows raised as he asked Hester what she thought of having the house built facing south, with the forest hill to the north behind it. Hester asked how she would ever see a sunrise if they did that. Why not face the east?

"And catch all the rain and snows?" Noah countered.

"What about a porch?" Hester proposed.

And so they bantered, planned, and dreamed, until Noah caught her up in his arms and told her he was marrying one of the bossiest women he knew, and Hester kissed him solidly to hush him up.

Hester felt a new freedom these days. She had been released from the troubling past, a blessing that was like the mighty flow of a waterfall, as unstoppable and as inspiring. With forgiveness came closure, bringing days of bright energy, a new spring to her step, a sense of purpose and fulfillment.

They had settled temporarily into the large stone house with Fannie, who had become fast friends with Barbara. They roamed the hills and fields of the Zug farm, trained the stubborn ponies, played church with the barn cats, and walked to school with Emma. It was as if little, deprived Fannie had never known another life. She bloomed like a wan flower, the sunshine and rain of the whole family's love allowing her to grow in ways no one had thought possible.

She even asked for a slice of cake, another molasses cookie, or a second cup of buttermilk, please. Every day brought a wealth of discovery as she saw the world around her through her friend Barbara's eyes.

Hester and Noah made a quick trip back to Lancaster to attend the wedding of Levi Buehler and Barbara King, a solemn affair that was held at the Buehler farm. The place had been painted, raked, cleaned, and trimmed until it was no longer recognizable. The hounds were now housed in their designated area, the chickens were cooped in their own yard, and there was the beginning of a profitable sheep industry. A flock dotted the green hillsides like balls of cotton.

Hester sat demurely, her head bent, her eyelashes brushing her cheeks, the twinkle in her eye completely controlled as the minister asked Barbara the usual wedding vows in German, and she answered in a less than humble—actually quite strident—"Ya."

After the service and seated at the wedding table, the place of her dreams, Bappie radiated an inner loveliness. Everyone agreed they had never thought of her as attractive, but that purple dress with her red hair gave her quite a shine, didn't it? Bappie and Levi ate their *roasht*, mashed potatoes, and the cooked slaw hungrily, enjoying every morsel of the wedding dinner.

Bappie opened her gifts, becoming quite boisterous when she received a set of green dishes from her Aunt Barbara, a namesake gift that far surpassed anything she had ever owned.

When she finally had a few moments with Hester, she gripped her hands and told her meaningfully that this was, without a doubt, the best day of her life, and did she see Levi's new hat? Whereupon, she opened her mouth and laughed in a most raucous manner. Hester joined in, thankful that Bappie had not changed at all.

While in Lancaster, Noah and Hester visited Walter and Emma Trout and Billy, who had arrived home a few weeks before. They left for Berks County that afternoon, full of hopes and plans for their own wedding.

Annie stood at the door of the stone farmhouse, shading her eyes from the glare of the evening sun, watching the advance of the two matched horses pulling the carriage behind them. The expression in her eyes was unfathomable. The Annie of old had changed in subtle ways, not yet noticed by anyone except the couple who was now approaching. A strange thrill, a sort of renewal, surged through her body.

Here was this couple, her children, brother and sister, and she was their mother. Anticipation beat happily in her breast as she looked forward to the responsibility of making a wedding for them as she had done for Lissie.

Hadn't that been a time of battles lost and won, though? Lissie is so powerful in words with a will of iron, and she is the same. Shameful. Absolutely shameful the way it went. But that was long before the time

Annie had spent with Hester, telling her of the dark past. Embarrassing the way she had told her so much.

Annie shrugged her shoulders, lowered her hand, and went to meet Noah and Hester, an unaccustomed gladness welling in her heart. As she neared the buggy, she hesitated. Would it be the same? Would they have discussed her and decided that none of that scene in the kitchen meant anything?

So she stood, her hands held loosely at her side, her back stiff and unbending. She had put on her usual scowl and wore it firmly, the armor that protected anything soft or insecure within.

But here was Hester now, her arms wide as she walked towards her, a gladness softening the black depths of her large eyes. Annie surrendered to the embrace, then stepped back with a soft, wobbly smile and examined Hester's eyes to make sure this was real and not some false follow-up to make her feel all right. For Annie was now a fledgling, a baby sparrow dependent on the food of love that Hester and Noah would continue to bring her. On her own, the old wounds and the anger that made them bearable would return, leaving her to starve, unable to grow.

Such a long and painful past could not be erased in one day. But with each day of their presence, and unknown to Noah or Hester, Annie received the bits of sustenance she needed. Mostly it was little things. Acts of unselfishness and kindness. Annie had never known kindness to have such an impact on her days.

Hester had brought a wrapped parcel, the brown paper tied securely with string. She handed it to her with a smile, her soft eyes shining.

Annie's hands began to shake, in spite of clenching her teeth, as she went to the cupboard for a scissors. Self-conscious now, she shook more until she dropped the scissors, which clattered loudly to the floor. "Ach," she said, impatient.

"I'll open it if it's all right," Hester said.

When the string was undone and the brown wrapping paper fell away, she saw four yards of beautiful blue fabric for a new Sunday dress.

"Why would you waste your money on an old ugly lady?" Annie croaked, emotion like sandpaper in her throat.

"Oh, Annie, it's the color of my wedding dress! You are the mother of the bride, so you and I will wear the same fabric."

"Ach." Annie held her mouth in a straight line, blinked furiously, and looked at Noah to avoid Hester's eyes. Then not knowing what else to say to hide her well-spring of pleasure, she scolded, "It's unnecessary. Too much money spent."

"Not for the mother of the bride, Annie . . . Mam," Noah said softly.

For Fannie, Barbara, and Emma, there was another large piece of blue fabric, along with yardage of black for their aprons. Peppermint candies were hidden in the folds, which created shrieks of excitement, a wild elation as the three girls scrambled onto the kitchen floor to retrieve them.

Hester watched Fannie, her cheeks pink, her large brown eyes alight with the joy of living, her dress stretched taut across her shoulders, which could not have been called thin any longer. Even her brown hair seemed to have thickened and taken on a luster. Her teeth had whitened from being vigorously brushed with bicarbonate of soda. With Barbara and Emma on either side, they resembled a trio of sisters, eager to live life with the carefree abandon of children.

Only occasionally at night, Fannie would waken, crying softly to herself until Hester pulled her close. She'd smooth back the tendrils of hair moistened by her tears and let her cry for whatever reason. After Fannie felt Hester's arms about her, she would become calm, a deep cleansing sigh would finish the tears, and she'd fall into a deep sleep.

Who could tell the loneliness of this little person? In a sense, she had been an orphan in a family of thirteen children, her parents mere shadows that passed over her.

And so wedding planning began in earnest.

Annie was a superb manager, saying, "First things first." The sewing would have to be taken care of immediately. They asked Magdalena to make the white shirts, as she was an accomplished shirt-maker. In the days following, they cut and sewed aprons, capes, dresses, and coverings in quick succession.

The date of the wedding was set for the thirteenth of November, too late, in Annie's opinion, but who had ever heard of getting ready for a wedding in less than a month? They even had to buy the chickens from Enos Yoders. She had never heard of not raising your own for a wedding. But there was a smile lurking in her eyes, Hester could tell.

The acreage that Hans had given them was an undeserved gift, a glorious remembrance from an imperfect,
tortured man, who had lived out a terrible penance,
suffering because of his sins, but redeemed by the grace
of Christ. He had given the land out of his love and as
restitution.

The land included acres of beautiful forest, lush and
green in the summer, with brilliant foliage in the fall.
Now, with winter's beginning, the cold winds whipped
the trees, leaving them etched against the sky and surrounded by a carpet of curling, brown leaves. Although
the grasses were yellow and brown, they still held the
promise of a new life ahead.

Noah staked the house facing southeast, the way
Hester wanted. The barn was to the left and set against a
hill, which allowed access to the top floor. Wagons could
also be pulled onto the barn floor by a team of horses to
ease the unloading of hay and corn fodder.

They would leave a few oak trees to provide shade in
summer. The pastures would fall away below the barn
where the incline was gentle. The cow stable would be
on the underside of the barn. The stones that would be
laid would provide sturdy walls to keep the animals
warm in winter and cool in summer.

They would rent the small house on the Henry Ebersole place for the first year, while Noah built the house
and barn. With neighborhood frolics and the help of
their brothers, they should be able to move within the
year.

Hester did not want a house made of stone. Noah
planned on a stone house, but Hester had wonderful

memories of the little log house with Kate, her mam, the babies, the fire on the hearth, and she wanted only that for the rest of her life.

"A small house, Noah, for we will have only Fannie," she said, a hint of sadness passing over her eyes.

Noah had seen this and quickly gathered her in his arms, kissed the top of her head, and assured her that Fannie was all they would ever need. He was getting far more than he deserved by having the chance to be her husband, to care for her all the days of his life. If he never had children of his own, that was as the Lord wanted. Hester was a gift, and enough.

She had remained in his strong arms, tears wetting the front of his shirt. How could she ever live up to this kind man's expectations? She told him this, felt his chest rumble with laughter, and smiled through her tears when he told her she'd have plenty of opportunities to throw her shoes at him.

As the days of preparation went by, their love grew more steadfast, more deeply rooted in the admiration they had for each other. Hester never failed to notice Noah's many acts of selflessness, how he gave of himself, not just to her, but to everyone he met. Especially to Annie. He seemed to understand the wounds she hid away from them, her eagerness to maintain a stance of strength, when in reality it was only a mask, and an ill-fitting one at that. Often as the days went by, the mask slipped, giving them a glimpse of the Annie that was to come.

The barn cats had always been a source of irritation to her. Woe to the cat that attempted to rub itself against her wicker laundry basket. Always, the cat was booted out of her way, sent into the air with a swift kick, and a firm "*Katz*!" If Annie had her way—except for the necessary extermination of rats and mice—no cat would have been on the farm.

So now, when Hester rounded a corner of the house and found Annie at the washline, bent over tickling a startled cat's chin before trailing a gnarled, shaking hand the length of its silky back, she stopped and reversed her steps soundlessly. She knew that if Annie was exposed, she'd resume her old ways and kick the unsuspecting cat for the benefit of her pride.

There was also the Fannie surprise. Fannie had developed a firm hold on Annie's affections. To see them together was a heartwarming vision. Fannie still hummed or sang softly, the way she always had, but now, Annie would join while they did dishes together. Annie's rough, patchy baritone pitched in to join Fannie's high angelic notes. Annie always stopped when Hester walked into the room. But it was all right. It was good to know that Annie cared for Fannie, took her under her wing, and kept her there.

The matter of her shaking hands came to a head, like a sore and throbbing boil, one morning when the tea kettle fell out of her grip, splashing boiling water on the floor, across her skirt, and all over the stove, sending water sizzling onto the hot stones of the hearth. With all the gathers in her skirt and the added protection of a heavy apron, Annie was not scalded, only frightened into a lip-trembling silence.

Hester had been folding wash, and with a shriek of fear came to her side, her eyes wide. "Annie! Are you all right?"

Grimly, with her wet skirts held out and bent at the waist, Annie nodded.

"You must do something, Annie. You will hurt yourself even worse as time goes on," Hester pleaded. She handed her a towel, which Annie used vigorously, rubbing the wet spots on the front of her apron. She turned away to lift the long heavy skirt and check for burns, but said it was only enough to redden the skin.

"What? What should I do?" Annie asked desperately. "The doctors all say the same thing. They call it palsy of the hands, and there is nothing to do for it."

Quietly Hester whispered, "There is something,"

What passed between them could only be called painful, a humiliation that could be felt, a nearly physical force.

Who could forget the agony of the past? Forgiveness was one thing—over and done with. But to forget completely was another. In a flash, they each relived the roaring sound of Annie's hatred as she refused Hester's remedy for palsy, forbade her from making any more tinctures, and nearly succeeded in burning the book of remedies above open flames, the precious book containing all the knowledge of her ancestors. Had Hester not torn it from her hands, Annie would have destroyed the priceless gift Hester had been entrusted with. The whole scene sat between them, thick and cloying, threatening to choke the life out of the flower of their forgiveness.

Annie lowered her eyes and turned her head away.

Hester felt the sting of remembering.

Silence hung between them, dense with unspoken words that were too loaded with danger to be uttered. Hester almost turned away and left the room, leaving

Annie to the demons of her past. That one incident had been the most cruel, and now to open that old sore and review it again in the light of day was almost more than Hester could do. She was afraid to try, but she was just as frightened to forsake Annie now.

Hester went to Annie and got down on her knees by her side as she sat slumped in a kitchen chair. She reached out, took her hands, and held them softly. She could feel the tremors.

Annie did not pull away.

"Let me try," she said simply.

Annie kept her face averted. Her throat worked as she swallowed. Hester kept her peace, watching Annie's face. When the glimmer of a tear appeared on her lower lash and hung there, trembling, before slipping down her papery cheek, Hester still did not speak.

Finally, Annie said, "Don't make me remember this."

"We won't. We will not remember together."

"What will you do?"

"First of all, since it is November, I suppose we'll have to pay Theodore and Lissie Crane a visit. Does she still have her store of herbal plants?"

Annie nodded.

"Then come with me."

"Now?"

"Now. The work will wait."

"I'm too ashamed. Lissie Crane knows what I tried to do."

"Lissie will be too happy to see us. I have not had the reunion with them that I wanted. I could only barely acknowledge them at the funeral. They are so old."

Annie turned. Unexpectedly, a smile lit up her face. "Not old, if you listen to Lissie."

Hester laughed outright, imagining the hefty Lissie moving about her house like a ship in full sail. "Does she still glide like that? Sort of float along on her tiny feet?"

"Oh, yes. She gets around."

"Then let's go see her."

They bundled into their heavy black shawls and bonnets, hitched up the trusty brown driving horse, and rode through the blustery November winds. The road wound in and out of the forest, past Sam Ebersole's and Crist Fisher's, the scenery so familiar, so dear, so recognized, Hester mused.

This was home. These rolling hills and cleared acres. These skies that were blue, scudding with gray and white clouds, like layers of freshly shorn sheep's wool. The air was pure and unhurried, the farms familiar, the new dwellings signs of prosperity. The very air carried an aura of acceptance, the hills and trees receiving her, protecting her, bringing a sensation she knew meant belonging. This was where she was meant to be.

She was home. Home in Berks County, close to the grave where Kate lay, and soon to be married to her son, the incarnation of Kate herself. Hester had been raised in kindness, with the gentleness and good grace of Kate's heart, cared for by her soft hands.

Theodore opened the door, his long, thin face wreathed with delight. Lissie lumbered across the floor behind him, her hands extended. Hester laughed, then cried a little, finally sitting at their small table with Annie beside her. She marveled at the vast person Lissie had become. Marriage must have given her a good appetite, as she was quite a bit larger than Hester remembered. Theodore wasn't thin either. A good portion of his stomach overlapped his broadfall trousers.

Hester and Annie could not get a word in at all. Lissie's face became an alarming shade of red as she talked, moving from stove to table, bringing hot cups of tea "to warm them," she said, along with a whole pumpkin pie, plates, forks, tumblers of ice-cold water, soft cup cheese, and slices of bread.

"*Schmear Kase! Frisha schmear Kase*," she yelled in a stentorian voice, punctuated by Theodore's vigorous nodding and repeating, "*Frish, frish.*"

Annie's hands shook so badly that her teacup clattered against the saucer, almost upsetting it. Quickly, both hands went to her lap.

"So, a wedding, I hear. A *hochzeit! Ach, du lieber.* You and Noah? Who would have thought it, years ago? You and Noah and Isaac all running around, with Lissie trailing on behind like an unwanted pup."

Hester nodded, smiling, and helped herself to a slice of bread and fresh cup cheese, that soft, pungent, spreadable cheese made from squeaky milk curds.

Theodore told them of his life with Lissie, the years going by so fast. He worked at tutoring the hard learners while Lissie kept the house clean and warm and put food on the table. He reported experiencing contentment and happiness he had never thought possible. His story was heartwarming, but out of respect for Annie and her disappointments, Hester switched subjects as soon as possible, asking if Lissie had sage and mustard seed on hand, which led to Lissie lumbering off to her storeroom and returning with two tin canisters.

"Now you have to be careful with the sage. You don't want too much. It can give you a bilious stomach. Lots of gas and cramping."

"No, I won't need it to be taken as a medicine."

"Oh?" Lissie lifted her eyebrows, a pained expression along with them; her curiosity made her miserable. Hester gave nothing away. She knew keenly Annie's pride and her reluctance to admit her one weakness, no matter how laughably obvious it was.

She paid Lissie for both herbs, and they were on their way home as soon as they could untangle themselves from the web of Lissie's talk. It never stopped, following them out onto the porch, down the walkway, and into the buggy. She was still calling out words they couldn't hear after the horse pulled the buggy away from the hitching rack.

Hester shook her head, laughing. Annie smiled and said, "That would be awful to have all those unnecessary words tumbling about in your head."

But they both loved Lissie, so they said nothing further about her.

At home, Hester boiled the sage and mustard seed into a decoction, the smell of it permeating the entire house. Annie busied herself with the sewing, keeping her eyes averted and saying nothing. When the mixture had cooled sufficiently, Hester asked Annie to place her hands in the liquid while it was as hot as she could possibly stand it.

She said the words quietly, forming a question more than a command, knowing how very hard this was for Annie.

She said nothing. She just sat at the table with the shallow basin of hot water and placed both hands into it, her face expressionless. The steam from the decoction alarmed Hester, who watched for any sign of discomfort, but there was none, not even a mere knitting of her brows or a flinch.

They repeated this quite often during the day, always being careful to avoid being seen by Noah or the children, for on that first day, Annie's furtive glances gave away her wish for privacy. But over the next few days, after mentioning what they were doing to the rest of the family, Annie felt comfortable enough to remain seated, no matter who walked into the house.

The children wrinkled their noses at the smell but said nothing much about it. Noah knew how much the effort meant to Hester and praised her deftness, saying that if she could accomplish a healing for Annie, imagine where this might lead! Perhaps that was why she had never borne children, that God had other plans for her with this gift of healing.

Annie was discouraged on the third day when she dropped half the pumpkin pie, and the custard slopped down the side of the table. Hester thought she might not be willing to continue further treatment, but Annie said she'd keep going till after the wedding.

As time went on, Hester developed a deeper respect for Annie's tenacity and her ability to keep trying in the face of doubt.

She also knew what this cost Annie—her pride, her painful memory, her admission of wrongdoing. It was a huge order for someone who had been as injured as she had been.

Meanwhile, the wedding preparation work continued—the cleaning and whitewashing, the raking and window-washing. Even the barn windows were rubbed to a gleaming luster, the furniture waxed and polished.

The baking took days—the loaves of bread, trays of cookies, cakes made with walnuts and molasses, ginger cakes, and white cakes decorated with icing and dried cranberries.

Through all the days of preparation, a sense of happiness stayed with Hester. She wore her sense of belonging like a rose-colored dress, confident in the way she went about her tasks, addressing every person with love.

CHAPTER 25

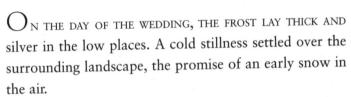

ON THE DAY OF THE WEDDING, THE FROST LAY THICK AND silver in the low places. A cold stillness settled over the surrounding landscape, the promise of an early snow in the air.

The sun melted away the frost on higher ground as the black buggies with brown horses hitched to them made their way to the Hans Zug farm. Excitement was in the air, everyone bathed and scrubbed and wearing their Sunday best, even if it was not the usual big event.

This wedding was not a full-sized, 200-guest wedding, customary for youthful couples. This was a widow marrying an older man, so there was no bridal party, no one to sit beside Noah and Hester.

Hester did not wear the customary white cape and apron, but black ones, signifying the fact that she had been married before. The blue dress she wore was a beautiful, tightly woven fabric, costing far above anything she had thought reasonable, but Noah insisted. It reminded him of the blue she wore when he met her and Bappie in the garden that day.

She had been a dream for him, belonging to his imagination and memory. But when she stood there, he knew his memory of her paled in comparison to the deep, black depth of her eyes, the deep, brown, toffee color of her skin, the blue sky matching the deeper blue of her dress.

If he lived to be a hundred, he would never be worthy of her, he said. Her beauty radiated from within. She was as sweet and unspoiled inside as she was beautiful on the outside.

Hester sat quietly and believed him, for that was how she felt about him. She would never tire of watching him move—the powerful swing of his shoulders, the height and breadth of him. Never had she imagined that the plane of someone's nose could thrill her. The way he talked, always with a half-smile of kindness and a chuckle at the end of so many of his words, belying a nature that was good.

Yes, they believed in love. In a love that could endure arguments and irritations, that was greater than trials and troubles. They had both come through so much and been blessed richly. Their forgiveness of each other was made sweeter as time went on. Now on this day, the love that was hampered in the past was given freedom to flow, a tumbling, rolling brook of purest water.

Annie had proved to be a capable manager, with everything listed and checked off as the days went by. On the *risht dawg*, the day of preparation, relatives and friends arrived early and plunged into the work, making the day festive with jokes and teasing, which was the custom.

It was Noah's job to behead the twenty plump chickens, safely housed in the coop. The fact that they had been bought was a well-kept secret. Enos Yoder pocketed the cash, his eyes twinkling, saying his lips were sealed.

First, the brothers hid Noah's hatchet. Six o'clock on the morning before his wedding, and Noah thought he had misplaced the carefully sharpened hatchet. He looked everywhere while the water bubbled away in the *eisa-kessle* and the *roasht-leid* arrived, and still he could not find the hatchet.

Hester had never seen her beloved Noah quite so rattled. She began to wonder if it was a bad omen, when she saw Solomon streak across the yard with Noah in pursuit, his powerful legs pumping. When he caught Solomon by the tail of his coat, he flung him to the ground and straddled him as Solomon screeched, "Uncle! Uncle!" The women clapped and cheered as Noah raised his fist, ready to pummel his brother, till in the knick of time, he yelled, "*Da cha shunk!*"

Noah released Solomon, ran off to the cupboard in the forebay of the barn, retrieved the hidden hatchet, and began to chop off the twenty chickens' heads, amid friendly ribbing from the *roasht-leid*.

That done, it was Noah and Hester's job to remove the clumps of celery, banked in long lines of raked-up soil, and bring them to the *kesslehaus* to be washed and sorted.

Alone in the garden, the cold, still air around them alive with the magic of the *risht dawg*, they worked in the freezing air, stealing kisses and laughing, the wedding day a beacon of joy over every task.

And so they were married in the great stone house Hans had built for Kate. Every piece of furniture had been stored in the shed to make way for hard, wooden benches, creating a wedding chapel, plain and austere, but warm with the love between them.

The service opened with the rousing German wedding song and closed with another song, also a traditional wedding hymn.

They stood side by side, Noah taller, his blond hair gleaming, cut and combed in the *Ordnung* of the Amish church. Much care and concern had been given by the church to this special day of being given in marriage.

Dressed in a snow-white shirt, black trousers, vest and *mutza*, he was indeed an *schöena bräutigam*, a young man who had waited longer than most to take a wife.

Beside him, Hester's beauty had never been more pronounced. Her face radiated true goodness from within, framed by the perfect line of her eyebrows, the perfect symmetry of dark lashes sweeping her golden cheeks.

They spoke their vows solemnly, as befitted the sobriety of the occasion. They never lifted their eyes or smiled until the last song had been sung. As the guests filed out, only then did they dare meet each other's eyes, speaking volumes to each other in their new freedom to love.

They said Annie smiled and laughed that day more than anyone could remember. And who was that young girl who sat with the bride and groom at their table?

Oh, that is Fannie Stoltzfus, others said.

Selly glay Fannie. Ach, ya. The women nodded, shaking their heads. That was the way of it, then. Her parents' house was full with too many mouths to feed, *arme leit,* yes, yes. She'll have a good home with *Hansa ihr Noahs.* But isn't it something how these two got together? Raised in the same house.

And so the day brought them many blessings, well-wishers, folks who wanted them to have a long and happy married life. And wasn't it so nice they had an *au-gnomma kind. Selly glay Fannie, gel?*

They praised the cakes, made a fuss about the cookies, said that Annie was something, now wasn't she? They shed tears thinking of Hans, barely cold in his grave, and here his son went getting married without him.

Only Lissie, Theodore's wife, had the nerve to say what many of them were thinking.

"It's a good thing," she said, her words clipped with disdain. Then she stretched her neck, her large head swiveling, and asked why it took the *freundshaft so hesslich* long to eat. She was hungry for *roasht.*

"Don't they know there are people here who didn't eat yet? Likely that ginger cake with brown sugar frosting will be gone till I get there."

She sat up straighter, her beady eyes peering worriedly from rolls of flesh. "Look at that Annie. She seems like another person. Laughs all day."

"Not all day," Elam Fisher sei Rachel said sourly.

Lissie turned to look at her. "You're hungry, too."

At dusk, the last buggy wound its way down the curving driveway. This had been a small wedding, so no evening meal was served, and there was no singing far into the night.

Annie, of course, was in the kitchen washing dishes. Solomon sat on a bench enjoying one last cup of coffee while Magdalena finished a slice of walnut cake.

The children were playing tag, dashing between the benches, fueled on an endless supply of cake and cookies. Daniel broke into song, his voice strong as he climbed the notes.

They cleared benches from the kitchen, then brought in the table and the cupboard. Annie said it was quite enough, they would be back the following day to clean up. She sat with them then, poured herself a cup of coffee, and talked about their day. Noah and Hester joined them, both radiant.

"We want to thank everyone for what you did, helping us prepare for our special day. We really appreciate it," Noah said.

Solomon waved a hand in dismissal. "It was nothing."

They had decided to spend the night together in the small rental house, and because it was a still, frosty evening, they walked.

Fannie stayed with Barbara and Emma, although Hester had warned them that sometimes she cried at night. They took this very seriously and promised to be very careful with her.

The night was dark with no moon. Only an occasional star shone from the black night sky. The silhouettes of the stark, leafless trees were even blacker, the road barely discernible.

Close by, an owl hooted its ghostly sound. The screech of a nighthawk followed, then another more drawn out one.

There was no need for words.

Both of them walked in perfect comfort, grateful for the holy moment. God had led them together, and now he was here to guide them, to give them strength, and to see them home by his grace.

Noah took her hand in his. "My wife, my love," he said.

"My husband, my love," she answered, releasing his hand to step into the circle of his arms.

Freed from the pain and confusion of her past, shedding it along with Noah's rebellion toward his now deceased father and the bitter Annie of his youth, their love was like a tropical flower, opening to the wonders of soft warm rains and brilliant sunshine.

After all they'd been through, neither one of them took their union for granted. As they continued their walk through the still night air, they talked of the times when they were apart, the times they suffered, missing their old home here in Berks County.

Hester told Noah that she had come home now. "This is my home, Noah. This place on earth is mine to call home. You are my home, my dearest husband. I love you for all time, here in these hills of my childhood."

The kiss they shared as husband and wife was sacred.

Annie's hands healed to a degree, enough that she was able to perform duties she had no longer been able to accomplish. She continued the treatment all winter, often thanking Hester quietly, with a touch of shame.

Noah and Hester brought Fannie to live with them in the cozy little rental house. She walked to school with Barbara and Emma every day, the same route Hester, Lissie, Noah, and Isaac had walked a generation before.

Fannie swung her little tin lunch pail as she ran to meet them in the morning, dressed warmly in her black coat, shawl, and bonnet, sturdy boots on her feet.

Hester spent her days arranging her furniture in the small, cozy house, the fire burning cheerily on the hearth. She thought often of her wedding day, of Bappie's tears, her raucous congratulations, and more tears at her parting.

She fixed a small bed upstairs under the eaves for Fannie, making sure there were plenty of quilts and sheep's-wool comforters so she would never be cold. She cooked good, nutritious meals and packed her tin lunch pail with honey sandwiches, dried apples, cookies, and canned pears.

The snow came early that winter, hard, biting bits of ice that pinged against the windowpanes and piled around the south side of the house like sugar. Hester threw logs on the fire, cooked a bubbling beef stew, and felt fulfilled.

Only sometimes she'd sit on their bed, the soft ticking crackling beneath her, silently stroking the white quilt Annie had given them, gazing out the window, her eyes seeing nothing. She would wonder, if only for a minute, how it would feel to be able to tell Noah they would soon have a child of their own.

Then she would turn away, scolding herself. It was not to be. Hadn't she been grateful, God giving her far more than she deserved? Here she was with all this happiness, longing for a child. Then she would refuse to dwell on this one small spot in her heart that yearned for a little boy who looked just like his father. Fannie's presence helped immensely—her humming, the way she never wearied of schoolwork or of Barbara and Emma.

The farm became a reality. The barn was every bit as magnificent as Dan Stoltzfus's in Lancaster County. The house made of logs with a steeply pitched roof was a true Dutch dwelling with a spacious kitchen and clever little nooks hidden away, to store extra linens, bedding, and towels.

A year passed. A year of happiness with Noah a constant source of joy, his love never once disappointing her. He had a love for her that he nurtured every day, always concerned for her welfare and Fannie's.

Which came first, then? The nausea or Annie's marriage to the widower Elias Lapp? She could never quite remember.

All she knew was that she woke one morning and thought surely someone had cooked onions during the night. The house smelled awful, just awful. She fussed and fumed, opened widows, and still that evening something smelled in this house, she said.

When she staggered outside very early in the morning, gagging and making horrible noises, Noah became alarmed and rushed to her side. He was elbowed quite sharply in the ribs and told to get away from her. This continued all week, till Noah stood stock-still in the barn, his eyes lighting up with a jolt of sudden knowledge.

Could it be? He remembered Kate. Tears sprang to his blue eyes as chills raced up his spine.

He couldn't tell her. It would be too great a disappointment if it were not so. A month went by before it dawned on Hester as she lay alone in their bedroom one rainy day, crying for no reason other than being so tired of this choking nausea. She called it a spring sickness at first. Or spring fever. Some vague ailment.

Could it be? Oh, she couldn't tell Noah because the disappointment would be too great to bear. She wouldn't say anything.

And so as she cooked, she almost always ran to the privy, the nausea in her throat, while Noah sat in the house wondering what to do.

They both became quite irritable with each other. She told him he needed to change his socks more often, and he said he was getting tired of potato soup.

One morning, Noah had had enough. He took Hester in his arms and whispered something in her ear.

"What?" she asked.

"Kate, our mam, used to be sick before another child came. Do you think it could be possible?"

She leaned back in his arms, her eyes wide and dark and fearful.

"Oh, Noah. She did, didn't she? Oh, Noah."

Then she cried, because tears came so readily these days.

Their baby girl arrived one still, frosty night in December, a dark-skinned little girl with a thatch of blond hair and the bluest eyes Hester had ever seen. Noah cried great sloppy tears, his emotion unchecked as he looked down at this perfect child of his and Hester's. A miracle.

Lissie Crane handed him a less than clean handker-chief and shooed him out of the room. She gave the baby to Hester, and Noah went.

They named her Annie.

Annie and Elias came to see her, pronouncing her the most beautiful child they had ever seen.

"You didn't have to name her after me," Annie said gruffly, so visibly pleased her eyes danced.

And then, like Kate, Hester bore many more children. She learned to laugh at the nausea, her soul fulfilled with the arrival of each one. Little Hans, all black hair and eyes. Albert, with only a sliver of dark hair, and blue eyes. Kate, the tiniest blond-haired one with black eyes.

Hester gained a bit of weight with each one. She rocked them all in the armless rocking chair, loving Noah, Fannie, and each of their children all the days of their lives.

The sun rose and set over Berks County in the late 1700s, the seasons came and went, the old passed away in due time, and the babies grew to become the children of the next generation.

The clock on the wall ticked away the hours, the house was filled with the happy cries of Noah and Hester's children, and God in his heaven looked down on what he had created and, someday, would return unto himself.

The End

GLOSSARY

A Hochzeit! Ach, du lieber! —A wedding! Oh, my goodness!

Ach, du yay. —Oh, dear.

Alta essel —old mule

An begaubta mensch —a talented person

An gute hoffning —a good hope for one's departed soul

An lot gelt —a lot of money

An schöena bräutigam —a good-looking bridegroom

Arme leit —poor people

Au-gnomma Kind —an adopted child

Aylend —trial

Behauft mit hexerei —mixed with witchcraft, or containing witchcraft

Bupplich —babyish

Bupply —baby

Da cha shunk —the dish cupboard

Da Levi sei Bappie —Levi's wife Babbie

Denke schöen. —Thank you very much.

Der Herren saya —God's blessing

Der saya —a blessing

Dess gebt hochzich. —There will be a wedding.

Die vitfrau —the widow

Diese hoyschrecken —the grasshoppers

Doddy —grandpa

Doo bisht, Hester King? —Are you Hester King?

Dummes —dumb thing

Egg Kuchen —egg cake

Ein English haus —A house belonging to someone whose first language is English, and who is, therefore, not Amish.

Eisa-kessle —cast-iron kettle

Elam Fisher sei Rachel —Elam Fisher's wife Rachel

Englischer —someone who isn't Amish or Native American

Eppa do? —Is someone here?

Ess vort dunkle. —It gets dark.

Eye du lieva, mon. —An old German expression, which translated literally, means "Oh, my love, man."

Fasark —To care for, look after

Faschpritz —burst

Frau —wife

Freundshaft —extended family

Geb acht. —Take care.

Gel?—Right?

Gewisslich—for sure

Goot. Goot.—Good. Good.

Goota mya!—Good morning!

Grosfeelicha—Proud, cocky

Gute Nacht. Denke, denke.—Good night. Thank you, thank you.

Guten Morgen.—Good morning.

Gyan schöena.—You're welcome.

Hansa ihr Noahs—Hans's Noah and family

Haus schtier—wedding gift

Heilandes blut—the Savior's blood

Heilig Schrift—The Holy Bible

Henn ma psuch, Mam?—Do we have company, Mom?

Hesslich—very much (as in extremely dark or cold, etc.)

Hexarei—hexes, curses

Ich bin Klein.—I am small.

Mine heartz macht rein.—My heart is pure.

Lest niemand drinn vonnen—Let no one live in here

Aus Jesus alein.—But Jesus alone.

Ich bin so frowah.—I am so glad.

Ich hab es shay Kott.—I had it nice.

Ich segne dihr.—I bless you.

Ich vill au halta fa fagebniss.—I want to beg for forgiveness.

In Gotteszeit—in God's time

Josiah sei Esther—Josiah's wife Esther

Kindish—childish

Komm mol—come now

Kommet rye—come right in

Krum Kuchen—crumb cake

Liebchenmaedle—lovely girl

Lied—song

Maud—a young Amish hired woman

Mein Gott, ich bitt—My God, I ask

Ich bitt durich Christchte blut—I ask through Christ's blood

Mach's nur mit meinem—Provide for my end of life

Ende Gute.—To be good.

Mit-tag—lunch

Mutza—coat, or Sunday suit coat

Na, do, veya isa deya fremma?—Now, here, who is this stranger?

Ob'l Dunkes Kucha—apple gravy cake

Oh, mein Gott. Bitte dich, bitte dich.—Oh, my God, please, I ask you, please.

Opp shtellt—forbidden

Ordnung—The Amish community's agreed-upon rules for living, based on their understanding of the Bible, particularly the New Testament. The *Ordnung* varies from community to community, often reflecting leaders' preferences, local customs, and traditional practices.

Panna kuchen—pancakes

Priest Gott.—Praise God.

Risht Dawg—day of preparation at the bride's home, just before the wedding

Roasht-leid—the people making the *roasht,* the main wedding dish made of bread filling and cooked, cut-up chicken

Rumspringa—a Pennsylvania Dutch dialect word meaning "running around." It refers to the time in a person's life between age sixteen and marriage. It involves structured social activities in groups, as well as dating, and usually takes place on the weekends.

S. gukt vie blenty.—It looks like plenty.

Schicket euch ihr lieben gäschte.—Behave yourselves, you loved guests.

Zu des lames hochzeit fest.—To the Lamb's wedding feast.

Schmücket euch aufs allerbeste.—Dress yourselves in your very best.

Schmear Kase! Frisha Schmear Kase!—Cup cheese! Fresh cup cheese!

Schmutz—fat or grease from meat

Schnitz un knepp—a main dish of dried apples, ham, and dumplings

Schnitzel Eier Kuchen—cut-up egg cake

Schöena yunga—a good-looking young man

Schpeck—fat from meat

Schpence—ghosts

Schpindlich—thin

Schrecklich mit—frightening with

Schtettle—town

Schtick—snack

Schtrubblich maedle—girl with the messy hair

Schtrubles—loose hair

Sell cutsich haus—that house full of vomit

Sell Indian maedle—that Indian girl

Sell is goot dunkas.—That is good gravy.

Sell suit mich.—That suits me.

Sell vowa so goot.—That was so good.

Selly glay Fannie—that little Fannie

Semmels—I have no idea. I'm sorry.

Siss unfaschtendich!—This is unbelievable!

Siss yusht.—It's just.

So gates. So iss es.—So it goes. So it is.

Socha—things

Tzorn—anger

Unbekannta—the unknown person

Unschuldiche mensch—innocent person

Unwort—untruth or lie

Veck mit selly.—Away with those.

Vell don.—Well then.

Vie bisht, meine liebchen?—How are you, my young friend?

Vonn anbegin—from the beginning

Voss gebt?—What's going on?

Voss hot Gott getan? Meine arme liebchen!—What has God done, my poor children?

Voss iss lets mitt sie?—What's wrong with you?

Wahrheit—the truth

Ya, ich bin Amos Schtoltzfus.—Yes, I am Amos Schtoltz-
foos.

Yung kyat psucha—newlywed visiting

Yung kyaty—newlyweds

Zeitlang—homesick

OTHER BOOKS BY LINDA BYLER

*Available from your favorite bookstore
or online retailer.*

"Author Linda Byler is Amish, which sets this book apart
both in the rich details of Amish life and in the lack of mel-
odrama over disappointments and tragedies. Byler's writ-
ing will leave readers eager for the next book in the series."
–*Publisher's Weekly* review of *Wild Horses*

LIZZIE SEARCHES FOR LOVE SERIES

BOOK ONE   BOOK TWO   BOOK THREE

TRILOGY   COOKBOOK

SADIE'S MONTANA SERIES

BOOK ONE

BOOK TWO

BOOK THREE

TRILOGY

LANCASTER BURNING SERIES

BOOK ONE

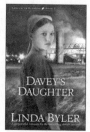

BOOK TWO

BOOK THREE

TRILOGY

HESTER'S HUNT FOR HOME SERIES

BOOK ONE

BOOK TWO

BOOK THREE

THE LITTLE AMISH
MATCHMAKER
A Christmas Romance

THE CHRISTMAS
VISITOR
An Amish Romance

MARY'S CHRISTMAS
GOODBYE
An Amish Romance

BECKY MEETS HER
MATCH
*An Amish Christmas
Romance*

About the Author

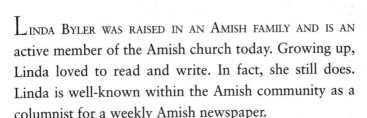

Linda Byler was raised in an Amish family and is an active member of the Amish church today. Growing up, Linda loved to read and write. In fact, she still does. Linda is well-known within the Amish community as a columnist for a weekly Amish newspaper.

Linda is the author of three series of novels, all set among the Amish communities of North America: Lizzie Searches for Love, Sadie's Montana (whose individual titles are *Wild Horses, Keeping Secrets,* and *The Disappearances*), and the Lancaster Burning series.

Hester Takes Charge is the third and final novel in a new series, *Hester's Hunt for Home,* which features the life of a Native American child who is raised by an Amish family in colonial America. The first two books in this series are *Hester on the Run* and *Which Way Home?*

Linda has also written four Christmas romances set among the Amish: *Mary's Christmas Goodbye, The Christmas Visitor, The Little Amish Matchmaker,* and *Becky Meets Her Match.* Linda has co-authored *Lizzie's Amish Cookbook: Favorite recipes from three generations of Amish cooks!*